I0630483

THE ZEAL TRILOGY

A New Kind of Zeal

THE ZEAL TRILOGY

A New Kind of Zeal

Michelle Warren

Discover other titles by Michelle Warren:

THE ZEAL TRILOGY Book 2: The Price of Redemption
THE ZEAL TRILOGY Book 3: The Crux of Salvation
Yeshua

Statement:

This novel is a work of fiction. Any resemblance of a character to a person living or dead is a coincidence apart from the clear characters of inspiration from two thousand years ago. Likewise, in the slightly futuristic poetic interpretation, the organisations, positions, places, nations, ethnicities, religions, ideologies, and customs explored do not represent any current reality today but represent a fictional future. Those portions set in the past are also fictionalized.

No offence is intended in the writing of the novel. The opinions upheld by the characters do not necessarily represent the opinions of the author, and any criminal actions or acts of war committed by the characters are not endorsed by the author.

This novel is not intended to incite violence or warfare: quite the opposite, the goal of the novel is to evoke peace.

Updated 2018
ISBN: 978-1-99-116960-0 (Paperback)
ISBN: 978-0-473-27828-1 (Kindle)
ISBN: 978-0-473-48481-1 (Audio)
Published by Michelle Warren

For Aotearoa

For New Zealand

Aotearoa/God Defend New Zealand [1]

E Ihowā Atua,
O ngā iwi mātou rā
Āta whakarangona;
Me aroha noa
Kia hua ko te pai;
Kia tau tō atawhai;
Manaakitia mai
Aotearoa

English translation
O Lord, God,
of all people
Listen to us,
Cherish us
May good flourish,
May your blessings flow.
Defend
Aotearoa

God of Nations at Thy feet,
In the bonds of love we meet,
Hear our voices, we entreat,
God defend our free land.
Guard Pacific's triple star
From the shafts of strife and war,
Make her praises heard afar,
God defend New Zealand.

Contents

Chapter 1

KERIKERI

Tristan tugged at the straps of his backpack, and wiped the sweat from his brow. The midday summer sun was getting to him now, despite the odd patches of shade from totara and pine trees. He had been walking for over two hours, after a mad salesman had dropped him off near Black Bridge Road. The guy was heading back to Auckland; no way was Tristan going to hitch a ride back there.

Ahead, the junction to Kerikeri came into view. Kerikeri? Surely he could make it further north than this. He took a deep breath and forged forward across the junction, watching for cars and darting back into the ditch as needed. Where should he go first? Whangaroa Harbour? Doubtless Bay? It didn't really matter. Just anywhere to get away from it all.

The tar-seal was starting to melt on the road. He smelt the fumes and grinned. Where could he score a joint? He wouldn't have to travel far, that was for sure. The thought spurred him on, one step at a time, and after another thirty minutes of slogging and sweating he crossed over to the left side of the road, and starting thumbing for a ride.

Now he was walking backwards, a little uphill and around a bend. He swore as a car nearly caught him, and he stumbled against a tree. Someone else tooted at him; he swore again. Then he noticed a Ute had pulled up at a parking bay a few metres ahead.

Tristan slowly walked toward the car. It was an old red Holden, and there were fishing lines strapped in the back.

"Sweet as," said Tristan, speeding up to catch the car. The driver's door opened, and Tristan reached out a hand.

"Hey, mate."

"Kia ora, 'mate'." An olive-skinned Maori man grasped his hand in greeting. "Need a ride?"

"Where are you headed?"

"Ninety Mile Beach."

Tristan grinned. "Ninety Mile Beach? More like 'Ninety Mile Rip', by now. Mind if I borrow one of your lines to go fishing?"

"Sure. Why not? There's still enough beach, and the warmer water's bringing more fish." The man smiled up at Tristan, a slight wrinkling creasing the corners of his eyes and a sprinkling of light silver dusting his short black curls. Tristan held his warm gaze, then suddenly reared backwards. The man was wearing a dog collar.

"No way," said Tristan, before he could stop himself. "You're a priest?"

"My name is Rau," the man replied. "Rau Petera, of the Ngapuhi tribe. And you are?"

"Tristan Blake, from…never mind."

"You look like you need some help, Tristan Blake. Do you still want a ride?"

Tristan looked the man up and down. "I don't know," he said. "What about that collar?"

Rau's brown eyes held his own. "Makes you nervous, does it?"

"Nervous?" Tristan laughed. "You have no idea!"

Rau's mouth twitched, and then he pulled the collar away and unbuttoned the first two buttons of his white shirt.

Tristan studied him, as Rau stretched out his hand again.

"Want a ride?"

"Okay," replied Tristan.

"Hop in then."

Tristan dumped his backpack in the back, with the fishing lines, and climbed into the car.

Rau pulled out and began negotiating the windy road. Tristan closed his eyes fleetingly, grateful for the air-conditioning.

Rau prodded him. "Here, have some coke."

Tristan looked at the half drunken bottle now in his lap. "This is yours?"

"You look like you need it more than me."

"You're drinking coke?"

"I'm an Anglican priest, not a monk."

Tristan sprayed the coke in his mouth and Rau smirked.

"Besides," he said, "you're helping my diabetes."

"Sorry," said Tristan.

"Ka pai," replied Rau. "Got family, boy?"

Tristan shifted uneasily, and didn't reply.

"My whanau's in Kerikeri," said Rau.

"Yeah?"

"My wife and two teen-aged kids. And then there's Auntie Ngaire, and three of my cousins…"

"Yeah, yeah," said Tristan, "I get it – the whole tribe."

Rau cast him a sideways glance, and Tristan stared out of the window.

At Kaeo Rau pulled off the highway.

"Want some food?"

"How about a beer?" Tristan smirked.

"Not on my watch. Kai?"

"Sure, whatever you're having."

Tristan watched as Rau crossed the road and shook his head. A priest – seriously? What weird twist of fate was that?

The empty coke bottle had fallen between the seats. Tristan reached down to pick it up, and as he sat back saw Rau at the driver's door.

"Here," said Rau, tossing him a paper wrapped parcel, "fish and chips."

"What?" chided Tristan, as Rau sat back in. "Won't we get plenty of fish later?"

"Depends how good you are! Personally, I'm not hedging my bets."

Rau smiled, and Tristan, despite his best efforts otherwise, found himself liking the man. As Rau pulled away from the curb and drove north, Tristan ate and passed Rau food.

"Where's the tomato sauce?" he complained.

"You Pakeha and your tomato sauce," replied Rau.

"Enjoying our potato chips, are we?"

"You got me, boy. But try a hangi someday – snapper and kumara. That's real kai."

Tristan broke apart a piece of fried terakihi and passed it to Rau.

"Fish and chips, fish and chips," he sighed. "All I ever see is fish and chips."

"Tired of fish?" asked Rau. "Your mother not giving you beef or lamb?"

"How old do you think I am, man?"

"Twenty?"

"I'm twenty-six. Fresh fish sure is better than army rations, but now I'm finally out of it I'd rather have a good juicy steak."

Rau's eyes glanced at him again and then back to the road.

"The army?"

"Five years."

"Why'd you leave?"

Tristan stared at the road ahead. Screams surrounded him; young faces dripping with blood filled his vision. He sucked in a breath and shut the memory down.

"Let's just say peacekeeping isn't all it's cracked up to be."

Rau lapsed into silence and Tristan watched him warily. "You got a joint, mate?" he finally asked.

"No," said Rau quietly. "I don't."

"Then how about your religion? Wanna try it on me now?"

Rau frowned, but still remained silent. Gratified, Tristan spoke into the silence.

"It's 2030," he chided, "and where is humanity at? The world's a crock! Temperature's rising, food's disappearing, people are fighting, and lunatics are still preaching."

Rau grimaced as Tristan's words became a torrent.

"The Middle East is still where all the action is," he said, "still! A brawling desert! We tried to help. We came this close to a nuke!" He pinched finger and thumb together, a mere millimetre apart. "A nuke, in the Holy Land! My God! You have no idea how close we came to World War Three…"

Tears pricked Tristan's eyes. He blinked them away furiously, as always.

"So preach it to me, priest. God exists, right? God loves us? Yeah, right."

Rau remained silent. Then he pulled over to the side of the road.

"Listen, mate," said Tristan quickly. "Thanks for the ride, and everything. I'll get off here, and hitch another ride, okay?"

He opened the door, eager to get away, but then suddenly Rau's hand grasped his shoulder.

"Hey," said Rau. "Where are you going?"

Tristan's body stiffened as the priest's grip reminded him of something, a distant memory, shoved away for too long. Rau's eyes searched his own and Tristan looked away, shaking his head.

"Hey, man," said Tristan finally, "it has nothing to do with you. I shouldn't have said anything."

"I know," said Rau, "but how about that fishing?"

Tristan hesitated, frowning, drawn back to his eyes. "What kind of fishing?" he asked.

"Only the best! You're looking at a Snapper champion."

"No way."

"2005 – I caught myself a whopper – a three-foot fish."

"2005? Twenty-five years ago? Forget that."

"Beat my record, and I'll give you the Ute."

Tristan stared at him. The Ute? Surely he wasn't serious. "You're bribing me?" he asked.

Rau shook his head. "Not a bribe, a prize."

Tristan tilted his head thoughtfully. What was the priest up to? "Think I couldn't get a car if I wanted one?"

Rau shrugged. "I guess your cash is stashed away."

"Getting pretty worthless, cash."

"Commodities are worth more."

"Missed out on the quarter acre section," said Tristan.

"I'll bet you can sleep in a car, if you have to."

Tristan frowned. "But why?" he asked. "Why would you offer me your car? Not to mention the petrol. Petrol's become as rare as hens' teeth."

Rau smiled. "Food's scarcer here as well. Fish well and live well, we say."

Tristan considered the offer, vacillated, and then finally shut the door.

"Fine," he said. "Have it your way."

Rau pulled back out onto the road and began driving hard around the bends.

"You're crazy," said Tristan.

"Aren't we all?" replied Rau.

They passed north, skirting the shoreline of Whangaroa Harbour and Doubtless Bay, and were soon heading northwest, beyond Kaitaia, toward Ninety Mile Beach.

Chapter 2

NINETY MILE BEACH

The sand ramp onto Ninety Mile Beach at Waipapakauri lay before them.

Rau smiled. Sandy dunes rose up on either side of the Ute, smothered with long yellow grass. Straight ahead, Rau caught his first glimpse of the damp brown sand and the sparkling blue ocean beyond. He took in a deep breath of salty air. At last he was back at his favourite spot! He had waited months for this moment.

Beside him sat the Pakeha, Tristan Blake, from who knew where? He had no tribe, of course, being a New Zealand European, but he seemed to have no whanau either.

Rau turned to face him. "Are you ready for this, Pakeha?"

Tristan shifted in his seat, peering through the windscreen at the ramp ahead. "You bet I am," he said. "Lay it on me."

Rau hit the accelerator.

The Ute jerked forward through the sand ramp, and suddenly out onto the wide expansive beach beyond. The vast dark blue ocean glimmered before them, and the wide, bright blue sky embraced them from above. Rau took a deep breath, and broke into a wide smile.

"Whoa!" Tristan cried out. "Stop the car!"

Rau slammed on the brake. Was the boy hurt? Instead Tristan leapt from the Ute and stood, stretching out his arms wide, gazing north. The sand stretched on and on, as far as the eye could see.

"Wow!" cried Tristan. "What a beach!"

Rau leaned through his window. "Easy, mate!" he said. "You're in the middle of a highway."

"What? Oh, yeah."

Rau could see the shimmering image of a distant bus, approaching rapidly. Tristan slipped back into the Ute, and Rau drove them closer to the water's edge. Waves rose to a metre, and then crashed on the shore. Beyond the layers of white froth the sea extended unhindered, to the horizon.

"Wow," said Tristan again.

"Different from the Middle East, eh?"

"So...beautiful." Tears pooled in his green eyes. "I've never seen it before."

Rau watched him. "Not everything in the world is war and famine, my friend."

Something in Tristan's eyes in that moment drew Rau to him. Peacekeeping, in the army? No, this boy was far from at peace. His talk of World War Three, his camouflaged memories; joints, and beer.

"Come on," said Rau opening the door, "let's get to it."

Rau reached into the cargo tray. Tristan was now kicking off his shoes, and dipping his toe into a broken wave. Rau gathered the rods and bait and joined him, delighting in the familiar northern warmth on his face and the gentle sea-breeze. The sun stood high in the sky.

"I never knew it could be like this," said Tristan, gazing out to the horizon.

"Like what?" asked Rau, laying down lines and bait alongside.

"I don't know...kinda free."

Rau nodded, and smiled. Tristan kicked some water in his direction.

"Hey," said Rau, "think I'm afraid of a little salt water? I'm a fisherman! Here, show me what you can do with a line."

And he tossed a rod to Tristan. He caught it, fumbled, recovered, and then cast the line far out beyond the waves.

"Not bad!" said Rau. "Try it again, this time with some bait."

Tristan wound the line in, attached a mussel to the hook, and cast out again. He had some skill, Rau noted, and then he cast out his own line, alongside him.

"I'll catch it!" Tristan insisted. "First fish, biggest fish: you name it."

"Whatever you say."

"How many fish do you catch?"

"Depends."

"I reckon…"

"Yes?"

"I reckon I could stay here for a while."

Rau looked at him – young face, blonde curls, white as, and utterly alone.

"Then you stay here for a while, Pakeha," he said. "See what your home, Aotearoa, has to offer."

An hour passed. Tristan had caught two kahawai, too small to eat, and had thrown them back; Rau had caught a foot long silver-grey trevally.

"I began fishing as a boy in Kerikeri," said Rau, winding his line in a little. "There were beautiful rainbow trout in the river."

"Kerikeri – 'The cradle of New Zealand'," said Tristan, looking at him. "You meet any of those missionary jokers?"

Rau smirked at him. "How old do you think I am, boy? Two hundred?"

"I dunno. Some of your ways seem as old as the hills."

Rau smiled. "Forget the army, mate – you should take up tourism instead."

Rau spotted Tristan smiling. At last, a smile! "Ngapuhi welcomed the missionaries," he explained. "Some of their families still live amongst us."

"And the Anglican Church."

"Ae."

"Ministers, and dog collars, and all that preaching. I've sure had enough of all of that."

"Enough?"

Rau watched while Tristan hesitated. There was more to him than just the army.

"What is it?" asked Rau.

"My…" Again he hesitated.

"Spit it out."

"I guess it's a waste of time hiding it from a priest."

"Hiding what?"

"My father's in the church."

Rau looked at him. He had a father?

"Where does he attend?"

Tristan grimaced, and then forced himself to continue.

"He's the Anglican Bishop of Wellington."

Now Rau stared at him. The Bishop of Wellington? The Right Reverend Mark Blake was this young man's father?

"I know of the man," said Rau, and Tristan shrugged.

"I'm sure you do."

"He recently became the head of the Church Council of New Zealand."

Tristan was staring at him. "Great," he said.

"Why…?" Rau quickly changed his question. "When did you last see him?"

Tristan grimaced, paused, and then continued, "About nine years ago."

"University?"

"Not exactly. I went to Victoria."

"Then…why…?"

Tristan's green eyes were on him, his expression a strange mixture of grief and indifference.

"Let's just say things took a turn for the worse after my mother died."

Rau frowned at him. What kind of turn for the worse? “Grief can sometimes change a man,” he offered quietly.

“That’s for real.” Tristan grimaced, shrugged his shoulders again, and turned away.

The sun began to lower in the mid-afternoon sky. Waves crashed around their knees. Rau shifted his feet in the water, and glanced back. The tide had risen enough to lap at the tires of the Ute.

“Look,” he said to Tristan, pointing to the grassy edges of the dunes. “There won’t be any room left for us soon.”

“We’ve only been here two hours,” said Tristan.

“That’s all we get now,” said Rau. “Low tide, that’s all. The tide moves fast. We'd better move.”

Rau waded back to the Ute with his rod, and picked up the bait from the bonnet. He heard Tristan splashing behind him.

“Where shall we go next?”

“Further north up the beach.”

“Why?”

“There’s a camp ground.’”

Rau shifted the Ute into reverse as Tristan got in, backed away from the water, and then began to move forward over the sand.

“Full tide is coming,” said Tristan, his voice tight. “What happens then? Does this place really turn into a rip?”

“We’ll get washed away well before ‘full’ tide.”

“What? When?”

“I’d give it an hour.”

Rau looked up the beach and saw the last bus coming their way. He was pushing it a little, he knew, and he closed his eyes fleetingly to murmur a prayer.

“The camp ground is twenty kilometres further up. We can stay there for the night.”

“What about your family?”

“They know they can’t stop me fishing.”

Rau smiled, and drove. He sensed Tristan's discomfort at his side.

"Have a little faith, mate," he said.

Tristan scowled. "You're crazy."

"Maybe. Or maybe I'm just inspired."

The bus passed them, on their right, and then left the beach. They were alone.

"What happens if we break down?" asked Tristan.

"Then we go for a little walk. And maybe a swim."

Up ahead Rau saw an unusual sight, a gathering of people. "Strange…" he murmured.

"What is it?" asked Tristan.

"People."

Rau pulled over and parked the Ute in front of a rock, next to an outcrop of yellow grass.

"What are you doing?" Tristan demanded, as Rau opened the driver's door. "We've got to get outta here! Where the hell are you going?"

"These people shouldn't be here."

"They must know, they're locals, aren't they?

"Come or stay, it's up to you," said Rau, and he left Tristan, with his stare and harsh breath, behind in the Ute.

A handful of people sat on the sand. Rau wandered up to them, and extended a hand.

"Kia ora!"

"Kia ora," a Maori woman replied, taking his hand, rising to her feet. "Pehea ana koe?"

"Pai ana."

"I'm Anahera," she said, "from the Cape." Her face was round, her eyes warm and sparkling brown.

"Oh," Rau said, "you're from Ngati Kuri. I'm from Kerikeri."

"Oh, from Ngapuhi!" she said. "Welcome." And she pressed her forehead to his, and her nose, and he returned the hongi to her.

"Are you fishing?" asked Rau. "The tide is coming."

"Ae," she said, "we are fishing."

"Any catch?"

"Not yet."

"But I think that will change soon." Rau turned to the new voice.

It was a Pakeha man. His face was a little hidden in a white hoodie, but he smiled in greeting, his dark brown eyes set on Rau.

Rau extended his hand to him. "Kia ora."

"Kia ora." The man shook his hand, but did not rise.

"Been here long?"

"Not so long. I'm Joshua."

Rau glanced over the hoodie framing his face. Was he hiding? No, not exactly hiding. And yet, he wasn't exactly visible either.

"Where are you from, Joshua?"

"Kaitaia. I'm hoping for a big catch."

Tristan joined them and stretched out a hand to Joshua. "Hi," he said.

Joshua's dark brown eyes shifted from Rau to Tristan. "Hi," he said, shaking Tristan's hand.

"What are you doing here?" asked Tristan.

"Fishing."

"Figures." Tristan shifted on his feet. "The tide's coming in, he reckons," he said, gesturing to Rau.

"Oh, yes?" asked Joshua.

"The tide! It's going to wash us all away!"

"So how important is the fishing to you?"

Tristan stared as Joshua rose to his feet. Rau could see him more clearly now: white face, dark brown eyes, brown curls, white sweater and jeans rolled up to his knees with bare feet.

"Let's go," said Joshua, and Anahera hastily followed him. The men also stood – two Pakeha and two Maori.

"Coming?" Joshua asked Rau, his eyes lingering on him.

Rau frowned, surprised. "It's dangerous," he said.

"There is still time."

Rau studied him. Joshua was surprisingly confident; certain. Who was he? Rau was drawn to him.

"Why not?" he said.

"You've got to be joking!" Tristan protested. "You don't even know the man!"

"Come and fish," replied Rau, smirking and gesturing him to follow.

Tristan shook his head. "Forget it, mate!" he said. "I'm looking for higher ground!"

"Fine," said Rau. "Have it your way. I'm going."

He grabbed his fishing gear from the Ute and followed Joshua, across the sand and back into the rising sea.

The water was getting cold as the afternoon sun dropped further in the sky. Waves splashed around their thighs. Rau shivered a little. He'd left his jacket in the Ute.

Joshua stood quietly beside him.

"Where's your line?" asked Rau.

"It's okay," answered Joshua. "I don't need my own line."

He gestured to Anahera and the men, who had all cast their lines out.

"These are your friends?" asked Rau.

"Yes."

"Family? Whanau?"

"Yes, Rau. They are my whanau."

There was something different about him: Rau couldn't decide what it was. "You can have my line if you like," he offered.

Joshua met his eyes, smiled sadly, and nodded. "Okay."

Rau handed over the line and bait. "Try this worm," he said. "Sometimes the fish like this best."

"Thanks," said Joshua. "But I think crab would work better here."

"No, seriously – use the worm, it will help you."

Joshua's eyes were on him. "Tell you what, let's try no bait, shall we?"

"No bait?"

"Just to see," said Joshua. And he cast the line, with an empty hook, deep into the ocean.

Rau scratched his head, staring at the water. “Why would you cast with no bait?”

“I have my reasons.”

“I don’t understand.”

“Wait and see.”

Rau shifted on his feet, in the deep water. His hands were empty – he had no line. Joshua was holding his line. Rau glanced up the beach at Tristan’s dark form; he was pacing backwards and forwards, eying the Ute.

“Do you want to go to your worrying friend?” asked Joshua. “Or stay here?”

Rau looked at him. “I’ll stay here,” he said instinctively.

“So you will,” said Joshua. “After all, here you are.” And he reeled in the line, and caught on the end was a three-and-a half-foot snapper.

Joshua released the struggling fish from the hook and lifted it into Rau’s arms.

“Highest quality snapper,” said Joshua with a smile. “I take it this will beat your three-foot record?”

Rau's mouth fell open. “How…?” he stammered.

Joshua returned his rod to him, as his friends also started reeling in a catch.

“Does it matter how?” he asked, his eyes dancing. “Isn’t it enough that it happened?”

Rau held his gaze. “Friend,” he said, “the tide is coming in fast. Do you need my Ute?”

Joshua’s face brightened. “Thank you,” he said. “But I need you to drive us.”

Rau tilted his head. “You seem familiar,” he said. “Do I already know you?”

“Maybe you do,” Joshua replied, “Rau Petera.”

Rau frowned, but Joshua had already turned his attention to his friends.

Rau tucked his rod under his arm, dragged the fish out of the water, and struggled up the beach, leaving a gash in the sand that would soon be swallowed up by the tide.

Back at the Ute, Tristan was jiggling from foot to foot. "Are you quite done?" he asked.

"Not quite," replied Rau, presenting the fish.

"What the hell…?" said Tristan, eyes wide. "No way!"

"What can I say?"

"Beginner's luck!"

"It wasn't me," said Rau.

"What do you mean?"

"Joshua used my line without bait, and caught it straight away."

Tristan's eyes widened further. "You're crazy," he said.

"Whatever you say."

"Shows how easy it can be to catch a massive one!" said Tristan.

"Shows how little you know about fishing."

Tristan scoffed. "Well go on, then!" he said. "What's your explanation?"

Without any warning he suddenly mounted a mound of sand, cupped his hands and shouted: "Hey, it's a miracle! Biggest fish in Rau's life – that proves it, there must be a God!"

Rau shook his head and tossed a shell in Tristan's direction, as Joshua wandered towards them and came to stand in front of Tristan.

Tristan shifted awkwardly and then met Joshua's eyes.

"You a believer, miracle man?" asked Tristan.

"You could say that," replied Joshua.

"Wanna catch me a great white shark?"

Joshua held his gaze. "You want a predator?" he asked.

"Food is food," said Tristan, "whatever the source."

"But not all food tastes as good."

"Beggars can't be choosers."

"What if I gave you the choice?"

Tristan frowned at him. "I…" he began, and then closed his mouth again.

Joshua seemed to be searching him. Finally he spoke. “Your friend has given me his Ute,” he said.

“What?” Tristan cast a foul look at Rau. “What did you do that for?”

Rau shrugged. “He beat my record,” he said. “Fair is fair.”

“Fair?” cried Tristan. “That Ute had my name on it!”

“Beat my record, and it’s yours again,” said Joshua.

Tristan straightened, a strange fervour in his eyes. “Beat your record?” he said. “Catch a bigger snapper? Then it’ll be goodbye to your ‘miracle.’”

“Try it,” said Joshua, smiling slightly. “See if you can win. Join us.”

Surprised, Rau surveyed them both. Join him? Tristan? And yet a purposeful expression was beginning to form on his face.

“Fine,” said Tristan, “I’ll join you! What the hell – I’ve got nothing better to do.”

Tristan grabbed Rau’s rod and launched himself toward the ocean, but Joshua suddenly seized his arm.

“Full tide,” said Joshua. “It’s coming.”

“Now you care about full tide?” scoffed Tristan.

“I do,” said Joshua.

Tristan stiffened at Joshua's look, and jerked his arm away. “To hell with your care,” he said.

“Do it in the morning.”

“I’ll do it now!”

“In the morning, Tristan,” said Joshua.

Tristan swayed for a moment, locked in Joshua’s gaze. Then he shivered.

“Fine,” he said. “I’ll be back at it in the morning.”

He threw the line down, and climbed into the Ute.

Rau now held Joshua’s gaze. “Who are you?” he asked.

Joshua smiled. “I am myself,” he replied. “Nothing more, nothing less.”

Then he bowed his head, turned, and called his friends over to the Ute.

Chapter 3

PARLIAMENT

The Right Honourable James Connor sat at his desk. A photo of his wife and daughter was the only thing sitting between him and Patrick Clarkson, and he was grateful for the distraction. Pam looked particularly elegant in the photo – a nice flowing floral summer dress showed off her figure, still slim in her fifties. And Rachel's smile was like her mother's, her jeans and floral shirt fitting for a woman in her early thirties.

As for Patrick? He was the spitting image of a typical politician: tall and thin, with worry lines wrinkling his face.

"...and have you even read the report from the Intelligence and Security Committee yet, James?"

Connor gazed at Clarkson's thinning hair. "Honestly, Pat, tell me I'm not getting as grey as you."

Clarkson shook his head, while Connor glanced fleetingly at his own reflection in the family photo. He still had a full head of hair! Miraculously some brown remained amidst the grey. Worry lines, yes. A bit of extra weight on board.

"James, for crying out loud, you're the PM! Now's not the time to talk about hair."

"And you're the Leader of the Opposition, but I'm not holding that against you."

"We're due in the Chamber in fifteen minutes! Come on, James, we've been at this for years. I'm starting to get worried…"

The air-con was failing again in the Beehive, at the peak of summer.

"Damned Global Warming," James Connor muttered under his breath, sweat dripping down his face. He rose to his feet.

"Come, Pat," he said. "Let's walk and talk." And he grabbed a folder of notes from his desk, and left his office.

They entered the lift from the ninth floor, waited for the door to close, and then turned ready for the opposite side of the elevator to open.

"You know what I'm talking about, James," said Patrick Clarkson. "Things are heating up overseas."

"Literally or metaphorically?"

The lift door opened, and Connor stepped out into an airy atrium but was hit by heat generated by the greenhouse effect of the windows. He glanced briefly outside, to the wide pavement and gardens. The sun was shining, and they were suffering.

"Literally and metaphorically, James! You know that!"

They made their way around the circumference of the round-shaped hall to the over-bridge, and across the black and white tiles chequering the first floor foyer of Parliament House.

"The Com' Security Bureau," Clarkson whispered into his ear, as they entered the Debating Chamber. "They're going too far with their surveillance, but boy, James, what are you going to do with their findings?"

Connor cast him a sideways glance, nodded him to his seat at the right of the Chamber, and then sat four seats forward on the left, the traditional place for the leader of the Government; opposite Clarkson, the Leader of the Opposition Party.

Other ministers filed in. Connor glanced at those seated behind him, his own members of the New Conservative Party. Politics in New

Zealand had changed over the last ten years; intensified and diversified. Across the way, Clarkson led a party quite different from the Labour party of old. It had shifted further to the left to become the new Socialist Party. Connor watched Clarkson as he gathered his papers. His old friend scared him a little now with his strengthening party line.

Connor glanced to his right, to the Christian Conservative Party, now allies, and across to the corresponding Clean Green Party, allies with his friend and rival, and now with increasing power in the current intensifying climate.

It was time. Connor stood, and everyone in the Chamber rose as the Speaker walked in, behind the Serjeant-at-Arms. The Serjeant-at-Arms placed the golden mace, the staff symbol of authority, onto its stand on the table, and the Speaker stood before his Chair and chanted the traditional prayer:[2]

"Almighty God, humbly acknowledging our need for thy guidance in all things…"

At this point Connor's thoughts drifted away, before returning for the final words.

"…grant that we may conduct the affairs of this house and of our country to the glory of thy holy name, the maintenance of true religion and justice, the honour of the Queen, and the public welfare, peace and tranquillity of New Zealand, through Jesus Christ our Lord…"

"Amen," Connor muttered, along with everyone else. The Speaker sat, and all the Members of Parliament followed.

Connor caught a flicker in Clarkson's expression. He knew what he was thinking: the Queen, still reigning at one hundred and four years of age. What use did they have for such a monarch? Nevertheless their entire political system acknowledged her authority, although in practice her authority remained to protect the integrity of the nation's democratic freedom.

Connor remained a monarchist, in the sense of their continuing Constitutional Monarchy.

Clarkson glanced at him, and his lips twitched condescendingly at the words of the Speaker. *We need no Queen*, his eyes said. *We need no Lord.* James steadfastly held his gaze, unshaken, and Patrick looked away.

The Speaker's voice lifted again.

"I call on the Government Order of the Day Number One."

The Clerk, sitting in front of the Speaker, spoke: "The International and National Crisis Surveillance Bill, Third Hearing."

"Mr Speaker," said Connor, rising to his feet.

"The Right Honourable Prime Minister James Connor."

"Mr Speaker, I move that The International and National Crisis Surveillance Bill be moved a third time."

Just one last time, James thought to himself, *to get this thing through*. The wheels of democracy moved slowly.

"The question," said the Speaker, "is that the Motion be agreed to."

"Mr Speaker."

"The Honourable Martin Hanks."

James sat to allow for the Minister of Defence, who was now standing to speak.

"I would like to thank the Foreign Affairs Defence Committee for considering the bill and attending hearings. The Committee recommended the urgent implementation of heightened surveillance, both off shore and on shore, in times of national crisis."

"Mr Speaker." Predictably, it was Clarkson.

"The Right Honourable Leader of the Opposition, Patrick Clarkson."

Clarkson rose to his feet.

"Mr Speaker, I have challenged this bill at first and second readings, and I challenge it again today."

"Mr Speaker," Connor interrupted.

"Mr Speaker," said Clarkson.

"I call on the Right Honourable Patrick Clarkson to continue."

"Mr Speaker," said Clarkson, glancing across the House to the other Members. "This bill, if passed, makes an unprecedented invasion of privacy into the personal lives of New Zealanders legal…"

"Mr Speaker," said Connor, rising swiftly to his feet.

"The Right Honourable Prime Minister James Connor."

Clarkson remained seated, as Connor continued. "Must I remind the Leader of the Opposition that this bill only applies to times of national crisis?"

"Mr Speaker," Clarkson promptly replied.

"The Right Honourable Patrick Clarkson."

"Does the Prime Minister consider New Zealand to currently be in crisis?"

James eyeballed him, clenching his jaw, thinking rapidly. Then he rose to his feet.

"Not yet," he said. "But if you gain power, our situation may deteriorate rapidly, and I want New Zealand to be ready."

Shouts from the Socialist Party filled the air, along with equally loud laughter led by Connor.

"Order!" said the Speaker. "Order!"

"Mr Speaker!" Clarkson responded, jumping to his feet. "The Prime Minister would have us all vote in a military state! New Zealand! We are talking about New Zealand!"

"Order!"

Back off, Connor thought, as he countered the attack. *We need this.*

"A military state!" he said. "What does the Leader of the Opposition call the state of Communist Russia, a walk in the park? Perhaps the Socialist Party should look more closely at their own policy suggestions, before engaging in a lover's quarrel over ours."

Again, Connor achieved the reaction he sought: anger, but greater laughter. They had a majority, surely. Would the same majority carry them through?

"I will have order!" said the Speaker, and Connor sat down, eying Clarkson as he took his seat again.

"Members," said the Speaker, "this debate has concluded. I now call for the Party Vote."

All members of the House rose to their feet.

"I'll ask the Clerk for the Vote," said the Speaker.

"Those in favour, seventy-seven," said the Clerk. "Those opposed, forty-three."

"Members, the Ayes seventy-seven, the noes forty-three. The motion is agreed to."

Connor took a deep breath, and let it out silently. It was done! At last! The first step.

The rest of the Chamber proceedings were relatively incidental. Connor participated, but constantly surveyed Clarkson. His old friend was disgruntled, more so than usual in defeat.

The session came to a close. The MPs rose, the Speaker left, and the MPs were free to leave.

Connor sat down to gather his papers, and when he next looked up Clarkson was standing over him.

"James," began Clarkson, and Connor scowled at him.

"Patrick," he said, rising to his feet and leaning in close to his ear. "Why such a fight over this one? You know as well as me what is happening overseas; you know we have to keep an ear close to the ground."

"I know the danger, James," said Patrick, "but how far will we let that threat drive our own response?"

"I expect purism from the Christian Conservative Party, Patrick, not from you!"

"James, I'm serious about this!"

The Chamber was emptying. Connor relaxed a little, and spoke more directly.

"You know the intel," he said. "The Communications Security Bureau…"

"Of course I know it, James! But does that give us the right?"

"The right?" Connor exploded. "Can't you see what's happening over there, Patrick? The United States is losing control. Economic collapse. They can't get themselves out of this one. China is growing in strength, but imploding at the same time: they can't feed their own workers.

Russia's clawing its way back to communism. Do you want to be like them, Patrick? And the Middle East – for crying out loud! There's the Intel and then I had it confirmed straight from a young retired army officer's mouth. He witnessed it himself, Patrick, we came this close to a nuclear Holocaust!"

He brought his finger and thumb together, only one millimetre apart. "This close!"

Clarkson grimaced. "I know," he said. "Add religious fervour onto famine, and you have a toxic mix."

"You would say that," said Connor, tongue in cheek. "Fervent atheist that you are."

"And what are you?" Clarkson chided. "Not exactly a faithful follower yourself. When did you last go to church?"

"Last Easter, if you must know."

"Easter, and Christmas – part of our culture, that's all. Christ and Santa Claus, as though they might save us."

Connor's eyes narrowed. "You are full of contradiction, Patrick. Here I am trying to save us, and you say, no, I have no right!"

"What kind of salvation is intel, James, at the end of the day? Look around you."

Clarkson gestured around the House, and then to Connor's own seat. "Who knows who is listening to you, right now?" He shook his head, and gathered his papers.

"At the end of the day, I'd rather die a free man than a prisoner of a national or international State."

Connor watched Clarkson leave the House, and then looked around the Chamber, taking in the plaques commemorating the wars New Zealanders had fought in. Did the plaques have bugs behind them? Was anything sacred anymore?

Connor wandered out of the House. He had stacks of paperwork to attend to, yet he wandered through the chequered foyer and down the steps to the courtyard before crossing the street to the aged Saint Peter's Anglican Cathedral.

The thought lingered: was anything sacred anymore? Christ, Santa Claus, international destabilization of economies and political systems, and weapons of mass destruction.

Connor gritted his teeth. No, the only thing sacred, in times of crisis, was survival. Survival of his people; survival of their way of life.

He turned abruptly and thrust himself back up the steps of Parliament, and back into the Beehive.

Chapter 4

SAINT PETER'S CATHEDRAL

It was ten thirty on Sunday morning, at Saint Peter's Cathedral in Wellington. The congregation, although still thin, had grown a little since the old Saint Paul's Cathedral across the road had merged with Saint Peter's, to become a new Cathedral.

The Right Reverend Bishop Mark Blake sat to the left of the pulpit, in front of the choir stalls. He wore appropriate bishop's dress: a purple cassock, covered by a looser white tunic, a layering of red, and a black scarf. A solid rimu cross hung around his neck, and he held in his hand the wooden bishop's staff.

In front of him, at the pulpit, the Dean of Wellington Cathedral, the Very Reverend Eun Ae Choo, was preaching. She wore a simpler dress: a white tunic over a black cassock, with a black straight scarf.

"The world is facing substantial challenges today," she said, "yet we are still blessed in New Zealand. We have food in our oceans, and water, although crops are sometimes failing, and livestock. Compared with many of our neighbours, we still have more than we need! There is much to thank God for."

Blake glanced over the empty wooden chairs in the nave. There was only a scattered attendance, as usual for an 'ordinary' Sunday, around fifty present.

"We should aim to be a source of peace, in a world passing through times of trial," Choo continued. "Consider our readings today:[3] the Gospel according to Matthew, Verse Nine from Chapter Five, 'Blessed are the peacemakers, for they will be called sons of God.' And the First Epistle of John, Chapter Three, from Verse Sixteen, 'This is how we know what love is: Jesus Christ laid down his life for us. And we ought to lay down our lives for our brothers.'"

Blake looked up at the picture of Christ on the cross, deep in the inner sanctuary, behind the altar. The tiles were fading and some had fallen off.

Choo continued: "'Dear children, let us not love with words or tongue, but with actions and in truth.'"

In actions and truth? Blake prayed silently to God. *We pour out church funds in food packages, from farm to City Mission, while your temple breaks apart and numbers continue to dwindle.*

"This is God's command, as John says," Choo continued, "'To believe in the name of his Son, Jesus Christ, and to love one another as he commands us...And this is how we know that he lives in us: We know it by the Spirit he gave us.'"

The Spirit. Blake stifled a grimace, and looked up at Choo's aging Korean face, radiant with faith in her own words. Why such faith, when presented with such gritty realism? The world's challenges presented a multitude of threats, unprecedented in history: famine, the threat of war and global catastrophe – what exactly did Choo see to rejoice in? Why such childlike devotion?

"And now let us affirm our faith, in the words on page four hundred and ten of the New Zealand Prayer Book,[4]" said Choo. Blake stood, at one with the choir on his left and the congregation on his right.

"'We believe in one God, the Father, the Almighty...We believe in one Lord, Jesus Christ, the only Son of God...We believe in the Holy Spirit, the Lord, the giver of life...'"

*We believe…*Blake frowned, eyes searching for his daughter. Where was she? He found her sitting two-thirds of the way back. What was she doing? Earphones? Surely not playing that wretched tini-pad again.

"Let us pray," said Choo, and Blake dutifully knelt along with the choir and congregation.

"'Lord Jesus Christ,'" he prayed, into the lapel microphone clipped to his scarf, "'we thank you for the universal Church, and for our Church here in Wellington. We pray for the world, and for our nation, that you might provide for our needs: bring us food, and health, and peace. We pray for our leaders, that you might guide their decisions. For your love and goodness…'"

"'We give you thanks, O God,'" all the people responded.

Choo moved away from the pulpit and walked between the choir stalls. She bowed at the altar, and then moved beyond it: behind the silver cup and silver plate with white wafers on top. Then she lifted her voice with a smile.

"'The peace of Christ be always with you,'" she said.

"'And also with you,'" the people responded.

"'The Lord is here.'"

"'God's Spirit is with us.'"

"'Lift up your hearts.'"

"'We lift them to the Lord.'"

Blake had heard the same words several times before. Choo spoke as if they were new every time; as though they held a new and special meaning. Her passion remained a mystery to him.

"'All glory and thanksgiving to you, holy Father,'" she prayed. "'On the night before he died your Son, Jesus Christ, took bread; when he had given you thanks, he broke it, gave it to his disciples, and said: Take, eat, this is my body which is given for you; do this to remember me. After supper he took the cup: Drink this, all of you, for this is my blood of the new covenant which is shed for you and for many for the forgiveness of sins…'"

It was almost over. Blake stifled a sigh.

"'We break this bread to share in the body of Christ,'" Choo proclaimed.

"'We who are many are one body, for we all share the one bread,'" the people answered.

"'Draw near and receive the body and blood of our Saviour Jesus Christ in remembrance that he died for us. Let us feed on him in our hearts by faith with thanksgiving.'"

Blake rose, and walked between the choir stalls. On either side the members watched him, each dressed in white and red. He led the procession, and the choir was poised to follow as he knelt at the railing before the altar, before Choo, the priest of Christ.

Choo held the silver plate with the wafers of bread in front of him, her priestly black scarf and white tunic making way for Communion.

"'The body of our Lord Jesus Christ which was given for you.'"

Every man needs a minister, Blake justified to himself, *even a Bishop*.

He took the wafer, closed his eyes, and placed it in his mouth. It dissolved quickly, as always.

Choo was before him now with the silver chalice: the wine.

"'The blood of our Lord Jesus Christ which was shed for you.'"

He sipped from the wine. The port was strong on his tongue.

The deed complete, Blake rose to his feet, turned, and walked back through the queuing choir members waiting to receive communion, rows of young boys and girls, and older men and women. Some looked bored. Others murmured words of prayer. Behind them the congregation lined up on both sides, joining the queue.

Blake sat, and waited. The choir returned and the choirmaster lifted his hands before them.

"'I Was Glad'" It was so familiar: Hubert Parry, 1902.[5] Psalm 122, 'I was glad when they said unto me: We will go into the house of the Lord.' Blake enjoyed the music, the sophistication of melody and harmony, not like that wretched hip hop rock Selena constantly pumped into their home. Noise! Why did the world love that racket? Blake thought. A little pop, maybe, to relax to, but nothing beat the classics.

Soprano voices lifted, beautifully blended with alto, tenor and deep bass. Blake was glad the church had brought women and girls into the choir: the diversity of the voices was a joy.

Finally Communion came to an end.

"'Go now to love and serve the Lord,'" said Choo brightly. "'Go in peace.'"

"'Amen,'" the congregation replied in unison. "'We go in the name of Christ.'"

The choir sang another song, and Blake walked down the aisle with Choo following behind. Blake paused briefly to shake a few hands, and then hurried down the side of the church, behind the choir stall, to the Robing Room. He'd let Choo handle the pastoral care, it seemed to be her forte.

Blake peeled off his robes, placed them on hangers, straightened the white shirt and black trousers he'd worn underneath, and strode back into the corridor and down to the front entrance, hoping for a quick escape with Selena.

"It was wonderful to serve with you today," said Choo at the door, smiling and grasping his hand in her own.

"Thank you, Very Reverend Choo," he said swiftly. "Always a pleasure."

"Would you like to join us for Sunday lunch?"

"No thank you."

"We've grown some oranges in our yard," said Choo. "My husband is giving out bags to families on our street."

"I'm very happy for you," said Blake. "Keep up the good work."

"Would you like some oranges?"

"No thanks."

"Tofu? We've managed to grow…"

"No. Sorry, must go. I need to prepare for the next Church Council meeting."

Blake pulled his hand away as he searched for his daughter. Where the devil had she gone?

He found her outside, milling about on the street with some other youths.

"What are you doing?" he questioned curtly. "I told you before, we have to get away quickly."

She turned to him, her white face framed by long curly black hair, her blue eyes cold.

"Whatever," she said, shrugging. Blake glanced at her friends and then looked back at Selena. Her earphones were still in.

"Get these out," he said, tugging them away from her ears. "Honestly, Selena, you've got no respect! No respect at all!"

He carried the tini-pad and earphones with him, striding toward the car, ignoring her protestations. At least now she would follow him.

The car park was deserted. Most people were forced to use public transport these days. Blake strode to his 2025 hybrid Mercedes. They were going cheap now, and he'd seized the opportunity.

"Get in," he said to Selena, over his shoulder.

"Go to hell," she replied.

Fury filled him, and he controlled it with his usual iron grip. "Get in, or you're walking home."

"Fine!" she said. "I'll walk!"

Blake looked back and saw a young man waiting: blonde, jeans, spiked hair.

"I'll bet he wasn't in the service."

"What's it to you?"

"That's not going to happen, Selena: you're only sixteen."

"So?"

"Get in now."

She scowled at him, and Blake stared at her. Who was this person? He remembered Selena as a child: gentle, obedient.

She was staring at him – and then finally she complied, getting into the back seat. He opened the driver's door, tossed her tini-pad onto the passenger's seat, got in, and reversed at pace, narrowly missing the young man in his haste.

Chapter 5

A STORM ON THE HORIZON

Tristan Blake stood on Ninety Mile Beach, at low tide. It was just after lunch time. The sun was high in the sky, beating hard on his face, but a light sea breeze took the edge off the heat.

He took a deep breath. The breeze, yes – the breeze would keep the warring memories of heat at bay.

Rau's rod was in his hand. Tristan pressed a worm onto the hook, and cast far into the ocean. It was low tide! Shallow water! Maybe a waste of time, but, even so, he was spurred on.

Joshua sat on the sand nearby. He was sitting with Anahera and the others, but he was closest to Tristan. The others were eating lunch, fish cooked over an open fire, but Joshua was not eating.

Tristan watched, out of the corner of his eye. Who was this man? Why did he irk him so much?

Dark clouds were gathering on the horizon.

"Looks like a storm's coming," said Joshua.

"Hmmm?" said Tristan, pretending not to be watching him.

"A storm."

"Oh. Well a little storm never hurt anyone. Might bring in some fish!"

Joshua was playing with sand now. Tristan couldn't help himself – he tilted his head for a better view, and Joshua smiled up at him. He was doodling, drawing figures in the sand.

"What's all that?" asked Tristan, and Joshua shrugged.

"My thoughts."

"You think in stick figures?"

Joshua's smile widened. "No," he said. And then he rose and stood beside Tristan, looking out to the horizon.

The grey clouds were deepening. "Thunder," Joshua murmured.

"You reckon."

"And heavy rain."

"Let's see if you're more accurate than our weather gurus."

Joshua smiled to him. "What would you say, Tristan?"

Tristan searched the clouds, took a deep breath, and sighed.

"Thunder and rain," he said.

"You don't like the rain?"

Tristan shrugged. "Too much of it in Wellington, I guess."

"Some nice days too?"

"Yeah, some nice days. I remember…"

Suddenly his mind unexpectedly shot into the past. It was his seventeenth birthday and they were on the beach at Days Bay. The sun shone bright and clear.

He didn't want to remember, and yet his mind was betraying him.

His mother was there, green eyes, smiling. It was warm and the sea was sparkling. She was reaching for his surf board, ready to try it herself – laughing and splashing the water.

Selena was there, too, seven years old, her long black curls jumping against her back as she ran around a huge sand castle adding shells. Her wide blue eyes were shining at him.

And…his father…

No. Tristan blocked this memory decisively, before it formed. He shook his head, clearing his mind. Where had this come from? He looked up, and Joshua's eyes were on him.

"What happened?" asked Joshua.

Tristan shuddered, and stared at the dark clouds on the horizon.

"What always happens," he muttered. "Life intervenes."

"You mean death," Joshua murmured beside him. "Death intervenes."

Tristan smiled sadly. "Yeah," he said. "I mean death."

Joshua was quiet for a moment. Surprised, Tristan glanced at him. A cloud had crossed Joshua's face, for a moment; the familiar smile was gone. His expression almost frightened Tristan in its sudden intensity.

"What is it?" Tristan breathed, before he could stop himself. Joshua was struggling, almost in a trance, as if seeing something else. And then his eyes found Tristan's again.

For a moment, in those brown eyes, Tristan saw a peculiar vast expanse: an ocean, and, in that ocean, in that moment, a strong swift current of grief.

"What do you see?" Tristan whispered.

Joshua's eyes lowered from him, and then, momentarily, drifted closed. When they opened again, and lifted to Tristan, the grief had gone.

"I see many things," said Joshua.

"What kind of things?"

Joshua smiled again. "Things that others are better off not knowing."

Tristan searched his face. It was a gentle face, unassuming – thoroughly ordinary and, simultaneously, thoroughly strange.

"You like talking in riddles?" said Tristan.

"Sometimes," said Joshua. "But with good reason."

"Let me guess," said Tristan. "Everything you do has good reason."

Joshua tilted his head and smiled, then backed away.

Tristan remained at the water's edge, fishing. The water rose steadily to his knees. He'd caught a light green-blue speckled kahawai, but nothing more.

Rau joined him. "Time to give it up, mate," he said.

"Just a few more minutes."

"You have a lifetime to beat him, you know."

"Whatever."

The clouds were approaching fast. The light had dimmed, and Tristan could hear a distant rumbling. He scowled, and looked at Rau.

"You know," he began, "your friend is…strange."

"Strange?" Rau smiled. "Is that all you have?"

"He…he seems to know nothing, and then suddenly knows everything."

"What do you mean?" Rau's head tilted thoughtfully.

"I swear he saw something: something important."

"Saw?"

"In his mind's eye, he saw it. It was bad."

Tristan swallowed. Rau was frowning now, obviously trying to read his expression.

"What do you think he saw?"

"You…you don't think he saw the end, do you?"

Rau laughed, but then quickly swallowed his reaction.

"The End of the World?" he said. "You believe in that?"

"Doesn't take much to believe in that now, does it?"

"I guess not, but…we've been waiting for that for two thousand years."

"What do you mean?"

"The Apocalypse, when Christ comes again. Our back is against the wall, and, hey, presto."

Tristan stared at him. "You see what I mean?" he said. "You people are crazy. You're actually looking forward to the End of the World."

"Not exactly – it's Christ we're looking forward to."

"Why?"

"Because he'll make everything right again."

Tristan studied him. "Everything right?"

"No more pain, or tears, or suffering, or death…"

A deep pain seized Tristan's chest at the words. He turned quickly away, and stared hard at the horizon, fighting a torrent of emotion.

"No more tears," he whispered. "No more death. Wouldn't that be nice to believe."

Rau stood silently beside him. Tristan suddenly envied him. He actually believed it! Oh, to have faith! Oh, to have hope, even in the face of utter disaster.

"Who knows what he saw," Tristan murmured to him. "Maybe he saw his own death, his own mortality: his own destiny into nothingness, like the rest of us."

"I don't think so," said Rau. "I don't think he's afraid of death."

Tristan glanced at Joshua. He was smiling, joking with his friends, helping to gather up the remains of the fish.

"Maybe you're right," said Tristan.

Rau tugged gently on his rod, and Tristan surrendered it to him. So be it: they would be travelling on with Joshua, for now. Yet curiosity still drew him.

Tristan strode up to Joshua, and tapped him on the shoulder.

"Hey," he said. "What did you see?"

Joshua's brown eyes were on him; Tristan stood his ground, as Joshua studied him.

"I saw many things," Joshua finally replied. "Many things that hurt. But there is one thing I can tell you."

"What?"

"I saw your mother."

Tristan stared at him, and then tears came from nowhere. He flushed, and Joshua's hand touched his arm.

"I'm sorry," Joshua murmured.

Tristan's eyes blurred. "It's not your fault," he whispered, blinking rapidly, trying to see.

"I know," said Joshua.

"I…" Tristan stuttered. "I…" How could he say it? Actually speak of love? No! He wouldn't do it. It was much easier to think the opposite! Much easier to say the opposite.

"I hate him," he said. "I hate him." His tears began to clear.

Joshua's eyes were on him, quiet, gentle, walking amidst Tristan's sudden searing pain. "I know," he said, "but it wasn't his fault, either."

Tristan arched back. He had a sudden urge to hit him. "What do you mean?" he cried.

Kind, firm eyes held his gaze. "You know what I mean," he said.

Tristan stood stiffly in the gloom, dark clouds forming over his head, light rain falling on his face.

Joshua's face darkened.

"I don't understand you," said Tristan. "What are you on about? But…but your words seem so real! And there's more! Something you're not telling me."

"Some things are better not to know," Joshua whispered. "Not until the right time."

A burden was in his eyes – a frightening burden. But then it was gone again, as fast as it had arrived.

He smiled, and turned, and joined the others. Tristan's gaze followed him.

"Well?" asked Rau, again at his side.

"Strange…" Tristan murmured. Then he shrugged his shoulders, and turned away.

Chapter 6

LAWFUL USE OF FORCE

James Connor sat in Select Committee Room Three, Parliament House. Gathered around him on either side were four of his Party, and across the large desk sat Patrick Clarkson and his representatives. To the left of Clarkson was one Member from the Clean Green Party, and to Connor's left was a Member of the Christian Conservative Party. Between them sat a Maori Party Member. At the far end of the desk was Police Commissioner Derek Peters, and Ms Kiri Rakena was seated at the computer which held all the public submissions for the matter at hand.

Connor's eyes swept the room taking in the wooden carvings of Maori ancestors, hanging on the walls. Then he brought his mind back to the task ahead.

"As Chairperson for the Law and Order Select Committee," he said, "I want to start by thanking you for your attendance."

Clarkson was grimacing – Connor ignored him.

"We are here to debate The National Lawful Use of Force Bill and The Extension of Maximum Sentences Bill."

Alongside him, the Minister of Law and Order, the Honourable Chin

Ho, stood.

"I am presenting these bills to the House," she said, with slightly clipped English, "in light of growing tensions in New Zealand. It is vital we maintain control, and I consider these law changes essential for sustaining peace in our land throughout the challenges ahead."

"What challenges are you talking about?" asked Kiri Rakena. "The public haven't been informed of challenges…"

"We've been warning the public of the implications of climate change for years!" said Tracy Harrison, from the Clean Green Party.

"Sure, the temperature's rising," said Rakena, lifting her hands to animate her words. "It's getting hot. We're having more droughts. Some farms have packed it in. But most of these submissions are asking what the Government is doing to help."

"The Government is taking stock of the situation," said Connor, bristling at the words.

"By trying to control the public," said Rakena.

"Exactly!" said Clarkson. "That's the Government the public voted in!"

Connor glared at Clarkson, whose face was annoyingly bright, and turned back to Rakena.

"The New Conservative Party supports individual efforts…" said Connor.

"…by not lifting a hand to help," said Rakena. "A lot of people have written in to say they are finding ways to help themselves: they're growing food in their own sections, sharing with their neighbours…"

"This is precisely the threat I am talking about!" said Connor, rising to his feet and jabbing a finger at Rakena, staring at Clarkson. "People are growing their own food and sharing! A few oranges here, a few apples there, sure! But what if this becomes the economy of the future? No declarations, no tax: no government!"

Clarkson rose to his feet, his eyes locked on Connor.

"Sit down, Right Honourable Prime Minister," he said. "You are the Chairperson of this debate, not the dictator of it."

Fury filled Connor. His temples throbbed as he stared back at Clarkson. How dare he? Yet there was truth in Clarkson's words. He took a deep breath and sat down, gesturing to his Minister of Law and Order.

Chin Ho stood again.

"New Zealand faces new threats," she began. "There is a rising dissatisfaction with the status quo. More people are hungry; more people are stealing. Inflation is rising. Violent crime has increased. Transport is limited, and jobs are out of reach. An entire redefining of our society might be ahead of us: the risk of civil unrest is high."

The Maori MP stood, Rawiri Heka.

"Perhaps a redefining of our society is what is required."

Connor took in Heka's greying hair, and the lines ageing his warm brown face.

"Any redefining of our society must be mediated through a democratically voted-in Parliament," said Connor. "That is why we are here! That is why we have been given the luxury of debating the issues. We have the freedom to determine our own fates.

"But what happens if neighbourhoods develop their own food supply, economies, and their own leadership? Destabilization! Local economy, local law, local politics; tribal wars. Do we really want to return to the Dark Ages?

"We must retain central leadership. We must retain order, and national cohesion, or we will be lost," said Connor.

There was silence. Satisfied, Connor saw he had broken through. Then Richard Holm, of the Christian Conservative Party, stood.

"But what is the purpose of central leadership?"

Connor's brow puckered. Holm was usually a reliable supporter of the Conservative Party.

"What do you mean?"

"What is your goal?"

Connor rose to his feet, smiling.

"What is our goal?" he said, gesturing to his other Party Members.

"Our goal is a happy, safe, independent, productive New Zealand."

"That's our goal too," said Clarkson.

"And ours," said Harrison.

"The devil is in the detail," said Holm, and Connor flashed a warning look in his direction.

Rakena shifted in her seat, as if uncomfortable, and then Commissioner Derek Peters rose to his feet.

"I represent the police at this committee," he began, "and I can tell you this: crime is definitely on the increase in New Zealand. There were twelve thousand, three hundred and four cases of serious violent crime last month alone. That represents an increase of three hundred percent compared with 2025, and six hundred percent compared with 2020. Theft has also risen dramatically. As things stand now, police do not have the resources to deal with theft. We are struggling to fully respond to all cases of violent crime. There have also been a number of political demonstrations that might have deteriorated into civil unrest. The police support both bills presented today. In our view, the police need the authority to implement increased force if it should be required."

Connor nodded at him, and looked around the faces at the table. Clarkson was silent – he seemed convinced by Constable Peters. Maori MP Heka also was silent. Harrison, of the Greens, was slowly nodding.

The only two looking uncomfortable were Holm, of the Christian Conservative Party, and Rakena, representing the public.

"Just what kind of increased force are we talking about?" asked Holm.

Constable Peters' eyes lingered on him, and then returned to Connor.

"Whatever force is required."

"Meaning?" asked Rakena.

Constable Peters shifted on his feet. He was a respectable looking man, thought Connor: early forties with short tidy brown hair. His police uniform was pressed, and his eyes were firm but kind.

He bowed his head at Rakena.

"Only what is required, Madam, and no more. At present, the police are able to use force to contain danger, to prevent greater harm. This bill only seeks to expand this application: the force must be clearly used to prevent greater harm to our communities, nothing less."

Connor could see the Constable had won Rakena's trust.

"...and so, Mr Speaker," said Connor, standing at his seat in the House of Representatives, "I would like to thank the Law and Order Committee for considering the bills, and attending hearings, and I now move that the National Lawful Use of Force Bill, and the Extension of Maximum Sentences Bill, be moved a third time. I commend the bills to the House."

"This debate has concluded," said the Speaker. "I'll ask the Clerk for a Party Vote."

The Clerk now stood, in front of the Speaker.

"Ninety-four votes in favour," she said. "Twenty-six votes opposed."

"The motion is agreed to," said the Speaker.

Connor nodded his head, and beat his fist in victory. Another step toward securing the safety of New Zealand! Soon they would establish stability! Soon he would safeguard their freedom.

Chapter 7

DAYS BAY AND THE NEW ZEALAND CHURCH COUNCIL

Mark Blake was glad to arrive home, after another Sunday church service. Climbing the internal steps from his garage to the hallway, he wearily made his way to the kitchen and dumped the keys to his Mercedes on the table. Selena scurried away to her bedroom – he let her be.

Mark kicked off his shoes, and wandered into the lounge. Before him, through floor to ceiling windows, was the massive expanse of Lower Hutt, with the Hutt River to the left and Wellington Harbour to the right. The day was clear, the water of the harbour sparkled in the distance, and wind whistled around the house. Mark drew in a deep breath, sat down on the leather couch, and reached for the paper.

There was an article on the front page, 'Parliament passes bills giving unprecedented power to police,' with a photo of James Connor smiling, in front of the Beehive. Mark studied his face for a moment: James Connor! He had actually made it to Prime Minister! Mark remembered their debates at Grammar. Oh yes, things had been different back then…Mark had been different. What had he argued for? That's right, for social care.

"The poor!" he had said to James, at seventeen, full of idealism and purism. *"Democracy is made to protect the weak!"*

"No, no," James had replied, *"you're missing the point, Mark – your faith is filling you with gushy sentiment. Democracy is for the rich."*

"It is to enhance the rich to lift up the poor."

James had laughed. *"Forget about politics, Mark: you should be a priest!"*

Mark had stared at him. A priest? He had thought about it, prayed about it, and then gone ahead and done it.

Now he was the Anglican Bishop of Wellington.

For a moment he felt a sharp pain deep in his chest. Tossing the paper aside, he rose and wandered over to the table beside the TV, where there was a photo in an old frame of his wife Teresa.

She looked young. Mark remembered the day: it was one of his best memories, and now was one of the most painful. They had been down the beach at Days Bay, on a perfect summer's day. Tristan and Selena had been there, and Tristan had actually managed to surf! Mark remembered his own laughter and his son's joyous enthusiasm. Selena had built the biggest sand castle Mark had ever seen, or at least the one with the prettiest shell decorations. And Teresa…

Mark held his breath now, at the memory. Teresa…her smile had been for him, as he had held the camera. Her happiness had been radiant, before…before…

Clenching his teeth, Mark shoved the photo down on the table, face down.

"I'm going out!" he called out, half choking, to Selena. "I've got another Church Council meeting!"

"Whatever!" her sixteen year-old voice replied as he grabbed his shoes and keys, and hurried back down to the garage.

The New Zealand Church Council. Usually they only met every three months, but lately, with the increasing demands, everyone involved thought they'd better meet more regularly.

Mark was hungry. He hurriedly ate a muesli bar from an emergency packet he kept in the glove box, and then walked through the deserted car park. Once again, his was the only car.

This time the meeting was being held at the Glen Road Baptist Church, in Kelburn. Mark wandered into the hallway, and then through into the auditorium. The Baptists often had a modern style of church – and there was the tiny cross, on the pulpit, at the front.

"Right Reverend Bishop Blake!" said a voice, and Mark turned to greet the grinning older man.

"Murray!" he said, reaching a hand to him. He looked homely, with a knitted brown vest and white shirt sleeves rolled up to the elbows.

"Welcome to our humble abode."

"I wouldn't say 'humble'…"

"I know you wouldn't say 'fancy,' either."

"Perhaps not…"

"Good to see you, Blakey."

Mark almost choked on his familiarity, but accepted it: Pastor Murray Simon was the head of the Baptist Council of New Zealand.

Murray motioned him towards a meeting room where eight other ministers were seated representing Catholic, Presbyterian, Methodist, Pentecostal, and other churches. Mark acknowledged them all, and then sat at the head of the table.

"Welcome, everyone," he said. "Thank you for coming again."

"Shall we open in prayer?" asked Murray.

"By all means, go ahead."

Murray bowed his head, and Mark glanced around at everyone present doing the same, before he followed suit.

"Precious Father," Murray prayed. "Thank you for your goodness. Thank you for your love. Thank you for bringing us all together here safely this Sunday afternoon. We pray that you might guide our meeting: help us to know what is right – give us your wisdom. We pray for New Zealand, that you might protect us and lead us, in Jesus Christ's name."

"Amen," said everyone, and Mark followed suit.

"Thank you," he said to Murray, and now he turned to the others. "What do we have to report?" he asked. "Who would like to go first?"

The Catholic Priest, Andrew Stead, lifted his hand.

"Yes, Father Andrew."

"We've noticed a lot of fear in our parishes," said the young man.

"Fear?" questioned the Presbyterian minister, the Reverend Robyn Peer.

"Well…they're wondering if this is the beginning of the End."

Glances passed between the ministers present. Mark looked at Murray, who had a glimmer of a smile, and shook his head.

"Honestly," said Mark, "a bit of heat, and people are already talking about the End of the World? People have speculated about that for almost two thousand years. The End is in God's hands – let's talk about today. How are the churches doing across New Zealand?"

"Well," began the Pentecostal minister, Luke Davies, "I want to praise God for everything that is happening in the Fullness of Life Churches across New Zealand. Our attendance has gone up three hundred per cent! God is giving us healings, and prophecies…"

"Good for you," Mark muttered, as Murray nudged him with an amused warning in his eyes.

"So the Pentecostal churches are thriving," said Mark. "And you, Reverend Robyn – how is the Presbyterian Church managing?"

Robyn shrugged her shoulders. "Much as it has before."

"Sounds like the Anglican Church," said Mark.

Now Murray was ambling around the table, as if in thoughtful prayer. Mark turned to him.

"What about you, Murray? How is the Baptist Church doing?"

Murray tilted his head, and gazed back at Mark.

"We're doing well, Mark."

"How so?"

"At least in this congregation…people are struggling more, but they're also helping each other more. Food is more difficult to find – but we seem to be more grateful for the food we do get."

He sounded like Choo, the Dean of Wellington Cathedral; even looked like her, in that moment. There was something in his eyes – something Mark did not understand.

"Curiously," Murray continued, "for us it is almost as though less is more."

Mark stared at him. "Less is more?" he said. "Sounds like an ad for losing weight!"

Murray held his gaze steadfastly. "Exactly," he said.

Mark felt uncomfortable. He looked away into the less challenging face of Father Andrew.

"And how are your finances holding up, Andrew?" he asked. The young man, blonde wavy hair, blue eyes, looked a little flustered. Mark wondered why the Catholic Church had not sent a more seasoned representative to the Council.

"Finances?" said Andrew. "What do you mean?"

"Offerings, Father: offerings! Are they falling off for you, as they are for us? Staff cuts, buildings wearing down, congregations dwindling – no perceived relevance anymore."

The young man's face looked bewildered. "What?" he said. "No, sir…"

Surprised, Mark searched him. "What do you mean?"

"Offerings?" Andrew continued. "I can't give you a figure, but I'm sure they've increased. More people are coming to church; they're looking for hope. Some people need more help, and other people are giving more. The rich are lifting up the poor."

Oh, damn, Mark thought, before he could stop himself. *The boy sounds just like me thirty years ago!*

"People are afraid, but they're also excited," said Andrew.

"Excited?" asked Mark.

"Well, yes, Bishop. We believe Christ is coming again soon."

Mark stared at him. A hard lump formed in his throat, and for a moment he couldn't breathe. He swallowed.

"Amen to that!" said Murray in his ear.

Mark forced himself to look at each minister in turn. Were they all expecting Christ's imminent return? Catholic, Pentecostal and Baptist were united – could it be possible? There it was. But others were wondering; they had doubt. Robyn looked particularly perplexed.

"No one knows the time or the place of Christ's return," said Mark mechanically, "but, in the meantime, here we are. How to manage with the resources we have? That is the question."

"No arguments there," said Murray, but still Mark could see a glimmer in his eye.

The meeting continued, talking about this and that: nothing of any great consequence, to Mark's mind. He dutifully continued as Chairperson, but was glad to finally draw the meeting to a close, an hour and a half later. Andrew recited a prayer but Mark hardly registered the words. Then it was over.

The ministers filed out of the room, but Murray did not let him escape so easily.

"Mark," the older man began, "is something going on with you?"

"What do you mean?"

"Your mind seems in a different space."

Every man needs a minister: even a Bishop.

Where had those words come from? His own words, suddenly in his heart – suddenly pressing. He resisted them.

"No," he said. "Nothing's wrong, Murray. Everything's fine."

Bullshit, his thoughts now betrayed him. *Nothing's been right with you for nine years. Not since...since...*

Grief threatened to overwhelm him, but he thrust it aside. Control was the only way to survive.

"Thank you, Murray," he said clearly, avoiding his eyes. "See you again next time."

And with absolute control, he straightened his shoulders, turned, and walked out the door to his isolated Mercedes Benz.

Chapter 8

AN EMPTY HOUSE

Selena lay on her back on her bed, her long black curls thrown erratically across the pillow, her white blouse dishevelled.

Her room was a mess. School books littered the carpet beside her desk. Maths was boring, music was a tedious farce, and in English she felt like a primary school kid playing with words. The teachers' assignments were a waste of time. She swept them aside in favour of something more stimulating.

Real music – that was the thing. Words of real life; the meaninglessness, the rage. Her earphones played out the heavy beat, in unison with her heart: searing tones of pain and death.

Her father had gone off to another pathetic church meeting. What was it with the robes, and the four hundred year old music? Why did he keep dragging her back there? She hated it, all the talk of the body and the blood. She hated the faces, drugged with the 'Spirit,' or, even worse, showing nothing at all.

She stared at the ceiling. She'd spent so many hours, just staring, like a prisoner in her own home. Where was he? She didn't care. Working here, working there; working everywhere. He brought home food and he paid someone to cook, and clean. What else was there? Apparently nothing. Apparently no one.

Her mother had gone. Selena had spent many years imagining she was still there with her, in her room; imagining what she would have said. But once she'd turned twelve, she had run out of inspiration. Her mother was dead. And as Selena had never experienced her as a teenager, she simply had no idea what to say to herself anymore.

Grief was a numb companion. And then there was nothing at all: nothing but anger, and this toward *him*. A perpetual, escalating anger, growing year after year after year.

Anger was now her closest ally.

Suddenly she was accosted – seized by a voice in her head.

Go, it said.

Go?

Now's your chance, it replied.

Excitement filled her, as refreshing as it was new. Could she leave? She could! She could use this imprisonment and turn it to her own favour!

She thrust herself from her bed, and headed down the hallway into the lounge, searching for her father's wallet before she realised he'd have it on him. Where would he stash cash? She went through to his study and found some cash hidden inside a book. A hundred bucks! That should be enough, to get her into town. Alex would meet her! He'd get her out of this hole.

She grabbed a key and her sandals, tugged her skirt down, and set off through the back door.

It was a long walk downhill to catch a train to Wellington Central. Excitement pressed her forward as she reached into her pocket for her phone. The network was down, again! Crazy! But surely it would come back on soon, and she'd be able to get through to Alex.

Eyes were on her as she walked – she ignored them. A brisk breeze embraced her, lifting her black curls. She drew in a deep breath, invigorated.

Halfway down the hill, a crowd was gathering. Surprised, Selena looked around. The police were there! Something had happened…

"What do you mean the petrol ran out?" a man cried out. He was short, and stumpy. "You're on a hill, idiot! Don't you know how to use the brakes?"

A red car had smashed into a wooden fence.

"It slid!" another man shouted, tall and muscular. "The gas ran out, the thing spluttered, and before I knew it I was sliding backwards…"

"Train not good enough for you, like the rest of us?"

"Don't blame me if you can't get a decent job!"

"Arrogant prick…"

The solidly built driver was about to throw his fists but a police officer, dressed in blue, stepped in. His face was haggard and his forehead creased into a frown.

"That's enough," he said.

"Oh, yeah?" said the driver. "Who says?"

"I do," said the policeman. "I'm Constable Stevens, and you're under arrest." He waved his badge.

"I don't think so!" said the driver. "From what I hear, there's no money left to imprison all the criminals."

The policeman grimaced. "That's not your problem."

"You bet it's not!" the driver said, pointing to the stumpy-looking man. "This joker's my problem!"

The policeman pulled out his baton and handcuffs.

"Just get on the bike."

The driver smirked. "What's the matter, no money for a car?"

"I don't have time for this!" said the policeman. "Get onto the bike now! I'll take you to the station, and then I need to move onto the next call."

The driver looked at the policeman, at the baton, and at the bike. An unusual expression came over his face. Then he put his hands out to be cuffed.

"Sure," he said.

Selena frowned. She glanced down the hill – could she easily slip past? She shifted her feet, uncertain, while Stevens cuffed the driver's hands and escorted him to the back of the bike.

The policeman sat on the front of the bike. Selena waited for him, watching while he fired up the bike, reversed, and shifted the bike into gear to move forward. Suddenly something changed. Selena felt it, before she saw it: the car-driver! He thrust his cuffed hands over Stevens' head from behind, dragging the chain tight around his neck.

Selena gasped. The driver was smirking, foolish man! He was stirring trouble, but not trying to murder the cop! He jerked Stevens back, by the neck, and the bike swerved, falling on its side.

The policeman rose, rage filling his eyes.

Selena swallowed. "Take it easy," she whispered. "Don't do anything rash."

The driver was still on the ground, trapped under the bike. The policeman grabbed his baton, lifted the bike away, and began to beat him.

Selena froze. He was the police! Charged to protect the public! Selena glanced at the fence owner, who was now backing away rapidly, and looked back again.

The driver was unconscious! His head was bleeding, and the policeman was still beating him!

"Stop it!" Selena screamed. "You'll kill him!"

The policeman stopped, stunned. He stared at the man lying unmoving beneath the bike. He fingered his own throat, and stared at his baton. Then he looked at her.

Terror filled Selena. What was he going to do? She fumbled at her cell-phone. Who would she call? The police? An ambulance? There was no network! There was nothing…

She longed to run, and glanced up the hill. Should she go back? Run back home to Dad? Conflict tore her heart: was that really her home? Was her father really safety?

The officer was approaching with regret in his eyes. His lips were parting, trying to form an apology. But it was too late. She wrapped her arms around herself – her body was starting to shake uncontrollably.

"Mum…" she sobbed. "What the hell is happening? Mum…"

And she ran down the hill, on and on and on.

A train was waiting, at the station below. Selena didn't question where it was going, but thrust herself on board – she only had to leave where she was. A lady appeared asking for a ticket, and Selena gave her the one hundred dollar note.

She stared out of the window of the train. The scenery was a blur. She had no idea where she was going. Her body was numb; her heart was numb. She jabbed randomly at her cell-phone.

The train arrived at Central Wellington Station, and the lady stood before her again, telling her to get off. She obeyed.

On the platform, Alex was waiting. When Selena saw him she almost collapsed, and his arm came around her shoulders.

"It's okay," he whispered.

"How did you…?"

"You called me."

"I…" She started to sob – couldn't control herself.

He grasped her hand and she followed.

"Where are we going…?"

"Somewhere where you'll be safe."

"Is anywhere safe anymore?"

"Yeah – some things can make us strong."

He took her away from the train station and led her down one street then another, and another. Selena felt like she was constantly about to fall, but he dragged her on and on until suddenly they were standing before a door.

Selena stared up at it. It had strange yet familiar symbols on its walls.

"I don't know," Selena whispered. "I don't like this place."

"Rather go to church?"

Selena shuddered. Church? No. Her father…But this place?

"Where do you want me to take you, Selena?" asked Alex. "To a pub? Give you alcohol? Speed? Addiction is weakness. This is the real strength."

Selena stared at him. She stared at the door.

"What is this place?"

"You know what this is."

You know.

"What do I know?"

Alex shook his head, and then gestured around them. "You know it all, Selena: you're a smart girl. Politics is impotent. The police are the real criminals. Education is control. And, worst of all, religion is lies."

"God…" Selena whispered. "God…"

"There is only one god," he said, pointing to the symbol.

Cold chills seized her body. She knew what this was, and it was not God. But who was God? Who was he, but an absent, indifferent, neglectful father? What did he know? What did he care?

"Who will be your god?" asked Alex. And drawing in a deep breath, legs wobbling, Selena reached out and thrust herself through the door.

Chapter 9

KAITAIA

Rau awoke lying in his tent, in a black sleeping bag. Tristan lay next to him, snoring.

Surprised, Rau shook his head and then he remembered: Kaitaia! They'd travelled down the night before, and now here they were camping in Joshua's home town.

The tent was stuffy. Rau dragged himself out of his sleeping bag. He checked the time; it was ten o'clock! Immediately he reached across to unzip the tent door, and crawled out onto the red rug beyond.

The sun was shining. Rau rose to his feet, stretched out his arms, and looked around.

His old silver-green two-man tent was pitched on flat yellow grass, sandwiched within a medley of colourful tents. To the left of Rau was the white office of the camping ground manager, and a handful of brown cabins. A long row of campervans were parked to the right. Rau remembered, now: this camping ground was down the road from Kaitaia Domain.

Rau searched for Joshua and found him sitting on a grassy slope under a pine tree, along from the row of campervans.

"Good morning," said Rau.

"Good morning."

"You're not at home?"

"I visited my mother last night – she knows I'm staying here with all of you."

He'd changed his clothes; full length black jeans, sandals and a T-shirt that said, 'I love Kaitaia!'

"Where did you sleep?"

Joshua pointed to the one-man tent next to Rau's site.

"Oh. Just the clothes on your back."

"What else do we need?"

Joshua smiled, and Rau studied him. Why was he lingering with this Pakeha? Why hadn't he returned to Kerikeri early this morning, as expected?

"It's Sunday," Rau muttered, half to himself. He wasn't booked to preach, but had expected to attend.

"Church?" asked Joshua.

"Well, yes."

"You are a priest."

Rau searched his gaze. What would Joshua's response be to his priesthood?

"I am a priest," said Rau, without shame. "Is it that obvious?"

Joshua's smile widened. "It is to me."

"Why?"

"I have a feel for these things."

Rau frowned. He was perplexed by this man – an emotion he had not experienced in a long time. Joshua seemed to enjoy avoiding direct questions, and maintaining a deliberate sense of mystery. But did he have any real substance?

"Stick around," said Joshua. "See what you think."

Rau stared at him for a long moment, and then Tristan joined them.

"Hey!" said Tristan. "Nice shirt."

"Thank you," said Joshua, tipping his head slightly. "Glad you like it."

"How's the fishing in Kaitaia?" asked Tristan. "I still need to beat your record."

"You tell me."

Rau watched as Tristan smiled at the challenge. "Okay," he said. "Watch this space."

The others were stirring now from the tents. The four they'd met from Ninety Mile Beach surrounded Joshua, and Anahera was there, too, sitting a little apart, quiet and attentive.

Rau cast his eyes around the campground. Some people were still resting in their tents. Others lounged on collapsible chairs outside tents, reading books. Kids threw balls to each other, along the lanes. The campground was particularly full. On some sites, two tents had been set up, and more and more people poured out of them.

"Just like Kerikeri," Rau murmured.

"Busy?" asked Tristan.

"Packed. Not just in the campgrounds, either. Did you see, on the way here?"

"Yeah."

"Tents in the parks, and along the streets."

"Something big going down?"

Rau frowned. "People can't afford rent anymore."

Joshua stood, and walked along the lane of campervans.

"What's he doing?" asked Rau.

"Don't know," Tristan replied. "But I'm going to find out."

Rau trailed behind him. Right now, in Kerikeri, his congregation would be singing hymns, and then their Vicar would lead them in prayer. Instinctively Rau began to hum 'Amazing Grace,' although he felt a sense of irony. 'I once was lost, but now I'm found'? He was feeling an increasing sense of being more lost, the more he followed this man.

Joshua glanced at each campervan as he passed by. These were the best powered campsites, plush with pines and pohutukawa, larger and more expensive, with larger, newer, and mostly hired vans. Rau had never travelled in one. Joshua paused for a moment, looking at one particular van – the largest, the family still within. Then he moved on.

Around a corner, to the left, was a hidden lane. The sites were smaller with a few weeds growing, and were filled with old campervans. These were the homes of permanent residents. Joshua stopped, and looked around.

"Here," he said, guiding his friends to a picnic area. "Let's have some food."

"Great idea!" said Tristan. "What are we having?"

"Brunch," said Joshua, looking straight at Rau.

"Brunch?" said Rau, and then he realised. "My fish…"

"What does everyone have?" asked Joshua.

"I've got avocado!" said Anahera. "Lots, at home!"

"Go and get it," Joshua replied.

"Meat?" one of the men asked. "I've actually still got beef, fresh from the farm."

"Go. Bring it back."

"And bread," another said. "I have a friend who owns a bakery."

"I have cheese."

"Bring it all!" said Joshua. "Bring it all, and let's have a feast. Time for a kiwi barbeque!"

The friends dispersed. Rau and Tristan wandered toward the campground's kitchen.

"So what are you bringing, mate?" asked Rau, and Tristan shrugged.

"I don't know, I don't have anything."

"Just in it for the kai?" Rau smiled gently.

"You can talk, you're only getting the fish he won for you."

Rau growled – Tristan was too quick off the mark! "I know," he said, "but isn't that the same with us all?"

"It doesn't matter," said Tristan. "He knows we're away from home."

"Each one should bring what he can…" Rau murmured. "This all seems so familiar, but I can't think why! He seems like the closest of friends and the strangest of strangers, all at the same time."

Tristan shrugged. "Why let it bother you? Why not just have a good feed?"

"Because there's more to life than a good feed, boy! Don't they give you food in the army?"

Tristan grumbled next to him, and Rau shook his head. "Sorry," he said.

"Forget it," said Tristan, as he strode into the kitchen. "Let's get that fish."

By the time Rau caught up, Tristan had already wrestled the plastic wrapped fish out of the large deep freeze unit and onto the floor.

"This thing weighs a ton!" said Tristan. "Gimme a hand!"

They struggled with the fish, out of the kitchen and toward the barbeque area, putting it down occasionally to warm their freezing hands.

Finally they reached Joshua, and laid the snapper at his feet.

"Done," said Tristan, and Joshua smiled.

"Good work."

"It's still frozen," said Rau.

"So it is."

"This fish is far too big for us to eat."

"You're right." Joshua's eyes wandered around the entire campground, before returning to Rau. "It is far too big just for us."

"You mean to feed everyone?"

"Why not? We have too much for ourselves."

"I…" Rau looked at his face, and then nodded. "I agree."

The others began to return. Anahera had brought other ingredients too, along with avocado: olive oil and butter, salad leaves and tomato, as well as plates, knives and tongs. The farmer laid down ten pieces of beef steak fillet. Another brought ten bottles of wine, and somebody else brought twenty packets of buns.

"Looking good," said Joshua. "Shall we get started?" And he rubbed his hands together and reached for the tongs.

Rau stood back, and watched as Joshua's friends hovered around and helped prepare the food. Anahera directed a lot of the food preparation, but the farmer joined Joshua barbequing the meat.

Tristan stood over the snapper. "What can I do?"

"Cut some fillets off the thickest part, first."

"The thing is frozen…" Tristan touched the skin. "No, hang on – it's starting to thaw." And he began to cut.

The sun was rising in the sky – it was eleven o'clock by the time the first fillets were cooked.

"Time for communion…" murmured Rau. Anahera put a bun, and salad and avocado, and a steak and snapper fillet onto a plate.

"Who first?" she asked Joshua, and he pointed to the old campervans nearby.

"There."

Anahera looked at him, nodded, and then walked over to a campervan. Rau watched her, from a distance. She hesitated and then walked up to the van and knocked on the door.

"What d'ya want?" a man's voice yelled out. "I'm busy!"

"We have lots of kai!" said Anahera. "And we want to share it!"

The door opened, and a dishevelled old man stood before her, with colourless skin and an overgrown grey beard, wearing a drab singlet and shorts.

"Food?" he said. "I haven't had a decent meal in weeks!"

"Here!" said Anahera, offering the plate. "There's more over here, too!" And she gestured at Joshua and the barbeque.

The man's eyes moved over the group, and their food, his gaze settling on the wine.

"You got grog?"

"Ae, but…"

"I'm in! Just wait, lassie." And he disappeared then reappeared, dragging on trousers and a shirt before joining them.

Anahera returned to prepare another plate. Joshua pointed to another of the old campervans, and off she went again.

The old man ambled up to Tristan.

"Give us a drink, mate?" he said. Rau could see Tristan's disdain.

“I don’t know,” said Tristan. “You look like you should give it a rest.”

“Wanna put a drink in front of an old man and then stop him?” said the man, pressing against Tristan.

Rau blocked his way. “Take it easy, mate,” he said. “This one has nothing to do with it. What’s your name?”

“Frank.”

“Where are you from?”

“Where does it look like, joker? I’m stuck here, I’ve been here all my life. Who brought the grog?”

“I did.”

Joshua was behind him. Frank turned to look at him.

“You wanna give an alcoholic a whiff of our quality Kaitaia produce?”

“This wine won’t do anything for you.”

“I’ll be the judge of that.”

“It’s low alcohol.”

“Yeah, right – not from our vineyards.”

“This wine is special – from my father’s vineyard.”

“Give it to me, and I’ll show you how special it is.”

Joshua held his eyes, smiled slightly and then handed him a bottle.

“Joshua!” Rau exploded, before he could stop himself.

“Rau,” Joshua replied calmly. “Watch and learn.”

Gleefully, Frank tore off the bottle's foil wrap, popped the cork, and took a swig. Then he spat it out.

“That’s sh…”

“Highest quality Kaitaia grapes,” Joshua interrupted him.

“To hell with the grapes!”

“Keep drinking.”

Frank took another swig and then started to scull the whole bottle.

“What the hell is this stuff?” he said, midway through the bottle, dragging his sleeve across his mouth.

“Not what you’re looking for.”

"The grapes…The taste is different. There's something about them."

"Good," said Joshua. "I thought you'd like it. And what about you? What have you got?"

"I'll show you. Come into my mansion."

"Okay then."

Rau watched as Joshua followed Frank into his campervan.

Tristan nudged him cheekily, from the side.

"Whad'ya reckon?" he said. "Think Joshua will try some real home brew?"

"I doubt it," said Rau, shifting awkwardly.

"I bet Frank has marijuana growing out of his toilet."

"You might be right."

"I might score a joint later."

Both Rau and Tristan watched the entrance of the campervan for movement. Frank emerged first, lost in thought.

Rau watched him closely. What had Joshua said to him? Frank marched towards the barbeque, and reached for the tongs.

"Step aside," he said to the farmer. "I'll show you how to barbe like a real man."

Joshua finally emerged from the campervan. He was standing high on the step, looking across at the gathering people. The crowd was growing.

"Amazing what some kai will do," Rau muttered, and Tristan laughed.

"Kaitaia, eh, mate? 'Plenty of food'?"

"You're more intelligent than you look."

"Whatever."

Rau's eyes were still on Joshua, who was now looking at the lane of the expensive campervans.

"Good luck," Rau muttered under his breath.

Joshua moved forward, received a plate of food from Anahera, and then wandered toward the first large campervan.

He knocked on the door. There was no answer. Joshua knocked again – still no answer.

"Are they away?" Rau asked, but Tristan shifted on his feet beside him.

"No way," he said. "Just ignoring."

"But why?"

"They want their space. It's a big city thing, bloody Aucklanders."

"Hmmm."

Joshua paused for a moment, and then wandered to the next campervan. He knocked – there was no answer. He tried again – again no answer.

He turned and looked straight at Rau, as if contemplating his next move. Then a door opened.

A woman stood there. She was in her thirties, her hair immaculately tied back, brow furrowed.

"What is it?" she asked.

"We have some extra food," said Joshua. "Would you like some?"

"No thanks," said the woman. "We have enough food."

"You are welcome to join us." He gestured across to their crowd. She glanced across to Rau and Tristan, and then looked back at Joshua.

"No thanks."

"We have some excellent Kaitaia wine."

"Is that what this is? Are you selling wine?"

Rau smiled to himself with irony, and watched as Joshua continued.

"No," he said. "I'd like to give you a bottle as a gift."

"What for? Are you expecting me to buy a crate later?"

"No, we have enough money."

The woman looked at him. "What do you mean?"

"What do you do?"

"I'm an account– none of your business."

She looked as if she was about to close the door in his face, when a child appeared; a girl of eight or so years, beautiful and vivacious.

"Hello!" said the girl.

"Hello!" said Joshua brightly. "What's your name?"

"Jesse."

"Wanna play?" Joshua looked back at her mother, as Jesse pleaded with her.

"I'm Joshua," he said. "Join us."

"Fine," she said, "just for a short time. I'm Claire. Jesse needs some time out of the van, anyway, but then we'll need to go to work."

Claire stepped down out of the van, and hesitantly walked over to the growing crowd.

"Kia ora," said Rau.

"Hello," she replied in a cool tone. She was wearing a tight knee length skirt, and a matching jacket, and walked awkwardly down the unsealed lane in black high heels. Jesse was wearing jeans and T-shirt with sneakers, and she ran to join in with the other kids playing ball.

Joshua moved on to the other campervans and knocked on doors. Some doors remained firmly closed. Others opened and he introduced himself, but no one was interested. Rau heard him wishing each one well, and then Joshua returned to Rau.

"Not much chance getting community out of an Aucklander," said Rau.

"Over one million people live in Auckland," Joshua replied. "Think they're all the same?"

Rau shifted on his feet, silenced, and then Joshua took his place in front of the crowd.

"Kia ora!" he said, raising his voice. "Nice to meet everyone!"

"Great," Rau heard Claire mutter from nearby. "Here comes the sales pitch."

"Help yourself to the food," said Joshua. "There's plenty more where that came from."

"Too much like my grandmother," said Tristan.

"We have wine – enough for everyone, low alcohol and great taste."

Rau noticed others looking, from around the camping ground: some through windows, others outside their tents. More began to gather in curiosity.

"Now," said Joshua, "I'm wondering, how many of you are living in a tent?"

A shout went up – hands went up.

"Living straight off the land," he said. "Good. How about a campervan?"

Claire didn't bother to lift her hand, but Frank did with great enthusiasm along with others who had joined the crowd from his lane.

"And who's staying in a cabin?" asked Joshua.

A few were joining in from the cabins further away. Anahera greeted them warmly, and offered food. Claire was grasping Jesse's hand, as if she was about to leave, when Joshua spoke again.

"What do you think?" he asked. "Tent, campervan or cabin – does it matter, at the end of the day?"

Now Claire looked at him and became still. Surprised, Rau watched her and saw Joshua notice her sudden attention.

Joshua wandered up to Frank's campervan and slapped his hand against it.

"Which is more important?" he asked. "The box, or the person who lives inside the box?"

Rau glanced at Frank – Joshua had his attention now too. He held a wine bottle affectionately at his side, but he was sober.

Claire was also looking at Frank, and now her face became cold and hard. Joshua wandered up to the wealthy campervans. He stopped next to Claire's, and turned to the crowd.

"If I hire this campervan," he said, "I get a microwave, ultra-high definition digital TV with one hundred and forty channels, blue-ray disc player, and a deluxe shower head. Cream spray and jet stream!"

He gestured toward Frank's campervan. "While that one down there is rusting with the basics."

Claire stormed up to him with Rau hovering close behind.

"Get out of my way," she said through gritted teeth. "My home and my life are none of your business!"

"Keep working like this," Joshua quietly replied, "and your daughter won't even know who you are."

Claire stared at Joshua, and Rau saw tears well up in her eyes. "You don't know what you're talking about," she whispered, and Joshua's face softened.

"I do know," he murmured. "You know it too, Claire. Love doesn't need all the extra trappings. Don't sacrifice the cake for the icing."

She stared at him, suddenly silenced. She looked around herself, suddenly aware of the eyes of the crowd.

"I have to go to work," she said. "I have to go to work!" She reached out to grasp Jesse's hand, and hurried down the lane.

"What is it with money?" Joshua cried out, across the crowd. "It promises to be our dearest friend, but then it becomes our harshest master! Is money what life is all about? If we spend our lives trying to get more and more of it, what will we sacrifice along the way?"

The crowd listened in silence. Rau thought perhaps they were also thinking about Claire, unable to stay to listen, unable to even rest while she was on holiday. Joshua had stopped speaking, and now everyone was murmuring to each other. Tristan stood next to him, munching on an apple.

"Did you even hear what he said?" asked Rau, and Tristan shrugged.

"Too much money isn't exactly my problem."

Rau smirked. "True. And yet…" He gestured to others in the crowd. "He seemed to reach them."

Joshua joined him, and Rau pulled him aside.

"You question money, Joshua?" he said. "You, a Pakeha?"

"Does my skin colour matter?"

"Your people hunger and thirst after money – that has always been the white man's way."

"You're wrong, Rau Petera – my people were not always this way."

Rau was struck by his brown eyes. They had a new intensity.

"And what is it with colour?" he asked. "We're all human, aren't we? Aren't we all brothers and sisters? Same vulnerabilities? Same needs? Same weaknesses?"

Rau frowned, suddenly aware of the state of his own heart.

"I'm sorry," he said. "I didn't realise…"

"It doesn't matter," said Joshua. "Rich, poor, Pakeha, Maori, from Auckland or Kaitaia – we're all in the same boat, the same waka."

"You're right," said Rau. "One massive waka. The past…"

"Shouldn't have happened the way it did."

"No. But the British – they didn't realise what they were doing."

"No, Rau – they did not. Just as the Maori didn't realise, until it was too late. We all lost our way. Time to find it again."

Rau lingered on his face.

"Something is changing within me," said Rau.

Joshua's smile was radiant. "Good."

"Brothers and sisters," said Rau, "ae! Brothers and sisters."

"Different, and yet together as one."

Joshua moved on and began to talk with some of the newcomers. Rau watched for a while, and then wandered up to a young muscular Maori man with a black spiral koru moko tattooed on his face and shoulders.

"Kia ora," said the man.

"Kia ora," Rau replied.

"I am Tane, of Tainui, from Waikato."

Rau raised his eyebrows in surprise. "I am Rau, of Ngapuhi, from Kerikeri. What brings you here?"

"I am visiting whanau."

"Have you had some kai?"

"Ae. Quite a feed you have here."

"Ae."

"And who is this man who speaks so boldly?"

Rau smiled quietly. "Joshua Davidson is his name."

"I like his words. They are very…"

"Maori?"

"Yes."

"And yet, not only Maori."

"He is a leader but not like the usual Pakeha leaders."

"Perhaps."

“I would like to hear more from him.”

Rau looked at him. “Then join us.”

Tane glanced at Joshua, and then turned back to Rau. Now Rau grasped his hand.

“Join us.”

Tane’s dark brown eyes held his. “All right, Ngapuhi Matua,” he said, “I accept.”

Rau pressed his forehead and nose to him, in a hongi, and Tane responded before wandering away, back into the crowd.

Chapter 10

THE GOVERNOR-GENERAL

Mark Blake was at a meeting at Saint Peter's. It was almost over. Gladly he looked around the faces of the Anglican Vicars of Wellington: young and old, men and women, some worried, some at peace. They had called the meeting, concerned for the rising tensions in their parishes. They had shared their concerns. Mark believed now they had got it off their chests, it was time to move on.

"We can handle a little heat," he said. "Don't worry, it's back to business as usual."

They gave him a long look, then rose to their feet and dispersed. Eun Ae Choo lingered for a moment, with an unusual expression on her face. She looked almost about to say something, but then she also moved on.

Mark gathered up his papers, rose to his feet, and wandered out of the meeting room and into the cathedral.

There a solitary person sat, in the middle of the congregational chairs. She was wearing a green blouse and matching half-length skirt. Mark did a double take. It was the Governor General! What was she doing here?

Her plain middle-aged face was fixed on the mosaic of Jesus on the cross, and her expression was surprisingly similar to Choo's – perplexed, and questioning. Mark hesitated, and then approached her.

"Right Honourable Anita Mayes," he began, offering a hand to her. "Can I help you?"

She smiled formally and rose to her feet. "Bishop Blake," she said. "Good to see you."

"Forgive me if I am intruding."

"It's not an intrusion."

"Indeed?"

"I am…contemplating a few things."

Mark politely waited, while she cast her eyes back over the cross and then back to him.

"Please join me," she said finally, "if time permits."

Surprised, he also glanced at the cross, and then back at her. "Very well," he said. "I have some time."

He sat next to her, and they both stared at the cross.

"I confess," Mayes began, "I haven't been to church in a while."

"Life can certainly get busy," Mark graciously offered.

"I had a few moments, so thought I would seize them."

"Good idea."

Now Mark was perplexed. Where was this conversation heading?

Mayes became silent for a few moments and then she spoke again.

"I have some concerns for our country."

Mark shifted slightly, next to her. "Oh, yes?"

"Will you keep my words confidential?"

Surprised again, Mark glanced at her. It had been a long time since someone had actually confided in him as a priest. He frowned slightly, at his own sudden awkwardness. He took a shallow breath, fleetingly closed his eyes before God, and then offered himself.

"Very well," he said.

Mayes rose to her feet, moved into the aisle, and began to pace, glancing from time to time at the closed glass doors. Mark also rose and moved to the aisle, leaning against a chair to give her his full attention as she paced.

"Our country is struggling," Mayes began. "Crops are failing, food is scarcer, petrol is escalating in cost and diminishing in supply – you know all of this."

"Yes."

"Crime is up, and understandably so. Theft is escalating, and disputes are leading to violence. Even the police, in some cases now, are succumbing to violence. I am a lawyer, Bishop Blake, but I'm not sure the Law is enough. I fear the Law is beginning to fail the people."

Mark stared at her. The Law failing the people? How could she say such a thing?

"The Law is vital," he said. "It provides safety. It provides the necessary external force, to stop us when we lose control."

"I agree with you," said Mayes, her eyes locked with his. "But what happens if the whole country starts to lose control? What happens if the law-keepers start to lose control? What happens if even the law-makers start to lose control?"

Mark swallowed. He looked away and wandered up the aisle, toward the cross.

"We are all, after all," Mayes voice continued, drifting over to him, "only human."

Now Mark stood at the steps leading to the inner sanctuary. There was sorrow in the face of Christ. He'd never noticed it before.

Fear gripped him. Mayes' words prickled his usual comfort of the status quo – 'business as usual.'

"What are you suggesting?" he said, into the inner sanctuary.

"I don't know," Mayes replied, right behind him. "That's why I am here. What do you suggest, Bishop?"

Pain stabbed at his chest. Where did it come from? It wasn't the first time. And why was the Governor General of New Zealand asking for his guidance now? Why, after all these years? Why now, at the very time he was least able to give it, after…after…

"I don't know what to suggest either," he whispered, staring at Christ, before finding strength to speak again. "We have what we already have.

We should use it well."

He turned back to Mayes.

"I agree we should use our system well," said Mayes. "My role is to ensure our democracy stands. To ensure, under the authority of our Queen, that our processes are not corrupted."

"The Queen is also the sovereign of the Anglican Church," said Mark. "Both Church and Government answer to her."

"Does the Church not answer to Christ?" asked Mayes, with a wry smile.

"Insofar as the Queen herself answers to Christ," Mark swiftly replied.

"Indeed," said Mayes. "And that is why I am here. In our constitution, both Queen and Government answer to Christ."

Mark looked at her. "In word," he said. "But in action? In reality? That is the question."

"Each person's faith is their own affair."

"I can respect that," said Mark, "when the scope of one's faith only influences oneself."

"Very good," said Mayes, her lips twitching, her smile faint. "Now you are certainly speaking as a bishop. My decisions could have enormous impact on our entire country."

Mark held her forthright gaze. What was on her mind?

"I signed a bill two weeks ago," she said. "I did not want to sign it."

"The National Lawful Use of Force Bill," Mark murmured.

"Yes," said Mayes. "I was wary of the bill – but I was obliged. I signed, and now the bill is an act: now it is law. Do you see what has happened since, Bishop?"

"Yes," Mark replied quietly. "I see."

"Escalating violence in the streets. The police, now, have been given the legal power to inflict more force. Two men are dead…"

Now a shadow crossed her face. "I am a lawyer, Bishop," she said. "Those men were innocent. We have deliberately avoided a death sentence in New Zealand for over forty years – we have maintained a system of due process. And now this new bill, which I signed into law, has thrown due process out of the window."

Mark had seen the articles: one of the men had been killed by a policeman on Mark's own hill!

"The police are not villains," said Mayes. "They are under strain, like the rest of us. We have given them too much power."

Her eyes shifted and set upon him.

Mark shifted uneasily under her scrutiny.

"You have the greater power," he said. "You are the Governor General – your signature is required for all changes of law. You represent the Queen."

"I do," said Mayes. "But my power is limited, Bishop. I am compelled to follow due process, and the Queen is compelled to let democracy have its way. Parliament, voted in by the people: Parliament determines the law, and Parliament voted for this law change. The Queen tips her hat and the Governor General upholds the true democratic process. Democracy decided, Bishop: but democracy made the wrong decision."

Now Mark suddenly realised why she was there. He flushed, and turned slightly away.

"You know who holds the real power in this country, Bishop," said the Governor General.

"The Prime Minister," replied Mark, staring at a wall hanging of Christ and his disciples handing out bread and fish.

"Is it not the Priest's role to inform the Head of State?"

The next wall hanging was Christ, standing before Pontius Pilate.

"To inform?" Mark asked under his breath. "Or to be crucified?"

"You know James Connor," said Mayes. "You both went to school together."

"Oh, yes," said Mark, giving a hollow laugh. She was shrewd! She'd done her homework! "I know James Connor! But tell me, Governor General, what message are you asking the Bishop of Wellington to bring to the Prime Minister of New Zealand?"

Now her face flushed, and Mark saw it, and was satisfied. His own actions were his alone – it was inappropriate for her to manipulate the pieces like a chess game, even if it was due process!

"You misunderstand me," said Mayes. "I am not putting words in your mouth. I am imploring you, Bishop, for God's sake, stop James Connor before it is too late."

Mark stared at her. Tears pricked the back of his eyes. In that moment, he saw what he had failed to see for so long: the greatest threat to the essence of freedom was dictatorial takeover. A rising Caesar…

"Your faith is filling you with gushy sentiment," James had said. *"Democracy is for the rich."*

"Talk to him," said Mayes.

"Democracy is to enhance the rich to lift up the poor," Mark had replied.

"Talk to him," she implored.

"All right," said Mark, "I'll talk to him."

It had been a long time since Mark had ventured into the Beehive. He stood at security, surrendering his wallet and belt to be X-rayed. Something beeped in his pocket, as he walked through the machine: darned keys! He obediently lifted up his arms to a guard, who passed a scanner down both of his sides, lingering on his pocket.

"What's in here, sir?"

He removed the keys, and the guard was appeased.

"Have a good day, sir."

"Thank you," he replied and walked through the glass doors.

He paused briefly at the reception desk, informing the lady behind the desk he was expected. She made a call, and then nodded to him to progress up the curving stairs to the reception hall where Connor was waiting for him.

"Mark!" he said, stretching out his hand, and Mark received its enthusiastic shake. "It has been too long!"

"Too long indeed," Mark muttered wryly. "Good to see you, James."

"Good to see you, too!" said James. "The Bishop of Wellington himself, fancy that! Come and we'll have lunch in the staff cafeteria."

Mark followed him into the lift.

The cafeteria was virtually empty. Surprised, Mark glanced around the empty chairs and tables.

"The Government running out of food too?" he asked, and James grinned.

"Don't you worry about that. What'll you have?"

"Ah…just standard coffee's fine."

"Not a cappuccino?"

"If you're having it."

"Cappuccino it is, then!" He ordered and then sat next to Mark.

His face had aged, Mark decided. Grey speckled his otherwise brown hair. There was a bit of a middle-aged spread, despite the food shortages. He wore suit pants, a light business shirt with sleeves still buttoned, his blue tie loosened a little. In all senses, he was average looking.

"How's Pam?" asked Mark, and James smiled.

"Good as ever. The garden's a bit more of a challenge for her."

"And Rachel?"

"Working hard, at North-East Hospital."

Mark braced himself, as the obligatory questions came.

"How's Selena?"

Mark shrugged. "Doing all right, I think."

"At Grammar?"

"No," said Mark, shifting uncomfortably. "She wanted to go to Hutt High."

James eyebrows shot up. "How's she doing there?"

"Top of the class. I'm sure she's bored, but she has to sleep in the bed she's made for herself."

James was smiling and then he tilted his head.

"I saw Tristan."

Mark swallowed. Connor had seen his son? How? Mark hadn't seen him in years.

"Where?" he asked, doing his best to sound nonchalant.

James looked puzzled. "You don't know?" he said. "He retired from army service."

Mark stared at him. Army service? How long…? He could have been killed! When did he…?

"What?" he said, resisting hard the impulse to shoot to his feet.

"Mark, don't you know?" asked James. "He was in the army for five years. Part of our Peacekeeping force, in the Middle East. We had a face to face meeting, and he told me of the atrocities there and the escalating conflict. How close the rebels came to securing a nuke…"

Mark's whole body went cold. His son, in the midst of a potential third world war?

"So he's back?" he whispered, his voice sounding mute to his own ears.

"Yes, he's back."

"Where?"

James shrugged, and looked uncomfortable. "I don't know, Mark – he's not my son."

The pain was back, deep in his chest and all-consuming. Where was Tristan? Was he safe? Was anywhere safe anymore?

The thought stirred him into action: his purpose for the meeting.

"James, what do you think about everything that's going on?"

"What do you mean?"

"You know what I mean, James: New Zealand! Everything is changing. We're not like this in little old New Zealand. We're a friendly country, beautiful, and a great get away, that's who we are. Self-sufficient. What's gone wrong?"

James held his gaze then glanced away, before looking back.

"Mark, the world's going to pot. Capitalism isn't working for the States, they're deep in the New Depression. Communism gives me the Heebie-jeebies. There's religious conflict, too – check out the Middle East, it might be the end of us all. What's the solution?"

"What about getting back to the basics?" said Mark.

"The basics?" said James, and then he laughed. "Here are the basics: there is no food or petrol. Our economy is being turned on its head. The threat is that we'll return to the Middle Ages with isolated tribal conflicts. Warring, across our nation. Is that what you want? We must maintain centralized control."

Mark frowned. The Middle Ages were a time of faith…

"Centralized leadership, yes," said Mark, "to serve the country's interests. To cultivate harmony…"

"You haven't changed," said James. "Still the idealist! Hold onto that."

Mark flushed, and persevered. "Centralized control only makes sense if it serves the interests of the country."

James paused. "We must maintain unity."

"Unity through freedom," said Mark.

"Sometimes freedom is a luxury we can't afford."

"James!" Mark rose to his feet, in dismay.

James stared up at him. "Sit down, Mark," he said quietly.

Mark remained standing. "James, you're starting to sound like a dictator."

James' expression did not change. "The Prime Minister is charged with the responsibility to ensure the security of the nation."

"The Prime Minister is voted in by the people and is chosen by the people."

"Once every three years."

"The PM serves the people, James, not the other way around!"

"Sit down…"

"If you're losing sight of that, maybe you should resign!"

"Sit down, Mark – now!" James exploded, thrusting himself out of his seat.

Mark stared into his face, flushed and angry. Had Connor unwittingly become a tyrant?

"Everything I do is to serve the interests of New Zealand," said

James. "How dare you imply otherwise?"

Mark remained standing. "Taking greater control always looks bad," he said quietly. "You're a politician – you know that."

"I do know that, Mark, but does that prove guilt?"

Mark smiled sadly, as Connor continued. "The people on the street have no idea of the bigger picture. The powers that be are organising, Mark – internationally, they are organising! Even Clarkson refuses to see what is in front of his face, he is too consumed by his increasingly communistic ideals. The international scene is ripe for complete conquest, can't you see? The Government has accurate Intel. If we don't remain united, we will fall, and all the nations with us."

"Fall to what?" asked Mark.

"To global totalitarian rule."

At this Mark swallowed, and sat back down.

"Do you have evidence?" asked Mark. "Or is it your fear talking?"

"I have evidence," said James. "They are hidden, but poised. They have food. They have petrol. They are listening to us, but they don't know yet that we are also listening to them. Our only defence is true self-sufficiency, and we can't do it unless we remain a cohesive whole! Our country must not fragment or we will be assimilated, as surely as a tsunami sweeps away everything in its path."

Mark grimaced. He looked out of the window as he considered James' words. Finally he spoke.

"James, I have known you since high school," he said. "We have debated, we have argued – we've even had the odd punch up. I can see you're genuinely concerned for New Zealand, and you're trying to protect us all.

"You have some kind of faith, behind what you are doing, don't you? Some kind of driving morality behind your actions? I say to you now, for Christ's sake, in all your efforts to save us, don't become the thing you fear most – don't succumb to becoming a Hitler."

James was still. He was listening. "I don't want to become a Hitler," he said. "But what if the future of New Zealand requires it?"

Mark stared at him, disturbed. Did the end justify the means? Surely not! Surely not…

"What is a future built on control," he replied quietly, "but the worst kind of imprisonment?"

"I don't have the answers for that," said James. "I'm a politician – you're the priest."

James rose, smiled briefly, and bowed his head. "It's good to see you again, Mark," he said. "Stay in touch."

Mark nodded, rising to his feet, and shook his hand. But after James had left the deserted cafeteria Mark sat back down, overwhelmed by a sense of dark foreboding.

Chapter 11

DARKNESS

Selena sat on her bed. Her room was dark – silent, and empty. She leaned heavily sideways against the headboard, and stared out of her small window. There was light out there, early summer evening light in the sky over Lower Hutt – but no light inside.

Books lay on her desk, abandoned, useless. They couldn't help her – nothing could.

Inside her, something stirred. Something deep; something horrible. It gripped her and gnawed away at her.

Go, it said.

"No," she whispered, gripping onto her duvet.

Do it.

"No," she repeated. Suddenly it took her, a flame, sweeping through her body, decimating her soul.

She rushed from her room, into the bathroom and hung over the toilet, retching.

Why bother protecting him? The voice now pounded in her ears. *He never protected you!*

"Leave me alone!" she gasped. "Go away!"

Her stomach heaved. Now she saw blood. Horrified, she began to shake, and it pressed closer.

You chose me, it said.

Selena clung to the toilet, and began to sob. “God!” she cried.

God? It laughed. *Why would a god bother to save a wretch like you?*

Her head was spinning. She closed her eyes. God? What did she know about God? Old music, old clothes, fancy words – so far away! So far, as to be pointless! So far, as to be impossible…

Her father…she still loved him! She still loved him, but he was so far away! So far away…

What's the use of his love? The voice said, penetrating her. *Impotent father! Does he care for you? No! Only for his wife!*

Selena wrapped her arms around herself, and began to tremble.

She is lost, and he discards you like shit!

Selena tried to cover her ears, but the voice became louder.

Show him what he has done.

She stared at the blood in the toilet.

“He doesn't know,” she whispered.

Show him.

Show him? Tears filled her eyes. No more innocence! No more childhood. Only hatred! Enemies! Enemies…

Bring him to our side.

A cold calm now came over her body. To her side, yes: no more God – no more religion.

She cleaned herself up with toilet paper, and then rose to her feet. There was no going back now.

She had already chosen her own fate.

Chapter 12

THE TIDE

Mark leaned back into his couch. The evening was still light outside, and sparrows were chirping. A few clouds hovered over Lower Hutt, beyond the windows, and the harbour was still. He put his feet up, and closed his eyes momentarily. Selena was in her room, no doubt studying. They had eaten dinner quietly together. Now he could finally relax.

Mark reached for the remote. The News was playing on Channel One. Mark glanced at it, and then picked up the paper and his cup of tea from the table. There was more bad news of attacks in the streets – two more in Lower Hutt, and five in Upper Hutt, not to mention the nine in the city centre.

"Crazy," Mark muttered to himself.

"…and in Kaitaia," the woman's voice drifted over him, from the TV, "a different kind of story. Campers had all their Christmases come at once, when they awoke last Sunday to a feast. A mysterious man invited campers at Kaitaia Kauri Camping Ground to indulge in brunch. Many said they had not eaten so well in years."

Mark watched as an old man wearing a singlet sidled up to a

young reporter.

"Best grog I've ever tasted!" he said. "And it didn't even make me drunk! That's saying something…"

"The news," Mark grumbled. "Where's the decent reporting these days?"

"Not to mention the biggest snapper we've ever seen," said a young man into the microphone, "right, Reverend Rau?"

A Maori minister stepped reluctantly into view. Mark frowned. He recognised him: it was Reverend Rau Petera! Mark never forgot a face. He had met him at the national AGM.

"What is this?" Mark muttered. "Some kind of church initiative up north?"

"Not my doing," said Rau. "The man beat my record."

"Sure did," said the young man, and Mark rolled his eyes.

"But who is this man?" The reporter asked, and now the young man was looking straight into the camera.

"I don't know," he said, smirking slightly. "God knows we need help. Maybe he's the Messiah!"

Mark stared at him and promptly dropped his cup. It shattered on the floor.

"My God," he whispered, rising to his feet, "Tristan!"

How old would he be now? Twenty-six? Yes – twenty-six. He looked like a grown man.

Mark hastily reached around for a pen and paper. Where? Kaitaia, in the campground. Which one? Kauri Campground.

He grabbed the laptop, sitting on the table, and dragged it open, searching for the campground. He found the number, grabbed his cell-phone, and dialled.

The phone was dead.

"Damn!" he said. He reached for the charger, and made a mental note to find Rau Petera's cell-phone number. Selena had emerged, Mark could hear her rummaging in the kitchen.

"There was steak, and bread, and cheese," Tristan continued happily to the reporter.

"But where is the man?" The reporter asked, turning back to Rau.

Rau hesitated. He glanced around the campground.

"I don't know," he said finally. "He has a habit of suddenly disappearing."

Now the reporter looked directly at the camera.

"And so," she said, "mystery man, or guardian angel? Either way, the people at Kaitaia Kauri Campground are feeling pretty good tonight. I think I'll try some of that steak! Ka kite ano!"

"Thanks, Julia," said the anchor woman. "Ka kite."

"What a load of crap." It was Selena's voice, from behind him. Mark was still staring at the screen.

"Well," he muttered. "Reporting's not what it used to be."

"Not the reporting!" said Selena. "A guardian angel! Like shit!"

Like shit? Mark turned to her. "Young lady, we don't…"

But her expression stopped him cold.

Her face was white. There were dark shadows around her eyes. The eyes themselves almost seemed a different colour from her usual blue – darker, almost black, as though…

Mark stared at her. "What happened to you?"

"Like you care."

"I'm asking you a question."

"And I'm not answering it."

Mark cast his eyes over her and spotted a tattoo on her hand.

He grasped her arm. It was the symbol of an eye, and the number 666.

"Shit!" he said, staring at her. "That's not funny, Selena!"

"Who's laughing?" she rasped.

"Quit it with the demonic act! What is it with you? You're a good girl!"

"See where that got me!"

"What do you mean?"

Her eyes were fixed on his now, empty; her soul was chilling him, a pit of darkness.

"My God," he whispered. "What I have done?"

"Bugger all," she said. "You've done bugger all."

"It's Alex, isn't it?" he cried. "That damned boy in the car park."

"And why not?" she asked. "It sure as hell was never going to be you."

Mark stared at her, dismayed, and let go of her arm.

"What have you done?" he asked, forcing himself to control his shaking body, his tone unnaturally calm.

"You know what I've done."

His vision blurred. Suddenly sweating, he swayed and then struggled to emerge again, as if through choking smoke.

"You know what I've done."

Her voice was hard. Her hand came to his shoulder and suddenly a creeping, drowning presence seized him.

"Get away from me!" he cried, desperately grasping the Bishop's cross hanging around his neck. "Get away from me."

Selena laughed. "Christ?" she said. "You're reaching for Christ now? You haven't trusted in him for years!"

Mark stared at her and shook his head, in a daze.

"You don't know what you're talking about."

"Oh yes I do."

"I have more faith than you think."

"No you don't."

"More than you think!"

"No. Not since her." She pointed to the family photo with Teresa at its centre.

Pain engulfed him.

"Don't," he whispered, knowing what she sought, knowing what she was about to unleash – the very thing he had fled for nine years. "Don't."

But she did not obey his plea.

"You killed her," she said.

His body stiffened, numbed by the words.

"It was an accident," he said mechanically. "An accident."

"You were at the wheel."

The tsunami in his heart was threatening to break, now. It was so close! So very close…

"It wasn't my fault!" he pleaded, his voice fading. "The brakes failed!"

"You were speeding."

"A hundred and ten!"

"A hundred and twenty-four."

The image was in his mind's eye, now – the image he had fled from for nine years. At 124 kilometres per hour, the car had suddenly spun out of control…

"How the hell do you know that?" he whispered. "How do you know?"

"You were reckless, and you killed her."

The tsunami reared up and then crashed, sweeping all his defences away. He cried out, his nails pressing sharply into his palms, while Selena's torturous words continued.

"You're a shell of a man," she said, "denying for so long your own responsibility! Hiding away! Forcing your children away! You stole their mother from them! You stole her away!"

"Shut up!" he cried out, shoving her back one step. "You're not my daughter! Get the hell away!"

"You're weak!" she continued. "Insipid! Full of deceit! You love the show, with your flowing robes, pretending to follow your God."

Pretence? Was it all pretence? Agony consumed him, but somehow he knew her words, so full of painful reality, were not actually fully true.

"You're wrong," he whispered. "I don't like the show. I don't like deceit. I follow because I still believe."

"You may still believe," she said, "but you no longer trust. Was it you who destroyed our family, or was it God?"

And now the most hidden part of him, the most concealed response, was unleashed.

"God!" he cried out. "God! How could you take my wife?"

"How dare he?" said Selena.

"How could you?" Mark cried out, clenching his fists. "For faithfulness you give a curse! A curse!"

He was a Bishop!

Hatred swelled in his heart and it frightened him. Hatred for God? What kind of slippery slope was that? And yet it beckoned. Selena's dark eyes were fixed on him.

"He betrayed you," she said, and Mark desperately fought the tide.

"No," he said.

"You gave your life to him in service, and he betrayed you."

"No!" he cried. She couldn't say that! It couldn't be true! "No."

"He has abandoned you, Mark Blake, as surely as you have abandoned your own children."

Her words were knives to his heart – and yet, in that moment, he could not deny them.

"No…" he whispered. But he felt himself suddenly, thoroughly, defeated.

Selena knew it, Mark could see it in the eerie aura of satisfaction on her face. She straightened, turned, and walked away. And he was alone.

In agony he slumped onto the floor. Just out of his reach was his cell-phone. The campground was written, there, on the table. Tristan! Tristan…

"Help," he pleaded, into the air.

Every man needs a minister. The words returned to him. A minister? But who? Eun Ae Choo's face appeared before him. Eun? Yes, it could be her. She would help! She could understand.

His cell-phone now had some charge. He would call her! But as he went to dial, his eyes fell upon the photo of Teresa.

Agony had its way.

It's your fault! A voice said inside his head. *You killed her! And God stood back and let you do it.*

"No!" he cried, and he threw his cell-phone to the ground, smashing it to pieces. "No!"

The cross was still around his neck. He dragged it off, and stared at it for a moment. What did it even mean? Nothing! Nothing, anymore. He threw it to the ground, after the cell-phone.

All that was left now was his wife.

In pain, Mark reached for the photo, and hugged it in his arms. He sank down against the wall and closed his eyes.

"Teresa!" he sobbed, his mind returning to the past. "Teresa! I'm so sorry!"

He pleaded with her for forgiveness, but forgiveness never came. He was locked in the past, without resolution, without reprieve.

"I'm so sorry," he said, weeping. And night time fell, but no rest came.

Chapter 13

WHANGAREI

Tristan stood under a kauri tree in Coronation Reserve. It was February now, and damned hot. He was sweating again. What's more, they were edging closer to Auckland, and Tristan was still keen to avoid the big city. The army! The past. Quite frankly, he could do without it.

The city of Whangarei was spread before him; a nice small city, scattered houses, green hills, with the harbour beyond. The surrounding bush sheltered him a little from the mid-day heat, but the air was stuffy.

Rau was arguing with Tane, the Maori activist who'd joined them in Kaitaia. Tristan watched, intrigued. Tattoos covered his face and arms, and probably his chest as well. He was a solid man. Not to be messed with, at least not if you weren't army trained.

"He's the one!" Tane was saying to Rau. "Descended from Potatau Te Wherowhero, and descended from King Henry the Seventh."

"Tane," Rau replied, in his familiar gentle but directly challenging tone, "you say this speaking from the tribe of Tainui, but here in Whangarei? That Joshua is descended from the first Maori king of Waikato, down south? Why should this bring joy to the ears of my tribe,

Ngapuhi? In this very place northern tribes defended against the southern tribes."

Tristan stared at him. What was he talking about? Maori wars, before the British came? Who cared?

"You are not understanding me, Reverend Rau," Tane replied, with sarcasm lacing his voice. "The issue is bigger than our petty tribal fighting. This one man can finally unite Pakeha and Maori! He is descended from both sovereign lines! Maori and Pakeha!"

What was he on about? Some weird mixed blood leader? Tristan almost laughed, Joshua hardly presented this way.

Rau was grimacing. "You are saying he is a king."

"Is he not?"

"A king – from up north?" Rau questioned. "A King of Kaitaia, perhaps. We already have a Queen of the Commonwealth."

"I have no interest in a King of Kaitaia," Tane replied, "I only have an interest in the Treaty of Waitangi. I only have an interest in our land, and our people. Te Wherowhero desired peace and justice!"

"That was a long time ago."

"So was the Treaty!"

"Joshua has no desire for power."

"Love, law and faith – these were the words of Te Wherowhero, Matua. Don't you see it? Don't you see that Joshua is the same?"

Rau was frowning. His eyes found Tristan.

"Let me guess," said Tristan in a low voice, "he thinks Joshua is this Te Whero guy back from the dead."

Rau raised his eyebrows, and Tristan returned the look. Then he wandered further down the track past some tall reaching kauri.

Another European was on the track admiring the trees. He wore grey suit trousers with a blue business shirt, the sleeves buttoned at the wrists. He shifted with the heat, and Tristan joined him.

"Wicked day."

"Yeah," said the man.

"You live here?"

"Yeah. You?"

"Ah…it's a long story."

The man stretched out his arms, and yawned.

Tristan couldn't help himself, he had to ask. "Why are you wearing a suit in a park, in the middle of one of our hottest days?"

"I'm working," the man replied.

"Here?"

"No! Down Central Ave." He gestured down toward the city. "It's my lunch-break."

"What do you do?"

"I'm an optical engineer." He seemed a little deflated.

"Tristan Blake," said Tristan, reaching out a hand to him. "Nice to meet you."

"John Robertson," the man replied. "Nice to meet you too."

Tristan thought that would be the end of it. John was gazing over the houses to the harbour, and Tristan was about to move on, when suddenly Joshua appeared.

"There must be something more to life than this," said Joshua.

John looked astonished. His tired green eyes took in Joshua's jeans and blue T-shirt. Tristan thought John looked about the same age as Joshua, mid-thirties.

"Sorry?" said John.

Joshua looked out to the hills, lifting his face to the sun.

"Life," he said. "There must be something more to it."

"Yeah," said John. "That's what I was thinking."

Joshua stretched his hand out to him. "I'm Joshua."

John reached for his hand, and suddenly stiffened, staring at Joshua. Tristan looked back at Joshua, but his intent gaze revealed nothing.

John was shivering in the heat. He held Joshua's gaze. Then Joshua released his hand, and John seemed to breathe normally again.

"So it is true," said John. "What that Maori man was talking about."

"True?" said Joshua, smiling slightly. "What is 'truth'?"

"Amen to that," Tristan muttered, but John was frowning.

"It is true," he repeated, and Joshua glanced at Tristan. He bowed his head to Tristan, and then to John, and walked away.

John frowned after him, and Tristan laughed.

"Don't worry about him," he said. "He's weird at times, but I'm certain he has a good heart."

Now John's eyes came to him. He looked in a slight daze, but now shook his head.

"You don't see him…?"

"See him? What do you mean?"

"I…I've never experienced this before…"

Now Tristan felt worried. What had Joshua done?

"You look like you need a minister," he said, pointing to Rau. "Talk to him, that one on the left, he's a good guy."

"Him?"

"He's an Anglican priest: Rev Rau Petera. Talk to him, I have a feeling he'll understand."

John followed his direction, wandering back down the track. Tristan watched him, shaking his head. That Joshua! He must have given him some kind of psychic thing, like he had done about Tristan's mother. Spooky! Weird. Rau would handle it.

Sure enough, he saw Rau stretch out his hand. "Kia ora," he said.

"Yeah, hi." John shook his hand.

"Kia ora," said Tane.

"Hello." John looked a little awkward with Tane.

"How can I help you?" Rau asked gently.

John hesitated then spoke to Tane.

"Joshua," he began. "You said he is a king. You're right."

Rau stared at him, while Tane broke into a wide smile.

"What are you saying?" asked Rau.

"I…" John struggled to spit the words out. "I just know it. It doesn't make any sense! But I know it."

Rau's brown eyes, gentle and curious, searched John's face.

"Brother," he said, "did Joshua himself show you this?"

"Yes."

"Then…maybe you should hang about with us for a while."

John frowned. "Take time off work?"

"Hard, is it?" asked Rau.

"Well…kind of. I own my own business."

"Time for a break, then?"

John stared at him. He glanced back at Tristan. He searched for Joshua, and found him.

"I…I'll need to sort some things out."

"We'll be here for another few days, that's all."

"Okay," said John, nodding. "Okay."

And he suddenly set off, back down the track, toward the city.

Tristan approached Rau. "What was that about?"

Rau seemed a little perplexed. "I'm not sure."

"Joshua is the king," said Tane, smiling widely. "It is as I suspected: our true leader has come. I will spread the news amongst the Iwi."

"What?" asked Rau. "Wait a minute, I don't think you've got it quite right…"

But Tane had set off down the same path, following John.

Tristan laughed again. "Mad!" he said. "You're all mad! But it's all very entertaining, and that Joshua, he's a hard man to pin down!"

Rau looked confused. Then his cell-phone rang. Tristan watched as he pulled it out of his pocket and answered, then fixed his gaze on Tristan with a strange mixture of amusement and concern.

"It's your father," he said.

Tristan stared at him. His blood went cold. "What?" he said.

"It's your father," Rau repeated gently.

Tristan wanted to push the phone away, but he couldn't avoid Rau's offering. He took a deep breath, reached for the phone, turned his back on Rau, and answered.

"Hello?"

“Tristan?” It was his father’s voice.

Tristan swallowed hard. He stared at the view, trying to focus far away.

“Dad?” he choked.

“Where are you?”

“Whangarei…”

“What are you doing?”

“I’m…” Tristan shook his head in irony. “It’s hard to explain. I’m just hanging out for a while.”

“Can we meet?”

“Meet?”

“Yes. Can I meet you, Tristan? I can come to you.”

“I…I’m not sure where we’ll be…”

“We?”

“I…I’m hanging out with some mates.”

“You don’t mean that guy from Kaitaia, do you? The one on the news?”

So he had seen him. He had heard his throw-away comment, designed for him: the one about the Messiah.

“Umm…” Tristan stuttered, and then he pulled himself together. “Yeah,” he said. “I’m hanging out with them for a while.”

His father was silent. For a moment Tristan thought he'd been cut off. Then he spoke again.

“I’ll find you, Tristan,” he said. “Is that okay?”

Tristan hesitated. Was it okay? No way! And yet a part of him wanted it. A part of him needed it.

“Okay,” he said, and then his father was gone.

Rau’s eyes were on him, warm and concerned, just like a minister.

“Everything okay?” he asked.

“Yeah,” said Tristan automatically. “Okay.”

But sweat was dripping from his face.

Chapter 14

THE PRISM

John ducked under some pohutukawa trees. He hastened down the track, away from Coronation Reserve, and then onto the road below.

What had just happened?

His heart was pounding hard. He needed something to prop himself up on, something to hold onto, but there was only open space and streets ahead to criss-cross on the way back to Central Avenue.

Joshua…He saw his eyes again: brown eyes, and beyond a vast ocean, stretching John's mind. It had been like glimpsing the entire Universe in one moment. It was too much, like drowning! And yet it was utterly wonderful. Overwhelming, and alien.

John shuddered. In that one moment, everything had changed – his mind had been turned inside out.

"Wait!" a voice cried out behind him. "Where are you going?"

A strong hand was on his shoulder. He halted, and the Maori man was there again, the big one with the tattoos.

"Kei te pehea koe?"

"Sorry?"

"How are you?"

John swayed. "What?" he gasped. "Oh…I'm all right…"

"Where are you going?"

"Back to work."

"How can you go back to work?" The man asked. "You've just met our king!"

John stared at him. "Our king?" he whispered. "I have no idea what that means."

The Maori face furrowed, as if disappointed. "Never mind," he said. "I'm spreading the good news! At last, the true King of Aotearoa! A new age is coming! Let's see what those reporters do with this!"

He slipped past John, and disappeared amidst the streets of Whangarei.

Sweat dripped into John's eyes. His trousers clung to his wet legs. Wearily he weaved his way through the streets, to his office on Central Ave.

Reaching for his keys, he unlocked the door, moved to his desk, turned the fan back on, and sat.

Prisms and lenses littered his desk. He had developed a new kind of lens, thinner than traditional plastic, and lighter – cheaper, too. Business had picked up, until global warming had taken hold. Now materials were scarce, and it was expensive to bring them in from overseas. He'd been exploring local solutions, alternatives to plastic with refractive properties, and perhaps even a new form of shatter-proof glass…

"You help people to see again."

John jumped at the voice, and looked up. It was Rau, the man with the gentle eyes.

John searched his face. What was he doing here? He must have followed him.

"I…" Rau looked like he was trying to find the right words. "I found what you had to say very interesting."

John shifted awkwardly on his feet.

"Yeah," he said. "Sorry about that."

"Sorry?" asked Rau. "Why?"

"Well, for butting in…"

"No need to apologise."

"It's just…"

"Yes?"

The brown eyes were upon him again. John felt he was being tested, and his awkwardness escalated. Should he speak? Should he share what was burning in his heart?

"I don't understand it," said John, "but…there's something about him. Something unusual."

"No argument there," said Rau, suddenly grinning. "'Unusual,' ae."

"No, it's more than that."

"More?"

Again, the eyes were upon him. John swallowed, and sat back down at his desk. He lifted a prism. Inspired, John raised the prism into the yellow sunlight streaming through his window.

"Look," he said.

Rau moved, to stand on John's side of the desk – as John held the prism to the light, with a blank white page behind it. The light shone through the prism, and then dispersed into every colour of the rainbow.

"It's like…" John struggled to spit the words out. "It's like Joshua is the prism."

Rau remained silent.

"Very good," said Rau at last.

John shrugged. "Not really," he said.

"Why do you say that?"

"I really have no idea what I'm talking about."

"I think that's what makes it so good."

The brown eyes were dancing, in that moment. John found himself smiling, and then he shook himself and returned to his prisms.

"What will you do now, John?" asked Rau.

John's hands began to tremble, as he reached for his other lens designs.

"I don't know," he whispered.

Rau picked up a prism. “You say Joshua is like one of these?”

“Yes.”

“Haven’t you been trying to focus light all your life?”

John swallowed. He knew what Rau was trying to do, but he wasn’t sure he could follow.

“You don’t understand,” he said. “This office is my life.”

“I can see that,” said Rau.

“I can’t just up and leave.”

“But how can you stay, now?” asked Rau. “Now you've found a real life prism?”

“He…” John struggled again. Why was it so hard to speak? It was because the perceptions were so indescribable…

“He makes me feel tossed! Like a boat on a massive wave. I have no idea where I’m going; no idea whether I might be crashed on the rocks…”

“Lost,” Rau murmured, and John nodded.

“Yes! I thought I had my life sorted, and now it’s all up in the air again! Lost!”

“I understand,” said Rau, his face changing again into that same thoughtful expression. “I was the same, but now…”

“Yes?”

“Now, suddenly, I’m starting to feel found,” said Rau, a growing certainty shining in his eyes.

“What do you mean?” he asked.

Rau broke suddenly into a wide grin. “I’m starting to get it.”

“Get what?”

“Him.” Rau’s face was radiant now. “I’m starting to get him!”

John could not understand, and was worried, for a moment, that Rau might break into a karakia: a Maori prayer. Instead Rau leaned toward him.

“What about you?” he said. “Don’t you want to get him, too?”

The ocean behind Joshua's brown eyes came into his mind's eye again. What did it mean? It was huge! Alien. Should he run? Should he stay away? And yet, there was such colour! Like light, dispersed: the spectrum of life. Such compelling light…

He looked down at the papers on his desk.

There must be something more to life than this. Joshua had spoken his very thoughts. But to follow meant to shut the door on his business; to shut the door on his life! To follow meant to risk everything.

"If you don't do this," said Rau, "you will regret it for the rest of your life."

John trembled. "It's easy for you," he replied. "You are a man of faith. I'm not."

"He is beckoning you, can't you see it? He is inviting you."

"I know," said John, "but I don't know the man! I don't know him, and you're asking me to give up everything."

"I'm asking you to gain everything, John! But to gain everything, sometimes you have to first let go of what you already have."

John rose and began to pace around his office.

"Shutting the doors spells death to a business!" he said. "I've built this place up for fourteen years!"

"I know it's a big ask."

"What did you give up, to be here?"

Now Rau shifted slightly. "Okay," he said. "You're right – it's easier for me right now than it is for you. But just wait until my Vicar starts asking questions. Why the extended leave? Why the sudden Sabbatical? Wait until she has to talk it over with the Bishop…"

"What then?" asked John. "Will you also need to give up what you already have?"

Rau swallowed. John was grateful to see some human frailty in his eyes – some doubt.

"My fathers have been priests for generations," he said, "ever since Samuel Marsden first preached the Gospel to the Maori, on the coast near Kerikeri, in 1814."

"That's quite a legacy."

"My father lived long enough to see my ordination."

"I guess you don't want to lose all of that, do you? Your family's reputation?"

"Mana…" Rau's face clouded. "My whanau mana…"

John's eyes fixed on him now. The test was unexpectedly reversed.

"Would you be willing to give it all up?" he asked. "If that's what it took to follow Joshua?"

Rau frowned. "Would I give it up?" he pondered. "I suppose if God required it…"

John was impressed by the sudden resolution in his eyes. "I would give up mana for God," said Rau. "I would choose a new path, different from the old, if God required it."

John nodded, beginning to understand him. "Then you are faithful to the God you believe in, Reverend Rau," he said, "but I don't share in your faith. My parents went to church at Christmas and Easter, that's all. We never spoke of God. Why would I suddenly risk everything to follow this Joshua?"

Rau studied him, and John purposefully held his gaze. Then Rau smiled.

"Because there's more to life than this." He gestured around the office.

John stared at Rau as he heard the same words again: his own words, Joshua's words, and now Rau's words. He agreed with them.

"All right," he said finally, succumbing. "I'll join you."

"Do it now," said Rau, his smile widening, "before you change your mind."

And John gathered up his papers tidily into a drawer, turned off the light, grabbed his keys, and walked to the door.

Chapter 15

WENDERHOLM

Tristan wandered across sand. The beach at Wenderholm was beautiful, much smaller than Ninety Mile but more hidden away. The ocean sparkled in the sun. Ahead, to his left, an estuary led to the Puhoi River, where Tristan saw a group of kayakers struggling against the current.

Tristan climbed the grassy hill, abutting the beach, and admired the view.

Grassland stretched in front of him, and behind this was the river. In the distance, to the left, tents were set up. Barbeque sites were scattered across the park. They were only thirty minutes' drive, now, from the North Shore of Auckland.

A large crowd of people had gathered together on the grass. Nowadays, surely, this whole area would flood at high tide.

Joshua stood in the middle of the crowd. Some people clung to him, others looked scared, but he seemed to take their fear away. Maori, European, Pacific, Asian, and Indian – all were there.

Tristan still found the man strange. There was certainly something about him, no argument there. He was compelling, though Tristan couldn't put his finger on exactly what it was. His words seemed to reach into the hearts of people. He could reach into the heart of the crowd.

"Why worry about what's going to happen tomorrow?" asked Joshua, his voice floating up the hill. "Worrying's not going to fix anything, is it? It'll give you an ulcer, or angina."

"Or worry lines!" a girl called out, and everyone laughed.

"Look at today, not tomorrow. See? It's a beautiful day. Each day is a gift given to us – we should use it well."

Rau was climbing the hill now, with John from Whangarei. They stood next to Tristan, and he sighed.

"You know he's an insatiable romantic," said Tristan.

Rau smiled. "That's one of the things I like about him."

"He seems to trust everything's going to be okay."

John shifted slightly beside them. "That's not it," he said. "It's not just blind optimism."

"Then what is it?" asked Tristan.

John frowned, looking at Joshua. "I'm not sure," he said, "but he's not blind. He sees everything."

"Exactly," said Rau. "He's a romantic, but his romanticism is built on reality."

Tristan shifted slightly, suddenly uncomfortable. "What do you mean?" he asked. "You're losing me."

John's green eyes turned to Tristan. "He sees it all," he said gently, "the good and the bad."

Now the image was there again. Explosions! Screams. The rifle was in his hands, firing – bodies were jerking, in front of him, bleeding, dying…

Tristan gasped, and stepped back. John's eyes were still on him, and then his hand came to rest on Tristan's shoulder.

"It's all right," he said.

"He sees it all?" Tristan choked. "How?"

"I don't know," said John. "But he does – and he's good. Not just a romantic, he is actually good."

Tristan's eyes drifted again to Joshua. He was moving from person to person, grasping hands, murmuring words, smiling at faces. He was good? Yes – good. Tristan could accept that. He already had.

Tane was close behind Joshua, following him everywhere he went. Behind Tane, a large group of Maori had gathered. Was Joshua their king? In a way he did look like a king. Was he like a politician? No – more like a king. There was something in his aura, something that went beyond being a leader of the State. Certainly many people already loved him. The only thing that was missing was the royal wave…

Tristan's mind drifted. When was the time of the kings? In the medieval era, before the Age of Reason…before computers, and cars, and nukes…

"Tristan."

The familiar voice dragged him back to reality.

"Tristan!"

Tristan jerked back to the present. His father was there, standing right in front of him! His face; he hadn't seen his face in nine years! How had he found him? How had he moved so quickly?

"Dad!"

His father had aged. His short black hair was peppered with grey, and there were permanent lines across his frowning forehead. The blue eyes now scanned over his face, and the frown softened.

"Tristan," his father said again, his voice gentle, "you have become a man."

Mark extended his hand. Tristan fumbled and took it. He had never shaken his father's hand before, not as an adult.

"It has been too long," said Mark, and Tristan shook his head, still in disbelief.

"Yeah," he said.

"Tell me what's been happening! Connor said…"

"Connor?" Tristan interrupted.

"You know, James Connor, the PM! He told me…"

"The PM?"

"…that you'd been in the army! The army, Tristan – I had no idea!"

Now Tristan swallowed. Memories threatened again, but he kept them at bay. What would a Bishop think of army duty? Tristan didn't know. He searched his father's face, but couldn't find any clue. All he saw was concern.

"I was in the army," said Tristan, "but I pulled out."

"Why?"

"I…" He grimaced slightly. Tell him? Tell his father? "I didn't like it."

Mark was silent, scanning him. Tristan saw compassion in his blue eyes. It hurt him. It reminded him of how things had been, before…before his mother…

"It must have been hard," said Mark.

"Yeah," Tristan replied.

"Good to be out?"

"Yeah. But not normal."

Now Mark's eyes moistened. He nodded. Then his gaze wandered over the crowd, and Tristan breathed a little more easily.

"What's going on here?" asked Mark, straightening beside him. "Who is this 'Joshua Davidson'? Everyone seems to know him – that's how I found you."

"Yeah," said Tristan, "he's becoming quite a celebrity."

"A celebrity?"

Reporters were on the outskirts of the crowd; Tristan could see them now. He thought he could see a medley of international presenters, too. Surely not?

Mark became silent again and then spotted Rau, who had slipped away while they'd been talking.

"Reverend Rau Petera!" he said. "Fancy seeing you here!"

Rau shifted awkwardly on his feet, and quickly extended his hand.

"Right Reverend Blake," he said. "Good to see you."

"Bishop Andrew know that you're here? Checking it out for him, are you?"

Tristan grinned. The cards had turned! But then he suddenly realised Rau was in a sensitive position.

"I'm on leave," Rau replied.

"On leave?" said Mark. "And you're spending it here?"

"We were in the neighbourhood," said Tristan wryly, and his father's eyes came back to rest on him.

"How did you two…?"

"I hitched a ride up north."

"I see."

Mark's eyes shifted over the crowd again. Tristan caught Rau's eye and smiled. He seemed a little stiff. There was silence. And then Mark spoke again.

"What exactly is he doing down there?" he asked. "Shaking hands like the Queen?"

Tristan smirked at how similar their thoughts were.

"Something like that," said Tristan, and Mark laughed.

"The Governor General would have something to say about that."

"I'll bet," said Tristan. "Maybe he should run for Parliament, then?"

"No point. Connor's totally ruling the roost there."

"I don't think it's his thing, anyway."

"Wise man."

"He's more the social worker type."

"As long as everyone's paying their taxes, he can do as much nice stuff as he likes."

Tristan was surprised at how easily their conversation flowed, after so long. Mark was smiling but there was something behind his eyes, a hidden tension.

"Where's Selena?" asked Mark, and Tristan straightened in surprise.

"Selena?" He hadn't seen his sister in nine years! Would he even recognise her? She had only been seven when he had left home.

Mark's eyes were searching the crowd, and then fixed on Joshua.

"What on earth…?" he said, and he abruptly left, striding down the hill.

Impulsively Tristan followed him. There was a girl standing in front of Joshua. Long black curly hair, blue eyes, could it be…? Maybe sixteen, the right age; quite beautiful! But her face – she looked white, deathly white! With black shadows under her eyes.

"What's wrong with her?" Tristan breathed.

Joshua took her hand, and something began to happen between them; something big… Mark cleared his throat obtrusively, and Tristan grasped his father's shoulder before he could intervene. They were only a few metres away.

"Wait!" he said. "Just wait for a moment."

Mark hesitated, and Tristan hastily searched Selena's face – her eyes! There was some kind of conflict going on, some kind of struggle.

"Help!" she cried, as she clung to Joshua's hand but then, suddenly, her expression hardened, and she scratched his face.

"Selena!" cried Tristan, as Joshua took hold of her head, muttering words over her Tristan could not hear.

Selena screamed. The sound sent chills up Tristan's spine. He rushed forward to protect his sister, but his father made it first.

"Get away from my daughter!" Mark yelled, dragging Selena away. Tristan staggered backwards when he saw her face. It was hard! Dark and eerie-looking, not the sister he had known. He threw up on the grass.

Mark was now standing in front of Joshua. He was angry, but Joshua was calm.

"What the hell are you doing?" Mark demanded. "What did you do to my daughter?"

"Nothing," Joshua calmly replied. "There was no time."

"You made her scream!"

"No," said Joshua. "It wasn't me who made her scream."

"What are you?" asked Mark. "Some kind of cult guru?"

"I am not," Joshua replied.

"I know who you are," said Selena, in an unnaturally deep voice that made Tristan shudder. "I know who you are!"

Joshua's eyes were firmly fixed on her now. Tristan had never seen him look like that before. The crowd were pressing in, watching; the cameras were running.

Selena laughed, loud and shrill. And then Joshua spoke.

"Darkness can never coexist with light," he said. "And one day, every dark corner will be lit up, like the brightest day. There will be no secrets, on that day. There will be no hiding place. Only truth; only honesty – only goodness will survive."

He walked easily past Mark, and brushed past Selena. Her back arched and she fell to the ground, screaming again. Tristan shivered, in the February heat.

Joshua had disappeared again. The ground was damp. The tide was coming in.

Tristan was perplexed by Joshua's words, but then he looked at his father's face, and saw utter fury.

The crowd dispersed.

Tristan stood on the hill. Behind him, seawater lapped halfway up the grassy mound. In front of him, the grassy plain was flooded. Joshua stood in water, up to his knees, in the middle of the plain. The current was strong. He was pushing hard against the tide.

Joshua's words to Selena, an hour ago, had changed his entire focus. As water had risen people had left, along with Tristan's father. He'd taken Selena with him, and angrily told Tristan he would be in touch.

Everyone loved comfort, and gifts. They were not so keen on exposure, and judgment. Was that what Joshua had meant, with all of his talk of darkness and light? Certainly his words had sounded like a threat. Had he intended them that way? Or had he just made a great mistake, in front of international media?

Tristan watched as a figure approached Joshua. It was John. He struggled with the current, but remained at his side. Then another more solid figure appeared. It was Rau.

Tristan hesitated, and then made his way down the hill and into the water. What was he doing? He wasn't sure. But he needed to understand.

The water was cold to begin with, but he pressed on, one step at a time. Once or twice he almost fell over, and then recovered, determined as he set his sights on reaching Joshua.

Before long, he stood beside him.

Joshua's face was impossible to read. John looked sad; Rau, cautious.

"What now?" asked Tristan, and Joshua steadily held his gaze.

"What do you mean?"

"Well – I think that was a real PR blunder, you know? If you want popularity…"

"Do you think I care about popularity?"

Tristan searched him. "No," he said, realising the truth as he said it. "I guess not."

Rau shifted in the water. "Joshua," he said, "the people weren't expecting…"

"Weren't expecting what?" Joshua interrupted him.

"Truth is truth," Rau continued. "It's all in how we say it."

"How we say it?" asked Joshua. "Or how we don't say it?"

"My sister," said Tristan, his heart suddenly pounding, "What did you say to her, to make her react like that?"

"That's enough!" It was John. Surprised, drawn out of himself, Tristan looked at him. His expression had become fervent – a little fierce. "You're both missing the point!"

"The point?"

"What if what Joshua said was true?" John asked. "Then he must say it! He must! For all of our sakes."

Now his eyes fixed on Tristan. "He didn't harm your sister!" he said. "You shouldn't be accusing him – you should be asking him what is wrong with her, and how she can be helped!"

Fear filled Tristan now, though he couldn't entirely explain it. Fear. He glanced at Rau, who was silent. And then he looked at Joshua.

There was sadness in his face, and a faraway look. He turned his back to them for a moment; he cast his eyes in the direction of the ocean. Then he returned, to look at them.

"My words stand," he said. "Like them or not, they will come to pass.

Full tide is coming, and I have come to teach people how to swim, before it is too late."

"Full tide?" asked Tristan. "What kind of tide?"

"If people are not ready, it will sweep them away: a tsunami unlike any before."

"You mean to warn us…"

"I haven't come to judge the world, Tristan Blake – I have come to save it."

Tears suddenly welled up uncontrollably in Tristan's eyes.

"Save it from what?" he cried. "Global warming? An asteroid? Weapons of mass destruction?"

"Do you think I mean a literal tsunami?" asked Joshua. "Yes, there will be flooding; yes, there will be war, and famine. These things have always been there. I'm talking about a more fundamental threat."

"What?"

"The darkening of the human heart."

Now Tristan was silenced. He remembered his sister's face: white, with dark shadows.

"Explain," he said.

"The times ahead will test the heart of humanity, unlike any other times before or to come," said Joshua. "Power is escalating, and so is desperation. Each person will need to choose, whether to aspire to the greatest good, or to succumb to the deepest evil. There will be no middle ground. The light will come and the darkness will be exposed."

"When?" asked Rau. "When will this all take place?"

"When?" Joshua repeated. "That is not for you to know, it's only for you to be ready."

"The light," said John. "It is already here."

"Yes."

"And the greatest good?" asked Tristan. "How can this be achieved?"

Joshua smiled sadly at him. "Only light can overcome darkness."

John stared intently at Joshua.

"I am the light," said Joshua. "I am also the boat, for the tide. Don't miss the boat! Turn on the light."

Tristan had no idea what he meant, but, once again, he felt certain his words were true. Light, darkness, flooding waters, desperation – disaster was coming! It was only a matter of time.

Chapter 16

JUDGMENT

Mark Blake stormed into the Beehive.

"Where's Connor?" he demanded of the receptionist. "I have to see him now."

"Sir!" The security guard called after him. "Sir – you can't barge in…"

Flushing, Mark straightened and then stretched his arms out, for the metal detector to move up and down his body.

"Clear," the guard announced, and then he moved away.

The receptionist hurriedly picked up the phone. Mark clenched and unclenched his fists, forcing himself to wait patiently.

"He will see you," she said finally, pointing towards the stairs.

Mark strode up them, two at a time.

James Connor was at the top. "How can I help you, Bishop?" he asked.

"I have some information."

"Information?" Connor's eyebrows shot up, in genuine surprise.

"Where can we talk that's private?"

"Probably nowhere on the surface of the planet."

"Then come over to Saint Peter's – I can't imagine anyone's dreamed of putting bugs there."

Connor hesitated, looking over Mark's face. Then he nodded.

"All right," he said.

Mark strode into Saint Peter's, with Connor in tow. They were alone, amongst the congregational seats.

"How can I help you?" Connor asked wryly, as he sat on a chair.

Mark stared down at him. "You won't believe where I have been."

"Where?"

"Wenderholm."

"Where?"

"Thirty minutes north of Auckland. I arrived back this morning."

"And you are pulling me out of a meeting to tell me this, why?"

"That man Joshua was there."

Now James stared at him. Then he laughed.

"You mean that guy on the news? Sounds like he could singlehandedly replace our social welfare fund: so much the better."

"I thought you were afraid of fragmentation."

Now a shadow passed over Connor's face. "What do you mean?"

"He's prancing around like a king up there."

Connor frowned. Then he smiled again.

"No matter," he said.

"No matter?" Mark repeated, exasperated.

"Let him act like a king. A little bit of shaking hands never hurt anyone. Heck, it's probably good for the morale right now. It might stop some of these altercations in the streets."

"James…"

Connor's eyes were dancing. "Let them hope, Mark! Let them have their warm fuzzies. He will reach his natural boundary, and then the thing will die out as quickly as it started. In the meantime, less violent crime! I'm all for that."

Mark frowned at him. "You treat faith as though it is a game," he said. "You always have."

"People will dream," said Connor, "and then they'll see the dream is false, and they'll turn back to reality. This Joshua is our friend, Mark. Why waste time making him our enemy?"

Mark shook his head at him. "You are a bloody enigma, James!" he said. "All this talk of your fear of political takeover from overseas, and here's someone in our own backyard acting like a king! What do you do? You just shake it off!"

Connor was grinning now, from ear to ear. His enjoyment filled Mark with irritation.

"Joshua Davidson is entertainment, Mark," said Connor, "nothing more! A bit of light relief, a bit of distraction, before we look at the threat of World War Three directly in the face.

"Thank you for the comedy, it's much appreciated! But now, really, I must get back to work."

Mark grumbled, and ushered Connor through the glass doors. He paused, watching his high school friend hurry down the steps, cross the road, and stroll back into the grounds of Parliament. Then he turned back into the sanctuary.

The church now was empty. Mark was grateful for the space.

Fury filled him. He strode up the aisle, hesitating on the pulpit steps, and then thrust himself into the inner sanctuary, and stood before the altar and Christ.

"How dare he?" he cried out to God. "How dare he?"

The image was before him: Joshua standing over his daughter, Selena's screams, and his outrageous words!

"Darkness can never coexist with light."

Those words had cut through Mark like a knife. Darkness? Was he insinuating that Selena was dark?

"Only goodness will survive."

It was Judgment. Judgment! Joshua Davidson was passing judgment on his daughter! How dare he?

"He pretends he is a king!" Mark declared, shaking his fist in the direction of Christ. "He pretends to know the state of our hearts! He doesn't know! Only God knows!"

Mark stared at the altar – the table of communion.

"Only God can judge, not any man! Only God!"

Even with his outpouring, Mark felt no relief. Instead he felt exposed. He trembled, and leant heavily against the railing: the place where people knelt, their palms held upward, to receive communion.

"Bishop?" It was Choo's voice.

Mark stared up at Jesus's face, on the cross. "Yes…?" he answered faintly.

"Do you need help?"

Help? He was the Bishop! Who could help him? A sudden surge of wilful determination coursed through him. He straightened his shoulders, and turned.

The Dean's face looked thoughtful. Her eyes were gentle.

"What's wrong?" she asked.

"Wrong?" Mark replied. "Nothing. Nothing at all."

"Only God can judge?"

"Instead of that man! That's what I meant. That man, up north."

"Joshua Davidson."

Mark frowned at her as he saw other ministers gathering behind her. Why? Then he remembered, they'd planned another Church Council meeting. Everyone was there, including the Baptist pastor, Murray Simon, in his usual casual shirt, and the Catholic priest, Andrew Stead, young and naïve.

"We may as well deal with this right now," said Mark, gesturing them into the choir stalls. "What do we do about Joshua Davidson?"

"Bishop," Choo murmured quietly. "This is a place of forgiveness, not judgment."

"You're wrong," Mark quickly replied. "Communion is all about judgment. Our sin is judged first. Only through judgment can we be forgiven."

He had silenced her mouth but not her eyes. The other ministers awkwardly took seats in the choir stalls. Choo shifted in discomfort, and then sat down.

"This Joshua Davidson," Mark began. "Have you seen him on the news?"

Murray's eyes were on him, his warm wrinkled face still smiling.

"I have seen him. He's helping the poor."

"And?"

"And what?"

"He's prancing about making judgments, as though he's God."

Now Murray's smile faded slightly. "What do you mean?"

"Making judgments!" Mark snapped. "I saw him myself! I went up, to see! He…" And now, suddenly, he didn't want to continue. Selena! No – he would not divulge this information.

"What judgment?" asked Murray.

"Never mind what," said Mark. "The point is, he's saying things he should not."

"I suppose we all do that?" said young Father Andrew.

"Yes, yes," Mark muttered. Darned purist! "We all do things we regret. But some of us do worse things than others. He is doing worse things! Anyway, forget I said anything. What other business do we have today? We should move onto that."

"Perhaps we should move into the meeting room?" Choo suggested.

"Yes, all right, let's move there."

Mark followed her out of the cathedral, through the corridor and into a meeting room.

Mark chaired the meeting, as always. Their talk about this and that bored him. When it came to an end, Murray stood before him.

"What do you have against this Joshua character?" he asked.

"What we all should have against him," Mark replied.

"What did he do to you?"

"Nothing."

"Why were you there?"

Mark shifted awkwardly. “To find my son.”

“Your son?” Murray looked astonished. “You’ve met with him?”

“Yes.”

“What was he doing there?”

Now Mark had to avoid his eyes. “I have no idea,” he muttered.

Murray shifted, and now he was sitting on the table, looking down at him, like a grandfather enquiring after his grandson.

“Is Tristan following Joshua?”

Mark swallowed. “What if he was?” he asked, eyeballing Murray. “Would that change your mind? What if you'd seen what I saw: thousands of people gathering around Joshua, hanging off every word he said, international media lapping it up, as though he was Jesus Christ himself. Would that bother you?”

Murray frowned. He glanced away and muttered some words under his breath, as if in prayer. Then his gaze returned.

“I don’t know,” he said. “I think that would depend.”

“On what?”

“On who he actually is.”

Mark stared at him, bewildered. And then he laughed.

“You can’t be serious.”

“How’s that?”

“The man is a fraud, pure and simple. A deceiver. A liar.”

“Then you have nothing to fear.”

Murray’s eyes were steady on him, challenging him. Mark held them steadily in return. Fear? What did fear have to do with anything? Nothing! Nothing at all.

“I am not afraid of the man,” said Mark. “I fear the deception.”

“I don’t think so,” Murray replied. “I think you fear the truth.”

Mark stiffened at the words. The truth? No! The truth was his friend, not his enemy: the truth was his foundation.

“Darkness can never coexist with light.”

Joshua was the darkness, not Selena! Joshua was the enemy.

Only goodness would survive.

Chapter 17

THE HOSPITAL

Rachel Connor's cell-phone was ringing. Frustrated, she laid the patient notes she'd been reading on the ward clerk's desk, and reached into her white coat pocket.

"Hello?" she said.

"Rachel!" her father's voice replied.

"Dad," she said, "I'm on a ward round. Don't you have meetings?"

"I'm about to head back in."

Rachel glanced up apologetically to her consultant, Dr Nigel Watts. He gave her a stern look back, and then gestured their House Officer, Sally Ng, to follow him.

"What is it, Dad?" she asked.

"You won't believe what happened."

"What?"

"Mark Blake just called me to Saint Peter's."

"The Cathedral? Why?"

"He's afraid there's a king taking over in Wenderholm."

Rachel shook her head, feeling a little dazed. "What?"

"Do you know Wenderholm?"

"Yes, I know Wenderholm! What are you on about?"

"A king, Rachel: a king! We're about to be taken over by the Northerners! Hold 'em off, will you? They should hit you first, there in Auckland, before they make it to Wellington."

For a moment, Rachel thought he was serious. Then his florid laughter filled her hearing, and she laughed with him.

"Had to share the joke, darling," he said. "Just too funny! Sorry to interrupt! Better get back to work."

"Yeah," she said, "you and me! Just keep any other jokes until tomorrow, eh, Dad? I'm on call tonight."

He had gone. She put her phone away.

Watts and Ng were talking to a patient in Room B. Rachel decided to leave them to it, and went to the first bed on the left in Room C.

A medical student suddenly appeared beside her, ready to jot down notes. Rachel admired his keen young enthusiasm with a pang of nostalgia: how quickly those days had passed by.

"Good morning, Thelma," said Rachel, reaching out a hand to the elderly woman. "How are you feeling this morning?"

"A bit better, thank you, Doctor Connor." Her dyed light blonde perm framed a polite smile.

"Good! How's that chest?"

"Not bad."

Rachel reached with her stethoscope to listen to Thelma's heart and lungs. The crackles she'd heard the previous morning were almost gone.

"It's sounding much better!"

"Does that mean I can go home?"

The House Officer, Sally, appeared and passed her the electronic chart. Rachel skimmed her eyes over it as Sally spoke.

"Temperature's been down for twenty-four hours," she said, "and O2 sats are back to normal."

"I think so!" said Rachel brightly to Thelma, and turned to Sally. "Good work. Discharge her today, with ten days of oral antibiotics."

Thelma's face lit up, her hazel eyes bright.

"I hope I never have to see you again," said Rachel with a smile, and Thelma nodded.

"Me too!"

Rachel reached for the small bottle of disinfectant in her pocket, and moved to the next bed, where a young Pacific Island woman in her twenties lay. She was dying of stomach cancer. Rachel sat on the edge of the bed, and reached to take the woman's hand.

"Good morning, Mary," she said.

"Good morning, Doctor Rachel," Mary replied, her voice weak.

"How is your breathing?"

"A bit better."

Rachel lingered on her face. The young woman's sister and aunt had also died of the same cancer. Her brown eyes were brave, lit from behind with her Christian faith.

"Has your pastor been in to pray with you?"

"Yes," said Mary. "I'm still hoping to be healed."

Rachel looked over her wasting body. Mary was well known to their team – she'd already had surgery, but the cancer had regrown and spread to her liver and lungs. From time to time fluid would build up around a lung, stealing her breath – she would return to hospital, and they would take out the fluid with a needle to give her relief.

Rachel was certain she had only a few weeks left to live, and yet what could she say without robbing her of her faith? A faith Rachel herself could not share?

She listened to her chest, looked at her chart, and patted her hand.

"Keep up the good work," she said, and with her grief masked she moved swiftly to the next bed.

A middle-aged Israeli man sat reading the paper. He looked up at her, and smiled. He was wearing a blue kippah cap on his head, with a Star of David.

"Greetings, Doctor Connor," he said.

"Greetings, Isaac," she replied.

Rachel moved to his side. "Would you mind?" she asked, and he shrugged, reaching to remove his cap.

"Go ahead."

She pulled back the dressing on his scalp. A tumour growing there had been removed, and the infection he'd developed afterwards was beginning to settle.

"News from the Middle East?" she asked, as she replaced the dressing.

"Tensions," Isaac sighed. "As always."

"Is there hope for peace?"

She found his gentle brown eyes, as he replaced his kippah.

"There is always hope for peace," he said, "with the Lord."

Faith, again, but a different kind. Rachel smiled sadly. "Shalom," she said.

"Shalom," he answered back, tipping his head respectfully.

As she moved to the sink to wash her hands, Rachel turned to Sally. "One more day of IVs," she said, "and then he can go onto orals too."

"Okay," said Sally.

Now Rachel wandered across the room to the foot of another bed, where a young Iraqi man was battling a continuing infection in the bone of his shin.

"The osteomyelitis is getting worse," Sally said quietly in her ear. "We've given five days of IVs."

"And the temp?"

"Still spiking."

"Blood cultures?"

"They've finally grown multi-resistant staph."

"Shit."

Rachel looked at the young man. Was he even twenty? His body was well toned, wearing black shorts and a green sports shirt, but his face was beaded with sweat. Rachel glanced at his chart – twenty-one. There was a notice pinned above his head: gloves to be used with any contact. She reached for some gloves, and drew back the dressing from his wound. Pus was draining directly from the bone.

"Vancomycin?"

"We've run out."

Rachel swallowed. She covered the wound again, and smiled at the man. What was his name? Abida.

"Can you fix me, doctor?"

Rachel felt her smile fading. What to say?

"Maybe surgery will help," she said. "Let me talk to my consultant."

His young eyes were fixed on her, she knew, as she washed her hands and left the room.

Rachel hurried into the corridor, taking a deep breath, and nearly bumped into Abida's parents, their smooth olive faces creased with worry.

"What are you doing for our son?" his father asked.

Rachel swallowed again. "I'm sorry," she began, struggling to find some form of comfort. "He has a resistant infection. The antibiotics we're using aren't working very well."

"Isn't there something else you can use?"

"We…" Grief threatened her. "We don't have anything else."

Medical supplies from overseas were restricted, now. All imports were drying up.

"Can't you do something?" Abida's mother cried. "He's getting sicker! Can't you see?"

She was grasping at Rachel's arm now, pulling her back into the room. Rachel shook off her arm.

"That's enough!" she exploded. "What do you want from me, a miracle?"

They stared at her, their mouths open, as her consultant came to stand beside her.

Rachel flushed, and fleetingly closed her eyes. Then she opened them again, girding herself again.

"Look, I'm sorry," she said quietly. "I'm sorry. Here's Dr Watts, he'll be able to help you."

But she knew there was nothing more he could offer.

The parents accompanied Watts, and Rachel retreated to the work bay. Sally sat down alongside her, with the charts, and Rachel threw her stethoscope on the table, staring at it.

"I hate this job," she said.

"You're not God," said Sally, and Rachel closed her eyes tightly again.

"Tell that to the patients who are dying."

Time was pushed – always pushed. Rachel opened her eyes, sighed, and then rose to her feet. "Radiology meeting," she said.

"I'll be there soon," Sally replied, "after I check the bloods."

"All right." And Rachel strode down the corridor and out of the ward.

Outside, the sun was shining. Rachel gazed longingly out of a window, to the blue expanse of Lake Pupuke beyond. Across on the other side of the lake was North Shore Hospital. She'd worked there once. Now, she worked in the newer hospital, serving the increasing population on the North Shore. 'North with Interest', the staff called it: North-East Hospital. Budget cuts, sixty hour weeks, medication tightly controlled. She needed a break, that's why she had exploded.

A large group of people had gathered on the lakefront. What was going on? She had no time to check it out – even her lunch-breaks were filled with beeps from the locator.

Reluctantly Rachel entered the dark radiology room. A large screen showed images of interest to be discussed. She cast her eyes over them: maybe sarcoidosis on the first chest X-ray? Maybe leukaemia on the bone scan?

Watts sat down next to her, his grey curly hair framing a smirk.

"Interesting episode on the ward, Rachel."

"Whatever you say," Rachel muttered. "That's what you get with multi-resistant staph."

"Shift him to the single room."

"We're getting a few cases now."

"I know. We must contain them. If we get an outbreak, we're stuffed."

"All right."

The radiologist began to talk through the X-rays. Soon they were looking at Mary's chest X-ray: half of her left lung was white.

"Progressed," said the radiologist. "The fluid is beginning to build up again."

"So I see," said Rachel.

"How is she clinically?"

Rachel smiled sadly, considering. "Better than she was when she was first admitted."

"She'll need another tap soon."

"Yes," Rachel sighed, "and another, and another."

"It helps her," said Nigel. "It's all we can do."

"I know," said Rachel. "It's all we can do, and yet she still prays and hopes."

She could feel Nigel's eyes upon her, as she stared at the X-ray.

"Have you told her the prognosis?"

Rachel swallowed. "Who am I to tell her how much time she has left?"

"It is your responsibility, doctor."

She avoided his grey gaze. "While she lives, there might still be hope."

"She is dying – there is nothing else."

"All right!" Rachel exploded again, now staring into his lined face. A fourteen-hour day, and this as well? "I'll tell her to her face she's dying!" she said. "I'll strip away any shred of hope she has! Is that what you want?"

Nigel's face hardened slightly, and then he softened.

"I'm sorry," he said. "I'll handle it."

"And what will you say?" asked Rachel. "You're an atheist! How will you comfort a Christian?"

Nigel smiled sadly, and Rachel instantly regretted her words. He had a heart! He knew their impotence.

"I'll tell her the truth, Rachel," he said. "It's all we can do. Even your agnosticism should tell you that."

Rachel swallowed, and moved her eyes from him to the new films: the CT scan of Abida's leg.

"The patch of osteomyelitis is also growing," said the radiologist, and Rachel nodded.

"Surgery," said Nigel. "Talk to the orthopods."

"I already have," said Rachel, feeling her voice dull. "They won't take him."

"Shift him into the side room," said Nigel. "I'll talk to his family again later today."

"All right."

The radiologist continued, presenting different films, and Rachel felt herself sinking into oblivion. Doom and gloom – that's all they had to offer! Soon broad spectrum antibiotics would run out, and then…

Sally suddenly burst into the room, her short black hair thrown back from her face.

"Rachel!" she said. "I need to talk to you!"

"What is it?" asked Rachel, thrusting herself out of the seat.

"I…" Now Sally's brown eyes drifted to Watts, and then returned to Rachel. What was in her expression: bewilderment? "I need to talk with you," she said again.

Watts stood up. "What are you on about, Sally?" he asked. "Did someone die? Spit it out."

"They're…" Sally hesitated. "I think they're…"

"What?" asked Rachel.

"Spit it out!"

"Oh, you've got to come!" Sally grasped Rachel's arm, and pulled her out of the room.

"We're in the middle…" Watts' voice trailed off, as Rachel was dragged down the corridor toward the lift.

"Something's happening," Sally gasped, on the way. "I don't get it – something weird. Abida and Mary went down to see this guy."

Now Watts had caught up behind them. "What?" he exploded. "How dare you let our patients go down to that freak show…?"

"What freak show?" asked Rachel. "What are you talking about?"

"You knew about this?" said Nigel, as they ran after Sally. "I'll have you up before the Medical Council…"

"I saw the people outside," Sally panted, entering the lift. "I heard the stories. But they went down there themselves, it wasn't me!"

The lift doors opened, and just outside the entrance, on the grass in front of the lake, was a large crowd of people. Even more had gathered since Rachel had looked out of the window.

"What's going on?"

Sally was searching for someone, and then she found her.

Mary stood before them, at the edge of the water. Her face was animated, and she was breathing easily.

Rachel stared at her. "Mary…" she stuttered. "What are you doing here?"

"I heard about the man," she said. "I thought he might heal me."

Confused, Rachel searched through the gathered crowd. What man? Her eyes returned to Mary – Nigel was reaching to take her pulse.

"Come upstairs again," he said. "You're unwell – the fluid is building up again…"

"It's gone."

"Come upstairs, we'll examine you again."

"You can examine me, but it's gone."

"You mean you can breathe?" asked Rachel, and Mary smiled at her.

"I can breathe. And the pain has gone."

Tears pricked Rachel's eyes. She blinked them away.

"Mary," she said quietly. "Can you please come upstairs? Let us examine you. Let us do another X-ray."

"Yes," said Mary. "I can do that for you."

Sally took Mary's arm, and escorted her back into the hospital.

Rachel met Nigel's grey eyes.

"Surely you're not thinking…" Nigel began.

"I don't know what to think. Maybe it's just hope! I don't know."

"Placebo effect!"

"Maybe."

Nigel grimaced. "A fluke, or whatever," he said, "Come on, Rachel – we're scientists. We study hard science, not delusions."

"I know that, but…"

Abida ran past them, grinning wildly. Rachel stared, as Nigel caught his arm.

"Hey!" said Nigel. "You should be in isolation!"

Rachel reached out to the covered wound on his leg.

"Gloves!" said Nigel, and Rachel hesitated. The dressing was still soaked. She reached into her pocket, found a pair of gloves, put them on, and pulled away the dressing.

The wound was gone.

Rachel began to shake violently. "How did this happen?" she whispered. "Who did this?"

Nigel held Abida's leg with his bare hands and stared at it.

"I must be going mad."

"If you're mad," said Rachel, "then all three of us are losing our minds."

"It's gone!" Abida cried. "I'm cured!"

Nigel took Abida's arm, and propelled him back into the hospital. Rachel pressed through the crowd, searching for the man. Finally she found him, his hands on an elderly lady's pained shoulder, murmuring over her.

Rachel stared at him. He was a European in his mid-thirties, wearing blue jeans and a faded grey T-shirt.

"Who are you?" she breathed, as his brown eyes settled on her. "What are you doing?"

The crowd peeled back as he took her arm and led her alongside the lake.

"I'm Joshua," he said.

Rachel frowned, confused. Joshua? She wasn't expecting a normal name.

"I'm…I'm Rachel," she stammered back.

"I have something to show you," he said, pulling a piece of paper from his jean pocket.

"Here's a DNA map," he said. "You're familiar with it?"

She nodded, struggling to focus as he unfolded it.

"I did a Master's in biochemistry, before I changed to Medicine," said Rachel.

"Do you know what this is?"

She stared down at his notes. It was a DNA sequence, scribbled hastily but understandable.

"I'm not sure…I don't recognise the specific gene."

"This is the sequence for aging."

Rachel frowned. Aging? The aging gene? That was only theory, wasn't it…?

"Do you have access to the human genome?" asked Joshua.

"Yes."

"This is it," he said, "the sequence for aging. This is the cause of aging for the entire human race."

Rachel trembled as she looked at the sequence, then Joshua turned the paper over.

"Do you know what this is?" he asked, pointing to the next sequence.

"No," she said.

"This is the original design."

Rachel swayed, peering down at the code. "What do you mean," she asked, "the original design?"

"The original design for that sequence of human DNA," said Joshua, "before it was changed to this." And he turned the page over again.

Rachel stared into his brown eyes. "What are you saying?" she whispered. "That this is the elixir of life? That with this gene no one would die?"

"No one would die from old age."

Rachel trembled before him, as he continued.

"Of course," he said, "you can't change the code of everyone who lives now…"

"But the next generation…"

"If you chose to, you could manipulate the genes of the next generation."

Rachel's jaw dropped. The page was lying in her hands – the page of his jottings. With this, she could change the world. But even as she considered it, she felt a new weight, a growing understanding.

"I can't use this," she whispered. "I don't have the authority! I don't have enough wisdom..."

He lifted the page from her hands, and put it back into his pocket, his eyes connecting with hers again.

"You're right, Rachel," he said gently. "None of you have the authority to use this."

She searched his eyes, as he touched her arm.

"Do you know what would happen, if you made people immortal, right here, right now, as things stand?"

Rachel shook her head. "What?"

"A multitude would die, Rachel – not of old age, but of starvation."

Dismay took her. Yes! Overpopulation!

"There is a time to live and a time to die, Rachel – do you understand this? You, a doctor? Do you understand?"

A time to die? Rachel reached instinctively to grasp his arm.

"Show me," she whispered. "Help me to understand it. You just healed…"

"We have the power to give life and to take it away."

"To take it away?" Fear suddenly gripped her.

"Are you afraid of me now?" Joshua murmured, grasping her arm in turn, "When you were so relieved by my healing before?"

Rachel cast her eyes over him. He looked like an average kiwi bloke, and yet he held life and death in his hands.

"I don't know," said Rachel. "Should I be afraid? Who are you?"

Joshua's face broke into a sad smile.

"That is the whole question," he said, "that you, and everyone, must answer."

Rachel struggled, and grasped for understanding. She suddenly felt in a different world! Like a baby, thrown into the water – everything had changed in a few moments.

"Are you…" she asked, "Are you some kind of alien?"

Joshua's smile widened, and brightened with humour. "I am alien to you."

"Are you – safe?"

His expression clouded a little. "That all depends, what do you mean by 'safe'?"

"Are you kind?"

Now sorrow suddenly filled his eyes – a deep, piercing sorrow: a grief that grasped her heart, and would not let her go.

"Are we kind?" he murmured. "Which is the kinder act, Rachel: to give you the DNA code for eternal life, or keep it away?"

Rachel reached out to touch his face. She felt like a child standing next to him, but strangely also felt embraced.

"I don't know," she whispered, and he nodded.

"Don't be afraid of me, Rachel," he murmured. "I am driven by love, not by evil – by a kind of love you can't yet understand. But even love, sometimes, must act strongly and be mistaken for evil, even while it is seeking a much greater good."

Rachel grasped his other arm. "So you are good, then?" she pleaded. "Not only powerful, but good? There is hope?"

Joshua touched her face, and suddenly tears filled his eyes. Tears! He was human! "Yes," he whispered, "there is hope. But you will see for yourself just how high a price goodness must pay in its outworking."

She searched his face: what did he mean? She searched his eyes. But now he turned away back into the crowd, and continued to heal them.

It was time for Rachel to return to the hospital.

As she walked back through the hospital doors, she reached for the stethoscope around her neck. Their methods now seemed like sticks and stones compared with his healing – her purpose seemed, now, like a faint shadow of his purpose.

For a moment she vacillated, and then she walked straight to the Human Resources Office, reached for a form, and signed her name.

Annual leave. It was time to take some rest.

Chapter 18

RISK

John sat against a pine tree. It was late. The sun had finally set on the long summer day, and darkness had settled. The park was almost deserted, and the lake was quiet and calm, sparkling in the moonlight.

John's eyes closed fleetingly. What a day! He'd never seen anything like it. Joshua had healed so many people! So easily, all in his stride! He healed, like…like…

Trembling, John shook his head at the thought. It was impossible. And yet, look at what had happened. What wondrous thing had they all witnessed?

Someone sat down beside him. It was Rau, his face radiant in the moonlight, his eyes lit with a joy John did not understand.

"Areruia," said Rau. "I have seen the coming of the Lord."

"The Lord?" John whispered. "Which Lord?"

"There is only one," Rau replied, smiling gently. "Only one, who has this kind of authority over us."

John swallowed, and shifted slightly on the ground. The Lord? John knew no Lord. And yet…and yet…

"Did you feel him?" asked Rau. "Did you see him?"

John wrung his hands in his lap. "I…I was too afraid to look."

"Look at him," Rau gently invited. "Look at him, now."

John raised his eyes, to search for Joshua. He found him alone at the lake's edge, dipping his hand in and out, making little waves in the water.

"So human," Rau murmured. "Do you see it? So human. And yet so…"

"Divine?" John interjected. "You might as well say it: I know who you think he is."

Rau held his gaze. "All right, then," he said, "I will say it. Yes, divine. I believe this is the Christ, returned to save us."

The words were like lead in John's stomach. He stood up, clenched his fists, and began to pace back and forth.

"You can't say that!" he said to Rau. "You can't claim this is Christ!"

"Why not?" asked Rau. "At Wenderholm, you were declaring his authority! How much more is his authority declared now?"

"It was different at Wenderholm!" said John. "We were alone!" Tears filled his eyes, and he rapidly blinked them away. "We can't hide now! Not with everything he's done."

Rau's hand came on his shoulder, from behind. "Don't be afraid, John," he said. "What can people do to us, with Joshua on our side?"

"What can people do to us?" John repeated, heart pounding. "People can kill us, Rau! People can kill us! He knows that!" Now he gestured in Joshua's direction. "He feels it."

John glanced back at Rau's eyes, to find a strange resolution there.

"I don't care," said Rau. "I've been following Christ all my life. I'm not going to stop now."

"Even if they crucify you for it?"

Rau's gaze was steadfast; strong. "Even if they crucify me," he said. "I'll die if that's what it takes."

"What about your family? Your wife? Your children?"

Rau swallowed, but his gaze remained. "Whatever it takes."

John admired him, as he saw the truth of his conviction. He truly believed; he truly followed. But John did not share the same faith.

"What do you see in him?" asked Rau. "Why do you follow?"

John looked again at the man standing alone beside the water. "I see someone I don't understand," he said. "Someone greater than I am – someone with great power, and heart."

"And the source of his power?"

"I don't know."

"Not God?"

"I don't believe in God."

Rau looked perplexed as he gazed at him. "How can you not believe in God, after what you saw today?"

John shifted again on his feet. God? What was God? An old man in the sky? Childhood fairy tales: Christ and Santa as one?

"God is for children."

"Not only for children!" Rau protested. "Christ was the most adult of adults!"

"Stories of an ark bouncing on the water," said John. "A flood and a dove. They're pretty stories for children."

"Unless you become as a child, you can't enter the Kingdom of Heaven.[6]"

"Exactly. Heaven is for children. Real life is for adults."

"Then who is Hell for?"

Surprised, John turned to find Tristan standing next to him. His face looked pale in the moonlight, his green eyes haunted. John frowned, as Rau put his hand on Tristan's shoulder.

"Are you all right, mate?"

"I don't know," Tristan whispered.

"What's going on?"

"Today…"

"Yes?"

Tristan was trembling now, and tears filled his eyes. "He fixed them!" he said.

John searched Tristan's face. What was wrong with this young man?

What had he seen, in his life? Some horror. Some source of great shame.

"Isn't that the point?" asked Tristan. "Isn't that what we need? Someone to care? Someone to fix us?"

"You mean someone to save us?" Rau murmured. "A Saviour?"

Rau's arms went around Tristan now in a strong Maori embrace. Tristan was crying. John was uncomfortable, and he backed away as footsteps approached.

"Where are they?" a woman's voice called out. "Where have the patients gone?"

John looked at her. She was a slim woman in her early thirties. She was wearing a white lab coat, and had a stethoscope around her neck under her straight brown hair. Fear struck him: she was a doctor.

"Ah…" he stuttered. "I guess they've gone home."

"Home?" she said, her face breaking into a pretty smile. "Don't tell me you've emptied the whole hospital!"

"Have we broken some kind of rule?" asked John.

"No!" she said. "It's up to them! They didn't sign out, though."

"Oh. Sorry."

She looked at him for a moment, glanced at Rau and Tristan, and then looked back at John, shaking her head.

"Sorry," she said. "That's not why I came."

"No?" asked John.

"No. I came to…" Now she seemed to be struggling a little, her blue eyes conflicted. "I had to finish being on call first."

"Busy?"

"No." Her expression was wry. "Quiet. And now I'm finished, and…"

"Yes?"

"I was wondering if I could help."

Surprised, John glanced at Rau and Tristan silently watching her. Their eyes met John's; they were wary. Could she be trusted? They didn't speak.

"How would you like to help?" asked John, looking back at her.

"Joshua seems to have things sorted."

"Oh, yes!" she said, seeming a little flustered. "I don't mean treating patients."

"What, then?"

"I could record them for you."

"Sorry?"

"I could record the healings. The diagnoses, the results, and the outcomes. I could document them and publish them."

Fear consumed John. Publish them? Make them known to the entire world?

"I don't know," he gasped.

Rau stepped forward. "I think it's a great idea."

"Really?" she said, smiling widely.

"Tell everyone. Join us."

Now the woman extended her hand to John. "I'm Rachel Connor," she said.

John hesitated and then shook it. "John Robertson," he said. "Nice to meet you, Doctor Connor."

Tristan nudged him.

"And this is Tristan Blake, and our leader, Rau Petera."

Tristan was clearly taken by the beauty of her enthusiastic eyes, and Rau was warmly receiving her. John nervously watched her. Documentation? She was a scientist. What place did a scientist have amongst them?

But then Joshua was there. He smiled and extended his hand.

"Rachel Connor," he said to her, "you are welcome here."

"Thank you," she said.

"Documentation," Joshua murmured. "An interesting idea."

"I just thought…"

"Do as you wish," he said. "Verify our proceedings with your science, as you see fit. I will not get in the way. But…"

"Yes?"

"You will find in time there are realms your science has not yet touched upon."

"Realms we cannot touch, or have not yet considered?"

Joshua's smile widened. "Both," he said. "Because both are inherently linked."

Rachel looked intrigued. Joshua had drawn her to them, John was certain. He had purposefully called her to join them – she had happily followed.

And John's interest in her also was rising.

Chapter 19

UNEASE

James Connor stared at the TV screen in the Beehive's staff cafeteria.

"What the hell…?"

The same damned young reporter was back, with another yarn to spin.

"Joshua Davidson strikes again!" she said into the camera. "Next on the agenda? Healings! Lots of them. Who needs a public health system, when Joshua is coming to town?"

Connor rose to his feet. "Great," he said. "Who needs fiction with reporting like this?"

People surrounded the reporter, jostling against her, trying to get air time.

"My foot!" said an elderly woman. "It was crook, and he fixed it! My GP didn't have a clue."

"And my head!" said another younger woman. "Terrible migraines, now gone!"

"Pity about the delusions," said Connor as he switched it off.

A sudden uncomfortable silence enveloped the cafeteria. Surprised, Connor glanced around his MPs – they had been watching!

"Back to work, people!" he said. "Happy hour is over."

Connor walked out and made his way to Parliament House. There, in the foyer, Clarkson joined him as expected.

"James," he said, as they made their way to the Debating Chamber. "Seen the news lately?"

"Tell me you're not talking about Joshua," said Connor. "I'm about up to here with all the stories."

"I like his style."

"What?" Connor glanced at his grinning face, and sighed. "Of course you do. Silly me."

"He's emptying our hospitals!" said Clarkson. "Nice social policies."

"Policies?" said Connor. "That's a new one."

"Food to the poor, healing to the sick. It sounds like he'll put us all out of a job!"

Connor did a double take. Put them out of a job? That was a bit close to the bone!

"Planning for retirement, Patrick?"

"Maybe he could take my job!" Clarkson's eyes were dancing.

"Yeah, right," said Connor. "He can have it!"

They arrived in the Chamber.

Connor tried to recall what was on the agenda. Ah, yes: the 'Emergency Reallocation of Public Funds' bill. All rose, for the Speaker. He prayed. All sat, Connor tuned out until the bill was announced, and then he rose to his feet.

"Mr Speaker," he said.

"The Right Honourable Prime Minister James Connor."

"I nominate that the Emergency Reallocation of Public Funds bill be read a second time."

"Mr Speaker," said Clarkson, rising opposite Connor.

"The Right Honourable Leader of the Opposition, Patrick Clarkson."

"I'd like to ask the Right Honourable Prime Minister whether now, finally, with the help of one Joshua Davidson, public funds might actually be in excess?"

Laughter spread across the House.

"Public Health pollution must be down," said Tracy Harrison, of the Clean Green Party, rising to her feet.

"I understand crime is falling," said Rawiri Heka, of the Maori Party.

"Hope seems to be rising," said a Christian Conservative Party MP, standing. "Morale hasn't been this high in our country for many years."

Connor rose quickly to his feet. "Point of order, Mr Speaker," he said. "We are not here to discuss Joshua Davidson."

He fixed his eyes on the Speaker. The older man looked between Connor, Clarkson, Harrison and Heka, and then nodded.

"Right Honourable Patrick Clarkson, withdraw your last statement."

Clarkson was grinning from ear to ear. "Mr Speaker, I withdraw my last statement."

"The question is that the motion be agreed to," said the Speaker, and now the Minister of Finance rose to his feet.

"Mr Speaker, I would like to support the Emergency Reallocation of Public Funds bill."

Clarkson rose to his feet.

"Mr Speaker, I would like to ask for more information regarding the powers rendered by the bill, and I ask where the funds might be allocated should the need arise..."

Connor girded himself. This one, as expected, would take more of a battle of wits. So be it.

The debate continued. The vote was taken. The Government coalition with the Christian Conservative Party was still in the majority. The bill was passed on to the Finance Select Committee, for consideration.

The Speaker left the Chamber. Satisfied, Connor hurried behind.

As he made his way back to the Beehive, Connor recalled Mark Blake's words.

"I thought you were afraid of fragmentation."

Connor shook his head. Fragmentation? No. There was no such threat.

"He's prancing around like a king."

A king. That thought struck more fear into Connor's heart. A king?

But again, no. There was no evidence of such a thing. Only a man, only a little mass delusion – food, and care. Nothing more. In many ways, the man was more like a priest than an actual king.

No wonder Blake was threatened. Let the priests work out their own quarrels; he had no interest in matters of God.

Smirking, Connor caught the lift, rose to the ninth floor, and entered his office. It was vital they nail this bill – time to prepare more information for the Select Committee.

Sitting at his desk, he reached for the bill's folder as his cell-phone rang. He answered, distracted. "James Connor."

"Dad?"

"Rachel!" Happily he looked at her photo, on his desk. "Unusual time for you to call."

"I've taken some time off work."

"Oh, yes? Everything okay?"

"Umm…" Her voice sounded hesitant, and then she continued. "Have you seen the news?"

"Yes, how can I miss it? Joshua Davidson's face is everywhere."

Rachel paused and then continued again.

"He was outside our hospital."

"Yes?" His eyes were drifting over the folder and he reached inside.

"I saw him."

Now Connor stopped, and focused fully on her. "And?"

Again, a pause. Connor frowned. "Rachel?"

"The healings are real."

Chills went up his back. "What do you mean, Rachel?"

"Dad – I think they're real."

His chest tightened. "Rachel, you can't say that. You're a doctor. You'll lose your job."

"I'm a scientist as well as a doctor," she said. "And as a scientist, I have to acknowledge what I see."

Connor's vision blurred for a moment. He blinked furiously.

"Rachel," he said. "Just keep this to yourself, okay? Keep it to yourself."

"What do you mean?"

"There's something going on with you. Don't tell anyone. I'll get Mum to visit you, or something – we'll help you."

"Dad, I'm not mad."

"We'll get you some help."

"Dad!" Her voice rose, strong and indignant. He'd never heard her speak so powerfully before. "You have to listen to me!" she said. "The healings are real! I'm a doctor – I know what I'm talking about! You have to listen."

Connor began to sweat. "But how can they be real, Rachel? What are you saying?"

Again, her voice paused. And then…

"I don't know what I'm saying, Dad – I don't know how to interpret the evidence. I'm just saying that the evidence is here. And…I thought you should know. You're our Prime Minister."

The grip on his chest tightened. It was heavy, a little frightening.

"Rachel," he said. "Did he make any mention of being a king?"

"No," Rachel answered.

"Do you think…?" Now he hesitated. Surely the phone was bugged. "Do you think he's dangerous?"

He heard her shifting, on the other end of the phone. Then she spoke again.

"No," she said. "Why do you ask?"

Now Connor was silent. He stared at her photo, at her beauty and smile.

"Keep me posted, Rachel," he said, conflicted. He could use her as an informant, but she would know it. "Let me know if you find out more."

He heard an almost inaudible sigh – and then, for the last time, her voice.

"Have a good day, Dad."

"Okay," he said. "Have a good day, Rachel."

Chapter 20

TAKAPUNA

Rachel sat on the grass, at Takapuna Beach. She was on the edge of the bank, her legs dangling over, her feet nearly touching the water below. It was high tide.

Behind her on the grassy bank, under plush pohutukawa trees, thousands of people were gathered around Joshua, along with a mix of national and international reporters.

Ahead the ocean sparkled, and beyond Rangitoto Island rose from the sea, a dormant volcanic cone laden with the largest pohutukawa forest in the world. The bright red spindle blossoms of New Zealand's Christmas tree were still blooming along Takapuna Beach. Rachel thought she could make out a little red amongst the deeper green of Rangitoto.

The sun was high in the deep blue sky – it was a beautiful, warm summer day.

Rachel glanced again at her cell-phone. 'Keep me posted,' her father had said. What was he on about? 'Dangerous,' he'd said. Why was he afraid? One thing was sure – she wasn't going to report to him, like an agent. There was no need, anyway; the media were everywhere.

She put her phone away, eyed the water at her feet, and tentatively dunked in a toe.

"Don't be afraid," said Joshua, his voice drifting over to her. "Hard times are coming but they are only the beginning of something brand new, and fresh. They might hurt! Like a mother hurts, when she is giving birth: she pushes, and pushes, and strains! But then comes the brand new baby! A wonder! A miracle. Joy comes in the morning, like the blossoming of the pohutukawa…"

Rachel's vision misted, for a moment. Childbirth. Then she turned, to look at Joshua. He was standing high on the bank, his voice carrying easily. The crowd was standing, or sitting, or lying on the grass – some people looked like they were sunbathing with their eyes closed, arms and legs stretched out. Children were running around, darting between people, and playing.

"A new time is coming," said Joshua, "when there will be no more pain, or suffering, or grief – no more hunger, or sickness, or war…"

Rachel's eyes found Tristan. He was standing very still, close to Joshua, listening intently.

"There will be no need to fight anymore," said Joshua. "No need to struggle on. There will be peace – real, full, complete peace."

Rau stood beside Tristan, his face radiant.

"The new season is coming," said Joshua. "It won't be long. But to reach it, we must learn to fight in a different way. Not with fists, or physical weapons. Not against an enemy out there – an enemy who is really our neighbour. No, we must learn to fight the true enemy: the shrewdest combatant. We must learn to overcome the voice of evil in our own hearts."

Rachel tilted her head, pondering over his words. The voice of evil? Our own hearts?

"There are different kinds of fighting," Joshua continued, "just as there are different kinds of love. There are different kinds of allies along the way. Some allies provide weapons of warfare for the fight. Some provide soldiers. Some allies provide strength, beyond our own strength – knowledge, beyond our own knowledge. Some allies are so strong, in the war that our only course of action is to join them – to become one, in the fight, with them."

John was there too, standing extremely close to Joshua, almost touching him.

"There is one Ally," said Joshua, "who is much greater than the rest: one Ally who can overcome the grip of the enemy, as surely as a tsunami wipes out everything in its path. What will happen, when that Ally comes? What will happen, when the flood comes?

"Every soldier needs to listen to his commanding officer, for the time when the ultimate weapon is dropped. Every soldier needs to take shelter, to survive while the enemy is taken."

Now Joshua paused before continuing.

"Who is that great Ally?" he asked. "That is the question we all must answer. When is the flood coming? No one knows but the Ally himself. Where is the shelter to hide?"

He paused again, and fixed his eyes on John.

"That shelter," he said, "is me."

There was muttering in the crowd. Joshua himself was a shelter? How could a man be a shelter for a flood? Rachel heard the people quibbling amongst themselves.

"I don't get it," said a young man beside her. "What's he talking about?"

"A tsunami!" said a woman opposite him. "There must be a tsunami coming! We should get away from the coast!"

Rachel looked down at her feet, dipped in the sea. The water was calm, and unmoving. A light sea breeze lifted her hair a little from her face. No, he wasn't talking about a literal tsunami, she was certain of that. But what about his talk of war? Wasn't that a little dangerous, in these tenuous times?

She glanced again to the reporters – the cameras, filming him. Had he meant a literal war? A literal weapon? She didn't think so. But what might others think? Surely he knew the potency of his analogies? Surely he knew the impact of his words?

Joshua's eyes roved over the crowd, and Tane stepped forward.

"You are our shelter," said Tane. "Our safety, for the storms ahead."

"I am," said Joshua.

"Then we will follow you!" said Tane. "You are our Leader – you are our Great Ally."

And he broke into a Maori karakia. A few others joined him, men and women. With Tane leading, they now began a waiata, singing to Joshua as the entire crowd listened. People rose to their feet.

Rachel watched them, and her vision misted again. She shook her feet to dry them, and rose to her feet. Aotearoa, New Zealand! Maori and Pakeha as one! This was her home.

The waiata, deep and soaring, came to an end. Then Joshua, in traditional response, began to sing.

Rachel stared at him, astonished. He was singing their National Anthem![7]

"E Ihowā Atua,
O ngā iwi mātou rā
Āta whakarangona;
Me aroha noa
Kia hua ko te pai;
Kia tau tō atawhai;
Manaakitia mai
Aotearoa"

What was going to happen to them? What would become of little old New Zealand, in the much bigger world scene? With Joshua around, everyone had begun to feel safe.

"God of Nations, at thy feet," he sang,
"In the bonds of love we meet,
Hear our voices, we entreat,
God defend our free land."

Voices joined in, now – thousands of voices – as one, with Joshua.

"Guard Pacific's triple star,
From the shafts of strife and war.
Make her praises heard afar,
God defend New Zealand!"

The song had become a prayer. The voices lifted and became united.

Rachel trembled with tears. What was happening, all around her? A new hope! A new passion! Joshua continued the National Anthem – he knew all the words, and the people followed him.

"Men of every creed and race,
Gather here before Thy face,
Asking thee to bless this place,
God defend our free land.

"From dissension, envy, hate,
And corruption guard our state.
Make our country good and great,
God defend New Zealand."

Then, when it was finished, a cheer went up – a loud, sustained shout of joy.

God defend New Zealand.

Something had changed, in that moment – Rachel felt it. Now there was no going back. Tane and the singers gathered tightly around Joshua as he pressed against their foreheads and noses, exchanging a Maori hongi with them all. Others flooded after them – Pakeha, European, Pacific Islander, Asian, Middle Eastern, people from all over. They loved him; maybe they even worshipped him. Rachel had never seen anything like it.

The cameras were there, as well, set back a little, watching: the world.

Rachel swallowed. What would happen next? She hesitated. But then she moved forward. She didn't want to be on the outside, anymore; she was a part of this movement, and she was safe, within it.

Quickly she joined the other people, and moved in closer to be with Joshua.

Chapter 21

THE LIGHT

John sat at the waterfront. It was late – most of the crowd had left. Some had stayed on and set up tents, on the grass. A few were trying to text their friends or family, and were struggling with the unreliable network.

John gazed out across the sea. Rangitoto was a dark shadow now; the moon and stars lit the dark sky.

Something remarkable had happened that historic day. Joshua had spoken, and the people had listened. They had heard him. They had seen him. And now they were following him.

The water had receded from the base of the grassy hill. A little sand was exposed now. John watched tiny crabs scamper across the sand, and felt the movement of air as someone came to sit beside him.

It was Joshua.

He looked tired – it was late. John smiled at him.

"Quite a day," he said.

"Yes," Joshua replied. "That's for real."

"They listened to you!" said John, and Joshua gave his sad smile.

"They listened, but they don't really understand," he said. "Not yet."

John searched his brown eyes, full of hidden meaning.

"The metaphors," said John. "A tsunami. A war."

"Big things are ahead."

"I get that, but…but what did you mean by the great 'Ally'?" Now John trembled. "What did you mean by the 'ultimate weapon'?"

The sadness in Joshua's face deepened. "Anyone who wants to find the truth will find it, John."

"What truth?" asked John.

Joshua's brown eyes were upon him. "Do you really want to know?"

John swallowed as he gazed across again to the dark shape of Rangitoto. The volcano was dormant, as were all the other cones in Auckland. Dormant now, but explosive a mere five hundred years ago. They were due for another eruption…

Do you really want to know?

Fleetingly John closed his eyes. Then he opened them again.

"I'm afraid," he said.

"I know," Joshua gently replied. "But you don't need to be afraid. Not if you stay with me."

And now Joshua took John's hand.

John was filled with discomfort at the physical touch of another man, but he knew there was nothing sexual in the act. It was something else Joshua sought, an entirely different kind of intimacy.

Something flooded over John, like a rushing tide passing right through him. Suddenly, in a haze, John saw a massive white sun rising behind Rangitoto. Light filled the sky, and the land; light passed over and through everything in its path. Joshua's hand gripped him tightly as John shook hard, the light passing through his body and soul. He cried out, as he felt his body and soul changing; being changed.

"What is it?" he cried. His hearing became filled by the light. All of his senses, his smell, and taste, and touch, were consumed by it. The Light wholly owned him. The Light was wholly joined to him.

"Not what," said Joshua. "Who."

And now Joshua let go of his hand.

Agony took him. Darkness rose up in his heart, a darkness that could not exist in the Light. Hatred, selfishness, murderous rage – where did it come from? Why? It was a purging! A purging, from the depths of his soul! It arose, and it was too strong, and he couldn't control it; he couldn't overcome it. He couldn't hide. His darkness was totally exposed, in the Light – it was fatal, in the Light.

Confused and dismayed, he groped around for Joshua. He was dying! Joshua's hand returned, and now John saw, in a haze, the darkness creeping as a disease from John to Joshua, infecting Joshua.

"No," John gasped, desperately trying to pull back his arm. "No!"

But Joshua's grip was stronger on him than his own retreat. The darkness spread to him, and John found himself relieved. Bewildered, he saw that his body, his own soul, was lit.

Joshua's face, in the haze, contorted. He looked ready to vomit. He turned his face into the Light, stretched out his arms, breathed deeply – his hand still grasped John – and then the darkness was gone.

All that was left was Light. John reached his right hand out to touch it, even as he still gripped onto Joshua with his left. The Light felt tangible – physical energy, warm, sweet, fragrant, musical; all the colours of the rainbow combined, and beyond this, more…

Trembling, John reached further into the Light. Who? Who…?

"Te Atua," said Joshua. "God."

"God?" John gasped. God? No! It couldn't be…

And then the vision disappeared.

Darkness surrounded him; it was night-time. The water was still, under a star-studded sky. Rangitoto was silent.

John pulled his knees up to his chest, and wrapped his arms around them. He was a child, now! Only a child.

Joshua was next to him, and John began to cry, overwhelmed. Joshua's hand was on his shoulder – a human hand.

"It's all right," Joshua murmured. "You're safe."

"Safe…?" John whispered. "What does that even mean?"

"I am the Bridge," Joshua murmured gently. "I am the Way into the Light."

"The Ark," John muttered, trembling. "The Ark, for the Flood."

"Children trust," Joshua murmured, "and so do the most adult of adults."

"You said you would teach us to swim."

"Faith is the swimming, John," said Joshua. "Trust is the way for all of humanity to survive."

John stared down at the sand at his feet. Faith? Not only an empty faith, not only trust for the sake of trusting; a specific faith – a specific trust. Trust in the one worthy of trust.

"Father," he whispered, a child trembling in Joshua's midst. Joshua's arm came around his shoulders.

"Don't be afraid," he said. "I am gentle, you see? I am gentle, and you can rest here with me."

John closed his eyes. The vision had been a massive event, overwhelming all of his senses, his body and heart. What was that Light? Who was the Light?

"I am the way," Joshua murmured to him. "Rest, John, it's late. Rest."

His hand came to John's head before he rose and wandered away, and John missed him, and was alone.

The moon was mirrored in the ocean, a pale reflection of what John had seen. He gazed at it for a long time.

Rachel came over to join him. "Are you okay?" she asked.

John glanced up at her pretty face – blue eyes framed by straight brown hair. How could he possibly begin to explain what had happened?

"I…" He gazed at her face then gave up, and looked away again to the ocean.

Rachel sat next to him. She was silent – he appreciated her sensitivity. He began to appreciate her presence, too. Then he spoke.

"Joshua," he whispered. "He…he showed me something."

"What?" asked Rachel.

"I…I find it hard to describe."

Her pretty face broke into a gentle smile. “I’m not surprised,” she said. “He’s quite an enigma.”

He smiled at her. “Yes,” he said, “but he’s so much more again.”

“What?” she asked again. “Try to find the words.”

“Why?” John asked, lightly joking. “So you can write them down? Part of your research?”

“Maybe,” she said, a little playfully, looking like a child sitting beside him.

“Quite the scientist.”

“Reality brings me joy.”

“Yes…” John murmured. “I think we might have that in common.”

He was holding her hand. How had that happened? He started and looked at her face, and began to stutter an apology, but she shook her head, and slipped her fingers between his.

This touch was very different from that of Joshua.

Flushing, he looked at her. He felt like a school boy. He had never been involved with a woman. She withdrew her fingers, grasped his hand, and then turned, shoulder to shoulder with him, looking out across the ocean.

“Tell me,” she said, “what did you see?”

Suddenly his words began to flow. “I saw light,” he whispered, “rising up as the sun, over the horizon. It was powerful light, and personal light; the source of life, and the threat of death. I was consumed, and then…”

“Yes?”

“Joshua saved me.”

He grasped her hand tightly. Her eyes looked perplexed, the eyes of a scientist.

“What do you say to that?” he asked.

“I don’t know,” she replied.

“Does science have a place here?” he asked, “in the realm of the unknown? In a realm beyond what we ourselves can see? Does science have a role to play?”

"I do have a role to play," she whispered, "as a partner in the quest for truth."

John's heart pounded at her words, and he saw her; suddenly wanted her.

"Yes," he said. "Yes."

Desire filled him, but not only desire. Impulsively he pulled her closer, kissing her, embracing her. Her arms were around him now. Her kiss was for him!

He pulled back, suddenly embarrassed, looking around them, but no one had noticed in the dark. Only Joshua had seen, and he was smiling knowingly.

Science, and…and what? He looked again across the ocean.

"What was the light?" asked Rachel and John struggled again.

"It's…hard to say."

"Energy?"

"Yes, but more."

"More?"

He swallowed, now, and then spoke. "Spirit," he said. "I think it was spirit."

"Spirit…" her face looked thoughtful. "Spirit, and science. Together? Why not? If spirit is energy – if spirit is light."

"More than energy," said John. "More than light."

"More?"

"I…" He struggled, painfully, to confess what was rising up within him. "God," he finally said. "I think it was God."

Rachel's eyes were on him. "God?" she said, and he began to writhe.

"I've never believed in God!" he said. "Not since childhood! I've never seen him! But now! Now…"

He felt himself surrender his final defences.

"I saw him," he whispered to Rachel. "I saw him, with my own eyes."

"Evidence…" Rachel murmured thoughtfully. "Empirical evidence."

"I can't explain it, but I saw him, and felt him, with all of my senses. It was overwhelming, and…Joshua was the only way to stay."

Rachel was silent, alongside him. Then she pulled out a notebook, and a pen.

"Are you serious?" John asked, nudging her. "I was joking when I mentioned your research before."

"You saw him," said Rachel.

"I know, but it was a vision, you know? Not my physical eyeballs?"

She shrugged silently. "I'll take down the information as it happened," she said. "The reader can decide what to do with it."

"A true scientist," John muttered. "The facts, pure and simple. The devil is in the interpretation."

Rachel smiled wryly, looking down into her notes, and John described for her now point by point exactly what he had seen.

Chapter 22

AUCKLAND

Sweat dripped down Tristan's face; it was another steaming hot day. He backed away from the melting tar-seal of the road, and the crowds of people, to shelter under the overhang of a bakery.

They were on Karangahape Road, in the centre of Auckland city. People were pressing into him on all sides. Where was Joshua? Tristan spotted him across the street. He was talking to some women wearing tight miniskirts and heavy makeup. Prostitutes? Joshua was talking to prostitutes, at a time like this?

Rau stood a few feet away.

"Hey!" Tristan called out. "Bro!"

Rau glanced his way, and smiled, and Tristan inched towards him.

"What's with Joshua now?" asked Tristan.

"All part of the territory," said Rau.

"Wadaya mean?" asked Tristan, staring hard at him, grinning from ear to ear. Rau shook his head.

"You know what I mean. He's talking with them."

"Got something to say?"

"Always. There is always something to say."

Rau's warmth silenced Tristan. Joshua was now gesturing the ladies to come forward. They hesitated, looking around at everyone, but then joined the crowd.

A car was struggling to slowly make its way through all the bodies. Behind the car was a large float.

"Come on," said Rau, grasping Tristan's shoulder, "that's our ride."

Bewildered, Tristan followed him, pressing between people to get to the float.

Somewhere ahead of them music was playing. Was it another car, maybe, with a stereo? Anahera was there, sitting on the outer edge of the float. John and Rachel were there, too, and a few others, on the other side. Rau pressed him forward, and Tristan awkwardly joined the team, dangling his feet over the edge.

"What am I doing here?" asked Tristan, and Rau patted his shoulder.

"You are following him, like all these people are following him," said Rau.

Joshua arrived and stepped up onto the float. Tristan looked up at him – he looked so ordinary! Wearing tidy jeans now, full length, and a smart short sleeved white shirt. There was a roar from the crowd, almost too loud for Tristan to bear, and then the float began to move slowly behind the car.

People steadily made way for Joshua. Tristan watched their faces, as they passed – they were captivated by him. They stretched their hands out to him, and Joshua stretched over to take their hands. Some cried out their need, and Joshua called out his comfort. The scene reminded Tristan a little of the Pope, except Joshua held no formal position, wore no formal robes, and had no formal training. Yet he was utterly adored.

Was he like Lady Diana? Tristan remembered reading about her once, in a history book: The People's Princess. Was Joshua the People's Prince? No, he was more. He had fed them. He had healed them. He'd even claimed to be their shelter, for the coming war.

Ahead came the sound of raised voices. Tristan stood up and saw a huge gathering of Maori wearing traditional dress, with feathers, beaded skirts, and tattoos. They walked in front, sometimes breaking into a haka, sometimes performing a karakia, sometimes singing waiata.

Tane was there, speaking to the group in Maori. Tristan knew he was proclaiming Joshua to be the King.

Tristan sat down again. Rau was quietly praying beside him. The float turned left, into Queen Street, and now there were more shouts. "Joshua!" they cried, whooping and whistling, and waving New Zealand flags in the breeze. Ticker tapes were thrown from the footpaths and buildings, descending all over the float. Tristan laughed, and reached out to grab a red streamer. What would be next? Fireworks?

Hands were waving and clapping, and voices were raised in song. Tristan had never seen such a display, not for over fifteen years. It was an utter extravagance, carried off by a city that could not afford transport. The people must have walked here from miles away. They had walked, Tristan knew, for the hope; they had walked, he knew, for their future.

The float travelled steadily down the main road of town and turned left into Customs Street, to more cheers and streamers. It was the same along Fanshawe Street, and then they turned left into Hobson Street, where the road had been roped off.

The parade was over; now people could return home. Tristan glanced back down the street and saw the masses moving, catching buses, trains, ferries, and walking. A few of the rich could still buy petrol for their cars.

Joshua stepped off the float. His face was bright, his eyes looked full of purpose. But there was something else too, a hidden sadness.

"Sir…?" Tristan began to ask, but then he turned and saw a group of people waiting for Joshua. Police were amongst them.

Tristan swallowed – were they going to arrest him? They watched and murmured a few words, and then two other men stepped forward. One was dressed in a dog collar, tall and slim.

"Joshua Davidson," he began, "I am the Right Reverend Richard Barker, the Anglican Bishop of Auckland."

Joshua tipped his head to him. "Nice to meet you," he said.

"I was wondering if you could please explain to me what happened here."

Joshua smiled, and shrugged. "The people have spoken," he said.

Now the other man stepped forward, also tall and thin. Tristan recognised him.

"Sir," he said, "I am Patrick Clarkson, the Leader of the Opposition Party."

"I know who you are," said Joshua. "I'm a New Zealander too."

"I understand what you're trying to do here, and I salute you for it."

"Thank you."

"Helping the poor, healing the sick, giving the people a voice: I support all of these things."

"Good."

"But do you realise what people are saying about you?"

Joshua didn't flinch at Clarkson's gaze, quite the opposite – Tristan noticed he grew in strength.

"What are they saying?"

Clarkson became silent, and now Bishop Barker spoke.

"Some say that you are the Christ returned to us, the one filled with God's Spirit – the one great high priest that we should all follow."

"And what do you say, Bishop?" asked Joshua.

The older man's face clouded with sadness. "I don't know," he freely admitted. "None of my years as a minister have prepared me for this."

Joshua laid a hand on his shoulder. "Then you are close to the truth," he said. "Keep searching for it. Keep watching. Keep seeing."

Barker looked perplexed at the words, and Clarkson stepped forward again.

"Priest or not," he said, "the people are starting to claim you are our king." He fixed his eyes directly on Joshua's again. "Are you our king?"

Joshua held his gaze, and once again Tristan saw the familiar sadness fill his expression.

"That is what the people say," he replied.

"Sir," said Clarkson, "I am a politician. In a democracy, people choose their leader. Not so in a monarchy. A monarch chooses himself."

Joshua smiled slightly. "Natural strength prevails," he said.

"Are you saying that you are stronger?"

"That is not what I am saying."

"Then what are you saying?"

Joshua looked at him, paused, and then spoke.

"There are different kinds of leadership," he said, "and different kinds of kingdom."

"Then you are a king?"

Joshua took a deep breath, and then released it. "I am," he said.

Clarkson's face flushed and Tristan swallowed. Joshua was directly calling himself a king, now? Where would that lead?

"You don't understand," said Joshua. "Your idea of a kingdom is different from mine. I'm not talking about a political kingdom – rather a spiritual one."

"Do you mean to do away with politics?" Clarkson asked him.

"I do not."

"Do you mean to override Parliament?"

"No."

Now Clarkson looked appeased. He tilted his head thoughtfully.

"How can you claim to be a king, and not participate in politics?"

"Political parties have their own form of power," said Joshua, "and God has his form of power. We should give to our politicians what they already possess, and to God what he already possesses."

Tristan was impressed with his words. Even Clarkson seemed intrigued.

"You are curious," he said. "Communistic, surely! Left wing! And yet, you let the status quo be?"

"A time is coming when everything will be turned over," said Joshua, "but that time has not yet come."

"The voice of the people; the power of the people."

"No," said Joshua. "The power of God, over and through the people."

Clarkson was silenced.

Barker spoke. "'Love the Lord your God with all your heart and with all your soul and with all your mind and with all your strength.'[8]"

"Yes," said Joshua, "I see that you mean it."

"'And love your neighbour as yourself.'"

"Love God and people," said Joshua. "That is the right way. That is the only way."

"And when we fail?" asked Barker. Tristan watched the same intensity appear on Joshua's face – the same deep sorrow.

"When you fail," he said, "I will carry it for you – I will see you through it. But you must hold onto me, or you will be lost. Darkness cannot coexist with light. Darkness will not survive."

Clarkson had lost interest, and was turning away. But Barker's expression held Tristan captive. His jaw was dropping, and his eyes were fully engaged.

"Are you the Christ?" he whispered. "The one we have been waiting for?"

Joshua gazed at him, searching, and then he answered.

"Who is the Christ?" he replied. "Each one must decide for themselves. But don't tell anyone your thoughts, not yet. The right time hasn't come yet."

Chapter 23

A POLITICAL THREAT

The House was in session. James Connor shifted in his seat, while Clarkson sat across from him. Connor fixed his eyes on Clarkson, but neither spoke. Around them, the Clean Green Party and the Maori Party were debating the finer points of the Global Warming Land Protection Bill.

Clarkson went to rise, and Connor briskly shook his head.

No! He mouthed, but Clarkson was already on his feet.

"The Right Honourable Patrick Clarkson."

"Mr Speaker," he began, "I urgently request the debate regarding the Global Warming Land Protection Bill be postponed, in favour of debate regarding Parliamentary action in response to a current crisis in New Zealand."

The Speaker hesitated, and Connor shot to his feet.

"Point of order," he said. "There is no crisis. I ask that the Right Honourable Patrick Clarkson kindly sit down, and let the House debate the issue at hand."

Now the Speaker looked at Connor, and then at Clarkson.

"Right Honourable Clarkson," he said, "please state the nature of the current crisis."

"Mr Speaker," said Clarkson, glancing at Connor, "I ask that I be allowed to present evidence directly to the House, to allow the representatives to decide for themselves whether they perceive a crisis of sufficient severity to warrant immediate debate."

"Very well," said the Speaker, "present your evidence."

Shit! Connor thought, sitting heavily. *Don't do this, Pat – you'll force my hand!*

Clarkson dragged a screen into the central area of the House.

"I present a recent high profile parade down Queen Street in Auckland," he said, pulling out a remote control.

Joshua Davidson filled the screen. He stood on the float, waving, while in front of him a Maori activist was shouting, alongside a group of Maori who were praying and singing. A huge crowd had lined the streets, waving to Joshua, and now the Maori leader was calling out in English:

"Joshua is our King! Descended from King Henry VII, and from Potatau Te Wherowhero of Tainui! He is the King of Aotearoa – the King of New Zealand! All follow the King!"

The image froze on a close-up of Joshua's face, his quiet smile.

The House was silent. Connor's eyes momentarily drifted shut. The Speaker was silent, and Connor looked urgently at him – he seemed lost for words. Then, finally, the Speaker spoke.

"The debate for the Global Warming Land Protection Bill is postponed. We'll continue with general debate regarding the promotion of a new king, Joshua Davidson."

Connor grimaced, and looked across to Clarkson.

Well? He thought. *Begin.*

Clarkson rose to his feet.

"Mr Speaker," he said, "the Communications Security Bureau brought to our attention the imminent parade in Auckland, and so I attended the parade myself. As a New Zealander, what I saw astounded me."

"Explain, Right Honourable Clarkson," said the Speaker.

"A ticker tape parade for a king, Mr Speaker," said Clarkson. "Last I checked we already had a monarch: is one not enough?"

There was muttering in the House. Connor shot to his feet.

"Mr Speaker."

"Right Honourable James Connor."

"There's no accounting for what Aucklanders will get up to sometimes, Mr Speaker," he said. "It is a different world up there, compared to the rest of New Zealand. I say allow them their delirium. It will quickly settle, in light of reality."

Clarkson's eyes were on him. "Mr Speaker," he said, "the security of New Zealand is at stake here."

"New Zealand is secure, Mr Speaker," Connor swiftly replied.

"A self-proclaiming king…"

"He is not self-proclaiming. Someone else was proclaiming it for him."

"He proclaimed it to me."

Now he had the full attention of the House.

"'A time is coming when everything will be turned over,' he said. 'Not the power of the people, but the power of God over the people.'"

Clarkson fixed his eyes on the Speaker. "A theocracy, Mr Speaker," he said. "Joshua Davidson wants to set up a theocracy."

Muttering increased in the House. A Christian Conservative Party Member, Stephen Gates, rose.

"Mr Speaker," he said, "do we not already exist as a theocracy? Our national anthem states 'God defend New Zealand.' You, Mr Speaker, open our sessions with prayer to God. The Queen is the head of the State and of the Church of England…"

"The Queen's role is only as a figurehead," said Tracy Harrison, from the Clean Green Party. "We function as a democracy, pure and simple."

Rawiri Heka, the Maori MP, rose. "The Treaty of Waitangi is an agreement between Maori and the British Throne."

"The Treaty would be obsolete, if we became a republic," said Harrison.

"We are not a republic," said the Speaker, "we are a constitutional monarchy. The Queen has authority, but stands back to oversee the democratic process."

"Much like God," said Gates of the Christian Conservative Party.

Clarkson's eyes were on Connor again.

"'The power of God over the people,'" he repeated. "This Joshua is a religious extremist."

"Let him dream," said Connor, "even if the dreams should be extreme."

"We can't let this movement continue to grow!" said Clarkson. "What might happen, if he begins to gain a substantial minority?"

"He already has a substantial minority," Gates commented.

"True enough!" said Clarkson. "And, Heaven forbid, what if he moves across New Zealand? What if he gains a majority? Our entire constitution would be on its head."

"Order," said the Speaker.

Connor stared down at his desk. On the shelf below, half hidden amongst his papers, was a small photo of Rachel. He had seen her on the news, sitting on the edge of the float, with Joshua rising above. She had not informed him of the parade, he'd been informed by others. Why had she joined in? Was she deliberately challenging his authority? Not as a father, but as the Prime Minister of New Zealand?

Connor knew this must not be the case. He knew there must be some other meaning to all this, some other reason that had captivated her so thoroughly. And yet she had not called; she had not explained. And he remained the Prime Minister.

"Mr Speaker," said Clarkson, "I ask the Right Honourable Prime Minister if he has received any international response to our national developments with Joshua Davidson?"

Connor swallowed. That very morning, the calls had begun.

He rose to his feet. "Yes, Mr Speaker," he said, "I have received multiple warnings from our allies overseas."

"Warnings?" asked the Speaker.

"They are not comfortable with Joshua Davidson's claims. They are also uncomfortable with our growing political instability. We are a test case – potentially the first country to have democracy fold, in the current international climate.

"We are being watched…and not only by our allies."

"What do you mean?" asked Clarkson, genuinely concerned.

"There are those with increasing power, internationally, who function outside the current political constraints. If we should fall, they will act. We will have no defence," said Connor.

Clarkson was silent now. Connor gazed around the House from the Speaker on his left, across the Opposition seated in front of him, to the Clean Green Party, forward right, to the Christian Conservative Party, to his right, and then to his own MPs. He took a deep breath. Then, with trembling hands, he set forward a paper.

"Mr Speaker," he said, "in light of this crisis, I move that a new bill, the Death Sentence Bill, be now read for the first time…"

The House erupted with raised voices.

Clarkson immediately jumped to his feet. "James!" he cried out. "This is over the top!"

"Our national security is at stake!" said Connor, clenching his fists under his desk. "Where did you think this would lead, Patrick?"

"We should arrest the man!" said Clarkson. "Arrest him! Put him away!"

"It won't be enough!" said Connor. "Activists can have more influence in jail than free!"

"He's not a political activist!" said Stephen Gates, the Christian Party MP. "He's more like a minister…"

"Ministers don't generally have ticker tape parades for themselves," said Tracy Harrison.

"Point of Order, Mr Speaker!" Connor tried desperately. "I am not asking for a bill for Joshua Davidson's death, only a general bill allowing for the Death Sentence in New Zealand. He would undergo a trial, if the police deemed it necessary…"

"The police won't touch him," said an Opposition MP. "They're too frightened of the crowd's response."

"James!" Clarkson's gaze bored through him. "You can't do this! This isn't what New Zealand is – this isn't who we are anymore! We avoid the Death Sentence with good reason!"

Connor swayed. Sweat began to drip down his brow. The Death Sentence? What was he doing? He didn't want this! Yet the threat! The danger of standing back and doing nothing…it was a danger he could not accept.

But what if Rachel got caught up in it all?

"Mr Speaker," he said quietly, "I commend this bill to the House and to the Law and Order Select Committee."

The Speaker stood, his face a rigid mask. "The question is that the motion be agreed to. Those who are of that opinion say Aye…" Connor's faithful MPs supported him with a firm response of 'Aye'.

"…Contrary, No." A loud barrage filled the House.

"The Noes have it," said the Speaker. "The Death Sentence Bill has failed to pass the first vote." He looked relieved.

Connor thumped his folder of papers onto his desk. He had failed, and so easily! Even with his own party's support! He would have to try again, and keep trying. Parliament must pass the Death Sentence in. There must be due process. Democracy must stand.

If not, they would all be lost.

Chapter 24

PRECIPITATION

Mark Blake stood at his lounge window. Wellington was spread out before him. Clouds were gathering over Lower Hutt, and the wind was chopping the water of the harbour. In the distance, the central city of Wellington was still.

The photo of his wife Teresa, and his young family, was still turned on its face. A perpetual replay of the procession down Queen Street in Auckland played out on TV – Joshua Davidson stood on a float, waving like royalty, with a Maori company leading the way, proclaiming him as king.

Mark clenched his teeth. A king! How dare he? All the talk of judgment was bad enough, but now? Actually parading down the centre of Auckland? How could that even be possible?

He frowned. Why had the man not been arrested? Why had Connor not acted in response to this provocation? Mark had thought he would be the first to act, yet he had not. Was Connor afraid of this man? Were the police themselves actually afraid?

Mark remembered the earlier reporting, the healings outside North-East Hospital. Surely they were false – surely the testimonials were set up, to stir up public support. Surely the man was a fraud!

And yet, what if…? What if…?

Mark trembled. How would it be, if this *was* Christ returning right now? How would he feel? Exposed, vulnerable; a wretch. He had rejected him!

This was a mistake he must not make. Mark reached for his Bible, and turned to the gospels. Jesus was descended from King David, of Israel. He emerged, amongst the people. He fed them, and healed them.

"Come to me, all you who are weary and burdened, and I will give you rest.[9]"

Fleetingly Mark closed his eyes. Joshua was acting in the same way, offering the same comfort. But was this enough to prove his identity?

"Truth," Mark murmured, opening his eyes. "What truth is he teaching them?"

Mark flicked through a few more pages.

"I tell you the truth," Jesus said, "the tax collectors and the prostitutes are entering the kingdom of God ahead of you.[10]"

Mark trembled. "Show me," he whispered. "Show me."

"Do not worry about your life," Jesus said, "what you will eat or drink; or about your body, what you will wear. Is not life more important than food, and the body more important than clothes? Who of you by worrying can add a single hour to his life?[11]"

Tears pricked at Mark's eyes. He kept turning the pages.

"A time is coming," Jesus said, "when all who are in their graves will hear the Son's voice and come out – those who have done good will rise to live, and those who have done evil will rise to be condemned.[12]"

"I tell you the truth," he continued, "whoever hears my word and believes him who sent me has eternal life and will not be condemned; he has crossed over from death to life."

"Crossed over," Mark whispered, reaching to lift Teresa's photo up again, off its face, "from death to life.[13]"

He gazed out through the window, at the choppy waters below and then to the sky above. There were a few light fluffy white clouds, but the sky was still blue. How would he know, if Joshua was the Christ? How would he really know?

"Give me some kind of sign," he prayed. "How can I know he is the one? Give me some kind of sign."

He kept flicking through the pages of his Bible. What would most define Jesus? What was the most defining feature of his life? Suddenly he found what he was looking for: Lazarus, Jesus's friend. He had died – and then Jesus had raised him from the dead.

"I am the way and the truth and the life.[14]"

Mark swallowed. A resurrection. If Joshua actually brought someone back from death, how would Mark be able to deny him?

There was movement behind him, and then Selena's voice.

"'A wicked and adulterous generation asks for a miraculous sign,'[15]" she quoted, and Mark grimaced, fixing his eyes on a ferry on the Harbour.

"None will be given but the sign of Jonah," he continued, paraphrasing. The sign of Jonah had been the death of Christ, his burial, and then his resurrection. Joshua's death? That wasn't going to happen, and certainly not a resurrection. But a resurrection of another? Yes, that would be the real test! A contemporary Lazarus…

"'Watch out that no one deceives you,'" Selena continued to quote, behind him, "'for many will come in my name, claiming "I am the Christ," and will deceive many.'[16]"

Mark swallowed again. Was he being deceived?

"'You will hear of wars and rumours of wars,'" she continued, "'such things must happen, but the end is still to come. If anyone says to you, "Look, here is the Christ!" or, "There he is!" do not believe it. For as lightning that comes from the east is visible even in the west, so will be the coming of the Son of Man.'"

The clouds in the sky were lit with the sun – it was a radiant day. How did the Bible depict the second coming of Christ? In the sky! Visible to all! Unavoidable! Wonderful, for those who wanted him, and terrible for those who did not.

"This isn't the Second Coming of Christ," Mark murmured to himself, exploring the clouds. "In the Second Coming, there will be no doubt and there will be no hiding place. No…" And now a kind of wonder struck him, as he reached up to finger the window pane between him and the sky. "It's almost as if…" He gasped, now, in realisation, "It's almost as if this is the *first* coming…"

"No," Selena's voice interrupted. "Not the first coming. He has already come."

"Of course," Mark continued in wonder. "He has already come: the true Christ has come, and he will come again. But this Joshua…it's almost as if he is a 'type' of Christ: a picture of Christ, for a new people – an expression of Christ, two thousand years later, for a new generation."

The thought began to stir hope within him. Could it be? Could it be that this new one was actually the same as the old?

"There's nothing new in what he is doing," said Mark. "Nothing new in what he is saying. It has all been done before! It has all been said before…"

"What use is there for a new expression?" Selena chided. "No! You must do away with him! You must sweep him aside!"

"What use?" Mark responded, breaking into a wide smile. "The same use as for the old expression! The old expression was once new – once fresh, and relevant, and alive. Why a new expression? We are a new people. The same truths need to be communicated in a new way. The same truth! Life giving truth! To all the nations."

Now Mark turned to face Selena directly. "He isn't overriding Christ!" he proclaimed. "He is communicating Christ! He is portraying Christ! He is embodying the same person – imparting the same God. A picture of the truth. A picture that bows down to the reality. What Santa Claus is to Saint Nicholas, Joshua is to Jesus, and both bow down to Christ.

"Why?" he continued. "For understanding! So that a new people can understand, and can respond. So that a new people can be shown how to live."

The realisation filled his heart with joy, but Selena's face was dark, her eyes almost black.

"To live?" she spat back at him. "What use is this 'understanding,' in a pursuit for life? Is Joshua seeking to give true understanding? Is God seeking to give life? He sets his people up to fall! He grants life, only to bring about death! You know this already, Father! You were at her side when she died!"

Now Mark was thrust back nine years – again his mind betrayed him, and he saw the unbearable. The car was upside down! They were trapped! Teresa was hanging, next to him, suspended by the seat belt. She had been knocked out! Still breathing, but bleeding from a gash that poured blood. Her head had smashed against the windscreen. The airbag had failed to fire.

"Oh God," he whispered. "Help us!"

He reached for her belt, but his left hand was trapped between the seats! His right arm was useless, broken – hanging down toward the shattered windscreen.

"Save us!" he cried. "Save us!"

Voices came from outside – hands tried the doors, but they were jammed.

Mark stared at Teresa. Her face was swollen; her body was twitching. And then she stopped breathing.

Desperately Mark tried again to reach her – he could not.

"Get us out of here!" he screamed. "Get us out – she's dying!" But the hands could not help.

In the distance Mark heard sirens wailing, but it was too late.

"Let me die too," he whispered to God. "Please! At least let me die too!"

But his prayer was not answered.

Now Mark looked into the dark eyes of his sixteen year old daughter.

"Does God really care about us?" she asked. "I don't think so, father."

He struggled to respond. "He kept me alive for you," he whispered. "He kept me alive for you!"

"And in this also you failed," she said.

Her words were knives to his heart, because he knew they were true.

"Joshua is deluded," said Selena, turning to the window and smirking at the sky. "He believes he is a king! He believes he is a god. But we know better than that now, don't we father." Now her eyes fixed hard on him. "We know there is no God."

Mark stared at her, and his heart flooded with agony. No God? No God? It couldn't be true! All of his life he had invested into God! All of his life, he had followed him! He was the Bishop! The Bishop of Wellington. And yet, now, in this moment, as he swayed on his feet, he began to falter.

"You killed her," said Selena, and Mark tightly closed his eyes and clenched his fists. "You killed her with your reckless driving. You killed her, not God, and now this Joshua is an imposter who needs to be swept away."

Selena touched his shoulder and agony consumed him. Darkness filled his heart.

"Kill him," said Selena, "and do away with the lies forever."

A strange stillness came over him. Mark opened his eyes. He could feel nothing now, nothing at all. He stared out of the window to the sky, and swayed.

"Kill him," said Selena again, and Mark struggled against it.

"I can't kill," he whispered. "I'm a priest."

"You know how to do it," said Selena. "You know who has the authority to kill."

Mark glanced now toward the central city, in the direction of the Beehive.

"Oh my God," he whispered. The weight of betrayal was crushing him. "Oh my God, I can't do this."

"You must do it," said Selena. "Joshua is leading our whole nation astray."

"He has done nothing wrong…"

"He has committed the ultimate sin," said Selena. "He is putting himself forward as God. It's blasphemy."

Blasphemy. An intense battle raged in Mark's heart. Was Joshua innocent? Was he guilty? Blasphemy was serious – perhaps the most serious spiritual crime to commit. And yet, was he a picture of Christ? Had he come from God?

"There is no God," said Selena. "Joshua is deceiving them all, as you also were deceived. False hope! False expectations! He is leading us all into death. He is handing our nation over to international conquest.

"Do we have a king? There is no monarch but Elizabeth. Do we have a priest? There is no God. 'Better that one man die than a whole nation perish!'[17] Do away with him. Do away with him, and set our nation free."

Better that one man die...Mark now felt himself girded – felt himself become strengthened with resolution. He was here for a reason! He was here for a time such as this.

It was time to act. It was time to save his nation.

Chapter 25

HELL'S WAY

Rachel stood on the waterfront at Lake Rotorua, admiring the black swans swimming on the blue water. Their white poop covered the pavement. Abandoned sea planes and children's water riders tipped up and down with the gentle waves – no one had spare money for rides anymore.

Rachel gazed out across the water to the bush-laden Mokoia Island, in the centre of the lake. The sky was a little overcast, threatening rain, but the view was still beautiful.

Behind her, as usual, a crowd of people were gathered around Joshua, on the dry grassy parklands. Rachel glanced back and remembered the days of her childhood, when markets, and fairs and circuses were held here.

Further along the pavement, John threw dry grass meaninglessly at the swans. He saw her watching, and wandered over.

"Nice day," she said.

"Not bad."

"There's a wonderful track around the lake, just over there." She pointed ahead, and he looked up.

"Down there?"

"Yes."

Now a mischievous smile lit up his face. "Wanna go?"

"Now?" Rachel glanced back at Joshua. He was busy taking people's hands, would he mind? Probably not.

"Okay," she said, and he took her hand, and led her to the start of the track.

The lake was blue-grey on their left as they began walking, ducking under branches and brushing past ferns. They passed through an abandoned car park, and then on to where the lake gradually transitioned into white milky water.

"Sulphur," said Rachel, drinking in the smell.

"Wow," said John. "Stinky."

"I love it," said Rachel, as they continued walking further around the lake. "It reminds me of my childhood. It's not as bad as it used to be!"

A flock of gulls abruptly took flight across the silicon-laden white water. Small bubbling mud pools gave off steam beside them. John paused, frowning, staring into the depths of the mud.

"What is it?" asked Rachel, as she watched him.

"Don't know," said John. "Must be hot in there."

"Boiling," said Rachel. "The whole area is thermal. Sometimes the pressure builds up underground, and there's an eruption! It happened in Kuirau Park, years ago – a little steaming pool exploded!"

"That's New Zealand, eh?" said John. "Made from the enormous pressure of two tectonic plates pushing against each other and volcanic eruptions everywhere."

"Isn't it beautiful?" said Rachel, squeezing his hand.

They walked further around the lake to where boardwalks skimmed over the white silica deposits covering the ground. They came to a viewing platform, and then wandered over the vast expanses of white sinter terraces, gazing out across the steaming white lake.

"Wow," said John, and Rachel squeezed his hand again. "See what

I mean?"

Rachel stood silently beside him, happy. She knew John was happy, too. Then a voice came from behind.

"Mind if I join you?" It was Joshua. He was grinning. Rau followed behind him, along with Tristan, Anahera, and a crowd of people.

Rachel blushed, but John still held her hand.

"We're moving on," said Joshua. "Rau and Tristan are staying here with these people, but I want you both to come with me."

"Where?" asked Rachel, and Joshua's gaze intensified.

"To Hell's Way."

"Excuse me?" said John, and Rachel broke into a grin.

"Hell's Way!" she said. "It's around the other side of the lake! Follow me!"

They stood at the entrance to Hell's Way. The old business that Rachel had visited as a child was now deserted. Red paint flaked from a sagging gate with the words 'Hell's Way' carved into the wood.

"Let's go," said Joshua, and he hurried through the gate onto a track.

Rachel looked at John, who was glancing tentatively back at her.

"I've got a bad feeling about this," he said.

"Joshua says to go."

"Then we should go." John took her hand, and they stepped inside.

The track was bare, the air hot. On both sides of the track little mud pools bubbled away, cute yet smelly. Rachel remembered the path well. A few Maori children played beside the track. Maori men and women sat quietly watching them, dressed in traditional flax skirts and feathers, with tiki, greenstone pendants of their ancestors, lying on their chests, and moko, tattoos, on their bodies and faces.

Rachel was surprised to see them – it was like looking back in time. She began to feel uncomfortable. The mud pools up ahead were much larger. She noticed the protective railing was falling away – the wooden structures were rotten.

Joshua was well ahead, swaying above a big steaming pool.

"What is he doing?" asked Rachel.

"I don't know," John replied, releasing her hand.

"He almost looks…" Surely not! "Suicidal…?"

"No," said John. "It's something else." And he quickly joined him.

Rachel approached slowly. What was Joshua doing? He'd die if he fell in – he'd be boiled alive. They wouldn't be able to save him.

Joshua's face was intense, as he stared down into the water. John had a hand on his shoulder, as if ensuring his safety, to make sure he didn't slip.

A child suddenly ran past Rachel, and she quickly reached for his hand. There were so many pools; surely the children were not safe playing here.

The little Maori boy laughed at her, and he pushed her away, but then he was slipping. Beneath him was a steaming hot pool. Rachel grabbed his arm again and he clutched at her, brown eyes wide with terror, crying out in Maori.

"No!" she cried, and pulled him away. He was safe! Relief filled her. But now she was slipping.

Panicking, she clawed at the ferns, but the leaves broke. She began to slide down towards the boiling water.

"Rachel!" screamed John, white-faced and racing towards her, thrusting out his arms to reach her. "Rachel!"

She fell, and hit the water.

The burning was agony. She screamed, but the burning filled her lungs.

"Oh, God!" she bubbled, desperately flailing her hands in the air. But the water engulfed her.

The burning swallowed her up.

Images flashed before her eyes: her mother, kissing her goodnight; her father's proud face, at her graduation.

Daddy, she moaned, *I'm dying…* His face faded as she sank into darkness.

She was tearing apart; she was being torn away. Horrified, she saw her body floating in the steaming water beneath her.

She was dead! She'd drowned.

But suddenly she saw a movement at the edge of the hot pool. Despite John's strangled cries Joshua entered the water, gasping as he dragged her body out of the pool and onto the bank.

He placed her gently onto her back. As she looked down at her body Rachel wondered if he would do CPR. Instead, he called her name.

"Rachel."

She felt seized. What was it? Someone was pulling at her.

"Rachel."

She saw a light. It was far away, in the opposite direction. Should she go?

"Rachel."

The voice was calling her back! Calling her back into her own body.

No…

"Come back," said the voice. "You're not ready! It's not your time yet."

She succumbed – she let go, and was drawn back.

"Rachel." Now she heard the voice again, this time calling from above her.

She opened her eyes, and Joshua stared down at her.

Stunned, she stared back. Where was she? Oh, yes! She had fallen! She had slipped into the boiling pool.

"Oh, God!" she choked. It had burnt! But she didn't feel any burning now.

She reached down, clutching her body. Her clothes were gone. She was naked, but she didn't care. Her eyes passed over her skin, looking for the third degree burns that would surely be fatal, but her skin looked normal. She could feel touch. There was no pain. Not even any redness.

Perplexed, she stared at her skin, and then looked up at Joshua. His hair was wet. His arms were bright red, and his legs. He was trembling – Rachel could tell he was in pain.

"You need morphine," she said instinctively, but he smiled slightly, and shook his head.

"No," he said. "I'll be all right."

Rachel stared at him, suddenly realising what he had done. Then she looked at John. His eyes were wide with fear and wonder.

"I…" She gasped, and continued. "I was dead…"

Joshua rose, swaying, as John took off his shirt and gave it to Rachel. The Maori people watched as the little boy came forward, tears spilling from his large brown eyes. He reached out and touched Rachel's arm, and then Joshua's. A woman came forward with a cloth, and wrapped it around her, and said something in Maori.

Rachel stood up. "You need to go to hospital," she said to Joshua. He smiled wryly.

"'Physician heal thyself'?" he said, before moving away.

A young Maori woman handed Rachel some clothes. "Miss, you can have my shirt and shorts," she said.

"Thank you," said Rachel.

"You saved my brother!" she said. "I saw it! I saw what you did! And then…"

She glanced at Joshua, and then back to Rachel. "I saw what he did, too."

"What did he do?" asked Rachel, wanting to hear the young woman's perspective.

Her brown eyes widened, as she held Rachel's gaze.

"He saved you, miss," she said. "You were a goner. Children die here all the time."

Tears filled up Rachel's eyes.

"Why don't you set up boundaries?"

"We can't," she said. "They don't work. The children are too small."

"Then why do you stay here? Why don't you move out?"

"Where else would we go?"

Rachel gazed at her and then saw Joshua approaching the others. He was still in pain, and yet he spoke to them in fluent Maori. She didn't know what he was saying, but they rose and followed him out of Hell's Way.

Rachel hesitated for a moment. She looked back down at the boiling hot pool. She shuddered and wrapped her arms around herself.

John was watching her. He swallowed.

"Are you okay?" he asked.

"Yes."

"What just happened?"

"I…" She shivered. "I died."

His green eyes intensified. "You actually died?"

"The water came flooding in!" she said, shuddering. "It was terrible! Into my lungs! I was above my body, looking down, and then…then…"

"Yes?"

"He saved me. I heard his voice – he called me back into my own body."

John's jaw dropped. He stared at her, and then looked at Joshua.

"Do you understand what this means?" he asked, and Rachel frowned.

"What?"

"It means…not only does he have the power to heal, he also has the power to bring the dead back to life."

Rachel struggled with his words. "I wasn't dead for long!" she said. "Just a few minutes! And yet…there was something about his voice. And…" She trembled. "My skin is normal, John."

"You didn't just come around," said John.

"There's no water in my lungs. My skin is normal. While his skin is burnt…"

A look came over John's face, now – a sudden understanding beyond what Rachel could see, and a sadness that came with that understanding.

"Let's get out of here," he said.

Gladly Rachel left the steaming hot pool behind, and followed again after Joshua.

Chapter 26

A NATION OR ONE MAN?

James Connor stood in the House of Representatives.

"...and so, Mr Speaker," he said, "I move that the Death Sentence Bill be read."

Perseverance! Perseverance.

"Right Honourable Prime Minister," said the Speaker, "you have used your authority to present this same bill twice already, though Parliament has voted and discarded it twice before."

"I understand that, Mr Speaker."

"You understand that I will not give you a fourth chance?"

"Understood."

"Very well." The Speaker turned his face to the entire House. "The question is that the motion be agreed to. Those in favour say, 'Aye.'" Again, Connor's faithful MPs complied with 'Aye.' "Those against say, 'No.'" And again, a barrage of 'Noes'.

"The Noes have it," said the Speaker. "The Death Sentence Bill will not be read and will not be presented again for at least twelve months."

Swallowing, Connor held the Speaker's resolute gaze and sat down. Across from him, Clarkson's eyes were rejoicing. The Speaker moved on to other business of the day, and Connor barely heard it. He had failed. Joshua Davidson would not be removed.

Eventually the Speaker drew the session to a close. Connor silently gathered his papers, and moved out of the Chamber. Clarkson trailed along happily beside him.

"The people have spoken," he said, and Connor gave a grim smile.

"The people have spoken."

Connor made his way steadily through the foyer, and into the Beehive. The people had spoken, but what if they chose Davidson? What if they chose to override their own state? Clarkson was afraid of him, wasn't he? Even he, with his communistic ideals – what would he do with a king?

Connor made his way to the lift, and rose up to the ninth floor. The people had spoken by supporting Joshua, and forcing the police to stay back; by prevailing with a no death sentence mentality. But did the people know what they were doing? Did they? How could they possibly know what the consequences might be of their short-sightedness?

The lift doors opened and Connor walked along the corridor. Parliament had tossed out his bill, like the hot potato that it was. He was humiliated, but what leader could persevere without handling a little humiliation along the way? What surprised him now, as he approached his office, was that he also felt relieved. The decision was out of his hands. The people *had* decided, or at least their representatives had decided. That option had closed.

He entered his office, dumped his folder on his desk and reached for the photo of Pam and Rachel. Relief flooded through him. At least now she was safe!

He replaced the photo on the desk, turned, and lowered himself into his chair.

Mark Blake stood in front him.

"What the hell…" Connor jerked in surprise, and then rose to his feet, offering his hand. "Mark!" he said. "What are you doing here?"

Mark shook his hand curtly, and then leant forward over his desk. "Connor," he said, "we need to talk."

Surprised, Connor stared at his face. He looked as if he had suddenly aged ten years. There were taut lines across his cheeks and forehead, and his eyes had a strange darkness within them.

Mark strode to Connor's door, and briskly shut it. Connor instinctively looked around, identifying the security button's location. Mark seemed on edge, dangerous even – almost as if he'd be capable of pulling out a weapon. Connor had never seen him like this before.

His dark eyes were intense now, and focused on Connor.

"Joshua Davidson‘s power is growing," he said, and Connor grimaced.

"I know," he said. "But I can't seem to do much about it."

"What do you mean you can't do much about it?" said Mark. "You're the Prime Minister, aren't you? You have ultimate power."

Connor frowned. Mark didn't sound like his usual self at all.

"I don't really have ultimate power," he said. "You know that, Mark! I'm the servant of the people."

"Bullshit."

Now Connor's skin pricked. This wasn't Mark! Not the Mark he knew.

"What's going on with you?" he asked, and now Mark's fists slammed on the desk.

"Deal with him!" he demanded. "Get rid of him!"

"I don't know how…"

"What are you, Connor – weak? Full of talk, but impotent in the outworking? You have all the power of New Zealand at your fingertips – are you too frightened to use it?"

Connor flushed deeply, as Mark continued. "'Democracy is for the rich,' you say, and then you go pandering to that idiot Clarkson! The people are trampling all over you! Soon Joshua will be right here in Wellington – soon his power will be infiltrating the Beehive itself. Soon there will be no Parliament, he will make it all obsolete. What are you going to do? Just stand back, and let it happen?"

Sweat pricked Connor's face as Mark's stare penetrated.

"I've tried," he said, "and I have failed."

"You mean the bill for the Death Sentence?" said Mark, laughing. "That's child's play."

"The political process…"

"Who cares about the political process?" said Mark. "Soon there will be no politics at all! Only rule! Only slavery!"

Connor swallowed hard, but persevered.

"We are a democracy!" he said. "Freedom! Freedom of speech! Public choice!" He still believed in it! Even now.

"The people have spoken, Mark – I'm not going to get in the way! New Zealand doesn't believe in the Death Sentence – they have chosen! So be it."

"So be it," Mark spat, now pressing his face close into Connor's. "No Death Sentence. But that doesn't mean no death."

Connor's body stiffened. "What do you mean?"

"You want due process?" said Mark. "I'll give you due process. This isn't a case of criminal law, this is much bigger than that. We are at war. Not a war of physical weapons, but a war for the minds and hearts of the people. This man Joshua isn't a criminal, he is an enemy of the state."

At this, Connor looked away. Mark was talking his language now, and he knew it: this had been the threat Connor had feared all along.

"If Joshua Davidson is allowed to continue, our whole nation will fall. One man, Connor! One man. Isn't it better that one man die, than an entire nation perish?[18]"

Connor closed his eyes as Mark continued. "He is a religious extremist," said Mark. "He must be contained."

"We live in a free society," whispered Connor. "Freedom of religion for all. If I kill him, our society has already fallen."

His body was shaking.

"If you don't kill him, you won't even have a society anymore!" said Mark. "Joshua Davidson will conquer Parliament. Who knows how many already follow him? Those who resist will fight – there will be civil war. We'll be thrust back into the Dark Ages, and the entire world will be watching, seeing the utter incompetence of your leadership – to not carry out the one act of execution required before it is too late!"

Now Connor slumped heavily into his chair, staring at the photo of Rachel.

"You know what you must do," said Mark.

"The army," said Connor.

"You are their superior officer," said Mark. "They answer directly to you."

Connor swallowed. "I don't know where he is."

"Even with all your intel?"

Connor grimaced. "He doesn't use electronics. And he tends to disappear, whenever you get a location on him. Crowds of people, and then, gone."

Now Mark was silent. Connor glanced up at him, and was surprised to see Mark in conflict, his face twisting in some kind of struggle.

"Mark…?"

The conflict settled, and his hard dark gaze returned. "I know how to find him."

"How?"

"Rau Petera follows him. He's a priest. And…there's another who will help you. In secret, not in public. You must do it in secret. No one must know."

"Who?" Nervously Connor avoided looking at Rachel.

"Tristan Blake."

Connor stared at him. Surely Mark had gone mad.

"Your son?" he cried. "You would incriminate your own son?"

"Whatever it takes," said Mark coldly, "to deal with the enemy."

"But Mark…"

"He is ex-army," said Mark. "He's there with Davidson. He'll know how to get the job done. Privately, Connor! No links! No civil war. A whole nation of suspects."

"Mark…"

"It's an easy solution."

"'Easy'"

"He will handle it discreetly, Connor! It will be just another job to him."

Connor frowned. Tristan Blake? Connor still remembered his face, the shadow of his memories, as he recounted what had taken place in the Middle East. Where was he now? Following Joshua? Seriously?

"Why would he execute him?" asked Connor, and Mark's eyes grew black.

"Because you will order him to do it."

Grief filled Connor, now: unexpected and deeply gripping grief. Did he want to execute this man? He did not. He seemed innocent! Good. But the rising movement he was causing was indeed an intolerable threat.

Should he do it? Should he execute his powers as head of the state?

He swallowed, closed his eyes fleetingly, and made a decision.

"All right," he said. "Find Tristan and start the ball rolling."

Chapter 27

NATIONAL SECURITY

Tristan stood on Mount Ruapehu. Behind him, a small group had gathered around Joshua. They had come a long way, most trekking from Taupo, but also from other towns and villages along the way. Joshua had led them here, up the mountain.

Behind rose the rocky crown of Ruapehu, with its many tipped peaks. There was no snow or ice. It was summer and the temperature was rising. The valley spread before Tristan, with its desert-like turf; it was a dry landscape that had become even drier over the years, with the increasing heat. Even so, the view was majestic.

It was a clear day. To the west, in the far distance, Tristan could see the single peak of Mount Taranaki. To his right, close by, was the single cone of Mount Ngauruhoe, and next to this the rugged peak of Mount Tongariro.

"Ready, mate?" asked Rau, appearing at his side.

"I dunno," said Tristan, looking dubiously up the mountain. "Am I?"

"Got to put your heart and soul into a hike like this," said Rau.

"Think I've done my dash with training. I'm happy to let my fitness slide for now."

Rau smiled gently. "Heat getting to you?"

"Always."

"We'll see you on the way down."

"Stay safe. Remember, you're not as young as you used to be."

Rau bowed his head towards him and, with a twinkle in his eye, set off after Joshua. Tristan could see John and Rachel, further up, holding hands.

"Damn," Tristan muttered under his breath, "she's taken."

The group took a slow diagonal course, up the face of the mountain, heading for the Crater Lake. Ruapehu was unpredictable – there were still rumblings from time to time, although the last eruption of rock and ash was over a year ago.

"Take it easy," Tristan muttered under his breath, looking at Rau's diminishing form. "Don't get blasted."

An abandoned chairlift, no longer operative, rose from the rocks to the left of the group.

"Joshua wouldn't have used it anyway," Tristan said to himself, "purist that he is."

Everyone had committed to the seven hour hike, even after the big stretch from Turangi. Joshua had left Rau's Ute at Taupo, and had gathered more people, inviting them to come with him all the way up the mountain.

"Good luck," said Tristan. And then he turned away.

What would he do now? Walk the walk down the mountain, back to Turangi? Wait for them there? If he stayed he'd only get more sunburnt than he already was, and for no good reason. But he didn't feel ready to leave.

Sighing, he found a rocky outcrop and sat underneath it, reaching for his water bottle and taking a swig. He thought about Joshua. What to make of him? He remembered the first time he had met him, on Ninety Mile Beach. That fish! He had been so determined to beat him, back then. Where was that determination now? It had dissolved somehow.

Joshua's faith…somehow Tristan had learned to live with it.

Tristan threw the water bottle backwards and forwards, between his hands.

"Looks like a storm's coming," Joshua had said, as they had stood, side by side, on the beach – as Tristan had tried to beat him fishing.

"A little storm never hurt anyone," he had replied. *"Might bring in the fish!"*

Tristan gazed at the water in his hands, now. "Such a mystery," he muttered. "You are always such a mystery."

He rose and emerged from the shelter of the rock. Further down the mountain he could see dust being thrown up into the air from Bruce Road. It had to be a car! Keen to get a lift, Tristan headed down towards the deserted car park, slipping on the gravelly mountainside in his haste.

The car came closer. Excited, Tristan watched as it approached. It was a newish Merc, a bit extravagant, but, hey, beggars can't be choosers.

As it came to a halt, Tristan wandered up to the driver's door. "Hey, mate, I was wondering if you could give me a…"

His words were cut off, as the door opened and the driver stepped out.

It was his father.

Bewildered, Tristan stared at him. "What are you doing here?" he asked.

"I found you," replied Mark. "Thought I'd give Rau a call."

"Joshua's not here right now…"

"I didn't come for Joshua."

Tristan frowned. Something was up: it made no sense.

"Why would you come again? We're on a mountain, for crying out loud."

"Can't I see my son?"

"You haven't seen him for nine years – except once."

"Time to fix my mistakes."

Mark's eyes were hard to read. Tristan eyed the Mercedes with its air-con with longing, but resisted the temptation.

"Why are you here?" he asked again. "I don't believe it's a social visit. A hot mountain isn't exactly your style."

Mark smiled. He nodded, and shut the door of his car.

"You're right," he said, moving toward Tristan. "There are other reasons I am here."

Tristan eyed him warily – his posture was suspicious. Tristan's training kicked in.

"That's far enough," he said curtly. Looking surprised, Mark stopped.

"What are you afraid of?"

"I'm not afraid."

"Good, because you shouldn't be," said Mark. "I'm not the enemy."

Tristan cast his eyes over Mark's face. Something had changed. Something was wrong with his manner.

"You want to explain that?" he asked.

"I don't need to explain it," said Mark. "You already know what I'm saying."

Now Tristan swallowed. He looked away, and then looked back.

"Explain it to me."

Mark's eyes were fixed on him. "You have served our nation for five years."

Tristan grimaced. "What of it?"

"You were trained to defend us, whatever the cost."

"So?"

"You need to defend us now."

Tristan directly held his gaze. "Defend us against what?"

Mark continued unfazed. "You must defend us against him."

Tristan's cheeks flushed. Defend the country against Joshua? What was his father thinking? Tristan laughed, and turned away.

"That's a good one, Dad," he said. "Defend our country against the only person who knows how to provide enough food, and heal the sick. Heck, I even heard rumours he brought someone back who died…"

Mark was silent. Surprised, Tristan glanced back at him. He looked white, for a moment, then pink flooded back into his cheeks.

"Lies!" said Mark. "Rumours. That's how a man like him gains power."

"Power?" said Tristan. "Oh, I'm sure he's not interested in power."

"How else do you explain the parade, and the float? He is gathering support – gathering power."

Tristan laughed again. "More like gathering need."

"He claims to be a king, Tristan!"

"A king?"

Tristan paused now, thinking back. A king? Had Joshua ever made such a claim?

"Oh," he said, "you're thinking of that joker Tane, and all his radical ideas. Some Maori king back from the dead, eh?"

"Joshua said it himself."

"I've never heard it."

"He wants to take over."

"I don't think so."

Mark's eyes were darkening. Tristan frowned – what was his problem?

"I don't get it," said Tristan, "why do you care? You're a priest, not a politician…"

And then Tristan began to understand. "Oh, now I get it!" he said. "It's the stuff he's saying! Something about light, and shelter – some people think he's actually Jesus Christ. I'll bet that's touching your buttons…"

"Never mind about that," said Mark curtly, "that's not important. What is important is your mother."

Now Tristan felt the familiar pain: his mother! Pain, in his chest, pushed away for so long, though not so much now, after Joshua.

"What about her?" he asked.

"Think this Joshua would have stopped her from dying?"

Tristan shuddered. "I don't know," he whispered, and now Mark was striding closer to him, pressing his face towards him.

"I do know," said Mark. "He couldn't have cared less."

Tristan frowned, his hands writhing. "I don't think that's true," he said.

"You think Joshua is God?"

"I don't know!" said Tristan, feeling confused. "God? I don't know…"

"What use is a God who would let Teresa die?"

Mark's words felt like a bombardment. Tristan shook his head and turned away, sweat dripping down his face.

"I don't know anything about God," he said. "I don't know what you're talking about."

"This Joshua Davidson is claiming to be God."

"What?" Tristan turned again to him. "Honestly, Dad, where do you get your facts from?"

"A shelter for the war to come," said Mark. "He himself, the shelter! Faith in him, to survive the storm! It is a claim to divinity, Tristan, pure and simple! Surely you remember enough of the Bible to see that?"

Tristan stared at him, and then looked away. Shelter. Storms. Faith.

"I am the way, the truth and the life.[19]*"*

Could it be? Could it be that Joshua was actually claiming to be God? Could it be that he, Tristan, had missed what was in front of his face all this time?

Bewildered, he shook his head.

"See it, Tristan," Mark impressed. "This man is the worst kind of liar."

Tristan struggled to focus on the dry turf on the horizon.

"Even if he is claiming such a thing," he struggled to explore, "why bother fighting him? Why the fear?"

"Because he is leading our entire nation astray."

It was a different voice. Tristan turned to look. From behind dark windows another man stepped out of the passenger door and stood in front of Tristan.

It was the Prime Minister, James Connor.

Tristan stared at him. "Sir…" he stuttered, and instinctively, wearily, provided a salute.

Connor nodded. "It's all right," he said, "you're not on duty."

What was he doing there? The Prime Minister himself, on Ruapehu in summer? He was even wearing suit trousers and long sleeves, although now he was rolling them up.

"Can I help you, sir?" asked Tristan, and Connor smiled sadly.

"That's what I'm hoping, soldier," he said.

Tristan glanced between Mark and Connor. "Just what exactly is it you want from me?"

For a moment neither spoke. Then Connor began.

"This Joshua Davidson," he said, "is a real concern to us, Lieutenant Blake."

"Sir?"

"We have serious concerns for the national security of New Zealand."

Tristan frowned. "How so, Sir?"

"We fear if this Joshua movement continues, it may result in civil war."

Now Tristan felt a heavy weight in his chest. Civil war? In New Zealand? The flashes were suddenly before him again: blood, screams, explosions…

"We can't have war here," he whispered. "Not here."

"We are safe," said Connor, "if we remain strong – if we remain united, and together. We stand alone; we stand together. But Joshua Davidson is starting to divide us – starting to create a movement in the opposite direction of everything we believe in."

"What do you mean?"

"People are starting to follow him as a king. You saw the parade, Tristan! You saw their devotion! Does he mean to visit Wellington?"

"Yes," said Tristan, instinctively.

"What will happen when he reaches the Beehive?"

Tristan frowned. The Beehive? Joshua? What were his plans? Did Tristan even know?

"Some are calling for his leadership, Tristan; many people! Hundreds of thousands, maybe even a million – what will happen?"

Tristan stared at him, and then turned away. What would happen? Why hadn't he thought of this?

"Do you want him to take over, Tristan?"

"No," said Tristan. "No."

"What if half our nation wants it?"

Tristan swallowed. "Then we'll be in trouble."

"You're right!" said Connor. "We'll be in big trouble! There'll be no going back, it'll be too late!"

Chills went up Tristan's spine as he realised why they were there.

"The police can't control such massive crowds," said Connor. "Our nation is in trouble! The army must act."

Then call up the army! Tristan thought, but stopped himself saying it. The army? Form an actual military state in New Zealand?

"We need a simple solution," said Mark.

"What kind of solution?" asked Tristan quietly, his back still turned.

"We need you," said Connor.

Tristan stared down at the rocks at his feet. His vision blurred in the heat. He blinked furiously, and his vision returned.

"You need me for what?" he asked.

"You're right beside him," said Mark. "You know where he is. You know where he will be. You're an insider."

"You want information."

"No," said Connor. "We need more than information."

Tristan closed his eyes tightly. Was this really happening?

"We need you to contain him for us."

"'Contain him'?" asked Tristan.

"Contain him," said Connor, behind his back. "Privately, securely: we need you to eliminate this threat."

Body stiffening, Tristan stared up the mountain, searching for them. Where were they? Could he still see Joshua, and John, and Rachel, and Rau?

He stifled a sob. Eliminate him? Eliminate Joshua Davidson? How?

Where? When?

"We will provide the weapon, when the time comes."

All of Tristan's memories suddenly came over him, like a flood – all of the memories of the last few weeks; all of the memories of the last five years. Like a flood, converging, as one, until he could see nothing else but blood.

"Do you have a joint?" Tristan whispered, and Connor patted him on the shoulder.

"We can get you a joint," he said. And Connor turned, with Mark, and returned back to the Mercedes.

The car drove away, pushing up dust, winding down, down the mountain. Tristan swayed, and fell down to the ground. What had just happened? The Prime Minister himself had asked him to kill Joshua! The Prime Minister!

Dismayed, he groped around, but he had lost his bottle of water. Kill Joshua? How could he do such a thing? Joshua was his friend.

And yet his father's eyes; and yet the Prime Minister's words:

"What will happen when he reaches the Beehive?"

The words plagued him now. Who was Joshua Davidson? Did Tristan even know? Did he know who it was he had been trusting all this time?

"We're in big trouble."

New Zealand couldn't falter, not like the rest of the world! Not now – not his home.

The threat needed to be contained.

Tristan hardened, his army training instinctively kicking in. Civil war? He would defend his nation, against the threat. He would always defend his home.

It was just a matter of when, and how.

Chapter 28

MOUNT RUAPEHU

Rau stood on the top of the mountain. His knees were aching and his body was drenched with sweat, but he didn't care. Before him lay Ruapehu's green-blue crater lake, still active, still steaming – dangerous, and vibrantly alive.

Rau turned – and stretched out, as far as the eye could see, was his homeland, Aotearoa. The single distant peak of Taranaki was to the west, the smooth cone of Ngauruhoe and rugged edge of Tongariro to the east, and the brown turf of the Iwi Tainui, the tribe of the Waikato, was expansive before him. This was the land of the Maori king! Rau smiled, remembering Tane, who had stayed in Taupo to spread the news of Joshua to his own tribe.

This was the heart of the North Island, of Te Ika-a-Maui, the great fish of Maui, as his people had named it in legend.

Tongariro…Rau recalled another legend: the priest of Arawa, Ngatoroirangi, had feared death on this very summit. Why? Rau pondered. Surely he hadn't yet known the One – the One greater than death.

Rau cast his eyes again across all the land.

"Areruia," he said. "Oh, Lord, you are majestic, over all the Earth."

He took a deep breath and broke into a karakia. When he'd finished, he turned and saw Joshua, away from the rest. The others were beginning to wander around the crater lake, but John lingered close to Joshua.

Rau made his way across the rocks to Joshua. His back was toward him, his hands held straight up, his face lifted to the sky. Rau could hear his voice – prayer, he was certain, though the melodic language he used was strange, and unknown.

Rau hesitated, now, behind Joshua's back. He shouldn't interrupt: this was Joshua's sacred joining to the divine.

He felt exposed, shabby, and sorely in need of a bath. Was it disrespectful, coming so unclean? Rau turned to leave, to allow Joshua privacy, but then Joshua turned and suddenly grasped his arm, looking into his eyes.

Rau gasped. Light flooded over him; light was penetrating through all of Joshua's being.

"Master," whispered Rau, sinking to his knees. "Master…"

The light searched the fullness of his soul, uncovering him. He trembled, and clung to Joshua's arm. He felt his hidden shame exposed, he writhed, but the light was stronger and melted his shame away.

"E te Atua," Rau breathed. "Te Wairua, Te Tamaiti: tapu!" he cried. "Tapu rawa!"

The light was sacred! The light was God.

"Ae," whispered Joshua, grasping his hand, pressing forehead and nose. "The Spirit is tapu, Rau. But Te Atua is here, and through me you can touch the light and live."

Rau closed his eyes tightly, and heard Joshua's voice murmuring words gently over his head – strange unfamiliar words. The light was now fully within; saturating him, owning him. But there was more! As Joshua murmured over him, Rau gasped again as his spirit was overwhelmed by love.

He began to weep, crying, as a child. Love! Divine love! Life-giving love. There was no hesitation, nothing was held back.

His soul was swept up by the love and swept wholly into oneness; swept wholly into joy. He was ecstatic; fully complete. He had found what he had trusted he would one day find. He had found Te Atua; he had found God.

Rau swayed on his knees, his eyes closed, still clinging to Joshua. He began to speak the same words as Joshua, worshipping with all of his being.

Joshua held him. And then, as the light began to fade, he opened his eyes.

Joshua's face was above him. His brown eyes were also filled with tears, his face lit up with joy. Human! He was only human, now. But, in those moments, Joshua had also been divine.

"Master," whispered Rau, and Joshua tipped Rau's head between his hands, as a mother to a child, and kissed him on the forehead.

"It's all right," he murmured. "You are safe, with me."

Rau grasped his hand firmly. "As the pikorua twists together for eternity," he said, "You are One."

"Yes," Joshua murmured. "Like a pounamu twist, we are One. And you also can be one, Rau, with us."

Rau gazed at him, and Joshua smiled back at him. Then Joshua rose to his feet. He glanced briefly at John, before moving away.

Rau remained on his knees. He held, in his mind's eye, what he had seen: the Light! The Light, around and through Joshua. He held in his heart, in his spirit, what he had felt: the Light and the Love! One heart! One spirit.

He stayed, bathing in the warmth of the sun; bathing in the warmth of the Spirit. John's face was white as he approached.

Rau smiled at him. "You saw it too."

"Light!" said John. "And…and love…"

"Personal," said Rau. "Not just a force: God is personal."

"A person?"

Rau glanced sideways to Joshua's back, and then returned to John.

"Open your heart to him," he said. "Trust him. And then you will know. Then you will fully know, and be fully known."

John was reading his eyes.

"God himself is light," said John. "God himself is love."

"Yes, John," said Rau. "Come closer to his light. Come closer to his love."

John glanced toward Joshua, and then looked back to Rau.

"Closer…" he murmured. "I never knew this could be."

"You did know it," Rau murmured gently, now rising to his feet. "As a child you knew it."

Tears filled John's eyes. "Yes," he said, "as a child."

"Know it again."

John's green eyes widened, and Rau searched him closely. This brother, from Whangarei – what would it take for him to return to a childlike faith? What would it mean for him?

John's face broke into a tentative smile.

"I should trust in him," he whispered, and Rau reached out to lay a hand on his shoulder.

"Yes, John," he said, "trust. Trust in what you have seen with your own eyes."

Rau could feel John's body trembling, under his hand. He showed such vulnerability! Such exposure.

"It costs to trust," whispered John, and now Rau patted his shoulder.

"Ae," he said, "it costs."

"He will take everything I am."

"Yes," said Rau. "Everything."

"My life will be changed forever."

Rau fixed his eyes on him. "Forever, my brother."

John hesitated, and Rau waited. Each person must choose for themselves. Then resolution came into John's eyes, followed by light.

"I've decided," he whispered. "It's done."

"Nau mai, haere mai," said Rau. "Welcome!" He embraced him, and now felt John accept his embrace.

"Thank you," said John, leaning on him a little. "Thank you."

Rau turned and saw Joshua had now joined and was talking to the rest of the group. He was gathering them, for the descent.

"Time to go," said Rau, and John's face looked a little sad.

"Time to go," he agreed, and Rau led him back, across the rocky mountain, to Joshua.

By the time Rau finally reached the car park, at the base of Ruapehu, his knees were killing him. Grinning to himself, he imagined Tristan's words: "Old man…"

Where was Tristan, anyway?

Rau surveyed the rocky terrain as the sun began to set, leaving them in shadow. The light in the sky was fading into twilight.

Tristan must have left already and headed back to Turangi. Rau shrugged. He sure had a story to tell him, when they met again! Light, and Love! What would the boy do with that one?

He smiled and then joined Joshua, and John, and the group, to set up camp at the base of the mountain.

Chapter 29

DISSONANCE

Tristan stood in the middle of Maidstone Park. They had made it to Upper Hutt, in Wellington. In front of him Joshua had gathered another new crowd and was speaking to them, as always. Tristan couldn't make out his words but he could see the faces in the crowd: wide eyes, full of hope and expectation for the future.

They were so close to the city of Wellington now, only twenty-five minutes' drive away from the Beehive.

Chills travelled up Tristan's spine. "Oh, God," he whispered, "what the hell do I do now?"

He had met up with them all again in Turangi, acting as though nothing had happened. But he was a spy now! Shit! A spy – how the hell had that happened?

He had acted the part well enough, but Rau had known something was up, surely! How could he not?

Tristan glanced over at his friend, and found Rau was already watching him. Tristan looked away, but Rau wandered over to him.

"You all right, mate?" he asked. Tristan reluctantly looked at him, absorbing his gentle wry smile, and his genuine concern. Something had happened to Rau, up Ruapehu! The aura of faith, that joy, that sun in his eyes, had intensified tenfold. Tristan had grown accustomed to it, had even grown fond of it, but now the light made him writhe.

"I'm all right," he muttered, keeping his face turned away. "Just hanging out for a joint."

Rau's eyes were inquisitive. Tristan tried to avoid him, but could not.

"Why?" asked Rau. "Why now?"

Tristan swallowed. "Just memories," he said. "My house is ten minutes' drive away, just down the road in Lower Hutt."

Now Rau's hand came to his shoulder, and Tristan forced himself not to flinch.

Don't touch me! You have no idea what's going on.

"Your father's house?" asked Rau, and a sudden sharp pain seized Tristan's chest. He closed his eyes.

"I'm sorry, Rau," he whispered. "Please leave me alone."

Rau was silent. Tristan opened his eyes again, to see the gravity in his face. Then Rau bowed his head respectfully, and moved away.

Tristan was surprised at the intensity of his own regret. He moved further away from the group, and lowered himself to the ground, against a maple tree. The leaves were beginning to change from green to yellow and orange.

His father's house…Now another torrent of pain took him. His mother! She had died only five minutes away! His father had driven her for dinner, while Tristan and Selena had stayed at home.

Tristan suddenly recalled the phone ringing that night, nine years ago. He had grabbed Selena and rushed to the hospital in the valley, where his father had sat ashen white, an arm in a cast, beside the body of his mother. A sheet covered her and there was blood! Blood, on the sheet…

He pulled his knees up to his chest, wrapped his arms around his legs and squeezed his eyes shut, hiding his face in his knees. He was feeling it now? Only now, on the eve of his decision to kill, he actually wanted to cry for his mother?

He had never felt it! Never felt it, until now…

Darkness surrounded him – with a stale, stagnant smell of death. He shuddered, fighting it, and staggered to his feet. Joshua stood beside him.

Bewildered, Tristan stared at him. They were alone. Why had he left the others? His face was close to his own.

Tristan suddenly remembered Joshua's words on Ninety Mile Beach.

"You said," Tristan whispered to him now, "that it wasn't his fault."

"No," Joshua quietly replied, "it wasn't his fault."

"Then whose fault was it?" Now agony consumed his heart, as he continued. "Was it God's fault?"

Joshua's expression shifted – the cloud had come again! The intensity.

"Do you need someone to blame?" he asked.

"If I did," said Tristan, "would it be you?"

Now Joshua was struggling again, the same struggle Tristan had seen within him on the beach, as if in a trance – like he was seeing something else.

"If it was me," whispered Joshua, "would that take the guilt away?"

Suddenly Tristan felt an inexplicable urge to touch him, to know what Joshua knew: to see what he saw. He vacillated, and then Joshua grasped his arm.

Light wrestled the darkness within him. Tristan cried out, pushing Joshua away, staggering backwards; staring at the man now on his knees before him. Joshua's face was ashen white, like his father's face had been on the night of his mother's death. His gaze was far away, and great sobs erupted from within him, until they were gone.

"Darkness," whispered Joshua. "It's everywhere! In everyone. It can't coexist with light! But I am the scapegoat."

Tristan trembled. "What do you mean?"

"I'll carry it," said Joshua, now looking up at him, from his knees. "All of it!"

"Carry what?" whispered Tristan.

"The guilt!" Joshua cried out. "The rage, the hatred, the crimes – the darkness! I have to get rid of it all!"

Tristan swallowed as he continued.

"The Light has to have its way!" said Joshua. "Don't you see? Love must have its way! I'll deal with the darkness, for anyone who will give it to me; I'll carry it, so that they can choose to live in the light."

Tristan was locked in his gaze – locked, neither for nor against this man whom he knew to be innocent. A scapegoat? What did he mean?

Joshua rose to his feet, his normal colour returning to his cheeks. He smiled, and turned away, and Tristan choked.

"Joshua," he said, reaching out a hand, before he could stop himself. "That vision, with me, on the beach…" A steel fist felt clenched around his heart as he continued. "Was that…was that…?"

He couldn't bring himself to state the deep fear rising in his heart. Had Joshua actually seen his own death, at the hand of Tristan?

Joshua hesitated, and then turned to him, meeting his eyes with an unreadable gaze.

"Some things are better not to know," he repeated his same words said on the beach, "not until their right time. But…" And now he grasped Tristan's shoulder, with steadfast gaze. "…do what you have to do."

Joshua quickly left, and Tristan stared after him. What did that mean, 'Do what you have to do'? Did he know? Chills again rose up Tristan's back. Had Joshua always known? Was he telling Tristan to kill him?

"So weird!" whispered Tristan, confused. What had just happened? What was the light? He didn't know. Tristan had that same sense he'd experienced on the beach: that there was more! More Joshua was not telling him; more to find out. But Tristan had no time left to look.

Tristan wandered away from the gathering towards the centre of Upper Hutt.

"Hey!" A voice called out to him, from behind. He ignored it, but it persisted, and then a hand grasped his shoulder. "Tristan!"

He turned towards the hand. It was Rachel. Her face was too inquisitive, but pretty. Tristan hated himself for the thought, and promptly discarded it.

"Oh," he said, "it's you. What's up, Doc?"

"Where are you going?"

"Ah…I don't know."

Her brow furrowed – and her eyes, now annoyingly doctorly, moved over his face.

"You don't look right," she said, and he smirked.

"Is that the best you have?"

"You look…" She hesitated, and then continued, "Stoned."

Tristan laughed at her. How ironic was that? "I wish!" he said, but now her eyes were looking further.

"What's wrong?"

He trembled, against his will, and closed his eyes. His mother was there: her body, the sheet. Those screams, from overseas! War! Never far from him. And now…now his damned father, and the Prime Minister of New Zealand himself, were asking him to kill a profoundly innocent man.

"Everything's wrong," he whispered, swaying on his feet – and he felt her hand on his arm, steadying him.

"Tell me," she said, and he shuddered.

"I can't."

"Tell me."

"I can't!"

Her hand gripped his arm firmly, and he opened his eyes to her physician's gaze.

"PTSD," she said, and he shook his head.

"What?"

"Trauma. From war."

He stared at her, and then swallowed. "I've been asked to do something," he said, "and it's the one thing I can't do! For so many reasons, I can't do it! But I must!"

She frowned. "Are you suicidal, Tristan?"

Tears filled his eyes. "No," he said. "I'm too afraid to die."

"Then what…?"

Her face was trustworthy. Her eyes were trustworthy. He found himself wanting to tell her, wanting to reveal the terrible conflict of his heart. Then came the sound of another voice.

"Tristan!"

This one he didn't recognise. He turned, surprised, to see a girl, maybe sixteen, striding up to him.

She had long black curls, and blue eyes. White skin. She seemed familiar…and then, suddenly, Tristan realised who she was.

"Selena!" His sister! She looked well kept, a young lady, with a short skirt and cream blouse. And yet there was still something wrong… Her blue eyes were dark, almost black.

Tristan swallowed, and found himself lost in the eyes. "Come with me," she said. "We have lots to catch up on."

She wasn't surprised to see him! Why not?

He glanced back at Rachel, and shook his head to clear it.

"I guess that's it," he said, and Rachel smiled sadly, concern in her eyes.

"I guess that's it," she repeated, looking at Selena and then back to Tristan. "Keep safe."

Safe…As Tristan followed Selena, he felt himself slipping more deeply into darkness, and death. Safe? Was there anywhere safe anymore?

"Stay with me, and you will be safe," Joshua had said, but his words were fading away.

"Follow me," said Selena, "and we'll get you sorted."

And he blindly followed, and left Joshua behind.

Chapter 30

WATER AND STONE

Mark stood on the bank of the Hutt River, in Lower Hutt. The river flowed past his feet in a quiet, dark torrent. The wind had lifted and he fought against it, to stand his ground.

Joshua was coming – Mark could feel it in his bones. The time was near.

Tristan…Mark swallowed, staring into the dark water. Tristan hadn't contacted them, since that meeting on Ruapehu. How would he act? Would he obey?

A crushing pain gripped Mark's chest. He gasped. Tristan might obey, now? Like this? Nine years later? Dismay filled him, but then he gritted his teeth, and clenched his fists, and willed the pain away. It was necessary! Whatever the cost, even if his son should be compromised, Joshua must be dealt with.

Mark turned his back on the river, walked down the bank, and strode across the large deserted car park beyond. He passed his Mercedes, not bothering to pay for parking, and weaved his way through the streets to Saint Luke's Anglican Church.

The Church Council of New Zealand: he had to get them on his side.

The church was quiet, filled with warm tones, light streaming through the windows, and an empty wooden cross behind the altar. There was a time when Mark had loved this church, years earlier, before tragedy had struck and meetings had taken over. Now that time was over.

He strode down the aisle to the waiting ministers, seated in the pews.

Murray rose to meet him. “Mark,” he said, extending a hand, smiling.

Mark nodded curtly to him and the others.

“Thank you all for coming,” he said. “This is an emergency meeting.”

He moved briskly to the pulpit to address them, with his back to the cross and the altar.

Murray was watching him closely and then sat down. “What’s going on?” he asked.

Mark surveyed their faces. The Church of New Zealand must be united and be one, against this imposter!

“Joshua Davidson,” Mark began. “He’s almost here. We have been slow to act, as the Church – we must act now.”

“What do you mean?” asked Reverend Robyn, the Presbyterian minister.

“This man is putting himself forward as Jesus Christ.”

Now he had their attention.

Young Father Andrew looked stunned. “What?” he gasped.

“You heard me,” said Mark. “Everything he is doing is the same.”

“Shouldn’t we all be aspiring to be like Jesus?” asked Murray, and Mark grimaced at him.

“Not if it means inviting people to trust in us for their salvation, instead of in God. That is not acceptable! I’m sure you’ll all agree.”

They were silent, and then the Pentecostal minister, Pastor Luke Davies, spoke.

“Jesus is our Saviour,” he said, “no one else. If someone else is claiming to be Jesus, he must be deceived! It must be Satan, not God.”

“Agreed,” said Mark. “This man is speaking the words of Satan, not of God. If he truly has powers, they must be Satan’s powers, not the power of God.”

He quickly looked over the faces. Reverend Robyn looked troubled, but she was silent. Murray also was quiet, obviously thinking. But now Father Andrew spoke.

"Aren't we waiting for Christ to come again?" he asked.

"Don't be a fool," said Mark. "If Christ had truly returned, we would all know it."

"Would we?" asked Murray. "'I come as a thief in the night.'[20]"

"'Be ready!'" Andrew quoted. "'Be ready.'"

"'Watch out that no one deceives you,'" Mark quoted easily. "'For many will come in my name, claiming "I am the Christ," and will deceive many.'[21]"

"Hmm," said Murray. "So, tell me, Mark, has he actually said that he is Jesus Christ?"

Mark stared at him, and flushed a little. "I'm surprised at you, Murray," he said. "Have you actually looked at what he is doing? Have you heard what he is saying? A claim to divinity need not be overt, it can be subtle: discreet, but clear."

"Like Jesus," said Andrew.

"'Darkness cannot coexist with light,' Davidson said. 'Only goodness will survive.'"

"True," Murray replied. "But I don't see the claim to divinity."

Mark fixed his eyes on him. "Just because you don't see it, Murray, doesn't mean it is not there."

Murray shifted in discomfort as Mark continued: "Have you watched the news? He talks of safety, for the tsunami to come. He says he himself is the boat for the flood. He talks of a coming war, and the dropping of the ultimate weapon – and he says that he himself is the shelter for when that weapon comes."

Murray swallowed, and Mark knew he finally had him. "Clearly the tsunami is God's Judgment. Clearly the great weapon is also Judgment. He is presenting himself as the Saviour of the world! He is putting himself forward as Christ."

Andrew's eyes were fixed on the cross, behind Mark's back. His lips were moving, as if in silent prayer, and then he spoke.

"What do you want us to do?"

Satisfied, Mark looked across their faces. "Firstly, we must take a clear message of his blasphemy to our churches, across New Zealand."

"Certainly," said Murray. "But those who attend church are already attempting to follow Christ. This man seems to be trying to reach those who do not yet know him."

"Which makes his deception all the more powerful," said Mark. "And that is why we must stop him."

"Stop him?" said Andrew. "How?"

Mark smiled slightly. "Don't worry," he said, "I have that part sorted."

"Sorted?" Murray asked.

"Yes," said Mark. "It's sorted."

Andrew was frowning, but remained silent. And now Reverend Robyn spoke.

"What are you planning?"

Mark absorbed her grey hair, and glasses.

"I'm going to bring about justice," he said.

"Whose justice?" asked Murray, but Mark promptly brought the meeting to an end.

The ministers wandered back out of the church, but Murray lingered, as always. Mark suppressed a sigh, as the warm eyes returned to him.

"What are you up to, Mark?" he said, and Mark smiled again.

"You'll find out soon enough."

Murray frowned. "I don't know who this Joshua Davidson is," he said, "but if we are to stop him, it must be through conversion."

"You do things your way, and I'll do them my way," said Mark.

"We are not the judge."

"Neither is he."

"Our job is to fight for the minds and hearts of men and women, not to condemn them."

Mark held his eyes with a steely gaze. “Each to his own, Murray,” he said. “You take the high way, and I’ll take the low way – someone has to act, when our backs are all against the wall.”

Murray’s eyes moved up and down Mark – he looked concerned. But Mark knew there was nothing Murray could do; he'd made up his mind.

“May God bless you, Mark,” said Murray finally, and then he nodded his head, and backed away, and was gone.

May God bless you. Mark gritted his teeth at the words, and glanced at the cross. Blessing? Mark shuddered. No! No blessing, only hatred! Only retribution.

“Justice,” whispered Mark, looking at the wooden instrument of Roman execution. “Someone must pay.”

His heart was girded, strong and resolute. Then he turned and saw Tristan had arrived with Selena. Mark stared, and then smiled. Fate! It was meant to be: the means for the execution walking in at the right moment!

Tristan looked bewildered. His eyes were fixed on the cross. What was he thinking? Some memory from the past? Could it be, Mark wondered with a growing sense of nausea, a memory of childhood faith?

“Don’t worry,” said Mark. “Your childhood days are over now.”

Tristan’s face twisted with pain, but Mark’s own heart was too hardened to care.

“Is he here?” asked Mark. “In Wellington already?”

“Yes,” Tristan choked. “He’s here.”

“Are you ready?” asked Mark.

“No,” whispered Tristan, but now Selena moved forward, and took his hand. Tristan’s body stiffened as she said something into his ear.

“If not now, then soon,” said Mark. “We must meet with Connor, to make the final arrangements.”

“The final arrangements?” Tristan moaned.

“The time, and place. The weapon.”

Tristan was swaying on his feet, now. He looked like he might vomit.

“Harden up,” said Mark. “You’re army, not some schoolboy. Why do you think I chose you?"

Tristan's eyes somehow met his and, for a moment beyond his own control, Mark was chilled by what he saw. Death!

"You have no idea who I am," whispered Tristan. "You're using me, using my training, nothing more. That's all this will ever be."

Regret threatened Mark's heart, but he thrust it aside.

"So be it," he said. "Do what you must do. The Beehive, in three days: one pm. Connor will be free."

Tristan's face flushed, and then turned to iron. "All right," he said, "the Beehive, in three days."

Mark nodded, and strode back down the aisle of the church.

The wind had lifted a little. Mark wandered across the pavement to cross the street, when he saw a small gathering in the council gardens.

"Joshua's here!" someone cried. "He's coming! He's coming!"

Tristan and Selena had caught him up and Selena laughed, loud and hard.

"'He's coming,'" she mocked. "'Let's all go and worship him!"

Tristan hit her lightly across the head. "Shut up," he said, but then she grasped his hand, and he shuddered.

Mark frowned at the gathering crowd. Joshua was closer than he thought! Tristan hadn't said where – he didn't need to say. In fact, the less Mark knew the better.

"Wait here," he said to Tristan. "Catch up with Joshua again and join his crowd."

Tristan grimaced, and nodded. "All right."

"You'll need to know where he is at all times."

"I think he'll be hard to miss."

"He disappears. It's those private times – they are your best chance."

Mark laid a hand on Tristan's shoulder. "Just get the job done, and get out of there. No one will ever know. Deal with him, and then you'll have your own life back again."

Tristan grimaced at him, and shook his head. "You have no idea, do you," he said. "You're asking me to murder an innocent man in cold blood."

"You're army!" said Mark.

"It's not the same!" For a moment Mark thought Tristan might hit him. "For God's sake, Dad – what the hell has gotten into you?"

Now fury filled Mark. His temples throbbed; his vision turned dark. He shoved Tristan.

"You also have no idea about me," he said. "You ran away."

Tristan's face hardened. "Why do you think I left?" he asked. "You turned into a bastard!"

Mark felt his hands clenching into fists, as Tristan continued with his unbearable tirade.

"You killed her, and then…"

"I hate you," said Mark. He coldly unclenched his fists, and watched the colour suddenly drain from Tristan's flushed face. "I hate you, and I never want to see you again."

It was said. It was done.

Tristan looked dismayed. Mark stared at him, furiously fighting the tide unleashing itself in his heart: no! It was enough! It was time to move on.

"Fine," said Tristan eventually, "if that's what you want."

"That's what I want," said Mark. "Meet with Connor, get the job done, and that'll be the end of it."

Mark turned his back on him, now, and he walked away, across the road, through the streets, back to the Hutt River car park. He wanted nothing to do with church now, or family.

"It's almost over," he whispered into the air as he drove home.

Tristan was left standing outside Saint Luke's. The wind was blowing again. It was cold. Drops of rain were starting to fall on his bare arms.

He stared at the place where his father had stood.

"I hate you."

My God, thought Tristan, had he actually said it?

"I never want to see you again."

It couldn't be, could it? One parent dead, the other rejecting…?

Selena was there, pulling flowers from the garden, pulling the petals off one by one, and then dancing around the small gathering, throwing the flowers over them. So sarcastic! So bitter! What had their father said to her? Had he even said anything? She had only been seven, when their mother had died.

"You killed her."

Why had he said it? In the heat of the moment! In the heat, he had said it! But he regretted it, now! He regretted it.

"I'm so sorry," whispered Tristan. "I'm so sorry."

Joshua's followers were gathering, there in Lower Hutt: there, in his home. Tristan would wait and then join with them again. He would do what he must.

Chapter 31

THE PLAN

James Connor stood waiting in the Reception Hall, in the Beehive. Autumn had finally come, and Connor was thankful for the cooler air. Through the window he could see the leaves of maples and other trees beginning to change colour to vibrant oranges, reds and rusty browns, before falling to the ground below.

He checked his watch: 12:57pm. Was Tristan still coming? Would he dare? Tristan must act soon, as Joshua Davidson was in the Wellington district. He was breathtakingly close now to the centre of political power.

Yet as Connor stared out of the windows at the trees, and glanced in the direction of Saint Peter's, he had his doubts. An execution? The thought made him suddenly want to vomit. This man, Joshua, seemed innocent – Pam had even talked about him with great enthusiasm. He was giving the people hope! He was giving them what they needed! She had implored him not to do anything rash, but Connor could not heed her words. He was the Prime Minister. It was his duty to act.

Footsteps sounded on the stairs. It was Tristan!

Connor offered his hand. He suddenly remembered their last meeting, on Ruapehu: Tristan had looked bewildered by their request – it was a clear request of betrayal.

“Hello, Tristan,” said Connor, and the young man's eyes narrowed.

“Hello,” he replied.

“Let’s get out of here.”

“All right.”

Connor led him down the steps and away, through the Parliament Gardens and beyond, weaving between the streets and down towards the waterfront.

“I hope you’ve given some thought to our request?” said Connor, and Tristan laughed slightly.

“Request?” he said. “Sounded more like an order to me.”

“Yes,” said Connor grimly. It was his own responsibility, and he’d better accept that. “It was an order.”

“All right,” said Tristan, his voice heavy. “I’ll do it.”

Connor glanced in both directions – surely the street was the safest setting as there was no audio monitoring – and then he looked at Tristan.

“You’ll need to pick up the weapon.”

“Yes,” said Tristan.

“It’s a CZ pistol.”

“Really?” said Tristan. “Not an army edition?”

“Certainly not,” said Connor. “There must be nothing linking Parliament to the incident, and also nothing linking you to the incident.”

“The ‘incident,’” scoffed Tristan. “You mean the ‘crime.’”

“No,” said Connor, “I don’t mean the ‘crime.’ This is a national duty, Tristan, for both of us. We are not criminals.”

“You reckon,” said Tristan, and Connor smiled sadly.

“I do reckon,” he said.

They continued to walk along Waterloo Quay. The sky was overcast and rain was on its way.

“Where?” asked Tristan.

Connor gave him a key to a post office box. “This parcel hasn’t been posted.”

“Understood,” said Tristan.

"Use gloves, of course," said Connor. "Leave no trace."

"Okay."

"It will be a random act."

"With no prints?"

"Unless you want to set up one of the others?"

"No," said Tristan, and Connor nodded.

"When you've finished," said Connor, "dispose of the weapon."

"Of course."

"A bin should do the trick," he said. "Nothing too extravagant – nothing too planned."

"All right," said Tristan.

They walked in silence. Connor wondered about the young man. How would he fare after this task? But he was army, so he should have the necessary emotional distance to carry it off.

He hesitated, and then continued.

"You will stay with Joshua?" he asked. "With his inner circle?"

"Yes," said Tristan faintly. "I will stay."

"How…" Connor made himself continue. "When will you execute him?"

Tristan's eyes closed fleetingly. "Soon," he said, "when the time is right."

"He's very close," said Connor. "You'd be wise to do it before he rallies up support here in the city centre."

"I know."

"If he brings on the same kind of following here as in Auckland, we might lose our chance."

"Yes," said Tristan, "I know."

"So you will do it soon, then?"

Tristan's eyes were on him, now, even as they walked.

"Yes," he said. "I'll do it very soon."

Connor's mind was set at ease.

They stopped when they reached the waterfront. Wellington Harbour spread before them, today an ominous expanse of dark, still water.

Connor watched as Tristan's eyes flitted across the surface.

"I'll return now," said Connor.

Tristan shrugged. "All right."

"Good luck."

Tristan laughed. "Luck has nothing to do with this."

"Confidence," said Connor, admiring him, and he shook his hand. "Goodbye, Tristan – all the best."

"Bye," said Tristan, as Connor walked away.

Following Waterloo Quay around to Bunny Street, Connor took several deep breaths and released them slowly. His plan was underway: now all Tristan had to do was execute it.

Better for one man to die, than an entire nation fall.

Chapter 32

PETONE

Rachel stood on the waterfront in Hikoikoi Reserve in Petone. A strong southerly blew from the harbour, lifting Joshua's brown curls and carrying his voice across the crowd.

Behind him, Rachel could see across the choppy water all the way to the ferry terminus on the right, with the high-rise buildings of the central city. Mount Victoria was across the water to the left. Beyond the high hill was Wellington Airport, and beyond this was the entrance to the harbour, the gateway to the South Island.

Would Joshua visit the South Island next? Picton, Nelson, Christchurch, Dunedin…there were many more people to meet.

Rachel looked back at the crowd. It had grown. Many people had followed him here from Upper Hutt and Lower Hutt, but there were also a lot of new faces, Maori and Pacific amongst them. Most would follow him into the city centre, but where would he go? Rachel smiled sadly, looking toward the Beehive. He wouldn't get much of a reception there.

Rachel's own home was across the other side, further west, in Churton Park. Would she go back? Would she visit her father? She hadn't decided, she was just taking one day at a time.

"Keep following!" Joshua called out to the crowd, from behind her. "Keep persevering! Don't lose heart, even when things get hard! Don't be afraid, even when war is at your doorstep."

Rachel looked at Joshua again. He was such an ordinary looking guy, still wearing jeans, even now. He had a cream long-sleeved cotton shirt on, with the arms rolled up to his elbows, and was shivering in the breeze but was otherwise oblivious to the cold.

He stirred people by reaching into their hearts; he had given to them, catered to their deepest needs, and offered them hope.

How many strong were they now? Ten thousand? All represented so many nations of the world, mixed up in a melting pot; a new society.

"This age will not last forever!" said Joshua. "A new time is coming, but that time will cost! Birth pains! There will be fighting, brother will rise against brother, father against son, daughter against father: all will be divided! But each must decide, before the time comes: before this age is ushered out, and the next age begins."

"What are you saying?" asked a short European man. "Aren't you bringing peace?"

"Yes!" said Joshua. "Peace! But peace always comes with conditions and a price. Peace always demands some form of allegiance. Where will your allegiance lie, when the testing time comes? Who will you hold to, when the battle is before you?"

A Maori man raised his voice. "Matua," he said, "Aotearoa has seen war before."

"Ae," said Joshua, "we have!"

"Are you wanting to bring war to our land again?"

"No!" said Joshua. "I have no desire for war! But sometimes a battle is necessary, to achieve the higher ground."

"Are you telling us to get weapons?" A Chinese lady called out.

"No!" said Joshua. "You yourselves must remain innocent! Be pure, as God is pure! If an enemy hits you, don't hit him back. Don't give evil for evil; overcome evil with goodness!"

Rachel felt moved by the words, stirred into greater goodness.

"And what if we fail?" It was a voice Rachel recognised. She searched and found him – it was Tristan!

Joshua's eyes moved to him. He was silent for a moment, smiling sadly; that same knowing smile.

"If you should fail," said Joshua, his eyes moving over the entire crowd, "then come to me, and we will fix it together. I will make it right! I will carry it! A loving father forgives when a child fails, if that child turns back again into the light."

His eyes moved back to settle on Tristan. "God is not a father of retribution," he said. "God longs to forgive, and to heal. If you follow me, you become my whanau; my family."

Tristan looked stricken by the words. Rachel watched him, concerned – there was obviously something going on between them. So often she had experienced this from Joshua, some hidden deeper meaning.

"Come to me," said Joshua, "and I will give you peace! Learn from me. Love one another; care for one another. Search for God, and you will find him. God is greater than humanity – God is our beginning and our end. Search for him, find him, and live.

"I am the bridge," said Joshua. "I am the bridge, between you and God! I am the doorway into light, and away from darkness. Walk across the bridge! Enter through the door! Soon I will open the door for you…"

Now his expression changed – his gaze became distant.

"Soon I will burst open the way!" he said. "But I can't make you walk through it! You must choose! You must choose to walk through the door, into the light! Into true life: life here and into the next age, now and forever."

"What do you mean?" an Indian man asked. "Are you talking about a spiritual life? Which god do you follow?"

Joshua looked at him, and smiled. "One God," he said. "One God, the creator of all. One Spirit, the source of life for all."

"Isn't that arrogance?" the man asked. "We Hindi have many gods – we choose our own gods."

"You may choose whatever gods you wish," said Joshua. "That

doesn't mean they are fit to save you. What is the truth? Choose carefully. The End is coming soon. Who will still be standing when the tsunami is upon you?"

The Indian man tilted his head, watching him. Rachel glanced back at the Harbour. A tsunami? It was a chilling metaphor for those who lived in Wellington. Everyone worried about 'the big one', a massive earthquake offshore, releasing a colossal tsunami.

Another European man spoke, this one with an English accent.

"Joshua!" he said. "How can humanity possibly know any truth about a 'God' with any certainty?"

"How much certainty do you need?" asked Joshua.

"That's not my point," said the man. "We cannot know! We are only human. Each person defines truth for themselves – there is nothing more than this."

Now Joshua's face became grim. "Reality is reality," he said, "and truth is truth. Is it not true?" He smiled wryly. "Humanity reads the truth – humanity does not define it. Men and women see truth as a grey haze, but they are not blind entirely."

"Impossible!" the man muttered, but Joshua continued:

"Use your vision," he said, "don't throw it away! Use what vision you have. Use it with humility – use it for good. Use it to seek truth: use it to find the way."

"But what is the right way?" a woman with a thick Russian accent called out.

"I am the right way!" said Joshua. "Listen to what I'm saying, I am telling you the truth! I am the way into life, and not only life here: life forever, in the next age. Hold onto me and don't let me go! Hold onto me, trust in me, trust in God, and you will live."

Rachel gazed at him, captivated, but now others were stirring in the crowd.

"Sir," said a Korean man, "you seem to be quoting Jesus Christ."

Joshua looked at him, and smiled. "You're right," he said, "I am. And you're not far from him."

"But…how can that be?" His gentle face was thoughtful, exploring, and then another spoke out.

"You are quoting Jesus Christ," he said, "and it's unacceptable! Stop now, repent, or you'll go straight to Hell!"

Joshua looked at him. "Do you want me to go to Hell?" he asked, and the young man straightened, looking unsettled.

"No."

"Neither do I want you to go to Hell."

Their eyes held. Rachel was surprised at Joshua's words, and so was the young man.

"Never mind Hell," said someone else, "it's just wrong! You can't put yourself forward as Jesus Christ!"

A few other cries went up, in support of this.

"And, anyway," said another, "what is all this talk of allegiance, and war? What are you planning?"

"Yes," others cried in unison, "what are you planning?"

"Are you planning a coup?" That voice was different – it was a young man, wearing suit trousers and a shirt and tie. Rachel recognised him – he was one of her father's MPs, the Minister of National Security, The Honourable Trevor Bates.

Now the crowd began to melt away, and Bates made his way forward until he was face to face with Joshua.

"Is that your plan?" he repeated. Rachel now saw there were ten or so police officers standing behind him; a lot, considering their stretched resources. What was her father up to?

"Are you marching into Parliament?"

A ripple of voices spread across the crowd. Joshua march into Parliament? Surely not.

"That is not my plan," said Joshua, holding Bates' eyes.

"Your ways threaten our democratic state!"

"My ways are not a threat to you," said Joshua.

"Talk of a monarchy!" said Bates. "Talk of a battle ahead. Listen carefully, New Zealanders! This man is stirring dissension in our peaceful land! He is stirring war!"

Rachel saw Joshua swallow at this, but he still held the minister's eyes.

"The monarchy is real," he said, "but not as you understand it. You yourself have your own queen, and she sits back and protects your freedom. Why would you be afraid of me?"

"I am not afraid," said Bates, "I am taking action."

"I have committed no crime," said Joshua, looking at the police. "Let anyone who has been following me testify against me, if I am lying."

The police looked around at the crowd then back at Joshua, and did not move. The MP glanced at them, and then back at Joshua.

"You are bartering," he said, and Joshua shook his head.

"I am gifting. There is no gift duty."

Bates grimaced. "You are familiar enough with our law."

"I am – I have not broken it."

"If you continue this way, our tax will be turned on its head. Parliament will fall – the government will have no power."

"I have no desire to overturn the government's power," said Joshua. "My power is of a different kind entirely. The power of secular rule, and the power of God: each to their own."

Bates shifted uncomfortably on his feet.

"Very well," he said, "you have committed no crime yet. Make sure it stays that way."

He turned abruptly and walked away, muttering to the police officers as he went.

Rachel frowned. Parliament: what were they thinking? Her eyes drifted across the water of the harbour again, toward the Beehive, and then her phone rang.

Embarrassed in the silence, she reached to turn it off – but she saw it was her father, and opened it.

"Dad?" she whispered.

"Rachel," said Connor.

"What the hell's going on?"

"Joshua is going on."

"What do you mean?"

"Stay away from him, Rachel."

"What?"

"Just stay away from him – it's not safe."

He had gone. Rachel stared at the phone in her hand and then looked up at Joshua.

"Don't be afraid!" he was saying again. "The battle is coming! Be ready! Know where your allegiance lies."

Suddenly, with a chill, she understood his meaning.

"My God…" she whispered. "Where is all this leading?"

Her allegiance: where did it lie? With her father? With the government? With New Zealand? There should be no conflict! There was no conflict – Joshua had said it himself! But they did not understand – they would use force! They would force a choice…

"Oh my God…"

Would she leave, or would she stay?

She studied Joshua's plain face, and his casual clothes. Did she believe in God? She didn't know! She still didn't know, despite everything she had seen – everything she had experienced. But she did believe in Joshua. Not exactly a divine belief, a human belief. And yet, he was more than human somehow. His humanity was greater.

Joshua was someone she aspired to – someone she wished she could be like.

Would she leave, now, out of fear?

"No," she whispered.

"Don't be afraid," Joshua called out to the crowd.

"I won't," whispered Rachel, "I won't be afraid. I choose to stay."

Chapter 33

MOUNT VICTORIA

John stood at the top of Mt Victoria. The temperature was dropping. John shivered, and drew his jacket closer around him. The sun was setting and blood red colours lit the sky, reflecting in the harbour.

It was beautiful. He took a deep breath, drinking in the view. Petone stood across the water to his right, darkening into twilight, with the faint flickering of lights of the houses. The majestic view of the city of Wellington rose in front of him: a multitude of lit high-rise buildings, the waterfront marina, the ferry terminus, and somewhere, behind those buildings, the Beehive.

The crowds who had flooded the high hill that day had gone. Autumn was settling in, and it was too cold to stay out at night. Leaves littered the ground, crunching under foot.

Now only a handful remained.

John made his way over to Rachel. She was sitting on a stone wall, her face reflecting the red hues of the sunset as she enjoyed the view.

"Lovely," she said, and he smiled gently, admiring her high cheeks and full smile.

"Yes," he said. "It is."

Her blue eyes moved to him, and became serious.

"John," she said, "do you think Joshua's in danger?"

John swallowed, glancing away to the darkening water of the harbour.

"I don't know," he said.

"My father…"

John shook his head curtly, moving back a step. "I don't want to think about it."

"We're so close!" said Rachel. "So close to the seat of power." And then she glanced over the wall.

Tristan was sitting on the grass on the other side, his back to Wellington and the sunset. He stared into the darkness toward the airport, and the mouth of the harbour – toward the South Island.

John climbed over the wall, and lowered himself to the grass. "Mind if I join you?" he asked.

Tristan shrugged. "Whatever."

John sat next to him, staring out at the same view. The sky had darkened on this side now, and the view was becoming pitch black.

Tristan was quiet and held himself stiffly. He must be cold, surely, John thought; he was only wearing shorts, and the T-shirt and jacket.

"Nice evening," John offered, and Tristan shrugged again, and said nothing.

"What are you thinking?" asked John.

Tristan grimaced, and then laughed. "More things than I'd like to say."

"It's a beautiful view over there," John said, gesturing back to Wellington.

"Not to me it's not."

"Why?"

Tristan took a deep breath. "Maybe ask Rau," he said. "Tell him I said it's okay. It doesn't matter anymore – it just doesn't matter."

And Tristan rose and moved away.

John frowned. What was going on? Where was Rau? And where was

Joshua? He walked around the stone wall, and down the hill.

He found Rau sitting on the grass, smiling into the fading red light.

"Must do some fishing down here sometime," said Rau, as John sat next to him.

"Something's up with Tristan," said John.

Rau frowned. "Ae," he said, "something's been wrong ever since we came here. It's his whanau."

"His family?"

"It's private."

"He said you could tell me."

Now Rau glanced sharply at him. "He did?"

"Yes – he said it didn't matter anymore."

Rau stared at him and then rose to his feet. "Where did he go?"

John gestured vaguely in the right direction. "Somewhere over there."

"It's not like him," said Rau, and he headed off to find Tristan.

John looked after him, and then searched around again. Where was Joshua? He wandered around the hill, and couldn't find him. He'd disappeared again. Maybe he needed privacy, too. John walked slowly back up the hill, and was near the top when he heard a sound under a cluster of maple trees. Something was happening; there was a tussle, and a groan.

He rushed under the trees, and found Joshua. He was sitting up taut against a trunk, his head lolling against the bark. Blood was smeared across his forehead, and his hair was matted with blood and sweat. On the ground, his hands grasped and released dead fallen leaves, his body writhing in pain.

"What is it?" gasped John, rushing to him. Was he wounded? Where was the blood coming from? John searched his body through the shirt, front and back. There was no wound in his chest.

"Do you need Rachel?" he said. "I'll get her…"

Relieved, John searched his scalp – had he been assaulted?

"No," Joshua whispered, grasping his arm, "that's not it…"

Agony flooded John. He gasped, and sank on his knees. “Master!” he cried, and Joshua jerked his hand away.

John sagged on the ground next to him. His pain had gone as soon as Joshua had released him, but it continued for Joshua! It was a torment John couldn’t understand! Physical, but not actually physical – emotional, or…or…

“Spiritual,” whispered Joshua. “It’s spiritual.”

“Spiritual?” breathed John.

“The spirit,” said Joshua. “Life or death! Life or death…”

And he crushed dead leaves in his grip.

John stared at him. There was blood on his forehead, but no source. What was that, spiritual?

“I have to face it,” whispered Joshua.

“Face what?” asked John, feeling a chill run up his spine.

“The end.”

Tears pricked at John’s eyes, and he hurriedly blinked them away. “Don’t say that!” he said, as Rau appeared.

His eyes moved between John and Joshua, and then he knelt beside Joshua.

“Master,” he whispered. “Tristan’s gone. What must we do?”

“Stay safe,” gasped Joshua. “Stay safe!”

“What’s going to happen?”

“We’ll gather,” said Joshua, “in the Gardens. We’ll all gather. So many, Rau – there are going to be so many! Everyone will be there!”

“But that’s good!” said Rau. “Your time has come.”

“Yes,” whispered Joshua. “My time has come.”

John stared at him with sudden dull pain, as Joshua continued.

“We’ll march toward Parliament.”

“But, Master,” said Rau, “they won’t accept you there.”

“You’re right,” said Joshua, and his eyes found John's. “They won’t.”

“You’ll die,” whispered John, grief filling his heart as he suddenly realised the truth of all he had feared.

“No!” said Rau. “Not you! You don’t need to die.”

Joshua's face contorted before them. "You don't know what you're saying," he said.

"You can live!" Rau insisted. "You have the power to live!"

"I have the power to give life, and to give it away…"

Tears flooded John's eyes now. Was it true? Was Joshua going to give his life away?

"Where's Tristan?" whispered John.

"Gone," said Rau, glancing at him before grasping Joshua's shoulders, not feeling Joshua's pain as John had – only his own.

"Don't go!" begged Rau. "We can find another way!"

"No," said Joshua, grasping onto his arm. "There is no other way."

"We can save you."

"I don't want you to save me."

"We can protect you!"

"Rau!" Joshua's voice was suddenly strong, suddenly commanding – he was grasping both Rau's arms now, shaking him. "This isn't you – you know better than this! You know better!"

Rau fell back. John watched as he swallowed and shook his head.

"Let me die instead," said Rau. "You are my whanau."

"No," Joshua whispered, his head lolling on the trunk again. "No."

"I…" John saw tears flood Rau's eyes. "I'll stay with you, until the end."

Now Joshua's eyes met Rau's, a deep, sad intensity momentarily overriding the pain.

"Oh, Rau," he whispered, "do you really believe you are strong enough to die for me? You're wrong! You're not yet that strong. Tomorrow, Rau! Tomorrow you will pretend you never knew me."

Dismay filled Rau's face. He stared at Joshua, and shook his head.

"It can't be!" he said, and Joshua grimaced.

"It is," he said, and Rau rose to his feet. He stared at John, and back at Joshua, and then he turned and ran away.

John propped himself up against the tree trunk next to Joshua, amongst the dead leaves, and closed his eyes tightly. Joshua heaved beside him.

"It's Tristan, isn't it?" said John. "Tristan's going to do it."

"Yes," said Joshua. "He's going to do it."

"How?" asked John.

Joshua grasped his hand, and John instantly saw an image of Joshua being shot.

"Oh God," he whispered, as he clung to Joshua's hand. The pain flooded through him again, but this time he could not let go.

"It's not the death I fear," Joshua whispered, his head now sinking for a moment onto John's shoulder, "it's the reason for the death."

"The reason?" John whispered.

"The darkness!" Now Joshua sobbed, and the sound cut John to the heart. His pain was tangible now – physical, throbbing, overwhelming.

"What is it?" John breathed. "What darkness?"

"All of humanity," whispered Joshua. "The darkness, everywhere! Of all of humanity gone wrong."

John squeezed his hand tightly, and saw a vision. Joshua was there! Hurting! He was in the middle of a street, surrounded by angry faces. There was something on his head! Some terrible weight, bearing down on him, pressing into his head, crushing him. Darkness was smothering him – darkness was penetrating into his body. Images flashed, in rapid sequence – felt and seen, experienced to the depths, though they were not his own. Murder, rape, hatred, fury – all took physical form: all were disease, stealing away his life.

Tristan! John felt him, through Joshua: his pain, his anger; his hatred! Mark Blake – Joshua knew him, and felt him, and was penetrated by his fury. John trembled: his own darkness was there, a more subtle shade but still adding to the weight. And now there were many other countless faces: countless people, from countless nations, burdening him with darkness!

"I am the scapegoat!" Joshua cried out. "I am the scapegoat!"

The darkness was too great! It was crushing him! It was killing him…

"Oh, no!" cried John. "God!" And the vision was gone.

Joshua remained, human and in agony – waiting to die, to save all of humanity from fatal darkness.

"Oh, dear God," John whispered, sinking down on his face at his feet. "Master! I'm so sorry! Forgive us!" And he prayed for him, and knew Joshua's bloodied face was pointed to the sky, as Joshua cried out to God. "Oh, Father," he cried, "help me! Help me."

Grief filled John. He lay face down in the dead leaves, at Joshua's feet. He drifted in and out of sleep. He prayed. Nightmares took him, and he jerked awake, only to find the real nightmare was still to begin.

"Oh, God," he prayed into the leaves, "save us! Save us."

And Joshua's hand came to his head, trembling, but strong.

"We will save you," he whispered. "We love you – we always have."

The sun felt warm against John's face. Filled with dread, John lifted his head from the leaves.

Joshua was beside him. He had washed his face and hair, and brushed off his clothes.

"I've found my strength again," he murmured. "I'm ready now. His light is stronger than the darkness."

John rose, swaying. Joshua's resolute gaze fixed firmly upon him.

"Time for my Coronation Ceremony," he said, and John shivered.

"Yes," he whispered.

"Will you stay with me?" Joshua asked, and John nodded.

"I will," he said, "I'll stay until the very end."

Joshua smiled, and John held his breath, lest the smile disappear. "I know you will," said Joshua, "and you will see for yourself, in the end, that the light is stronger, John. Don't be afraid! Trust! Even in the darkest night, trust!"

John held his gaze, swallowed, and nodded. His choice was made! It was already made.

"I will trust," he said, and he straightened up, brushed down his own clothes, and followed Joshua up the hill.

Chapter 34

THE PROCESSION

Rau stood in the Botanic Gardens, with thousands of people from all over the Wellington region. Word must have gotten out! Of the five hundred thousand in the region, Rau was sure a hundred thousand had assembled, covering the pavements, spilling across grass, pressed between redwoods, oaks, pine trees, and flowering plants. Many people watched from the road.

Police were scattered amongst them, nervously eyeing the crowd. Politicians were there too, he was sure of it – wearing suits, in the cool day.

Rau stood close to Joshua, and was comforted to see John and Rachel also standing close by. There'd been no sign of Tristan since Rau had last seen him the night before, on Mount Victoria.

Joshua's words echoed through Rau's mind. *"Do you really believe you are strong enough to die for me? You're wrong!"*

Was Joshua truly going to die today? Every day was vulnerable – every day was precious. He stood before the crowd, his arms stretched out.

"Tomorrow you will pretend you never knew me."

How could it be? Rau was certain he would step up to protect him; if someone pulled a gun, he would take the bullet. He loved Joshua! He loved him as friend, as brother – as precious master.

"I'll never betray you," he whispered. "Never."

"Decide!" Joshua called out to the crowd. "Who will you follow? Who will you trust? Decide, for time is running out!"

"What decision?" A woman asked, in a business jacket and skirt. "I am Tracy Harrison, of the Clean Green Party. What are you doing here? Where are you going with this?"

"I'm going to my own kingdom," said Joshua, and Rau shifted on his feet. Did he have to be that direct?

"Your own kingdom?" Rau recognised the Leader of the Opposition, Patrick Clarkson. "We don't believe in your kingdom – we believe in our own!"

Now a few angry shouts went up. "Let him speak!" some said.

"No way!" others argued. "He's talking about a kingdom, here! He can forget it!"

Rau glanced at John, who was also looking at him, his face grave.

"You won't be able to come," said Joshua, "where I am going! I have to go first, and then you can follow."

"Where to?" asked Clarkson. "Parliament? We're ready for you, if you try it!"

Rau stared at his face. What did he mean, ready?

Joshua continued, unabated. "I'll go first, but follow me now!" he said. "Follow me, as far as you can, and then no further. See what you must see for yourselves."

And he moved down the driveway and out of the gardens, into the street.

Rau rapidly followed closely behind, with John and Rachel. The crowd pressed in, jostling them forward onto Salamanca Road.

"Stop shoving!" someone called out.

"He's moving away."

"Follow him! Don't lose him!"

As voice after voice shouted out, Rau's ears rang with the din. He stumbled on, forcing his way through more bodies until he was close enough behind Joshua to be able to hear what was being said.

"Sir," said a man, "I am Rawiri Heka, of the Maori party."

"I know who you are," said Joshua.

"Please tell us what your intentions are."

"My intentions have always been peaceful."

"We understand that, Sir, but you seem to be bringing a hundred thousand people to Parliament."

Joshua smiled wryly. "Isn't this country a democracy?"

He continued walking, and Heka stood aside, making way for Clarkson.

"Stop this!" he ordered. "Or your actions will be interpreted as an act of war!"

"An act of war?" someone cried out. "How stupid is that?"

"The joker thinks he's a king!"

"Don't insult him!"

"Do you really think that he's a king? Your majesty!" The speaker performed a mock bow, but the crowd kept pushing forward, and people fell over him.

"Hey, get off!" he cried, as he shoved them aside.

Fists started flying, but the crowd continued to push Rau forward. Behind him police officers intervened, breaking up the fight.

Joshua made his way to The Terrace, and then down to Bowen Street.

Rau swallowed. Why did he have to go to the Beehive? Why did he have to make such a bold statement? Behind him the crowd continued with their jibes.

"You know where he's going!" someone called out, laughing. "He wants to take over Parliament!"

"Don't be ridiculous!" said another woman.

"It's time for Joshua to rule! I choose Joshua as king!" yelled a man.

A chorus joined in, and the words became a chant. "Joshua as king!

Joshua as king!"

"Shut up!" cried others. "Can you believe it? Royalists, in our capital city! God save the Queen!"

"Joshua is King!"

"Don't be stupid!"

And now fighting really broke out. Rau's heart pounded as he watched police officers slipping into the crowd, separating the fighters. Punches landed on the officers, and now they pulled their batons out.

"God," Rau whispered in prayer, "help us."

Suddenly there was a cry from Joshua. "We're coming in peace!"

His voice drifted over the crowd. "Don't fight! What can you achieve with fighting? Only bruises! We haven't come to fight, only to show."

He continued walking, and the crowd calmed down.

Joshua turned right at Bowen Street, and now Rau saw his first glimpse of the Beehive through the metal rail fence. He stared at the brown ten-storey structure. From here the Government ruled! The front entrance to the Parliament buildings was still a five minute walk away.

A peaceful demonstration, Rau thought to himself. That's all this was! There was nothing to fear.

Joshua continued, and turned left into Lambton Quay. The first gate was locked shut – he walked past it. But the sight beyond the gates chilled Rau. There, gathered in the Parliament grounds, was the army.

Rau hesitated. The crowd continued to push forward, but Rau began easing himself away to the periphery of the crowd.

Joshua was walking up Molesworth Street, and now he stopped outside the second gate.

The army stood at attention – perhaps two hundred officers waiting for him. They reached for their rifles, as one man, and laid them ready against their shoulders.

Rau hurried past the gate and stood back, watching. Saint Peter's Cathedral was nearby. It could be a refuge! A refuge, if they needed to run.

"What's going on?" someone called out. "What's the army doing in

Parliament gardens?"

"Stay back!" an army officer called out, from the front row, rifle ready.

"You can't do this!" said someone else. "We're New Zealand citizens! We have a right to enter the grounds!"

"Stay back, or we will fire!"

"Like hell you will!" A tall young man angrily stepped forward. "Stuff this for a joke!"

And he thrust himself through the gate.

"No!" Joshua cried, but the army's response was swift. The officer drew tall, his rifle ready, and shot the man.

A ripple of shock passed through the crowd. Joshua hurried forward, lifted the man in his arms and stepped back, laying him on the ground. Rachel rushed to help, but Joshua laid a hand on her arm, passed a hand over the man's chest, and prayed.

The man opened his eyes and stood up. Rau gaped as the crowd exploded.

"Look!" a woman cried. "It's a miracle! Joshua has come from God! Parliament's going to fight him! The army's going to attack him! Fight! Fight for Joshua! Fight!"

"No!" Joshua's voice cried, but the woman ran forward, and she was shot.

Now the crowd lost control. They swept forward, pushing the gates. Some of the army was smothered, other officers were firing, and police began to beat people in the crowd outside the gates.

"Do you believe Joshua is Jesus Christ now?" A voice spoke into Rau's ear.

Rau tore his eyes away from the carnage, and found Mark Blake, the Bishop of Wellington, standing beside him. His face was hard, his eyes intense and accusing.

Rau swallowed. The crowd had lost control! They were being killed! Their own people were being killed. Was this was he had expected? No! He had expected peace! He had longed for peace.

Was Joshua really the Christ?

Rau saw Joshua's face was pale. His voice was raised, but now his words were achieving nothing. Rau still believed in him! He still believed. But as he looked at Mark Blake, as he felt the bishop's stare, he remembered his family, and their humiliation if he should be excommunicated from the church. His throat constricted. It was all over. There was no going back, now – not for Joshua. Rau's only hope was to return up north, and pretend nothing had ever happened.

"No," he whispered. "I don't believe he is the Christ."

"Tomorrow you will pretend you never knew me."

Never knew…Rau suddenly realised his meaning. Not the simple 'knew' of ordinary acquaintance – the true knowledge! The true knowledge of his identity.

He had done it! He had pretended Joshua was not Christ, when he knew, in his heart, he was.

He had betrayed him.

Blake's face broke into a knowing smile – a smile of satisfaction. Rau's vision blurred. He had denied him! The one he loved! He had denied him.

Pain filled his heart, but so did fear. What would happen now? He couldn't bear to stay and find out. He couldn't bear to watch Joshua die.

He turned and ran, and Blake's smile was etched in his mind, following him everywhere.

Chapter 35

THE CORONATION

Rachel stood inside the gates of Parliament.

In front of her, four people lay shot on the ground. She rushed toward them to help, to check their pulses, but was shoved away by army officers.

"Stand back!" they ordered.

Rachel stared at them. "I'm a doctor, for Christ's sake!" she said. "Let me pass!"

But they shook their heads. "No exceptions."

The four extra shootings, after the first, allowed the army to gain back control of the crowd. They were surrounding the people, now; ushering them out of the Parliament grounds and back onto the street.

Rachel was pressed back too, by a wall of army officers. She almost stumbled, but somehow kept her footing.

"Our army is supposed to protect *us!*" someone called out in fury. "Not bloody Parliament!"

"Parliament *is* us, bloody monarchist!" someone else yelled.

The black iron gate was in front of her. A few people tried to clamber over it, but they were pulled down.

"Back!" the army officers called out, lifting their rifles in aim. "Or we will use force!"

Rachel stared at their faces: hard, focused and oblivious to killing. Four innocent people lay dead! One had been saved by Joshua – only one. How the hell had it all happened?

Through the gates, Rachel saw a movement behind the wall of army officers. A man in a suit was walking to the Hill Street gate. She recognised his walk and greying hair. Was it her father? Rachel pushed through the crowd, until she reached the edge.

Army officers were spread across Molesworth Street, holding people back. Rachel looked between their shoulders. At the intersection of Molesworth, Hill and Aitken Streets, with Saint Peter's Cathedral looming above, stood Joshua at its centre. Surrounded by army officers, his face was white but unreadable.

Rachel's heart pounded in fear. He was alone, isolated out. She suddenly noticed his white shirt: 'I love Aotearoa,' fading in the sun.

"You can't kill him," Rachel instinctively whispered to the army officers. "He has committed no crime."

"We're the army," an officer replied, "not the police. We act in times of war, to establish national security."

"We are not at war!" said Rachel, and now Joshua's eyes were on her.

War…

"He's done nothing," said Rachel. "He's a pacifist, for God's sake! You can't kill him! It would be an act of murder, if your actions were unprovoked! You'd be held to account – taken to court…"

They shifted on their feet and Rachel knew they agreed.

"He is a New Zealand citizen," she said. "You must protect him: you know that."

Rachel's eyes roved the street. John was standing only a few metres away from Joshua. John! His loyalty! He was exposed, and Rachel could see the fear in his eyes, but also his gritty determination. He was staying, and no one was going to move him.

Rachel caught his eye, and they smiled grimly at each other. Then

Rachel looked away. Where was Rau? She couldn't see him anywhere. Had he been hurt?

A man stood on the steps of Saint Peter's, wearing Anglican robes. Rachel vaguely recognised him – it was Mark Blake, the Bishop of Wellington; a friend of her father's. As she watched, a Korean woman wearing simpler robes rushed down the steps. It was the Dean, Eun Ae Choo. Rachel had met her one Easter, when her family had attended church.

"What's going on?" cried Choo, looking across the crowd and into the grounds of Parliament. "Are those people dead?"

"Joshua Davidson killed them," said Blake, pointing to Joshua. "His uprising is destroying our nation."

Rachel stared at the Bishop. He was blaming Joshua? Where did he think it would lead? The Bishop and the Dean should be diffusing the situation! Proclaiming a blessing from God, or healing words, or forgiveness! But Blake's face was hard, and Choo's forehead was furrowed as she whispered what Rachel could only imagine was a prayer.

Rachel remembered the politician she'd seen leaving Parliament grounds. Surely he would represent the people? Surely he would act?

Finally she saw him emerging from the crowd, opposite the steps of Saint Peter's. It was James Connor.

Rachel pressed against the army officers. "Let me through!" she said. "That's my father!"

"No exceptions," said the officer, but Rachel suddenly dove between their legs.

She was through! On her knees, on the road, with nothing but space between her and Joshua. She scrabbled on her knees, crawling towards him until she felt the cold tip of a rifle on the back of her head, stopping her from rising to her feet.

Rachel saw Joshua's eyes widen, and then he stretched out a hand.

"No," he said, "she's not the one you want."

The rifle left her head, allowing her to stand, but now it was prodding the small of her back.

"Leave her!" her father's voice called out. "That's my daughter!"

"She's a rebel," the officer called back. Rachel flushed, looking at her father. His face was taut, his forehead creased.

"What the hell are you doing?" Rachel cried out to him. "The army, Dad? What are you thinking?"

Now the officer was forcing her down to her knees again, the rifle again at the back of her head.

"Leave her," said Joshua calmly. "No one else needs to die today."

Rachel shook. She locked eyes with her father. Then his eyes shifted to Joshua.

"You are a curse," he said, spitting. "A curse that is bringing our people to ruin!"

Joshua did not speak. Confused, Rachel searched his face. He was innocent! He was good, not evil! How dare her father accuse him, when his own actions had precipitated the riot?

"You're a bastard!" Rachel shouted. "An incompetent bastard!" And she felt a blinding, sharp, painful blow to the back of her head.

She fell, gasping – her vision blacked out, but she could still hear her father's voice.

"Stand down, officer!" he ordered. "I am your commander!"

There was a hand on her head. The pain disappeared, and her vision returned. Confused, Rachel looked up to see Joshua standing over her, his face breaking into his familiar smile. He reached out a hand and pulled her back to her feet.

"Don't argue anymore," he said quietly to her. "Don't fight them. You'll get yourself killed."

He had always said it! Don't fight! Don't use weapons! Overcome evil with good! Swallowing, Rachel nodded and stepped away, with her back to the iron gate.

A figure had appeared, next to her father. It was the Governor General, Anita Mayes. Surely she would stop this! She held the most power in New Zealand: she was the guardian to ensure the diplomatic process continued unhindered.

"Right Honourable Prime Minister James Connor!" she said, loudly.

"Do you really think this is legal?"

"The nation is under threat, Right Honourable Governor General," her father replied. "I have taken the necessary actions to ensure our nation's survival."

Rachel longed to hate him, but could not. He was the Prime Minister! He was responsible! He was afraid! He had acted in good conscience in New Zealand's interests.

Blake shifted on the steps of Saint Peter's. "Connor!" he boomed. "Do something! Deal with this man, before it is too late!"

Rachel stared at him. What did he mean? Her father, with a grim face, lifted his arm in the air. Rachel noticed a movement in the crowd, to her right, and now Tristan stepped between the officers. He was carrying a rifle,

Rachel swallowed. "Oh my God…"

Tristan's face was hard – his eyes distant, his gaze far away.

Tristan!" she whispered. "What are you doing?"

She had known something was up with him, but she hadn't acted! She should have sectioned him, or something; kept him safe!

"Tristan!" her father cried out. "Why now? Why like this?"

"Now!" Tristan replied, his voice hard. "Here! A public act, ordered by the Prime Minister himself! An army weapon, so no one can hide!"

A lead weight grew in Rachel's stomach, and began to twist in her gut.

"Oh my God," she whispered. Her father had organised the assassination of Joshua.

A girl was with Tristan, strangely flitting around Joshua, chanting, goading; laughing eerily.

"King Joshua!" she mocked, bowing. "Your majesty!"

"Witch," whispered Rachel, fighting back the urge to vomit. There was a black intensity to her eyes; an aged calculation to her actions. She appeared young, but came across as ancient; bitter and conceited. She was carrying a round ornament made of some strange grey metal Rachel had never seen, with ancient symbols and a pointed design.

"Your majesty!" she said, bowing, placing it on Joshua's head.

It was a crown.

Rachel stared. Joshua's face turned a sickly shade of grey. His brown eyes fixed on her, and she saw his sudden agony. His head tipped back, he clung the crown firmly to his head, and began to stagger.

"What is it?" whispered Rachel, and then she cried out. "Poison! Thc girl is poisoning him! Get that thing off him!"

But now John was shaking his head and stretching his hand out toward Rachel.

"No," he said. "Don't!"

Rachel stared at him. John's eyes were full of tears, his face contorted. Rachel wanted to rush forward, but knew she must not! Something was happening! Something she could not understand. John knew! John understood. She had to trust that he knew what to do.

She remained still, clenching her fists, and now Blake sounded over Joshua's head.

"Kill him, Connor!" he shouted. "Do it now!"

"Not yet!" John cried. "Not yet! It's not the right time!"

Joshua was groaning, now. He staggered, still trying to keep his footing, his face pointed up to the sky, his hands clutching the crown to his head.

Tristan was staring at Joshua now, shaking.

"Kill him!" Blake cried out. "Kill him, and we will all be safe! Kill him, and we will all find our peace!"

"The scapegoat…" Tristan whispered. "Oh my God, the scapegoat…"

Rachel thought the rifle might fall from his shaking hands.

"You can't kill him!" Choo cried out, from the Cathedral. "Killing is a sin! This man is innocent! He is innocent!"

"Enough!" Blake shouted. "I'll dismiss you for disgraceful conduct! You'll never work in the church again!"

Choo stared at him. She looked as if she was about to tear off her robes, but then a strange calm came over her. She stepped away from him and retained her robes, grasping them firmly.

"Don't kill him!" she called out to Tristan. "In the name of God, I say to you: this is a crime! This man is innocent!"

Rachel felt tears pricking her eyes. A woman of God! At last, a true bold Christian voice! Blake shoved her, and propelled her back into Saint Peter's. At least she would be praying, thought Rachel. At least someone would be praying.

"Kill him!" Blake repeated. "Execute him! Now!"

"Prime Minister!" The Governor General cried out. "Our state is a democracy! We have a Law! We have a court system!"

"To hell with the Law!" Blake shouted. "This is about our survival! Our survival, as a people – even as a race! What are you waiting for?"

He was staring at Connor.

Rachel saw reluctance in her father's eyes. At last, reluctance! He wasn't evil! He wasn't a tyrant! He didn't want to do it.

"Do this," Mayes declared loudly, "and I will use the powers invested in me to dissolve the Government! This is not your role, Connor! You are way out of line here!"

Connor's eyes moved over the crowd and the army, his gaze passing through the iron gates to the four dead bodies beyond. Then he straightened with new resolution.

"Let the people decide!" he said. "This won't be my responsibility! Let the people decide!"

"Connor!" Mayes cried out. "You call this due process?"

"People of New Zealand!" Connor called out. "What is your decision? This man, Joshua, has stirred up our nation! Four are dead! We are fighting each other – we are divided! We are all New Zealanders. What should we do? You decide!"

There was silence – and then a response.

"Oh, to hell with it!" someone cried out. "Get it over with! Get him out of the way, so we can all go home."

"Kill him?" asked Connor. "How many say yes?'"

"Oh, you can't be serious," Rachel muttered under her breath. Then a swell of anger overrode her thoughts as she saw the girl straightening beside Joshua, her dark eyes hard and cold. She was adult – she was ancient.

"Kill him!" she commanded. "Kill him!"

"Just kill him!" the people cried. "Get it over with! Kill him!"

Others struggled! Others shouted for his life! Rachel raised her voice, loud and strong.

"No!" she cried. "Kill him, and it will all be over! We will never be the same again!"

Joshua's eyes were on her, now! He was suffering. His grey face was sweating, and bleeding! Bleeding…

"Hematohidrosis," she whispered. "Rupturing, from the stress…"

Tristan stood before Joshua. Rachel watched, as Tristan looked at Joshua's staggering form and saw the blood – Tristan's face contorted. Joshua was looking at him, now! His eyes were clouded with pain, but gracious! There was no anger! No resentment! No fear! Rachel was drawn into his expression. It was love! Tristan saw it, too: looked stricken by it! Love.

Joshua reached out a hand to grasp Tristan's shoulder – his body stiffened. He fell to his knees, his back taut; his face pointing to the sky.

"Father!" he cried to God. "Don't hold it against them! They have no idea what they are doing!"

Blood dripped down his face. The crown fell off his head, and now he stretched his arms out wide.

"Where are you?" he cried, his face now contorted with terror! "Oh, God, Daddy – I can't see you! Darkness! Darkness…"

Rachel's eyes filled with tears – she blinked them furiously away. Joshua! Joshua…

Tristan was rigid. Dismay flooded his face. Then he stepped back, gathered the rifle, and fired.

Rachel choked. Bullets landed in Joshua's chest, jerking his body backwards, throwing him to the ground.

She rushed forward now to where he lay gasping on the ground, his body jerking with pain. She tore away his blood stained white shirt, and found five bullet wounds – two to each lung, and one to the heart. There was no sign of the bullets leaving his body.

"Oh, God," Rachel breathed, shaking. "No…"

She reached for his neck and felt for his pulse. It was still there, but faint and fading rapidly! He was bleeding badly from the chest and heart.

Rachel took off her jacket, and pressed it into his wounds. Pressure! But she knew it was useless. His heart had been penetrated! And his lungs! There was no way he could survive.

He grasped her hand, now. Rachel sobbed, as he met her eyes – as he struggled, on his last breaths.

"It's finished!" he gasped. "It's sorted!" And his face broke into a beautiful smile.

Rachel held him in her arms. "Don't go!" she cried. "Don't go!"

Peace slowly filled his eyes. His head fell back, and his hand fell from hers.

He was dead.

Rachel sank to the ground beside him. Resuscitate? She crossed her hands over his chest and began to pound his heart. But then she felt a hand to her shoulder.

It was John. His eyes were overflowing with tears. He held her gaze, and shook his head.

"It's over," he whispered. "Don't try to bring him back."

She stared at his face and began to weep. She shrank back away, from John – away from Joshua's body. And then she looked at the crowd.

They were silent.

"Enough!" cried the Governor General's voice. "By the power invested me, as the representative of the Queen, I now announce the current Prime Minister has acted outside of his jurisdiction! I am dissolving Parliament! The Queen will rule directly, until time permits to allow for an election – until democracy is effectively established again!"

Democracy, freedom, choice: they were gone! Fear had ruled – corruption had acted.

Joshua was dead.

Chapter 36

CRISIS

Mark Blake stood on the steps of Saint Peter's, staring down at the street. The Governor General had dissolved the Government! Connor stood next to Mayes, his face white and rigid. The crowd began shifting about, muttering backwards and forwards. Mayes was ordering the army to dismiss the people – to send them home. They were dispersing quickly, and in what seemed like only a few minutes, most of the people were gone.

Tristan had fallen to his knees. He'd thrown the rifle down, away from himself, and was staring at the ground. Mark swallowed – Tristan's eyes looked haunted.

Selena was smiling and circling the body, holding the crown. Her eyes lifted, and now she looked directly at him, her black eyes penetrating.

Chills crept up his back. He tore his eyes away and tried to find some kind of refuge in the other woman, kneeling next to the body. It was Rachel, Connor's daughter. A doctor. She'd tried to save him.

Another man Mark did not know sat next to Joshua's body. He wanted to avoid looking at him, but found he could not take his eyes off him. He was sitting close to the body, crying. Mark had never seen a man cry like this before. His entire body was shaking, gripped, totally immersed in the tragedy.

Mark felt numb. He didn’t look at the body – he couldn't bring himself to do so. And yet he couldn’t leave it, either.

Choo was beside him. “One of us should go to him,” she said quietly.

Mark swallowed, and could not answer her.

“You dismissed me,” she said. “It has to be you.”

Mark stared at Rachel, the doctor, on her knees – the one who had tried to help.

“I’m not fit,” he whispered to Choo. “I just murdered him.”

His body began to shake uncontrollably, the earliest tremors of a catastrophic explosion. Selena was there now! Selena’s voice was whispering in his ear.

“Look at him,” she said. “Look at what you have done.”

She took his hand and led him down the steps of Saint Peter’s Cathedral. She led him where he dared not go, but where he no longer had the strength to resist.

The body was there, now, at his feet. His eyes moved, against his will, over it. There was blood! He was standing in it! It was soaking into his purple tunic. Joshua's white shirt was torn from his chest – there were five bullet holes.

Mark contorted, as he looked at his face. It was peaceful.

“He was innocent!” Tristan’s voice wailed behind him. “We just killed an innocent man!”

But there was more – Mark knew, so much more!

“The scapegoat,” Selena whispered into his ear. “You know who this is!”

Mark looked down to his feet, at his robes now soaked in blood.

“Joshua,” said the man crying beside him. “You know his name is Joshua. You know him!”

“Even the name is the same,” Selena whispered.

Mark ran.

Away from the body, away from the grieving man, whose presence was so true, away from his son, wretched, on his knees after his crime, away from…from the One…

Joshua…'The Lord saves!' Joshua…

Mark ran up the steps of Saint Peter's past Choo, thrust his way through the glass doors, and emerged into the nave. He stood in the aisle, between congregational chairs. The cross was before him – distant, in the inner sanctuary. Jesus, on the cross…

Mark's shaking intensified. He forced himself to approach the cross – one shaking, unsteady step at a time. What had he done?

The glass doors sounded behind him. Who was it? Which one? The accuser? The faithful friend? Choo? Which one would reach him first? Which one would try to dictate his fate first?

It was Selena. "You know who I am," she said. "You know what you deserve."

Agony crashed upon his heart, powerful enough to sweep his life away.

"I know," he said. Hell whispered to him: torment, judgement – an eternity of retribution. "I know."

"An eye for an eye," said Selena. "Death for death. There is no grace, only justice! Only judgment. Only the Law.'

She was behind his back, and now she was putting something into his right hand.

"Why be a hypocrite?" she asked. "Death for death! Execute justice! Execute judgment."

He looked down, and found himself holding Tristan's rifle. With horror, he stiffened, staring at it, and then he looked up again at the cross. He was halfway down the church – only halfway to the inner sanctuary.

The door sounded behind him again. He turned, with pain, and saw Choo's concerned expression change to dismay.

"Mark!" she whispered, tears suddenly filling her eyes. "No!"

Her tears unleashed his own. He blinked the tears away, but his eyes filled again and again.

"Everything I am," he whispered, "is lost."

"No!" she pleaded. "There is always a way back!"

"Not always," he said. "There is a point of no return."

Her face was kind, her eyes forgiving. He regretted dismissing her, but at least this crime could be undone.

"Maybe you'll get my job," he whispered, smiling whimsically. Then he turned back to the cross.

The rifle was heavy in his hand. He gripped it, awkwardly, and moved closer to the cross. Death! Death…

The door sounded again, jolting through his melancholy.

"Leave me alone," he called out without turning, his voice resonating around the cathedral.

"Selena!" Tristan's voice sounded, loud, authoritative. "Get that rifle off him now!"

Her voice resonated laughter. "Get it off him yourself!"

Loud determined footsteps came up the aisle. Mark turned and raised the rifle, pointing it at Tristan's chest.

Tristan stopped short, staring at him, and Mark's gaze locked with him.

"You're not going to shoot me," said Tristan, his eyes filling with tears. "I know that for certain."

Mark's eyes also filled with tears. "You're right," he said, "but…" And now weeping threatened to overpower him. "…don't make me kill myself in front of you."

Now Tristan's eyes widened in grief-stricken terror, and it was agony to Mark's heart.

"I'm so sorry," Mark whispered to him, "you've seen too much already! I'm so sorry, Tristan, but…even protecting you isn't enough to keep me alive anymore."

Tristan began to weep, and Mark shook his head.

"Leave," he implored. "Leave."

"If I leave, you'll kill yourself!" said Tristan.

"I'll kill myself anyway!" said Mark. "Please, Tristan: leave!"

Dismay filled Tristan's face. His eyes moved, to Selena, and back again to Mark.

"She did this!"

"She did this?" Mark laughed with pain. "No, Tristan! Life did this! And…and I did it. I'm so sorry!"

"Selena…"

"She's too far gone, Tristan. But you – you can still live."

Tristan's eyes held his. Mark was relieved to see, Tristan was strong in that moment! He was strong. Tristan swallowed and then he nodded.

"All right," he said.

"I…" Mark choked on the words. How much he had failed him! "I love you."

Tristan's face contorted as he wept silently, then smiled sadly.

"I love you too," he whispered – and then, swiftly, he turned and walked down the aisle, and out of the doors.

Choo was on her knees in the last row, her lips moving, her eyes open; her face stricken. Mark gave her a wan smile and then turned back to his purpose.

He was almost there, at the altar! Before the cross. He had arranged the execution of Joshua! He had demanded his death.

The scapegoat…All of Mark's anger! All of the hatred he held inside he'd poured over Joshua's head! All of his guilt! All of his rage, at…at…

And now, Mark trembled. His rage at whom? At God? Yes! All of his rage at God, he had unleashed upon Joshua! When – and this admission was agony – he'd known all along Joshua was an expression of Christ. When he'd known Joshua was seeking to open a way to God.

Mark had betrayed him: the one he'd vowed to follow – the one he had vowed to serve.

He had killed a son of God.

Mark sank to his knees. He leaned heavily over the communion rail, his right arm hanging loosely, clinging to the rifle; his blood stained robes spread out over the polished wood.

"Hypocrite," said Selena, and Mark tightly closed his eyes.

"I have sinned," Mark whispered, and Selena laughed.

"You have sinned?" she said. "By killing a son of God? Without doubt. But why should we be surprised? After all, you killed her!"

Suddenly Selena's grip was on his shoulder and he was thrust back into the memory again: the car, upside down. Teresa, trapped! Her face, dripping blood! Her breathing, stopping…

Agony overcame him. He screamed, his pain resonating throughout the cathedral, but suddenly Selena's hand was forced away.

Mark clung to the railing, trembling as he saw the man, the one who had loved Joshua, grip Selena's shoulders with both of his hands.

"Get out!" he ordered, his eyes holding the fire of pure rage.

Selena's face contorted, and her voice rose to a shriek.

"Who do you think you are?" she shouted. "John of Whangarei? If I can kill Joshua, I can kill you!"

"Get out!" he said again. "I don't care about my death anymore, only his death! Only him! Leave now!"

Mark stared – Selena began to scream as John held her arms, like she had screamed with Joshua. Her body jerked, and Mark stiffened along with her, gripping the rail. Then suddenly she collapsed.

Bewildered, Mark watched as John caught her body. She was stirring, now, in his arms! She was staring up at his face! Her eyes were blue – wide, as they had been as a child: afraid! Tears were flowing…

Mark longed to rush to her and scoop her up in his arms. But he could not.

John lifted Selena into Choo's arms. What had just happened?

"Maybe I should have been Catholic," Mark muttered, "or Pentecostal, or something…"

Was it some kind of evil spirit? A demon? What did he know of this? For a strange moment, he imagined asking Father Andrew, or Pastor Luke. Then his own guilt descended back upon him, like a black cloud.

He buried his face in his arms, over the railing. The rifle was still in his hand. It was a comfort, now – it gave him control over his own fate; power to undo his guilt.

A hand landed on his shoulder, a different kind of touch.

"You didn't kill her," said John, and his words were agony to Mark.

"I was speeding," Mark whispered, lifting his face from his arms, looking up at Jesus's sad expression on the cross. "I was speeding, and I killed her."

"You were speeding," John murmured over him, "but the rest was a terrible accident."

An accident. Grief flooded his heart. An accident?

"If I'd been going at the right speed…"

"…she wouldn't have died," John finished. "But God wants forgiveness, not condemnation! God wants forgiveness!"

Mark felt weeping threaten him. "What do you know about God's forgiveness, 'John of Whangarei'?" he cried out. "What do you know about God's Law? Have you even stepped into church since childhood? What do you even do in Whangarei? Herd sheep?"

Tears filled John's eyes – the grieving man.

"I know as much about it as anyone!" he cried. "Maybe it's you who knows nothing!"

Mark shifted uncomfortably as John's words poured out.

"Joshua chose to die!" he said. "He chose to die, to carry all of our mess! Don't you get it? You've been in church all your life! I saw him die! I saw what he was doing!"

Now John grasped his arm.

"All the crap that goes through our heads and our mouths, and the ridiculous things we do," he said, "Joshua took it onto himself! So we could be free of it! So God's anger at us could be relieved! So some kind of justice could be done! So…" And now John hesitated, as if he was considering his own words. "So we could be fixed."

Mark gazed at him for a moment. "'The punishment that brought us peace was upon him,'" he quoted, "'and by his wounds we are healed.'[22]" Mark enjoyed John's ignorance of the old, even as the new was thrusting Mark into utter humility.

The cloud of his guilt re-emerged, still deep, still dark. Mark took a deep breath.

"Even if I was innocent of her death," he said painfully, "or even forgiven of her death, I killed him! I killed Joshua!"

How the pain intensified with the thought! This was the bottom line. He rose to his feet, now, holding the rifle – leaving John behind, entering into the inner sanctuary where John was not free to follow.

The altar was before him – the sacred wooden table, covered with white linen for purity. In ancient times the priests had sacrificed animals, to carry the evil of the people and save them from God's judgement.

Someone had left a silver chalice and plate on the white linen. Wine was in the cup, and white wafers on the plate: the body and blood of Christ – the Lamb of God, to take away the sins of the world.

Behind the altar was the cross. He was very close now. Mark stood at the foot, looking up the fading tiles, to Jesus. Sorrow…sorrow, for the sins of the world…

Mark's face contorted as he lifted the rifle and pointed it at the head of Jesus.

"It's as though I shot him myself!" said Mark. "I did! I handed him over! And…and…" How unbearable to actually say it! "…and that makes me Judas!"

The dark cloud descended. It filled every inch of his body, emotions and thought. Judas, the one who had betrayed Christ to his enemies, with a kiss! Who had handed him over to be crucified.

Mark had believed and betrayed. He had believed, and executed the one he had professed to love.

"I *am* Judas," he whispered. "My God! My God…"

Judas had killed himself.

Mark had been pointing the rifle at Christ. Now he drew it down, and turned it upon himself. Through the mouth, upwards, into the brain…

He swayed, his heart pounding. He was afraid of death, but fear was not enough. This was right – it was fitting. A second Jesus; a second Judas, offered at the altar. John from Whangarei could not begin to speak to the depth of his understanding.

But then there was another interruption.

Mark felt he might go mad. Quiet, please! Solitude, in the last moments before his death! But God would not give him solitude.

Rau Petera was bursting into the inner sanctuary.

Mark stared at him. His face was wet with tears, his eyes red. He was still weeping, even now, as he grasped Mark's blood stained robes and gazed into his eyes.

"Don't be like Judas," Rau implored him. "Be like Peter!"

"Like Peter?" Mark breathed. Peter was the one who had denied three times even knowing Christ! The one who had denied him, and had wept with remorse, and had returned, and later died for him.

"Be like Peter!" Rau pleaded. "Come back! Come back!"

Mark found himself grasping for Rau's arms as sobbing erupted from within him. They had both failed! Mark could see it so clearly now in Rau's transparent face: he had denied him! He had left him to die! Rau's regret flowed through his tears. Mark could see he had known him, and had left! But he had returned. Seen his body! He had returned to the altar; returned to his position.

Mark sagged down to his knees before the Kerikeri priest.

"I am worse than you," he choked. "Much worse."

"I was closer to him," whispered Rau. "I knew him, without a doubt, and still I denied him."

The rifle…Rau was touching it! Mark's body shook hard.

"Don't," he pleaded.

"Let it go," Rau murmured over him.

"You don't know what I've done."

"Tell me."

"I convinced Connor to kill him."

Now he had confessed it. Rau's face contorted, but then he shook his head.

"What else?"

"I played on his fears!" Mark writhed. "Manipulated him into it! I hated God…"

Now Mark closed his eyes as everything began to pour out.

"I sped, and Teresa died, and I blamed God, and then I shut out my children…" He trembled. "Tristan was in the army – I never knew! He could have been killed! And Selena…" He began to sob. "I'm a useless father…"

Rau was pressing his forehead to him now and murmuring a prayer in Maori. Mark clung to him, vulnerable, eyes still closed. The rifle was gone! Mark was afraid, but he didn't want to die. Rau's words soothed him. He felt something stirring in his heart; it was new, spiritual, it felt like…like love…

"God loved us so much that he gave his son,[23]" Rau murmured. "This is Christ's body, given for you. This is Christ's blood, given for you."

Mark opened his eyes, to look up into Rau's.

"Christ's body and blood?" he whispered.

"Given for you," said Rau, "for the forgiveness of sins.[24]"

His eyes were offering, inviting. Mark trembled. No death, but a road to forgiveness? That would mean facing the full grief of everything he had done! That would mean living with it, day by day, until…until one day the grief was finally gone…

Grief…but no burden. No judgment. No condemnation. No hatred, no anger, no murder, no neglect, no…sin…

Rau turned to the altar, and turned back holding the body and the blood of Christ.

Mark reached out his hands, and Rau placed a wafer in them.

"The body of Christ, given for you."

Mark closed his eyes. He took it in his mouth, and swallowed it; received it. Christ's death, for him! To carry his guilt! To carry his darkness.

"The blood of Christ, given for you."

Mark received the silver cup and drank from it. The sip of strong alcohol warmed his chest, even as another kind of warmth penetrated his whole body.

Rau's hand was on his shoulder now.

"The blessing of God, the Father, the Son, and the Holy Spirit, be with you now, and forever more."

"Amen," whispered Mark.

It was finished.

Peace. On his knees, Mark felt peace: a kind of peace that wholly filled him; a kind of peace he had never known.

"And you?" he murmured gently, looking up into Rau's face. "Will you receive communion from me?"

Rau smiled sadly. "I would," he said, "but I'm not yet ready."

Mark tilted his head, looking at him. "Not ready?" he said, surprised. "But…you just helped me…"

Tears filled Rau's eyes again. "I'm willing," he whispered, "but I'm not yet ready."

In humility, Mark reached up to touch his face. "May God bless you," he said, "for the right time."

"For the right time," Rau whispered as Mark rose to his feet.

Rau bowed to the cross, and then turned and stepped out of the inner sanctuary. Mark watched him grasp John's hands, and both men cried freely with each other.

"Tristan," said Rau, and John glanced up at Mark.

"Go," said Mark, and both Rau and John quickly walked down the aisle and out of the church.

Mark hesitated for a moment in the inner sanctuary. He looked at the altar, with its leftover wafers and wine. He wandered up, murmured prayer over the emblems, and took them into himself – they were sacred! They were not to be randomly discarded. It was their tradition, and he agreed with it.

He looked up into the eyes of Christ on the cross.

"'By his wounds, we are healed,'" he murmured, as a new joy filled his heart, like the glory of a very first sunrise seen on a clear, fresh morning.

He bowed to the cross, his heart and tradition as one, and then left the inner sanctuary.

Outside Eun Ae Choo had her arm around his daughter. Selena's face was hidden in her shoulder.

As he approached he could see Eun Ae's eyes were filled with tears. He disrobed, revealing his shirt and trousers beneath.

"I'm sorry," he said. "I was a fool to dismiss you."

She bowed her head graciously. "Then I am reinstated?"

"So far as I'm concerned, you never left."

She smiled sadly and now his eyes moved to Selena.

Eun Ae lifted her arm and Selena curled her legs up onto the chair, wrapping her arms around them. Mark felt drawn to protect her, as he had before Teresa died.

Eun Ae stooped to lift Mark's robes from the ground, and he grasped her arm.

"You don't have to do that," he said. "You're not my servant. I'll deal with them later."

"No," said Choo, "it's all right – I'll do it."

"Joshua's body," said Mark. "He might still be outside."

"We'll give him a service?"

Mark took another deep guilty breath. Could he attend Joshua's funeral? And yet, yes, he would.

"If God wishes it," said Mark.

Eun Ae made her way to the other side of the church, and slipped out of sight into a changing room. Then she reappeared again, walked down the side aisle and left the Cathedral.

Selena remained curled up, her face buried in her bare knees. The green shirt she was wearing was dishevelled, and her long black curls were thrown over her legs. She was shivering.

Mark sat beside her. "Selena…"

She didn't respond. Sadly Mark laid a hand on her shoulder, and she flinched.

How long had it been? How many years had they lost?

Nine. Nine years…

Mark wanted to hang his head in shame, but instead he lifted his face back to the cross, prayed for her under his breath, and tried again.

"Selena," he murmured, "I'm here for you now."

"Don't," she gasped.

"I'm so sorry," he whispered. "I'm so sorry."

"It's not your fault," she moaned. "It's my fault."

"No," he breathed, "not your fault…"

She stiffened and lifted her head, her face contorted.

"My fault!" she said, through gritted teeth as she dug her nails into her arms. "It's my fault! It's my fault, it's my fault…"

And she dug and dug, until she was bleeding.

Mark reached forward to grasp her arms, and she fell off the chair and started to hit him. Mark held her to his chest, rocking her and singing, as he had done when she had been hurt at age seven. She struggled against him! She fought him! Mark felt her adolescent rage! But he knew there was more. He knew to look deeper.

"Oh, Selena," he whispered with tears, "I'm so sorry! Mummy's gone! Mum's gone…"

Now her voice lifted into a wail, and her fighting ceased. "I know Mum's gone!" she cried. "But where's Daddy? Where's Dad?"

The words were a knife to his heart – a knife he knew he must endure.

"I went away," he whispered, shaking hard. "I had to go away! I'm so sorry, Selena! But now I'm back! Now I'm back…"

She lifted her head from his chest and looked into his eyes. She was sixteen, her blue eyes intelligent, insightful, and haunted with agony.

Mark touched her face. "My beautiful daughter," he said, and she closed her eyes tightly, shaking her head.

"I don't believe you," she whispered.

"I was a fool," he said. "A fool to leave – I didn't even see."

"I…" She choked, and opened her eyes again; held his eyes again. "I hated you." Her blue eyes filled with tears and pain. "I hated you, and I became Satan incarnate, and…and now I want to die."

Tears filled his eyes. How similar they were!

"I know you want to die," he said, reaching to stroke her black curls, "but I want you to live."

Her face contorted with her struggle. "Please," she whispered, "don't preach to me!"

Pain seized him. "I won't," he whispered.

"I couldn't stand it…"

He wanted to cry. "I won't!" he insisted. "I promise."

"I don't need you to be a priest right now."

"I know…"

"I need you to be…"

"Dad."

The word made her stiffen. He reached to hold her face in both hands – to press his forehead against hers.

"I'm sorry," he whispered. "I'm so sorry."

Sobs began to erupt from within her. "I'm so sorry, Daddy!" she gasped, and he felt her pain as his own.

"It's all right!" he murmured. "It's all right…"

Her face was in his shoulder now, her head lolling on his chest. Torment! Her voice rose to a wail – he ached with her agony, but he remained.

"It's all right," he kept murmuring to her. "It's all right…"

Her fingers were digging into his arms now. He closed his eyes tightly but still held her, and began to rock her again. A song came to him – a song he had sung before the accident.

She straightened suddenly, and looked into his eyes.

"Dad?" she whispered.

"Selena," he whispered back, "I'm going to look after you now."

She trembled. "Really?"

The tears pricked his eyes again. Fatherhood! He hadn't grasped it! He hadn't understood it.

"I'm here now," he said, and a kind of painful wonder lit up her face.

She touched his face.

"I've missed you, Daddy," she said – and then, suddenly, she curled up on his chest.

Mark looked down at her black curls.

Daddy…

This was another deep truth he had locked tightly away.

"I've missed you too," he whispered, and Selena closed her eyes, and soon she was asleep on his chest.

Mark sat there in the first row of the church, holding his daughter. What had happened to her? Some terrible thing: isolation, desperation – evil! But it hadn't finished there! It wasn't over! There was still time.

He trembled, carrying her – he stared at the cross. He murmured over her, drawing her closer, and then closed his eyes to pray for her.

Selena stirred. She was in a haze – almost in sleep.

Something had happened to her. What was it? That man, John, of Whangarei – he had pulled her! He had grasped her shoulders – he had felt just like Joshua!

The light! The same burning light – it hurt! She clung to the light, and the darkness couldn't stay! And…and then, suddenly, with a scream, he was gone.

Emptiness swallowed her. She was alone! But…but, no: not alone. Someone was there – home was there.

Her head was on his chest, now. He was praying! Light! Light…

"Daddy," she whispered, still in sleep. "Daddy…"

"I'm here," he whispered, "I'm here."

The light was stronger than the darkness! Stronger! She tried to touch it, but sleep was taking her – she was so tired! So very tired…

"Sleep," Mark whispered over her, stroking her hair. "Sleep, my beautiful girl."

"Sleep?" Selena whispered back, shifting in his arms, hiding her face in his neck.

"Sleep," Mark murmured, shifting his arms around her. And she obeyed him, and sank deep into sleep.

In wonder Mark gazed down at her. In wonder he gazed at the cross. Then, suddenly, he remembered his other child.

Carefully he lifted Selena in his arms, rising to his feet, and walked down the aisle.

Chapter 37

GRACE

Tristan sat next to Joshua's body. There was blood on the ground – blood was in his mind. He lifted his hand, sticky with it – he laid his hand on Joshua's shoulder, and groaned.

Death. It was everywhere! Death. Touching Joshua did nothing now! His lit eyes were closed. His warm smile was gone.

"What have I done?"

There was a hand on his shoulder, and then a strong arm embraced him. Tristan glanced up – it was Rau.

"Oh, God!" Tristan pleaded, pain twisting his heart – did Rau know? He was holding the rifle!

Rau drew him into his arms. Bewildered, Tristan's control fell away and grief took him. He sobbed, his body shaking hard as pain consumed his soul.

Rau was rocking him. Tristan clung to his shirt, hiding his face in his shoulder.

"Kia tau i te rangimarie," Rau whispered over him. "Kia tau, kia tau i te rangimarie. Be at peace, Tristan. 'By his wounds, we are healed.'"

"I killed him!" Tristan pleaded. "I killed him!"

"We all killed him" Rau murmured. "Be forgiven – be at peace."

Rau's hand moved over his face, while Tristan hid in his shoulder. He was murmuring over him in Maori, praying for him! Tristan tightly closed his eyes. What did he know of God? Nothing, he thought. Nothing but the agony of life. And yet Rau's words soothed him – Rau's care began to heal him.

Tristan became still. He didn't know what this new calm was – something spiritual? He didn't know. Was it some kind of trust? Some deep kind of love? It was something he had never known before.

Rau asked nothing of him. He only held him, only murmured over him; only loved him.

Rau grasped Tristan's hand. Tristan stiffened – it was sticky with Joshua's blood! He was passing it to Rau! He tried to pull back, but Rau grasped him more firmly.

"It's all right," he said. "We'll carry it together."

And now Rau was pulling him to his feet.

Tristan stared at him. He felt strong now! He felt like he could survive what he had done.

Rau smiled gently at him, and the smile reminded him of Joshua. Tears filled Tristan's eyes and he cried, without stopping himself. Then he stepped back.

Rachel was there, beside Joshua. Rachel. Tristan searched her face – he knew she was avoiding him. She was angry. She was keeping watch over Joshua, protecting his body…

"I'm sorry," Tristan whispered, and she shook her head and looked further away.

John was standing behind her. Tristan met his eyes, face to face, over Joshua's body. John! He looked upset, and yet gracious too.

"What do you say to me?" asked Tristan, and pain flooded John's face. Tristan felt his pain, and did not block it.

"You did what you had to do," he said.

Tristan wrapped his arms tightly around himself. "I shouldn't have done it!" he cried. "My God! How could I do it?"

John's face softened, and his hand came to rest on Tristan's shoulder.

"How could you not?"

Tristan was seeing Joshua again, staggering; clutching the crown to his head. Darkness! Darkness was surrounding him! Darkness was killing him…

Tristan moaned, and spoke. "I still shouldn't have killed him."

"You're right," said John, "but it still had to happen."

Tristan reached out and grasped John's shoulder in return.

"Thank you," he whispered, and John nodded, with tears.

Tristan looked down at Joshua's face. Joshua: kind, insightful – seeing what others did not see; being what others were not. What was it about him? A light – a light, frightening sometimes. A power greater than it should be, suggesting something more – suggesting something much bigger, or even someone much bigger.

"I am the boat for the coming tsunami: with me, you will be safe."

What had it been, that darkness? What had he been carrying, in his last moments? Tristan couldn't comprehend it, not as John did. He couldn't comprehend the magnitude of what had taken place. But he remembered the person: his words, his eyes, his face…his smile…

Ninety Mile Beach…The storm had been coming, on the horizon: that smile had suddenly disappeared, and in its place had been intensity.

"What is it?" Tristan had breathed. *"What do you see?"*

"Some things are better not to know – not until their right time."

Now Tristan stared at his dead blood-stained face. He had known! Dismayed, Tristan suddenly realised Joshua had seen his own death, after all! And…and he had seen Tristan pulling the trigger…

Tristan swayed, and sagged down to his knees beside Joshua's head. What kind of death was this? What kind of life? Living with one's own murderer and embracing one's own death? Joshua had loved him! Even knowing what he would do, he had loved him.

Tristan remembered those last moments now; he remembered them with agony. Joshua had grasped his shoulder! Had fallen to his knees in front of him.

"Father!" he had cried out to God. "Don't hold it against them! They have no idea what they are doing!"

The darkness! As if drowning! As if drowning…And then, the shots.

Tristan reached a trembling hand out to Joshua's chest now – to the bullet holes – and tears filled his eyes.

"I'm so sorry!" he cried to him. "My friend! I'm so sorry!" And he wept.

The images of war were before him again, now. Screaming! Death! His rifle, shooting! Shooting, as though…as though they were not human beings he was killing…He shook as he regretted his actions, his hand remaining on Joshua's bullet holes, his eyes closed. Death! Death!

"I'm so sorry!" he whispered. "I'm so sorry!"

The scapegoat! He felt no terror, now! No fear. He could look at the images! He could feel them! He knew he was carried – the boat, for the tsunami! He was carried, and grief filled him, and the grief was good, and right.

But there was a final image: the hardest to look at – the hardest to resolve.

It was his mother.

He saw her now – her body, on the stretcher. Her face, dead, dripping blood, like Joshua's…He saw her, and cried, and then saw his father, sitting next to her, his shoulders sagging, his face in his hands.

"It wasn't his fault." Joshua was before him again, on Ninety Mile Beach.

"What do you mean?" he had cried.

"You know what I mean."

It wasn't his fault…Tristan realised it now, painfully, clearly – he had blamed his father for his mother's death! He had blamed him! He'd cut him off and had joined the army, in his fury.

"I hate him," he'd told Joshua.

Now there was no hatred, only regret! Such regret, for all of his life! All of his life…

He moved his hand from Joshua's wounds to his forehead, and closed his eyes.

"Forgive me," he prayed. "My precious friend, forgive me."

And then he opened his eyes.

Someone was standing on the other side of Joshua. Tristan looked up, from the leather shoes, up the grey trousers, to the creased shirt, and then to the face above.

Mark Blake held his eyes. There were no bishop robes, only the simple clothes of an everyday man. His face was transparent! Vulnerable! Tears were in his eyes! Grief passed between them: grief, and deep regret.

Mark's hand was reaching for him now – Tristan was pulled up and into his father's arms, beside Joshua's body.

"I'm sorry," Mark whispered into his ear, and Tristan shook in his arms.

"I…" Tristan stuttered, and couldn't find the words! "I was wrong…"

"So was I."

"I…I loved her…" His heart twisted. It was such agony, to lose her!

Mark drew back from him now, grasping his hand. Joshua's blood was sticky between them, but Mark didn't flinch. He was crying, his eyes wet but filled with strength.

"I loved her too!" said Mark. "So much, Tristan! I loved your mother so much!"

Mark's body shook, and Tristan grasped his other hand, and folded both arms on his own chest.

"She was beautiful!" said Mark, and Tristan nodded, tears flowing freely.

"Beautiful."

"I shouldn't have sped…"

Tristan quickly shook his head. "Oh, Dad," he whispered, "when I had my car, I sped all the time…"

Mark laughed gently, even as he cried. And his eyes changed into an expression Tristan hadn't seen for nine years.

"Stay with us, Tristan," said Mark. "Come back home."

Tears filled Tristan's eyes – tears that would not stop.

"Home?" he whispered.

"Where will you go now?" asked Mark. "Now that Joshua has gone?"

Tristan hadn't given it a thought. He stared into his father's eyes, into his sudden yet familiar love.

"I killed him," he whispered. "I killed him, and he forgave me."

"So did I," Mark whispered.

"I pulled the trigger – I should go to prison. I'm willing to go to prison."

"Maybe so," said Mark, "but where is your accuser?"

Tristan looked around himself. Rau was standing aside with John, both quiet. The crowd had left! The army had dispersed – he had acted as one of them! The police had also gone. Who would they arrest, their own prime minister?

James Connor was there! Tristan saw him, standing in Hill Street, watching from afar; still looking shocked. The Governor General had left. A female minister stood praying on the steps of Saint Peter's.

Even Rachel's anger had eased, replaced by the deepest of grief.

Where is your accuser? Selena lay on the ground, but now she stirred and rose to her knees, reaching out to touch Joshua's face, looking confused. Tristan remembered how her eyes had been: black as death, bitter, evil.

The accuser was gone.

"Home?" Tristan whispered, looking back into his father's face. "Give me some time! I think I need more time…"

"I'll give you time," said Mark gently. Tristan released his hands and stepped back, and as he did so he felt a strange sense of peace, and it was good.

Mark now knelt next to Joshua's body. Tristan watched him, and stiffened as he suddenly remembered his father had been on the verge of suicide. How had he come back? Tristan glanced at Rau, and at John, and then back down to his father.

Mark was reaching, to touch the face – to touch the bullet holes.

"'By his wounds we are healed,'" he murmured, and then he unbuttoned his own shirt, leaving himself naked and shivering in the autumn air, and laid it over Joshua's chest and head.

"Reverend Rau," he said, looking up again, "let's arrange his funeral."

"His family!" said Rachel suddenly. "Where are his family?"

"We are his family," John replied. "He always said so."

"His mother," said Tristan, with tears. "He had a mother, in Kaitaia."

"I will find her," said Rau. "I will bring her down. His father has passed on. But, Bishop Blake…"

"Yes?" asked Mark.

"No one will attend a funeral service – they will be too afraid."

Mark swallowed, and Tristan saw the understanding in his eyes.

"Very well," he said, and called over the other lady minister who had been waiting. "We'll make it a private burial. We will bury him here, Eun Ae – in the burial ground of Saint Peter's."

Her face broke into a sad smile. "I'll make some calls," she said.

"Thank you," said Mark.

Tristan watched his father rise to his feet again. He quickly reached to unbutton his own shirt for him, but Mark laid a hand on his shoulder.

"I'm all right," he said.

Selena was sitting quietly next to Joshua's dead body. Tristan reached out a hand to lay it on her head. She was hidden away, and yet…and yet she was Selena again…

"What happened?" he murmured, and Mark's gentle voice replied.

"More than you need to burden yourself with."

"Will she be all right?"

"I believe so – now I've finally worked out what to do."

Mark reached down to her and lifted her to her feet, murmuring in her ear, and she shrank away with him from the body.

Tristan was almost alone, now, with Joshua – soon he would be buried! Soon he would be gone.

Only one remained: Rachel.

She was gazing down at Mark's shirt, resting over Joshua. Her face was contorting with the finality of the gesture. Then Tristan watched fury enter her eyes, as she turned to look at Connor.

"Don't," whispered Tristan. "Don't make the same mistake I made…"

But she rose to her feet, leaving Joshua behind, and he couldn't stop her from striding toward the shocked man.

Chapter 38

FURY

Rachel strode toward her father. Anger filled her – fury owned her. Joshua was dead! Joshua was dead, and her father had killed him! It was his fault!

Connor was standing alone. His face was pale – she didn't care. She hated him! She hated him for what he had done.

"How dare you?" she cried as she reached him, pressing her face into his. "You bastard!"

He looked bewildered at her onslaught, and struggled to speak.

"I…I didn't know what to do…"

"So you chose this?" said Rachel, jabbing her finger back toward Joshua. "You're a murderer, Dad! A murderer!"

"The people chose it!" Connor tried to defend himself.

"Don't give me that crap!" said Rachel. "It's your fault! You set them all up…"

"No," Connor whispered.

"You killed an innocent man! You're corrupt! A dictator of the worst kind – killing anyone who gets in your way!"

Connor was shaking hard now – tears were forming in his eyes, his forehead creasing into strained lines.

"I'm not a dictator," he whispered, "I believe in democracy! Democracy!"

"Bullshit!" said Rachel. "It's your kingdom, that's all! Your kingdom, and curse anyone who resists."

He was silenced – she had silenced him! But now someone approached – it was Mark Blake, still without his shirt.

"If you must blame someone, blame me," he said.

Rachel stared at him. "You?"

"I forced him to do it."

Connor was staring at Blake now. He shook his head.

"You have destroyed our nation," he whispered. "You have destroyed me!"

Blake's eyes widened. "James," he said, "this wasn't your fault – it was much bigger than you."

"Much bigger than me?" cried Connor. "What's going to happen now, Mark? Our constitution has been dissolved! The Queen to rule – how? With the army! A military state! Brother will fight brother!

"Our army isn't big enough, Mark! War will come! Civil war. Our nation will be divided, and then…" His eyes clouded with utter dread. "Then we will be conquered."

Blake frowned at him. "James," he said quietly, "there's nothing we could do to stop this."

Connor swallowed. "I listened to you!" he said. "I should have followed my own judgement!"

"You're right," said Blake, "but now it is done."

"Done?" cried Connor. "How easily you dismiss it! You took me to Hell, Blake! You took me straight to Hell!"

Blake's face drained colour, and now Connor looked back to Rachel.

"Hate me," he said. "Do whatever you like. We're in trouble now! We're in trouble, and there's no going back."

He gave a sideways glance to Blake then turned on his heel to walk back into the Parliament grounds.

Rachel frowned, now confused. She looked at Blake. Had he led her father astray?

"Don't hate him," said Blake. "His hands were tied."

"Did you tie them?"

Blake took a deep breath and then released it. "In a manner of speaking, yes."

Rachel's anger grew again, now against this man before her. "Then you were the one?" she asked. "Who led him to public disgrace?"

Mark straightened and swallowed. "Yes," he said. "What you're saying is true."

Rachel stared at him. Who was he? The Bishop of Wellington, a friend of her father since high school. She knew him! Regal robes, high and mighty position.

"You make me sick," she said, "bloody ministers! Hypocritical, standing up there preaching and then leading us all astray…"

Blake's face flushed, but he remained silent as she continued.

"…always thinking you're better than we are, always judging, always condemning…"

"I'm not condemning…" said Blake, and Rachel scowled, jabbing her finger back toward Joshua.

"Oh, yeah?" she asked. "What do you think you did with him?"

Blake fleetingly closed his eyes and then opened them again.

"You're right," he said. "I did condemn."

"You stand up there at the altar, as if God himself is speaking through you," she said, "when it isn't God! What is your voice, but the pathetic mutterings of a twisted man? You're not a child of God – you're twice the child of Hell I am!"

His eyes widened – she had reached him! She had caused him pain, at least some of the pain he had caused her! But now another voice was intervening.

"Rachel!" It was John, his voice strong and penetrating. She looked at him – he was shaking his head, his gaze intense.

"Don't do this," he said. "This isn't what he saved you for!"

What he saved her for?

Rachel remembered, then, the boiling water at Hell's Way! The agony, and death, and…and life again…Joshua, burnt! Burnt, having saved her…

Shame filled her. She was hatred, when he was love! She was bitterness, when he was forgiveness…

She turned, weeping, to run away, but Blake was grasping her arm.

"Wait," he said quietly, and she shook her head.

"Please let me go," she whispered.

"You're right about me," he said. "Everything you said was right."

She trembled. "But everything about me is wrong."

"That's why he did it," said Mark. "You do know that, don't you? That's why he died for us."

She stared into his eyes. That's why he died?

"I can't bear to be saved," she whispered, "not if it means that he should die! Not if it means that he should be shot!"

The memory was there again: that terrible crown, and his suffering! His body jerking back with the bullets! She couldn't save him!

"I'm a doctor," she said, "but he was the real healer, not me! He was – and now he's dead, and…and I hate us all…"

Mark's face was drawn with grief. She tore herself away, and ran with the sound of his voice at her back.

"Rachel!"

Pain drove her, through the streets of Wellington. She ran and ran until her heart heaved in her chest, but she could not stop until she reached Wellington Harbour. She stood on the edge of the water staring down into the depths.

His face, when he died! *"It's finished!"* he had said. *"It's sorted!"* He had even smiled! But she fought his offering. They weren't worth it – none of them were! They weren't worth it, if this should be the cost of their salvation!

She sank down to the water's edge, dangling her feet over. Did she want suicide? No – no. Only some kind of peace, some kind of resolution – but it never came.

"Love…" She whispered into the water. "What's the use? It costs too much! Too much." Life cost too much. Humanity cost too much! And yet…and yet she knew Joshua would not see it that way; she knew he had not seen it that way. He had been more than she could ever be. Why had she not died, or any one of them? Why him? Why him?

"It's a travesty," she whispered, and terrible grief threatened her heart – and then someone lowered himself to sit beside her, dangling his leather shoes.

It was her father.

Connor sat shoulder to shoulder with her, at the water's edge, staring down into the water. He reached over and took her hand. He squeezed it.

"You followed me?" asked Rachel, and he shrugged.

"Got nothing better to do," he said, and Rachel elbowed him, and he actually smiled.

"What the hell happened?" she asked, and he shook his head.

"I don't know!" he said. "I'm out of a job! I…" And now he released her to bury his face in his hands.

Rachel looked at him, at his sagging shoulders. She laid an arm around him.

"Maybe it's good to be out of that job for a while."

"Maybe," he whispered into his hands.

"I shouldn't have said the dictator thing."

He shrugged painfully. "You're not the first."

"I…" She considered him, considered Joshua – considered the whole situation. "I love you."

He lifted his head from his hands, and looked at her.

"I'm scared, Rachel," he whispered. "I don't know what's going to become of us now."

Rachel held his eyes – his fear. Joshua's words were with her then! The tsunami! The war. Fear! And…and trust…

"Maybe it's not up to us," she said. "Maybe none of this has been up to us."

"Resorting back to our church days?" said Connor with irony. "Blake getting to you now?"

"He said something."

"Oh, yeah," Connor replied, "I'll bet."

"I…I basically called him a bastard, and…and he agreed."

Connor stared into her eyes, and then he suddenly laughed. "He admitted he was a prick?"

"Well, he didn't quite put it like that."

"No kidding!"

"But…he took the blame, Dad."

Now guilt filled Connor's face. "You know I don't agree with that."

"I know."

"But…maybe there's some hope for Blakey after all." And his face broke into a wide grin.

Rachel sat with him at the waterfront for a long time. She knew John, Rau and Blake would be moving Joshua's body, but she couldn't bear to watch. Instead she sat with her father, talking about nothing but feeling everything, at the same time as him.

His arm was around her shoulders now, and she leaned against him. Neither spoke of what had happened to Joshua – neither could.

The water was deep, and still. Father and daughter stared down into it. There was no resolution, but at least they were together.

Chapter 39

REST AND PEACE

John stood in Saint Peter's Cathedral. Joshua was there, his body lying in an open wooden casket. John stood next to him, in the aisle, before the pulpit – facing the cross. He laid his hand on the white linen covering Joshua's chest, and trembled. Under his hand, under the linen, the bullets remained in Joshua's body.

John lifted his eyes to Joshua's face. He was clean now, with no trace of blood. His brown curls fell loosely around his white face. His vibrant eyes were closed; his tender voice was silenced.

Grief gripped John's chest. He stretched his fingers to touch Joshua's face. He was at peace now! It was finished! It was done.

Tears filled John's eyes and his vision blurred, but he didn't care. The tears fell down his cheeks, and onto Joshua's body.

A woman's hand took his. Surprised, John looked up at her, standing on the other side of Joshua. This was his mother! Dear God, his mother! Her brown eyes held his, her brown hair framed her light brown face.

"Madam…" he whispered, "I am so sorry…"

Her hand tightened on his! Tightened, while his body was flooding with regret! While her eyes were flooding with tears.

"It was meant to be this way," she whispered.

"Meant?" John choked.

"From the beginning," she said, "he was different! From the very beginning…"

John swallowed. "You knew he was going to be killed."

Her face contorted with grief. "I knew," she whispered, "I just didn't know when."

Astounded, John began to weep, but now Rau's hand was on his shoulder.

John tightly shut his eyes. Pain engulfed him! The vision, on Mount Victoria! Joshua, in agony, under the tree! And then just outside, staggering, under the crown – staggering, under the darkness. The evil was smothering him! And then, the shots – then, his body thrown back, choking…choking, and dying…

John groaned, and choked, and Rau's arms wrapped around him and drew him away to a chair.

"You were there," Rau whispered. "You felt it all."

"I couldn't leave him," John whispered back. "I knew! I knew how bad it would be, but…I couldn't leave him…"

Rau was silent alongside him. Where had he been? John didn't know, caught somewhere in the crowd, most likely.

Rau grasped his hand now, and lifted him again to his feet. He was the leader! John had known it for a while: Rau was their leader.

John watched him, and then, with Rau, cast his eyes over the Cathedral. Reverend Choo was standing at the pulpit, preparing for the service. Mark Blake was standing near her, in his full regalia. John would have resented those robes, but suddenly realised he wore them out of respect for God. It had nothing to do with Mark himself. It was their way! Richness and beauty, worn to express the richness and beauty of God.

Rau turned, then, and looked towards the back of the church. Tristan was standing with his arms wrapped tightly around himself. He had come! John admired him – to be here took courage. What pain was in him? What regret? He couldn't come closer, but he remained with them, in the same way he always had.

Rau moved down the aisle, to speak with him. John watched as Rau said a few words and even gently punched Tristan in the arm, his face breaking into a grin. Tristan managed a sad smile, but still shook his head. He couldn't do it! Rau let him be.

Sadness filled Rau's face as he walked back up the aisle, a sadness reflecting Tristan's own. And then John suddenly wondered about Rachel. Where was she? He had last seen her arguing with Mark Blake! He remembered…

"Everything about me is wrong."

She had run, and she hadn't come back.

"Where are you?" he murmured, with fear, and then he turned.

Eun Ae Choo began the service. John listened to her gentle voice as she recited the set words.

"We have come together to remember before God the life of Joshua Davidson, to commend him to God's keeping, to commit his body to be…"

Now she hesitated, and Mark looked at Joshua's mother. "Buried, or cremated?" he asked quietly, and more tears filled her eyes.

"Buried," she whispered.

Eun Ae continued. "…to commit his body to be buried, and to comfort those who mourn with our sympathy and with our love; in the hope we share through the death and resurrection of Jesus Christ.[25]"

Her brown eyes were alive, although also sad, her face reflecting both joy and grief. John was surprised at her – she was so different from himself, and yet, in those moments, wholly one.

Now Rau was standing tall, next to Joshua, facing the congregation – facing John, and Tristan.

"Hear the words of Jesus Christ our Saviour," he said, "'Ko ahau te aranga, me te ora: ko ia e whakapono ana ki ahau, ahakoa kua mate, e ora ano: e kore ano hoki e mate ake nga tangata katoa e ora ana, a e whakapono ana ki ahau.'"

Joshua's mother began to cry, with the words John did not understand, and Rau began to translate:

"'I am the resurrection and the life,'" he said, quoting Jesus, "'even in death, anyone who believes in me will live."

"The boat, again," John whispered, "for the tsunami…"

He began to tremble, then, looking again at Joshua's face. Would he live? Would Joshua actually live? He had faith in God – would that faith be enough to raise his spirit into Heaven to be with God?

A resurrection? God raising Joshua's spirit? Yes – John could bring himself to trust in this.

He sank down to his knees, in the church, and closed his eyes. Faith, in death, was painful! Why was it so painful?

"'Set your troubled hearts at rest,'" Rau continued, and John knew he was looking at him. "'Trust in God always; trust also in me.'"

Trust…John took in a trembling breath, and let it out again. *Trust.*

"'God so loved the world that he gave his only Son that whoever believes in him should not perish but have eternal life.'"

John could trust that God would not let Joshua perish.

With relief he looked up, still on his knees. Rau was smiling gently at him, as he continued.

"God our Comforter," he said, "you are a refuge and a strength for us, a helper close at hand in times of distress. May your Holy Spirit lift us above our natural sorrow, to the peace and light of your constant love; through Jesus Christ our Lord. Amen."

John rose to his feet. He could trust in that light, and love, for Joshua, although not for himself. Joshua would be safe! Joshua would live.

"Our Father in Heaven," Rau began to pray, "hallowed be your name, your kingdom come, your will be done, on earth as in heaven…"

Here John's mind drifted again, into his own grief; into his own exhaustion. His eyes drifted closed, and he swayed on his feet.

"…Save us from the time of trial, and deliver us from evil. For the kingdom, the power, and the glory are yours now and forever."

"Amen," John whispered instinctively as Eun Ae spoke again.

"Now, therefore, Joshua Davidson," she began, and John's eyes opened with new tears. This was it! This was the end. "We commit your body to be buried, earth to earth, ashes to ashes, dust to dust…"

His mother's voice lifted now into an open wail, and John's grief rose up in sobs to meet hers.

"…in the sure and certain hope of the resurrection to eternal life in Jesus Christ our Lord."

"Amen," his mother and John said, as one.

It was over.

John stood, still and stiff, as Mark now walked up to the coffin. He looked at Joshua's face and his own contorted.

"Blessed are the dead who die in the Lord," he murmured, "for they rest from their labours." And then reached down, lifted the lid of the coffin and placed it over Joshua's body, sealing him in.

John stared at the coffin. It was being lifted. Mark himself was lifting it, onto his shoulder, and Rau. John rushed forward to help them. The three struggled with the weight. And then suddenly Tristan was there. He glanced across at John with a grief-stricken frown, as he also lifted the coffin onto his shoulder.

They carried Joshua down the aisle, through the glass doors and down the steps to the street, where they turned right, passed through a gate, and entered a small private graveyard alongside the Cathedral.

A fresh grave had been dug out; a large heap of soil lay alongside.

John swallowed as they lowered Joshua's coffin to the ground, and then gently into the hole. Another man, who'd been waiting, leaned over the coffin and sealed it shut, with hammer and nails.

Eun Ae stood at the foot of the grave, Joshua's mother beside her.

"We have entrusted our brother Joshua into the hands of God," said Eun Ae, as the man reached for a spade and began to throw soil over the coffin. "We now commit his body to the ground."

It wasn't long before the coffin was completely buried.

"'The Lord is my shepherd,'" said Rau, "'therefore I shall not want.'"

"'Though I walk through the valley of the shadow of death,'" Joshua's mother murmured, "'I will fear no evil.'"

"'Surely your goodness and mercy shall follow me all the days of my life,'" said Mark.

"'And I will dwell in the house of the Lord forever.'[26]" It was Tristan.

Surprised, John looked at him. Tristan? He searched his eyes. The words were familiar to him – where from, another funeral? John saw it in him: his mother's funeral. Did he believe? Not a full belief, and yet, somehow, in that moment, a partial belief: in that moment, somehow, a trust for Joshua's wellbeing with God, and the wellbeing of his mother.

It was over.

The funeral director moved his hammer and spade away, and he left them in privacy. Eun Ae moved amongst them, gently grasping everyone's hand, and then she also moved away. Mark looked at each one in turn, he smiled sadly, grasped Tristan's hand, and led him away.

Only Joshua's mother and John remained.

She looked at him and touched his face. "You were his brother," she said, and John cried.

"I don't want to leave him," he whispered.

"Then stay," she said. "It is the Maori way."

"Stay?"

"Stay here." She gestured to the grave. "Stay, and keep watch over his body."

"If the army finds out," John whispered, "they might take his body away."

She nodded and then smiled sadly. "Don't worry, John," she said, "he is safe in the hands of te Atua now."

John watched her bow her head, and then move away from him, through the gate and out.

John was alone.

The grave was fresh, and silent. He gazed down at it. There were others, old, with large, engraved tomb stones. Joshua's had no expensive stone, only a simple wooden cross pressed into the soil over his head.

John sat down next to the grave. It was beside the tall white stone wall, which hid the graves from the city. He leaned against it; the stone chilled his back. He shivered, and closed his eyes. Joshua! He remembered him – he slipped into a restless doze, recalling his face and his words. Time passed, he couldn't tell how long. One time he awoke it was dark, and cold. He looked up to see Mark Blake placing food beside him, and laying a blanket over him.

John wasn't hungry. He left the food on the plate on the ground, and fell asleep.

Exhaustion had its way with him. Dreams and nightmares wrestled in his heart – dreams of Joshua alive, and the light in his eyes; nightmares of his staggering, his cries, and his body jerking back into death…

When he woke again, morning had come and Joshua's mother was there.

"It's all right," she said, "I'll look after him."

John frowned, and felt his body's needs. She sat, and he rose and stumbled out through the gate. His legs were stiff! They hurt! Mark was there, without the robes, and the sleeves of his shirt were rolled up.

"Come," he said, grasping his hand, and John stumbled after him. Mark led him back into the church and down the side aisle into the changing rooms, where robes were hanging up, and there were toilets, and showers…

"Am I allowed in here?" John whispered, and Mark smiled gently.

"You are now," he said.

Mark had arranged a change of clothes. Surprised, John stared at them.

"Why are you doing this?" asked John, and Mark laid a hand on his shoulder.

"I can't fix what I did," he said. "I can't bring Joshua back. But I can help his followers."

Tears filled John's eyes. "Thank you," he choked, and Mark patted his shoulder.

"Get ready," he said, and John obeyed him.

Refreshed, John walked out of the robe room.

The Cathedral was silent; empty. John wandered down the side aisle, toward the glass doors, but then he hesitated. He instinctively turned, and slipped between the chairs into the central aisle.

The cross was far away, in the inner sanctuary – Jesus was hanging there, painted on tiles. John gazed at it and wandered closer, up the steps toward the railing; toward the table before the cross.

Someone cleared their throat, near him. It was Mark, sitting in a wooden chair on the inside of the railing, near the table.

"Should I not be here?" John whispered. Mark opened his mouth, and closed it again. His eyes passed over John, and then moved to Jesus on the cross.

"The veil has been torn away," he murmured to himself, and John did not understand him. Then Mark rose to his feet and ushered him in.

"Come," he said, and John entered into the inner sanctuary.

The table was there, with white linen – a silver cup and plate, with wine, and wafers.

"I never understood Communion," John murmured, reaching tentatively out to touch the silver. "Not really."

"Neither did I," said Mark, his voice sounding wry.

John lifted his eyes over the table, to Jesus hanging on the cross.

His eyes, his face…

"He looks sad," John murmured quietly.

"He's carrying the sins of the world," Mark replied.

"Sin is such a judgmental word," said John, with pain. "It makes it sound like God hates us; like he wants us to go to Hell. Like he wants to punish us."

"No," said Mark, his voice choking.

John looked at him. "What is it?" he asked.

"Something I didn't understand before," Mark replied.

"What?"

"The love."

"Love?" asked John, and he shrugged slightly. "What does it even mean? It's a cliché – all the doorknockers use it."

Mark was silent. Then he rose to his feet and moved closer to John, so they stood side by side. Mark's eyes went up the cross, and John followed his gaze – back up to Jesus.

"That's why he did it," said Mark, "to show us! To show us what God's love actually means."

John frowned, gazing at him. "A man, hanging on a cross?" he said. "I don't understand."

"What about a man shot?" asked Mark. "Do you understand that better?"

Grief gripped John again; hard, stinging. His body, thrown back! The blood.

He gasped, and Mark gripped his shoulder.

"You know why he did it, John," he said. "You told me, in this very place! All the 'crap,' you said – he died to take it all away! He died for God to forgive us, and fix us."

"All the darkness," John whispered, staring up at Jesus's face. "So much darkness!"

"He has carried it all," said Mark. "'It is finished.'"

John reached up to touch the bottom of the cross. "I think I get it," he said. "I think I'm starting to get it."

"You get it for all the darkness of the world," said Mark, "but do you get it for yourself?"

John frowned. "For myself?"

Mark walked now behind the table and lifted the silver cup and plate.

"That's what these mean, John," he said. "That's why he gave them to us. They represent his body given for us, so that we could live. And when we eat and drink, we take into ourselves what he has done. We trust in it, and we confess our own darkness, and we live. No more darkness! No more guilt. Time for the light! Time for goodness, and fullness of life – eternal life, here first, and then forever."

John looked at the bread and wine – the body and the blood.

"Do I have to eat bread and drink wine," he asked, "to be safe? To be right with God? To live forever? Do I have to eat these to live?"

"No," said Mark, "they are symbols. In our hearts and minds, we need to know it! In our hearts and minds, we need to receive it. These symbols are one way, but there are others…"

"Other ways…" John murmured, looking at the silver cup and plate. "If he was here right now, how would he express this? What would he use?"

"To place the truth into your body – to place it into your mind and heart?" said Mark. "Such intimacy, John! To offer one's own body and blood to save another. Do you see it?"

"I do," said John, "but it's not our language! It's not our way."

"Then find it in your language," said Mark. "Find it in your way. Find it, John, and then pass it on."

John gazed at him, and then came the familiar tears. "Who am I?" he asked. "To find it? It's not my body – it's not my blood! It was his! His…"

Grief took him again, and he ran – away from the altar, away from the cross, out of the Cathedral and back into the graveyard.

The day passed slowly. John sat with Joshua's mother next to his grave. He sat and thought about Mark's words, and remembered the sad face of Jesus on the cross, and remembered the pain of Joshua's death. He had died for everyone, John knew that! He had died to carry the dark thoughts and actions of everyone! But how to explain that, to a nation in upheaval? How to put it into the right words…?

And how to explain the tragedy of his death – the finality! The scapegoat, gone: the injustice, with no resolution.

Twilight was upon him. Joshua's mother had gone. John's vision was fading, and his stomach was groaning.

"Eat," said Mark's voice. "You haven't eaten since he died."

"Can't," John whispered. Mark's hand was offering food to his mouth and John obeyed, but he choked on the crumbs. Mark was sitting with him now, offering him water, and John swallowed. He sat against Mark for a while, feeling faint. Mark offered him more water and food, and he followed.

John sank into sleep. It was a new kind of sleep – strangely new. It felt like he was in a different place. He breathed, and turned, and rested, and then heard a voice.

"John."

Was he dead? He felt relief – dead? Could that be the resolution?

"John."

He shifted, on the ground. The ground! It was still there, but he felt different! He struggled to follow the voice, and then he felt a hand on his shoulder, and gasped: it couldn't be!

"John."

John opened his eyes, and Joshua's face was before him. His hands were grasping his arms.

John stared at him. His smile! Oh, dear God, his smile – it was so wide! There was joy in his eyes; joy in his face! John trembled, and reached out to touch his face – it was such a vivid dream! Such a wonderful vision to see the yearning of his own heart; the longing of his soul. It had never happened! The death had only been a nightmare.

John sank against him, and laughed, but then cried. No! No – the death had happened! It was this that was not real! This that he could not trust…

He straightened, on his knees – he drew back, but now he was being shaken.

"John!" said Joshua's voice. "John!"

Surely Mark's face was about to appear. Surely it was him again shaking his body.

But the face remained, the eyes changing to intense purpose. His hand was being grasped and he was being pulled to his feet, and moved a few steps, next to…to the…

The grave had been disrupted! The soil was sitting again in a pile alongside the grave. The coffin was open, with the lid on top of the soil, and…and the body was gone.

"My God," John breathed, "the army – they must have come! Stolen the body."

"While you were sleeping?" Joshua's voice murmured. "And they left you to sleep?"

"They don't care about me," John explained to the one he was certain was only in his mind. "They only care about you."

"They'll care about you soon," said Joshua, and John stared at him. Those were words John's mind would not have created.

"What do you mean?"

Joshua was smiling again, a wide grin, and for a moment John didn't fight it – for a moment he allowed himself to believe he was actually there. He reached in wonder to touch his face again, as a child, and then he heard running footsteps.

It was Rau. He looked stunned as he stared at Joshua. As if he was there! And then he fell to his knees before him.

"Master!" he said. "E te Ariki!"

"Rau," said Joshua, laying a hand on his head.

Rau began to sob, and John couldn't understand why – surely it was all a dream! Surely all of it was a vision.

"Do you love me, Rau?" asked Joshua, and Rau's face contorted in pain.

Joshua turned back to John. He was grasping his hand again and, with his other hand, he began to unbutton the clean white shirt he was wearing.

"Look, John," he said, and he drew John's fingers in between the unbuttoned shirt edges. There were bullet wounds in his chest! Cavities, and yet healed! Scars, healed…

Joshua pulled his fingers over the scars and into the cavities.

John stiffened, and was jerked out of his daze. Dear God – his bullet wounds! His wounds were still there – they were real! Real…He could feel them! He was touching them…

Now Joshua reached into his clean jeans' pocket, and pulled out the five bullets. He reached for John's hand and he placed them in his palm.

John swayed, staring at them. The bullets were out of shape. They'd been used, crushed, and now they were out of his body! They had been removed.

John's wonder shifted to become terror. He was alive? Actually alive? Not only a spirit, he was physically back?

Shock filled him. He sank back to his knees. Joshua caught him, and lowered him gently to the ground.

"My God," John whispered, "Master – you're alive? You're alive?"

"I am," Joshua murmured over him, "and now you must tell the others."

"Tell them?" John breathed.

"Tell them," said Joshua, "and I'll catch up with them soon."

He stepped back away, glanced again at Rau, and then suddenly disappeared.

John was fixed to the ground, on his knees. He stared up at Rau, whose face was serious.

"I'm dreaming," he said, "I have to be dreaming."

Rau shook his head. "No," he said, "I knew this would happen."

"You knew?"

"It is written."

"What did he mean, asking you if you loved him?"

Rau's face clouded, and then he turned and ran away.

John was alone. He noticed, now, the early morning light, and the fresh cool of the new day. He saw the soil of the grave sitting tidily back in its pile, with the lid of the coffin neatly placed on top, upside down, the nails pointing straight through the lid, as if unused.

There was no sign of any disruption in the graveyard at all.

Had it been a vision? Had Rau himself been a vision? No, Rau's grief had been real! And the bullets were still lying in his hand…

John trembled, now, looking at them. Five bullets. Joshua was dead, but now he was alive! Buried, but now walking again!

The injustice of the death had been undone.

A sudden surge of hope thrust John to his feet. Life had overcome death! Light had overcome darkness!

It was finished! It was over! And now there was no going back.

John placed the bullets safely in his pocket, and strode out of the graveyard.

Chapter 40

VICTORY IN DEFEAT

Rau sat outside Saint Peter's. He was away from the graveyard, away from the cross and the altar, leaning against the wall of the church with his face in his hands. Shame! Shame. Their beloved friend was alive! Joshua was alive! And he had denied him…

"Do you love me, Rau?" Joshua had asked, and his words had been agony to him.

From his place, Rau could see across the road to the intersection where Joshua had died, through the black iron gate into the Parliament grounds beyond, to the Parliament buildings, and the Beehive. There were still army officers, patrolling the ground! There was no functioning Parliament now, only the Governor General and an emergency council; only the Queen of England, ruling direct.

Rau shifted his eyes over to Molesworth Street. It was there he had denied him! It was there he had run away.

"Aue te whakama," Rau whispered, "I have brought shame upon my whanau."

Generations of priests! And he had failed them all. When the ultimate test had come, the peak of ministry choice, he had failed.

His mana was lost – he had brought humiliation to his own.

Pain filled him, but this was not the greatest pain. Not only had he brought shame to his whanau in Kerikeri, he had brought shame to his whanau here! He had brought shame to Joshua! He had brought shame to God.

He buried his face back into his hands, but now someone was sitting beside him.

"Rau." It was Joshua's voice.

Rau writhed in his presence. "Master," he whispered into his hands.

Joshua's arm was around his shoulders now. "Rau," he said, "look at me."

Look at Joshua's victory? Look at his love? Look at his goodness, when Rau had missed it all? He had fled! He had abandoned him, at the peak of his offering!

Rau lifted his head to look at him, and shame flooded him as Joshua's eyes met his.

"Do you love me?" asked Joshua, and Rau moaned with his confession of the truth.

"Yes," he whispered.

"My whanau needs your help," said Joshua.

Rau tilted his head, looking at him. His whanau? The others?

Joshua grasped his hand, and searched his eyes.

"Rau," he repeated, "do you really love me?"

Rau swallowed. "Yes," he said.

"Then take care of all my whanau."

Joshua's eyes were finding him and then Joshua grasped both of his arms, and lifted him to his feet.

"Rau," he said, and Rau held his eyes. "Do you love me enough to take care of all of them?"

He gestured around the Parliament grounds, and Wellington, and beyond – Rau knew, to all of Aotearoa. Tears filled Rau's eyes, now, and a profound, deep love suddenly filled his heart.

"Ae," he whispered, sinking to his knees. "I love you, Master. Anei taku aroha!"

"Then take care of my Iwi, Rau," said Joshua. "My body and my blood are given! My tribe is born."

Relief filled Rau, a painful, releasing relief. He was back! Joshua was back! And Rau was back. Released! Released to lead! And...and there was more...

Joshua's eyes were changing from intense purpose to deep, girding grief.

"One day," he said, "some men will kill you, Rau, because of me."

Rau gazed up at him from his knees, and the words, intended to warn, were also freedom to his heart. Joshua's face was close to his, and Rau pressed his forehead to Joshua's; his nose to Joshua's.

"Amine," he said. "E te whanau, we are the body of Christ! We are bound by the love of Christ."

"Amine," Joshua whispered, and he lifted Rau again to his feet.

Rau noticed John, now, coming around the corner of the church. John was gazing at Joshua, utter wonder in his eyes, like a child. Rau could read his thoughts – his amazement that Joshua was alive!

"What will happen to him, Master?" asked Rau, and Joshua's gaze became far away.

"He will still be here," he said, "until he sees the end."

"The end?"

"The end is coming," said Joshua. "The tsunami! The war. Birth pains! And then, the next age. Light will overcome darkness – only those in the light will survive. He will see it! He will know it."

Rau looked at John. He would be alive, until the end? Surely the end was coming fast! Surely there was little time.

Rau looked back at Joshua, but he had gone.

John ran over to Rau, and grasped his hands. "Can you believe it?" he said. "It's real! He's actually alive!"

Rau smiled at his new discovery. "Oh, yes," he said, "I believe it all right."

"We have to tell everyone!" said John. "This changes everything!"

"Wait."

"We have to tell everyone!"

"First things first, John: wisdom! Wisdom. Don't rush in yet."

John gazed at him, listening to his voice.

"Don't rush in," he said, and Rau gestured to the Parliament grounds. John looked at him, and then broke into a grin.

"I'm telling Mark Blake!" he said, and he rushed into the church.

Rau rushed after him, into Saint Peter's. Mark was there, between the choir stalls, behind the pulpit, wandering backwards and forwards, with his hands clasped behind his back. Rau was sure he was praying.

"John," Rau whispered, but he couldn't stop John's younger exuberance.

"Mark!" John called out, launching himself beyond the pulpit. "Mark!"

Rau hastened his step – the Right Reverend Mark Blake's response to news of a resurrection of Joshua Davidson! This Rau had to see!

Mark turned, and looked surprised. "John!" he said. "I see you're revived?"

John was grinning from ear to ear. "Not me!" he said.

Mark's eyes were set on him, and Rau watched his gaze pass over John's face, and body, with a flicker of bewilderment followed by a dawning thought.

"Don't tell me," he said wryly, and John slapped him on the arm.

"He's alive!" he said. "He's alive!"

Rau closely watched Mark's face. How would he respond?

"Alive?" Mark asked, with complete control. "Who?"

"Who do you think?" said John, and Rau thought he might start jumping up and down on the spot. "Joshua! Joshua's alive!"

Mark's blue eyes widened slightly and then came to rest on Rau.

"Alive?" Mark asked, and Rau nodded.

"Yes," he said. "We both saw him, together."

"The grave!" said John. "Come and see!" And he grasped Mark's sleeve, and tugged him down the aisle.

Rau made way for the bishop, and then followed after them. Mark was allowing John to drag him but he cast a questioning glance back at Rau.

At the gravesite Mark's eyes roved over the mound of dirt, the lid resting on top, and the open empty coffin lying in the ground. He stared at John, and then at Rau. Then he tipped his head back, face to the sky, and erupted in resounding laughter.

"Hallelujah!" he cried. "All over again – he is risen! Victory! Victory!"

And now his eyes came to settle on Rau, his face lit up as Rau had never seen it before.

"The sign of Jonah," said Mark. "The only definitive sign: dead, in the grave, and risen again!"

"Yes," said Rau quietly. "Death swallowed him up and spat him out again."

"I have no idea what you're talking about," said John happily, "but I know he's alive! And I'm going to tell everyone about it!"

He turned and moved toward the Parliament buildings, but Mark caught his arm.

"Wait, my friend!" he said. "Think about what you're doing."

"No need to think!" said John. "Time to tell!"

"How are you going to explain this?" asked Mark.

"No need to explain it."

"That works for Israel two thousand years ago, but here?"

John smirked at him. "What part of 'back from death' do you think people won't understand?"

Mark was smiling at him, now – Rau knew his thoughts! The arguments! The endless debates! John had forgotten, Rau saw – had instantly forgotten that he had once been a sceptic! But then the conversation was interrupted.

Tristan walked into the graveyard.

Curious, Rau wandered up to him.

"Kia ora, mate," he said, and Tristan smiled in memory.

"Hey, old man," he replied. "How are the knees?"

"They've got a new lease in life."

"True…?"

"Got something to show you, I have." And Rau ushered Tristan over to the empty grave.

Tristan's eyes settled on the open coffin and widened.

"Oh, boy," said Tristan, looking at Rau. "That's a biggie."

"Yes," said Rau, straightening to his full height, "and so it begins."

Tristan stared at the grave. "I missed out on that darned fish!" he muttered, and Rau bowed his head.

"He dodged the bullets."

Tristan's eyes suddenly widened further, shifting again to Rau. "My God," he whispered, "you're right! He beat me! He actually beat me, and I'm glad! He's won! Thank God he's won…"

And relief flooded his face.

Joshua's mother was walking in now, looking at the grave, lifting her voice with joy. Selena had appeared and was hiding behind Mark, who was smiling. Tristan was studying Rau.

But John's face was lit up.

"Careful," Rau warned, but John would not listen.

"There's someone I have to tell!" he said. "Someone before all the rest."

And as he launched himself through the little gate, Rau knew he was heading to find Rachel.

Chapter 41

THE CULMINATION

Rachel stood on Molesworth Street. The iron bars were in front of her, the Parliament gardens behind. The army was still patrolling the grounds, backwards and forwards. They reminded her of the Changing of the Guard outside Buckingham Palace.

The New Zealand flag was at half-mast – and, alongside this, at full mast, was the British flag: the Union Jack! The flag of the Queen.

The Governor General now was in absolute power over the nation. The army had been stationed at key locations across New Zealand, and the police were working closely alongside. Everyone had seen the shootings at Parliament! Everyone knew now they must not resist.

Her father had entered the Beehive, to gather his belongings. Rachel waited outside the gate. Why was she there? She had known she must come.

People had died there. What had happened to their bodies? Surely the army had made the necessary arrangements. And Joshua had died there too.

Rachel wandered over to the intersection, the place where he had died. She crouched down to the ground. His blood still stained the ground. Swallowing, she reached out to touch the stain on the concrete. Gone! He was gone.

She lifted her eyes and looked at Saint Peter's. Had they taken his body there? Had there been a service? Was he buried there? She had missed it all! The one funeral she absolutely should have attended, she'd missed!

She wanted to visit him now, to see his grave. And then, at the same moment, someone emerged from a gate alongside the church.

It was John.

His eyes quickly found her. His face was lit up with joy! How could he be happy now? John rushed to her and lifted her off her feet, away from the ground; away from the place of death.

"Rachel!" he cried. "Have I got something to tell you!"

Rachel frowned at him, her head beginning to hurt.

"What are you doing?" she asked. "It's only been a few days since he died."

"Yes!" he said. "And everything's okay now!"

"What do you mean?"

"He's come back! He's back!"

Rachel stared at him. He was delirious. Now she was back on her own two feet, she reached to grasp his arms.

"Oh, John," she murmured, "it's okay! It's okay…"

"I saw him!" he said, his face radiant.

"In a vision," said Rachel.

"I touched him!" said John. "He put my fingers on his wounds."

"What?" Rachel shook her head, to clear it. "What are you saying?"

"I saw him, Rachel!" Now his face was close to hers. "I felt his body, as surely as you feel mine now." And he reached, and grasped her fingers, and slipped them through his shirt, to his chest.

Rachel's heart suddenly pounded fast. She tried to draw her fingers away, but John was holding her hand on his chest.

"Where did you go?" he asked.

"Away!" said Rachel. "I had to get away!"

"Why?" asked John. "Why for so long?"

There was a new strength to him – a kind of fire, a passion, a certainty, a daring…

"I couldn't bear his death," she whispered, and now his hands were holding her face, his eyes looking at her lips.

"He's alive," he whispered, and his face lit up into a majestic smile. "He's alive."

"It can't be," she whispered back, and his fingers were moving through her hair.

"That's kind of the point," he said with a grin. "That's the beauty of it."

"Five bullets. Oh, John!" She sobbed, and now his expression changed to compassion and he gently kissed her forehead.

"It's all right," he whispered. "It's over now."

He was reaching into his pocket and he pulled something out.

"Five bullets," he murmured gently, and now he reached for her hands and laid them onto her palm.

Rachel stiffened. The five bullets! Deformed! Used!

"John," she gasped, "what have you done?"

But now he was curving her fingers over the bullets – now he was drawing her hands onto his chest, over his shirt.

"Nothing," he whispered ardently, his eyes wholly genuine. "I promise, Rachel, on my life: I didn't do anything to his body. He gave these to me."

Rachel stared into his eyes. Was he really saying it?

"Where's the scientist now?" asked John. "Rau and I both saw him – we both touched him! The grave is empty. He gave me these bullets…"

Now Rachel began to feel a deep panic rising up from within her, but John held her and breathed into her ear.

"Don't be afraid," he whispered. "You don't have to be afraid."

"Evidence."

"I'm giving you the evidence."

"Give me more."

"I am more evidence!" His warm breath on her face was quickening! Quickening. "I was dead, with him! And now I'm alive, with him…"

Her body was aching for him; her soul was aching for his words. He was transformed! From agony, to ecstasy!

"Stay with me," whispered John. "Give me your mind. Give me your science! Join with me, and we can make this miracle known to the world."

"Give me everything you have," whispered Rachel. "Tell me everything you know."

"Everything," whispered John. "I'll give you everything."

And their mouths were together – their passion joined.

His strength was within her – his certainty! His faith! Stronger, than her horror! Stronger than her fear! His love was inside of her – stronger than her bitterness! Stronger than her hatred.

She gave her certainty to him! The death! Certain death! His certainty he gave to her: he was alive again! Joshua was alive.

They kissed; their hearts were one. And then John was reaching for her left hand, as he kissed her, and although her eyes were closed she felt his heart, his passion, and his fingers reaching her own.

"Marry me," he whispered into her ear, placing a greenstone ring on her finger. "I found it just now, in the church."

Rachel gazed at him. "We only met a short time ago…"

"That doesn't matter," said John. "We both know it is right."

"So soon…"

"There isn't much time." He grasped her hands again to his chest. "It's going to get dangerous, Rachel! Love means loyalty! Love means commitment! Until death! Until death."

There was no other way, with him! His entire being! Body and soul, and spirit…

"He owns you," whispered Rachel, "more than I! Always, he will own you more than I."

"Yes," whispered John. "Always."

"My love for him will never be as strong."

"I understand."

"I don't get God! Only Joshua."

"Understood. But I have to ask you, Rachel."

"What is it?"

"Look with your eyes! Listen with your ears! Think, with your mind, and feel with your heart."

"My heart?"

"Search for the truth, Rachel – be a good scientist! Search for the truth, even where you didn't expect to find it! Even if it surprises you – even if it shakes everything that you believe!"

Her heart was pounding hard, captured, as he continued.

"Show courage, and join with me!" he said. "Be my wife."

Rachel gazed at him. She glanced down at the ground, at the blood stains. She glanced up at the church. And then she looked back to John.

His eyes were lit, vibrant with purpose and love. Suddenly he had emerged, overnight! Suddenly he had become the one she could marry.

"Stay with me," she whispered. "Stay with me, and join with me: be my strength, be my light."

"I will," whispered John over her. "I will stay. And stay with me! Stay with me, and join with me: be my wisdom – be my love."

Their mouths were one, their bodies drawn together. His ring was on her finger.

They were whole.

Chapter 42

NEW IDEAS

James Connor sat in his old office in the Beehive. Once the Prime Minister's office, it had now been made obsolete. Connor could still not fully grasp the reality that Parliament did not actually exist anymore. Instinctively he wanted to attend meetings, and join the House of Representatives – it was hard to believe the House had been shut down.

The Governor General of New Zealand had only acted this way twice before, the most recent time more than one hundred years ago!

Connor was humiliated, but more than this he was worried.

Quickly he gathered up his papers and his personal items, including the photo of Pam and Rachel, put them in a box and headed down the empty corridor.

The Beehive was deserted, an eerie reality. Connor knew the Governor General was busy in Parliament House. He also knew the New Conservative Party was busy reinventing itself, ready for the upcoming election. What would Patrick Clarkson do now? This was his great chance. Would he secure communism? Connor shuddered at the thought.

The Clean Greens and Maori party, there wasn't much threat there. But what about the Christian Conservative party? Would they suddenly rise up, in this climate of religious extremism? Would they suddenly become a power to be reckoned with?

Connor stepped into the lift, and turned around. Joshua Davidson…He swallowed. Tristan had shot him, in public! In public, for all to see! Connor had never intended that! Never wanted it. Tristan had secured Connor's dismissal! On purpose, Connor was sure. And yet, Connor couldn't blame him. And yet, Connor agreed with him.

Joshua Davidson was dead.

Connor emerged from the lift, and wandered out to the reception area. He could see the army guarding the Governor General's quarters and the New Zealand flag at half-mast, while the British flag flew at full mast beside it. The humiliation! The shame. And such utter uncertainty for the future.

He walked down the steps to the exit, past the security guards at the entrance. Clarkson was outside in the gardens, gathering support. Connor let him be. His time was over, now. He was finished.

The black iron gate stood before him, where four New Zealanders had been shot dead. It was his fault! Their blood was on his hands. And the blood of Joshua Davidson.

Rachel was waiting for him, outside the gate. She was sitting on the ground, near where Joshua had died. He wandered over to her.

"How about a trip to Stewart Island?" he asked – it was the furthest place from Wellington that he could think of. But then he saw a funny expression cross Rachel's face.

She rose to greet him, her eyes bright. She was quite beautiful, in that moment – she reminded him of Pam.

"Ah, Dad," she began, and he frowned, perplexed.

"Yes?"

"I have two lots of news to tell you."

"Fire away."

Her face was a little flushed, almost as if…

"Don't tell me you're in love," said Connor. "Impossible! After all the hell we're going through…"

"Not impossible," said Rachel, smiling wryly, "only improbable."

Connor stared at her. "You look stunning, Rachel," he said. "If it was any other time but the impending demise of our nation, I'd be happy for you!"

"I'll accept that," said Rachel, grinning, but then her expression changed and she became serious. "There's something else I need to tell you."

"What, you're pregnant?"

She hit his arm. "No! Come on, Dad, I'm a grown woman."

"Spit it out, then."

"It's about Joshua."

Now he shifted on his feet. "What is it?"

Her expression was unusual, he couldn't quite place it. Was it intrigue?

"There's going to be talk," Rachel began. "There will be new ideas."

"What kind of new ideas?"

"Well…" She hesitated for a moment and then continued. "Some people are saying that they have seen him alive again."

Connor dropped his box. The frame – had it shattered? He stooped to check. Rachel was standing over him now.

"I'm going to write it all down," she said, her voice firm, "so that everyone can decide for themselves what they think."

"Have you converted to this new religion?" asked Connor, reaching to turn over the frame.

"No," said Rachel, and Connor saw the frame was still intact! Not shattered! Pam and Rachel were still smiling into the camera. Connor quickly picked it up, with his box, and rose to his feet to face her.

Her eyes were bright. "I haven't converted," she said, "but I'm open to it! I'm open, and I'm going to write about it, and I'm going to stick with it."

Connor's eyes drifted down and he saw there was a ring on her wedding finger. He swallowed.

"Shouldn't I be giving you away?"

Tears filled her eyes as she took his hand.

"I love you, Dad."

The words hurt, but he smirked. "All I can say is, thank goodness I'm not the Prime Minister anymore."

"Agreed!" she said quickly.

"Which one is he?" asked Connor, and Rachel smiled sadly.

"The one who was crying, next to Joshua. His name is John."

"Fitting," said Connor. "Someone's got to match that fire inside of you."

She was smiling and crying at the same time. Connor smiled sadly at her.

"What should we expect from this movement?" he asked, and she shook her head.

"I honestly don't know."

"Will I ever see you again?"

Pain filled him now – a deep pain. She was going! She was leaving. She was choosing a dangerous path!

"You will if you come with us."

Connor gazed at her, and then laughed. Beautiful! Kill Joshua, and then join him. Why not? Lose his job as Prime Minister, and join a King.

"I'm sorry, my precious girl," he said, "but even my mind can't cope with that many twists and turns within one week!"

She was grinning, and now he grasped her hand.

"Rachel," he said firmly, "make sure John keeps you safe, okay? I love you! And if he gets you into deep water, he'll have to answer to me."

Irony filled her face, and he enjoyed it, and he pulled her into a hug.

"Go now," he said. "Be with him. Find out what's going on with Joshua, and do what you must."

Her arms squeezed him and then released him, her face shining.

Connor moved away towards his car, glad for his wife and the shelter of his home. Rachel must choose her own path. And who knew what bizarre twists lay ahead with the Joshua Movement.

"Besides," he muttered under his breath, "I thought you said there were going to be *new* ideas…"

Chapter 43

THE BREATH OF LIFE

John wandered down the side aisle of Saint Peter's. A meeting was taking place in one of the side rooms. John could hear Mark's voice, rising up above the others.

"Yes, I know, Murray!" said Mark. "I was totally against the man! What can I say, 'God works in mysterious ways!'"

"'Mysterious ways'?" said Murray. "Mark, I'm seriously concerned you're developing some kind of multiple personality disorder."

John poked his head around the corner – was he serious? But the older man's face was warm, and smiling.

Mark laughed. "Can't blame you for that one, Murray."

"I still think this Joshua is an imposter!" said Pastor Luke.

"Yes, yes," Mark replied, "and tell me, what do you know about demonic possession?"

"Demonic possession?" pondered Luke. "Well, the person has to submit to Christ to be delivered."

"Apparently not," said Mark.

"Not?" asked Father Andrew. "A person can be exorcised by a priest, by God's Spirit, but faith is important…"

"I don't think this one had faith, though I might be wrong."

"Who was it?"

"My daughter."

The room was silent. John stood still, in plain view, and Father Andrew spoke again.

"Does she need prayer?"

"Always," Mark murmured. "I will always pray for her."

"And the exorcism?"

"Already done."

"By which priest?"

Now Mark turned, and looked straight at John. "By which priest?" he murmured, rising to his feet toward him. "This priest."

He reached out his hands, and grasped John's between his own.

John flushed but held Mark's eyes – his gratitude.

"Join us," said Mark, and John shifted a little awkwardly.

"I don't know…"

"That's all right," said Murray. "You are free to come and go as you please."

John bowed his head, and looked amongst the faces. So diverse! So many different churches.

"Diversity makes as stronger," said Mark.

"I agree!" said John. "As long as we follow the same Master."

"Yes," said Mark brightly, "as long as we follow the same Master."

John shook the hands of the ministers present, held their gaze, and then he moved toward the door.

"You still have that project to work on," said Mark smiling, and John remembered. Then he wandered out of the room, down the side aisle, and into the church.

The altar, and the cross, remained.

John wandered up to the inner sanctuary. The silver cup and plate were still there: the blood of Christ! The body of Christ.

He pulled out the five bullets from his pocket. Death – a symbol of death, but not of life…

He heard raised voices, now, in the meeting room alongside. Then he heard one voice: the familiar voice of his beloved friend.

He laid the bullets on the altar, and then Joshua was there beside him.

"The body and the blood," John murmured to him. "What should I do, Master? What new symbol can we make?"

Joshua passed his hand over the bullets, and they were repaired, and had now become gold.

"The bullet is the sign of my death," he said, "and the sign of your life."

"Like the cross…" John murmured. "But how can we take it into our bodies and hearts?" he asked. "Your offering into us, like the bread and wine?"

Joshua breathed over him. "Breathe deep, John," he said. "God's Spirit is the breath of life. I gave up my breath for you; I give God's breath for you."

John took in Joshua's deep breath. It was for him, now! Cleansing; bringing life.

"Not new," John murmured, and Joshua smiled.

"No, my beloved friend," he said. "Not new at all."

And then he was gone.

John laid his hand on the cup and the plate – over the wine and bread – and breathed deep. The love of God! The light of God! He knew them, now! He felt them! He housed them. He longed to share them.

Breathe deep…

It was time to pass it on.

Chapter 44

AROHA

Rau stood on the steps of Saint Peter's, and then moved into the graveyard alongside.

Joshua's grave was still empty. The soil was starting to slip into the empty coffin. Soon the coffin would be full, and the grave site would have no worth.

Rau considered it. What was the message to bring, now? The same message it had always been. The witness of Joshua alive again; the witness of Christ alive again. There was no grave to visit, no tomb to see. There was the record, in the living witnesses – and, in time, a written record, for generations to come.

"Do you love me, Rau?"

"Ae, my precious Master," Rau whispered. "Aroha!"

"Then take care of my Iwi." And Joshua stretched his arms out to embrace all of Aotearoa.

Rau considered the Land of the Long White Cloud, and he smiled. This was his land! This was his home. This was his calling, all coming together as one.

"E te whanau," he said, "we are the body of Christ!"

And he moved himself forward, away from the grave, and out through the gate.

Parliament was before him. The army still marched inside the gates.

"One day some men will kill you because of me."

Was he ready to take the risk? Was he ready to pay the price? Here he had run away! Here he had denied Joshua!

"Breathe deep," John had said to him. *"God's Spirit is the Breath of Life!"*

The hongi! The breath of God.

"He gave his breath away," Rau murmured in the direction of the guards. "He gives us his breath today."

Rau took in a deep breath and then he moved forward.

"Kia ora!" he called out to the guards. "Pehea ana koe?"

Some of the soldiers glanced at each other, but others responded.

"Pai ana," they said.

"You fellas ever have time off?"

"Ae," some said.

"Well, how 'bout we catch up over some kai later?" He had their attention now. "I'll be over here, see, on the other side of the gate? Boy have I got some news to tell you!"

He smiled, and moved to set himself up outside the gate, near where Joshua had died. The guards were watching, and Rau was pretty sure a camera or two wouldn't be too far behind.

"E te Ariki," Rau murmured to God. "My life is in your hands."

Across the intersection, on the other side of the place where Joshua had died, Tristan stood on the steps of Saint Peter's. He looked at Rau, standing at the iron gate, and he smiled.

"Not wearing a dog collar now," he said quietly. "We've both come quite a way from Kerikeri, my friend."

Now he lifted his voice to reach him.

"Hey, you – joker!" he called out, and Rau turned to him, "I hear you've got some news to tell!"

"Got that right, mate!" Rau called back. "Where's your whanau?"

Tristan grinned at him. "You are my whanau, mate!"

"Then what are you doing over there?"

Tristan hesitated, glancing at the army. Go along for the ride? Still go along, and risk death? Joshua had moved on, but Rau was now standing up to the mark – taking his place! Taking the lead.

Tristan's father appeared alongside him, now – his whanau! His other family.

Mark was smiling quietly, looking at Rau.

"Here or there?" Tristan asked him. "What would you say?"

"For me, the answer is here," said Mark, gesturing to the church. "For you, the answer is different."

"Does it have to be one or the other?"

"No – it can be both."

"Both?"

"You belong to both whanau, Tristan: both worlds."

Tristan gazed at him, tilting his head. For nine years he had lost his first family and now he had gained them again: father and sister! Yet there was another whanau drawing him now: another family.

Rau's eyes were on him, and his face was lit.

"Come on, boy!" he said. "Want a ride? How about that fishing?"

"Where are you headed?"

"Dunno – I'm not driving! Let's find out together!"

Tristan broke into a wide smile. "Okay!" he said. "I'm in!"

And he strode down the steps of the church, across the street, and joined Rau on the other side.

###

Next in The Zeal Trilogy:

THE PRICE OF REDEMPTION

Alex is the mastermind, but his father is the tyrant. Who will win?

Alex is caught in a nightmare. His mother is dead, his sister troubled, and his father Kensington's angry fists are gaining strength. The killing of spiritual leader Joshua Davidson has left New Zealand in crisis. The Queen is ruling through the Governor General, but now Kensington's eyes are turning to Parliament. With Alex's brilliant mind, he can invade; with Alex's vulnerable heart, he can conquer.

Kensington's rage is murderous. He thrusts a gun in Alex's hand, but Alex is torn. He remembers his mother. He remembers love.

Another way beckons Alex, but at the highest cost. Will he betray his father? Will he overcome him, before someone else dies?

The Price of Redemption is the second in *The Zeal Trilogy*, a spiritual psychological suspense for people of all walks of life. If you enjoy compelling characters, powerful drama, and stories with a New Zealand flair, then you'll love Michelle Warren's books of loyalty under fire.

Connect with the Author,

MICHELLE WARREN

Michelle Warren was born in Wellington, New Zealand. She lives 1.5 hours away from Matamata, otherwise known as Hobbiton. She is glad to live in Middle Earth, and loves The Hobbit and The Lord of the Rings.

Michelle has visited many places, most notably of late Ghana, for which she is grateful for warm hearts and excellent cocoa beans.

Michelle writes spiritual psychological suspense, in which she expresses journeys into Christian spirituality. She seeks to provide a medium in which people of different perspectives, faiths or outlooks can be entertained and need not fear to tread. Michelle believes that friendship in the midst of our differences is vital and mutually beneficial, and so she seeks to write fiction representing and allowing for the coexistence of all.

In her newsletter, Michelle explores different challenges facing New Zealand and the world, exploring different human outlooks and potential.

Contact Michelle at **michelle@michellewarren.kiwi** or grab a free copy of her novel *Yeshua* and sign up to Michelle's Newsletter here: **https://BookHip.com/ZBSVHAX**

Books by

Michelle Warren

THE ZEAL TRILOGY

Available as ebooks, paperbacks and audiobooks.

A New Kind of Zeal

The Price of Redemption

The Crux of Salvation

Yeshua

ENDNOTES

1) Thomas Smith, Timoti Karetu and Thomas Bracken. 1878, 1979 and 1876. 'Aotearoa/God Defend New Zealand.' Manatu Taonga Ministry for Culture and Heritage, http://www.mch.govt.nz/nz-identity-heritage/national-anthems/god-defend-new-zealandaotearoa: accessed 22 December 2013. Used with permission. Also 'God Defend New Zealand.' Wikipedia, http://en.wikipedia.org/wiki/God_Defend_New_Zealand: accessed 22 December 2013.

2) Speaker R M Algie and Bishop Eric Gowing. Wellington: New Zealand Parliament, 1962. House of Representatives. 'Prayers.' New Zealand Parliament, http://www.parliament.nz/en-nz/about-parliament/how-parliament-works/ppnz/00HOOOCPPNZ_141/chapter-14-business-of-the-house#footnote_4: accessed 22 December 2013.

3) Scripture taken from the HOLY BIBLE, NEW INTERNATIONAL VERSION. NIV. COPYRIGHT 1973, 1978, 1984, 2011 by Biblica, Inc. Used by permission. All rights reserved worldwide.

4) This copyright material is taken from 'A New Zealand Prayer Book – He Karakia Mihinare o Aotearoa' and is used with permission. The Anglican Church in Aotearoa, New Zealand and Polynesia. A New Zealand Prayer Book – He Karakia Mihinare o Aotearoa. Christchurch, New Zealand: Genesis Publications, 1989, 410-429.

5) Hubert Parry. I Was Glad. London: Novello & Co Ltd, 1902.

6) Mark 10:15 Paraphrased.

7) Thomas Smith, Timoti Karetu and Thomas Bracken. 1878, 1979

and 1876. 'Aotearoa/God Defend New Zealand.' Manatu Taonga Ministry for Culture and Heritage, http://www.mch.govt.nz/nz-identity-heritage/national-anthems/god-defend-new-zealandaotearoa: accessed 22 December 2013. Used with permission. Also 'God Defend New Zealand.' Wikipedia, http://en.wikipedia.org/wiki/God_Defend_New_Zealand: accessed 22 December 2013.

8) Mark 12:30-31. Scripture taken from the HOLY BIBLE, NEW INTERNATIONAL VERSION. NIV. COPYRIGHT 1973, 1978, 1984, 2011 by Biblica, Inc. Used by permission. All rights reserved worldwide.

9) Matthew 11: 28. Scripture taken from the HOLY BIBLE, NEW INTERNATIONAL VERSION. NIV. COPYRIGHT 1973, 1978, 1984, 2011 by Biblica, Inc. Used by permission. All rights reserved worldwide.

10) Matthew 21:31 NIV.

11) Matthew 6:25, 27 NIV.

12) John 5:28-29 NIV.

13) John 5:24 NIV.

14) John 14:6 NIV.

15) Matthew 12:39 NIV.

16) Matthew 24 NIV.

17) John 11:50 Paraphrased.

18) John 11:50 Paraphrased.

19) John 14:6 NIV. Kenneth Barker, ed. The NIV Study Bible New International Version. Michigan: Zondervan, 1985.

20) Luke 12:39-40 Paraphrased.

21) Matthew 24: 5. Scripture taken from the HOLY BIBLE, NEW INTERNATIONAL VERSION. NIV. COPYRIGHT 1973, 1978, 1984, 2011 by Biblica, Inc. Used by permission. All rights reserved worldwide.

22) Isaiah 53:5. Scripture taken from the HOLY BIBLE, NEW INTERNATIONAL VERSION. NIV. COPYRIGHT 1973, 1978, 1984, 2011 by Biblica, Inc. Used by permission. All rights reserved worldwide.

23) John 3:16 Paraphrased.

24) This copyright material is taken from 'A New Zealand Prayer Book – He Karakia Mihinare o Aotearoa' and is used with permission. The Anglican Church in Aotearoa, New Zealand and Polynesia. A New Zealand Prayer Book – He Karakia Mihinare o Aotearoa. Christchurch, New Zealand: Genesis Publications, 1989, 410-429.

25) This copyright material is taken from 'A New Zealand Prayer Book – He Karakia Mihinare o Aotearoa' and is used with permission. The Anglican Church in Aotearoa, New Zealand and Polynesia. A New Zealand Prayer Book – He Karakia Mihinare o Aotearoa. Christchurch, New Zealand: Genesis Publications, 1989, 827-841.

26) Psalm 23. This copyright material is taken from 'A New Zealand Prayer Book – He Karakia Mihinare o Aotearoa' and is used with permission. The Anglican Church in Aotearoa, New Zealand and Polynesia. A New Zealand Prayer Book – He Karakia Mihinare o Aotearoa. Christchurch, New Zealand: Genesis Publications, 1989, 841.

REFERENCES

God Defend New Zealand/Aotearoa

Thomas Smith, Timoti Karetu and Thomas Bracken. 1878, 1979 and 1876. 'Aotearoa/God Defend New Zealand.' Manatu Taonga Ministry for Culture and Heritage, http://www.mch.govt.nz/nz-identity-heritage/national-anthems/god-defend-new-zealandaotearoa: accessed 22 December 2013. Used with permission. Also 'God Defend New Zealand.' Wikipedia, http://en.wikipedia.org/wiki/God_Defend_New_Zealand: accessed 22 December 2013.

Chapter 3

Speaker R M Algie and Bishop Eric Gowing. Wellington: New Zealand Parliament, 1962. House of Representatives. 'Prayers.' New Zealand Parliament, http://www.parliament.nz/en-nz/about-parliament/how-parliament-works/ppnz/00HOOOCPPNZ_141/chapter-14-business-of-the-house#footnote_4: accessed 22 December 2013.

Chapter 4

Kenneth Barker, ed. The NIV Study Bible New International Version. Michigan: Zondervan, 1985.

The Anglican Church in Aotearoa, New Zealand and Polynesia. A New Zealand Prayer Book – He Karakia Mihinare o Aotearoa. Christchurch, New Zealand: Genesis Publications, 1989.

Hubert Parry. I Was Glad. London: Novello & Co Ltd, 1902.

Chapter 20

Thomas Smith, Timoti Karetu and Thomas Bracken. 1878, 1979 and 1876. 'Aotearoa/God Defend New Zealand.' Manatu Taonga Ministry for Culture and Heritage, http://www.mch.govt.nz/nz-identity-heritage/national-anthems/god-defend-new-zealandaotearoa: accessed 22 December 2013. Used with permission. Also 'God Defend New Zealand.' Wikipedia, http://en.wikipedia.org/wiki/God_Defend_New_Zealand: accessed 22 December 2013.

Chapter 21

Kenneth Barker, ed. The NIV Study Bible New International Version. Michigan: Zondervan, 1985.

Chapter 24

Kenneth Barker, ed. The NIV Study Bible New International Version. Michigan: Zondervan, 1985.

Chapter 30

Kenneth Barker, ed. The NIV Study Bible New International Version. Michigan: Zondervan, 1985.

Chapter 36

Kenneth Barker, ed. The NIV Study Bible New International Version. Michigan: Zondervan, 1985.

The Anglican Church in Aotearoa, New Zealand and Polynesia. A New Zealand Prayer Book – He Karakia Mihinare o Aotearoa. Christchurch,

New Zealand: Genesis Publications, 1989.

Chapter 39

The Anglican Church in Aotearoa, New Zealand and Polynesia. A New Zealand Prayer Book – He Karakia Mihinare o Aotearoa. Christchurch, New Zealand: Genesis Publications, 1989.

www.ingramcontent.com/pod-product-compliance
Lightning Source LLC
Chambersburg PA
CBHW021445240626
47153CB00001B/307
9781991169600